TEMPORARY WIFE
Joan Kilby

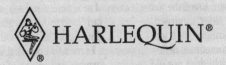

HARLEQUIN®

TORONTO • NEW YORK • LONDON
AMSTERDAM • PARIS • SYDNEY • HAMBURG
STOCKHOLM • ATHENS • TOKYO • MILAN • MADRID
PRAGUE • WARSAW • BUDAPEST • AUCKLAND

ISBN 0-373-70832-7

TEMPORARY WIFE

Copyright © 1999 by Joan Kilby.

"Ms. Dutot is required to leave the country without delay."

The immigration official spoke in a stony voice. "Given Ms. Dutot's widowed status and expired work visa, we have no choice but to deny her further residence."

Burton held up a hand. "Pause. Rewind. Are you saying she can't stay because she isn't married to a Canadian citizen?"

"That is correct." The official turned to Veronique. "You are required to file a deposition at the Customs and Immigration office. We can accommodate you immediately."

Before she could answer, Burton put his arm around her waist and drew her to his side. "That won't be necessary, will it...darling?" She glanced up, eyes wide. He held her gaze, hoping she wouldn't flinch.

"Wh-what are you talking about?" She tried to tug away, but he held her fast.

Smiling through gritted teeth, he replied, "I'm talking about our forthcoming marriage, of course."

She was speechless, thank God.

Dear Reader,

Years ago I sailed to Tahiti on a fifty-five-foot yacht built and captained by my father. I've been fascinated with the tropical French colony ever since. So when I needed a foreign heroine for my "green card" marriage, Tahiti seemed the natural homeland for my heroine. Or perhaps more accurately, *Temporary Wife* became home for a heroine in search of a story, for Veronique has resided in my imagination for quite some time. I can readily relate to her homesick feelings, living as I do in Australia, far removed from family and friends in Canada.

I had a lot of fun writing *Temporary Wife*. At one point I was calling television stations, trying to interview a producer and having little success. Then, through a serendipitous turn of events, a producer called *me,* looking for a romance writer to appear as a celebrity guest on a local cooking show! Naturally I leapt at the chance. Not only did I experience on a small scale what my heroine faced as a television chef, I also got to visit the studio and talk to the director, audio and visual technicians, camera operators—in short, everyone involved in producing a TV show. During my cooking episode—which included Veronique's mango salsa, by the way—I pumped the producer/interviewer almost as fast as *she* could ask *me* questions. My questions were edited out of the final tape, of course, but I got my information and had a ball doing it.

Like my hero, Burton, I spent my childhood in a rural area outside Vancouver. Like him, I enjoyed the sunshine and ignored the rain, loved the juxtaposition of mountains and sea, and as I grew older, mourned the loss of farmland to houses and industry. But farmers are a tenacious lot, clinging to the land with a love that sometimes defies economics. I fervently hope that when my grandchildren are old and gray, farmers will still be tilling the rich and fertile soil of the Fraser Valley.

Sincerely,

Joan Kilby

To Michael,
who knows "the Secret,"
with love and gratitude.

ACKNOWLEDGMENTS

I would like to thank Nieve Jones and the crew at Optus Local Vision; Janna M. Dieleman and colleagues at Delta Cable TV; and Lawrence McDonald for providing information and insight into the world of television.

Thanks go to Fraser Valley potato grower Robert Swenson, and to Ruby Friesen for interviewing him. Thanks also to John Friesen, whose pursuits include farming as well as sailing, for information and inspiration.

Joan Hunt told me all about the trials of broken hips, and Cheryl, from the Department of Customs and Immigration, explained the intricacies of work permits and immigration.

Special thanks to Ghislaine Jauselon for correcting my French, and for sharing colorful stories of life in Tahiti.

Any technical errors in this book are mine.

CHAPTER ONE

MONDAY MORNING AND Burton O'Rourke had a lot on his mind. Just when he'd thought his life couldn't get any better, it had suddenly turned very, very bad.

Torrential rain drummed on Vancouver's gray and soggy downtown core, beating an unrelenting tattoo on Burton's big black umbrella and hampering his long-legged stride down Burrard Street. Although the weather matched his mood, it was incidental to his problems.

Roughly forty-eight hours ago, his maternal grandfather, the person he loved most in the world after his mother, had been alive and feeding his flock of prize-winning Rhode Island Reds. Sometime before lunch on Saturday, Granddad's heart had seized while he was lifting a heavy piece of lumber. And he was gone, just like that. Slumped on the sagging steps of the farmhouse he'd built with his own hands almost sixty years ago.

Burton sidestepped a puddle, bumping umbrellas with a faceless passerby. He stepped up his already-brisk pace amid the stream of workers hurrying to their dry, well-lit offices and shops. Pointless, futile anger—directed at himself as much as at fate—drew a spontaneous muttered curse from him. He should have been there to carry that lumber. Because of him, perhaps, Granddad had been cheated out of seeing another spring turn to summer, seeing his crops grow and ripen.

Granddad's death also left question marks around Burton's half-finished documentary about the history and future of farming in the Fraser Valley. He had a nasty feeling Murphy would come up with an answer. One he wouldn't like.

Burton ducked out of the rain and into the Channel Seven television station. Granddad hadn't lived to see the dramatization of his life's work, but by God, Burton would make sure the old man was remembered.

He shook out his umbrella in the doorway, and collapsed it into clammy nylon folds as he crossed to reception. Halfway there, he did a double-take. Lillian Spencer, the station's attractive elderly receptionist, had changed her hair. Normally fluffy and white, curled in a fashion befitting a grandmother ten times over, it was now cut in a youthful, spiky style.

"Good morning, Burton," Lillian said, glancing up from her computer to greet him with a smile. "Still raining, I see."

"A morning fit only for ducks and native Vancouverites," he said as he balanced his briefcase on his knee and popped the latches. Removing a single stem of yellow freesia, he added it to the vase bursting with spring flowers on Lillian's desk. He kept the vase full by adding one flower every day. Rain or shine. Life or death. "You've had your hair done."

Lillian pulled the freesia toward her and inhaled. "You're a darling, Burton." Straightening, she gingerly touched her hair. "Do you like it? My grandniece is going to hairdressing school. I think it makes a change from my plain old-lady style."

"Nobody would ever call you plain, Lillian," he said, hoping she wouldn't notice he hadn't answered her question.

He shrugged out of his coat and slung it over his arm. The cuffs of his long-sleeved navy cotton sweater and his black denim pants were damp, as were the socks inside his black Rockports. He ran a hand through his short hair and flattened the annoying cowlick that curved over his right brow.

"Is Murphy in yet?" Grief, briefly suspended, resurfaced in a frown. He hated having to deal with this now, but he couldn't rest while the future of his documentary was uncertain.

"He just went up." Lillian peered at Burton over the rims of her half-glasses, her gray wisps of eyebrows knitting in concern. "Is something wrong?"

There was no reason to keep Granddad's death a secret, except that it hurt like hell to talk about it, and Lillian had an attentive way about her that drew a person out. "My grandfather died on Saturday."

"Oh, Burton. I'm so sorry." Lillian discreetly punched a button to save the spreadsheet on her computer screen.

"Thanks, Lil, it's okay—" He stopped, wiping a hand across his eyes. "Actually, it's not okay, but I can't do anything about it." Intentions, good or bad, never did anything.

Lillian shook her head gently, watching his face. "Very upsetting. Was it unexpected?"

"Yes." His voice sounded harsh and suddenly he found he couldn't talk about it, after all.

Lillian's gift lay in knowing when to offer sympathy and when to offer a distraction. She touched his hand. "Ernest has arrived."

"Ernest?"

"Your new production assistant. He's setting up his desk in Jim's old spot."

"Good. I'll see him in a few minutes. First I've got to talk to Murphy."

"Yes, of course. *Lost Harvest.*" Lillian had instantly understood the ramifications of his grandfather's death.

Burton nodded, one hand clenching into a fist. Everyone at the station knew how much this project meant to him. Maybe some didn't know it was a tribute to the man who'd

been his greatest influence, but they were aware it would
be the first piece he'd written, as well as produced.

The phone rang.

"Good morning, Channel Seven," Lillian said in her
well-modulated telephone voice. She listened a moment,
then glanced up at Burton. "Your mother," she whispered,
a hand over the receiver. "I'll put her on line one."

Burton nodded and started down the corridor. He could
hear Lillian gently murmuring her regrets over his
mother's recent loss. He was worried about Mother; she
and Granddad had been very close. Her grief, like
Burton's, was as fresh and deep as a newly dug grave.

The key ready in his hand, he unlocked his office door
and swung it open in one motion. The space was a scant
ten-by-twelve, mostly taken up by shelves lined with rows
of boxed videotapes. The file cabinet in the corner was
stacked high with more videos. Three walls were covered
with photos, mostly black and white, relics of his early
years as a photojournalist. On the fourth wall was a window that overlooked a parking lot. Burton didn't care
about the view, or lack of it. He had a highly developed
inner vision that lent color and shape to his world, and
provided him with abundant mental images. Sometimes
more than he could cope with.

Kicking the door shut, he rounded the desk, scooped up
the telephone receiver and punched line one. "Hello,
Mother," he said, sinking into his chair. "How are you
this morning?"

"I'm fine, Burtie dear," Catherine O'Rourke replied,
her voice clear and high. "Just fine."

Anyone else would think she sounded like her normal
cheerful self. But Burton heard the note of strain, knew
she was barely hanging on to her control. He took a leaf
from Lillian's book. "I arranged with Granddad's neighbors to look after the dog until we can figure out what to

do with him. They'll feed the chickens and collect the eggs, as well.''

''That's nice of them. Did you…cancel the phone and the electricity?''

He understood her hesitation. Mundane details like a name in a phone book or on a hydro bill gave a certain solidity to life, provided proof of existence. And when they were cut off for good… It had been the same when Dad had died five years ago and they'd had to cancel his car insurance and credit cards. It was hard to let go.

''Let's keep the utilities going for a while,'' Burton replied. ''At least until you've sorted through his things. Until *we've* sorted through them,'' he amended, knowing how hard it would be for her to do it alone.

''All right. Thank you.''

''How is it going with the funeral arrangements? Can I do anything?''

''No, I'm fine. I like to keep busy. It takes my mind off…things.'' The quaver in her voice was now clearly audible. ''I just wish I'd been there when he died. I wish…''

Burton's throat thickened with his own intertwining of grief and guilt. The image of Granddad as he'd found him replayed itself before his mind's eye as it had done countless times over the past two days. For months he'd been meaning to get out there and help fix the front steps of the farmhouse. Why hadn't he made the time to just go and do it? When he finally had gone, it was too late.

Old Doc Perkins had insisted that at Granddad's age, cardiac arrest could have come at any time. Sure, Burton thought. One could also argue that death was inevitable, a fact of nature, a peaceful end to a full life. But no matter which rationalization he applied, William Armstrong's death still felt like his fault. Granddad had always taught Burton the meaning of responsibility. Death was the final lesson.

"We're reading the will tonight," Catherine said. "You'll be there, won't you?"

Burton covered his face with his hand and swore silently.

"Burton? Did you hear me? I said—"

"I heard you." He cleared his throat. "What time? It's going to be chaos around here today—" He broke off. Every day was chaos, a battle to stay ahead of a breakneck schedule constantly being undermined by the unexpected.

"Eight o'clock. Now, Burton…" Rather than reproach him, her tone implied she expected him to do the right thing.

Burton flipped open his daily planner to the ribbon that marked last Friday's date, April 30. He turned the pages forward to Monday, May 3.

Every time slot until seven-thirty at night had something penciled in. Snatching a pen out of the bamboo holder on his desk, he made a slash through tonight's seven-thirty entry. And wished for the zillionth time there were forty-eight hours in every day. "Don't worry, Mother. I'll be there. I'll come straight from the station since I'll be working late."

Catherine sighed. "When are you not? You're so much like your grandfather."

Burton's gaze moved to the opposite wall, to a photo he now realized he'd been avoiding looking at since he entered the office. Sandwiched between the stark images of a Belfast bomb blast and a group of Israeli soldiers bristling with Uzis, was a color portrait of Granddad.

William Armstrong's weathered brow was almost as stern and unyielding as the soldiers'. But his sense of humor, honed as fine and dry as the prairies from whence he'd come, was evident in the curving lines around his strong mouth. His hair, once a dark copper like Burton's, had turned to a thick shock of white, but his eyes, the same brilliant blue he'd passed on to his grandson, had barely dimmed with age.

"I'll take that as a compliment." Burton pressed his thumb and forefingers to the inner corners of his eyes. "I imagine whatever he had will go to you as his only child, but if his chess set isn't spoken for, I'd really like it to remember him by."

"I know he would want you to have it," Catherine said, her voice warming. "You were only nine when he taught you how to play. The pair of you used to sit under that horse chestnut tree in the side yard, brooding over the game for hours."

Burton remembered it well—the old man's quiet chuckle as he applauded Burton's first unassisted checkmate, his own bursting pride at his grandfather's approval. The silence on the line stretched. Burton felt the sting of tears. He reached into his pocket for a handkerchief.

"He was a great guy," he said at last. "I have to go," he added, tucking the handkerchief back in his pocket. "Call me if you need anything."

"I will. And don't forget—eight o'clock at Mr. Bingham's house."

Burton wrote down the address of his grandfather's lawyer and said goodbye. Then he strode back down the hall to the elevator, and jabbed the button for the fifth floor. There had to be a way to keep the project going.

The elevator inched upward, past Research and Public Relations, past the cafeteria and whole floors of offices. Burton shut his eyes and tried to visualize Murphy waving aside the objections and difficulties inherent in continuing a show whose main character had died.

The elevator jolted to a stop, the doors opened with a *ping*, and the image of a benevolent and risk-taking Murphy disappeared in a puff of mental smoke.

At the outer desk, Sylvia murmured into the telephone receiver cradled between her neck and shoulder while her long lacquered nails tap-danced across the computer keyboard. She glanced up, her cinnamon-colored mouth a startled "O" as Burton walked past her, knocked once on the double oak doors and pushed his way into the plush-carpeted corner office.

Odd. The air, usually so full of cigar smoke that breathing was a health hazard, smelled conspicuously fresh this morning. "Excuse me, Murph, can I have a word?"

Ponderous and bulky, Ed Murphy leaned back in his leather swivel chair and grunted acquiescence. "What's up, O'Rourke?"

Burton pulled out one of the guest chairs in front of Murphy's big oak desk and leaned forward with his elbows on his knees. "It's *Lost Harvest*. Something's happened. Something that'll affect the show."

"Get to the point," Murphy demanded in his cigar-stoked growl. He took a swig from a giant-size mug printed with a black silhouette of the Vancouver skyline.

Impelled back to his feet by a sudden tightening in his chest, Burton said, "My grandfather died. On Saturday."

Murphy's responding grunt contained sympathetic overtones. "Sorry to hear that. You want a day or two off, you got it."

"Thanks, but that's not what I need right now." Burton paced restlessly across the room, unimpeded by furniture or implements of work. At the far side he turned and faced his boss. "I want to keep going on *Lost Harvest*."

Murphy's fleshy face settled into a scowl. He reached a thick hand across his desk to extract a handful of jelly beans from the brass humidor that, until recently, had contained the finest Cuban cigars. "How the hell you going to manage that?" he barked, popping a bright purple bean into his mouth.

Burton strode back to Murphy's desk. "I've got hours of taped interviews—Granddad in his kitchen, out in the barn. I've got interviews with local marketing boards, the minister of agriculture—''

''A bunch of talking heads. What you need are shots of your grandfather on a tractor. A farming documentary needs to show him planting, harvesting…all those things farmers do.''

''I've been waiting for the weather to cooperate.'' Burton rubbed his jaw with the frustration of it all. Granddad had been held up by the rain, too. One hundred acres were plowed and ready to plant with potatoes. Both he and Granddad had thought they had plenty of time. ''I'll just have to find another farm to use for location shots. No big deal.''

''I dunno, O'Rourke. This project was supposed to be finished weeks ago. Channel Seven is about entertainment. I had a helluva time convincing the board to take a chance on a documentary in the first place. It's going to be damn near impossible to get them to agree to another delay.''

Burton moved to the plate-glass window and gazed out at the rain-soaked corner of Burrard and Comox. ''The Fraser Valley has some of the richest soil on earth, and our farmers are being forced out of production by high taxes, cheap imports and the demand for further development. We should be growing food, not houses.''

''Spare me the rhetoric, O'Rourke. And sit down. You make me nervous always moving around like that.'' Murphy popped the rest of the jelly beans he was holding into his mouth. Then he flicked the flame on the silver cigarette lighter shaped like an ocean liner that plied the sea of papers on his desk.

Burton looked at the jelly-bean-filled humidor. ''You've quit smoking again. No wonder you're in a foul mood.''

''Don't be a smart-ass,'' Murphy said. ''Cut your losses, O'Rourke. It's not as though you don't have anything else on your plate.''

''This is my grandfather's *life* we're talking about.''

"That's exactly what I never liked about this project."
Murphy jabbed a pudgy finger at him. "You're too involved. No disrespect to your grandfather intended, but it's
a waste of time to carry on. You've had a tough break,
but don't let it affect your judgment."

Burton resumed pacing. "There's nothing wrong with
my judgment. You want entertainment? *Lost Harvest* is a
show that's informative, interesting and suitable for the
whole family. It has human interest coming out its ears.
Old farmers retiring, younger family members reluctant to
take on a way of life that provides little financial incentive
and a ton of hard work. Loss of heritage, the changing
identity of a region. Give me a week. I'll find one of
Granddad's cronies. We'll redo the entire show."

"Stop talking, goddamn it, before you start making
sense. This project is going back on the shelf. It's been a
ratings risk all along, and the odds just went up. We have
a responsibility to our sponsors. Hell, we won't *have* any
sponsors if we don't come up with the goods."

"And just who are these sponsors?" Burton demanded.
"California tomato growers? Housing developers? People
who have a vested interest in seeing a show like this fail?"

"Fact one," Murphy said, ignoring Burton's question,
"Channel Seven is in a slump. Sponsors are getting nervous, and that means tighter purse strings. Fact two, the
board of directors wants something fresh and exciting.
They came up with some suggestions at their meeting last
week." He leaned over to pull open a side drawer and
rummage through the files. "Why the hell they pay me to
be vice president of programming, I don't know," he muttered. "Here we go," he said, pulling out a file folder and
opening it. "One of their ideas is not half-bad—a cooking
show."

Burton stared in disbelief. "A cooking show?"

"You betcherlife. And you're going to produce it."

Burton gave a short, mirthless laugh. "What I know

about cooking wouldn't fill a measuring cup. Get Trudy to do it."

Murphy grunted. "You're lucky it was me who heard that sexist remark and not the lady in question."

Burton gestured impatiently. "I only meant because she likes cooking shows. She told me she watches them all the time."

"Trudy is booked up. You've got a hole to fill. Summer's coming and it's always slow what with reruns and fill-ins. We've got to give the ratings a kick up the backside."

"You think a cooking show is the answer? Come on, Murph."

"You'll make it happen."

Burton pushed a hand through his hair. "I'm not a miracle worker. The documentary was at least something I could get my teeth into."

"Don't be so quick to write off cooking shows. Trudy isn't the only one who watches them. This food craze is even bigger than exercise. In these lean, mean times, people want comfort, and comfort means food." Murphy popped another half-dozen jelly beans into his mouth and sat back to chew.

Burton resumed pacing. "I've got the crew assembled for *Lost Harvest*. The schedule is finalized. Everything's done but the final shooting. All I need is the green light from you."

"Save your breath, O'Rourke. I'm giving you the cooking show because it's important, and because you're the best damn producer I've got. So quit your bellyachin' and get on with it."

Burton snorted and furrowed a hand through his hair. "I'm beyond cooking shows, Murph, and you know it. I've done game shows, news, sports, soaps..." He turned and pointed a finger at Murphy. "Remember the miniseries I did last year that got picked up by CBS? And what about that L.A. production company that's been sounding me out to do a movie-of-the-week?''

"What about it?"

"I could go elsewhere," Burton said quietly.

Burton held Murphy's gaze for a full five seconds. Then he started for the door. It was a heavy bluff, and he wasn't at all certain it would succeed, but he was desperate. He was almost through the double portal and starting to sweat when Murphy cleared his throat with a phlegmy rumble.

"Don't go off like a cheap firecracker, O'Rourke," he grumbled. "I didn't say you couldn't ever do your blasted documentary. Make this cooking series a success—and by that I mean a significant jump in the ratings—then, if you find yourself another farmer, you can have the resources to finish *Lost Harvest.*"

Burton broke his stride. If he'd learned anything in seven years of television, it was to recognize a final offer when he heard one. Keeping his expression carefully neutral, he turned and held his ground. "A cooking show would have to be prime time to earn a jump in the ratings."

Murphy waved a pudgy hand. "We'll move things around if we have to."

Burton stepped back into the office. "And the budget? I can't raise ratings on a shoestring."

"You'll have a budget appropriate for a half-hour prime-time slot." Murphy leaned back in his leather swivel chair and belched. "That'll have to be good enough."

Burton put his hands on his hips and stared at the floor. A cooking show was beneath his experience and talent. But prime time was not. It might work. Damn it, he'd make it work. *Lost Harvest*—and Granddad's memory— depended on it.

"I want this deal in writing," he said, lifting his head. "Shooting of *Lost Harvest* has to start no later than August first if we're going to get enough outdoor shots with sun in them.''

Murphy's face creased into a bulldog grin. ''Maybe you should take yourself to Hollywood, O'Rourke, where the sun always shines.''

Burton grinned back. ''Maybe I will.''

But he knew he wouldn't. His career was important, and he was working for the day he'd be able to pick and choose his projects. But he loved Vancouver, rain and all, and besides, now that Granddad was gone, his mother had no family but him.

Murphy scowled again, but Burton knew this time it was purely for effect. He and Murph tussled on a regular basis; it didn't stop them from being friends.

''You've set yourself a helluva schedule, O'Rourke,'' Murphy said. ''You're the only guy I know who comes in here and demands to be overworked.''

Burton shrugged. As his career had progressed from camera work to directing to producing, the demands of his job had tightened around him. He'd tied the knots himself, every rope the challenge of a new project he couldn't back away from. That was the way he liked it.

He strolled over to Murphy's desk to lift the lid on the humidor. ''I see you don't like licorice.''

Murphy gave a wheezy chuckle. ''Help yourself. Then get outta here. And next time, knock before you barge into my office.''

''You got it.'' Burton popped a black jelly bean into his mouth. Then he carefully moved the guest chair back to its proper position. Before he shut the double oak doors behind him, he poked his head back through. ''Thanks, boss. Give my regards to Mrs. Murphy.''

Out in the reception area, Sylvia's glossy mouth was now busily chewing gum, her lacquered nails drumming the desktop as she waited for a printout.

''Morning, Sylvia,'' Burton said as he went past.

"Morning, Burton." She flicked her shining fall of chestnut hair behind her shoulders and gave him a parting smile.

Burton bypassed the elevator and took the fire stairs to the first floor.

Lillian glanced up as he pushed through the heavy door. "How did it go?"

"Do you like cooking shows, Lil?"

"Love them. Why?"

"Because that's what's replacing *Lost Harvest*."

Her kindly face twisted sympathetically. "I'm so sorry, Burton."

He shrugged. "That's show biz. What I need now are fresh troops. Send in my new assistant, please."

THE ALARM CLOCK RANG, long and shrill. Bleary-eyed, Veronique Dutot peered over her hot-pink comforter at the window. Rain sheeted down the pane and drummed on the roof, dripping steadily from the eaves. Did it never stop raining in this horrible country?

With a groan, she hit the off button, fully intending to go back to sleep.

A sneeze took her by surprise. *Mais, non!* Not a cold. She snuggled under the covers and tried to recapture the dreamscape of a white coral beach fringed with palm trees and lapped by crystal-clear turquoise water.

The telephone rang.

Veronique snuggled deeper, but the phone was not as easily silenced as the clock. Muttering in French, she sneezed again, then snaked an arm up through the bed-clothes to drag the receiver into the muffled warmth of the down-filled quilt. *"Allo?"*

"Veronique! *C'est moi,* Ghislaine!"

"Ghis!" Veronique sat upright, her chill forgotten in the excitement of speaking to her sister, half a world away in the South Pacific. She answered her in French, glad to use her native tongue. "I didn't expect you to call. Nothing's wrong, I hope?"

"I just wanted to talk," Ghislaine replied. "How are you? What are you doing?"

"Wishing I was in Tahiti with you." Veronique sighed, her mind filling with images of the island—the color and bustling heat of Papeete harbor, the heady scent of frangipani filling the air at dusk, the chickens pecking at coconuts in her sister's yard....

"How is Donaldo?" she went on. "And Coralie? And *le petit* Hugo?" She'd never met her baby nephew, but on top of the refinished walnut dresser opposite her bed stood a photo of him—a wisp of hair and a gummy grin—cradled in his three-year-old sister's arms.

"Everyone's fine. Coralie asks about you all the time—when is Veronique coming again? And Hugo is growing a tooth."

"A tooth! Already! You better send a new photo. Tell me, did you get the part-time job at the bank?"

"No, they wanted someone with more qualifications."

"Too bad—"

"Poof! Who wants to be all buttoned up, anyway? I'm better off sticking with the airline for now. Yesterday Donaldo and I took our sailboards and windsurfed halfway to Moorea." She paused. "I wish you were here, Vero. Remember how we used to windsurf for miles, nothing but the wind and the sea and the sky? Listen, can you hear that?"

Veronique listened hard. She heard a soft rushing sound that rose and fell rhythmically. It called to something deep in her soul. Something fundamental, like the relaxation of the mind that came only from conversing in her native tongue. "What is it?" she whispered.

"Have you forgotten the sound of the ocean already?"

Veronique flopped back on her pillow with a groan. "Don't torture me!"

"Oh, Vero, I know you hate it in that cold, wet country. Donaldo's cousin, Jean-Paul, is building a floating-restaurant at the marina. He's looking for a head chef and asked if you were available. Head chef, Veronique!"

Head chef! Her dream was to someday have her own restaurant, but for now... She could go home, be among her family and friends. "What did you tell him?"

"I said I would talk to you." She paused, then said, "Your husband, that horrible Graham Gerritson, is dead. Why don't you come home?"

"I want to. I will—soon. Marion is getting out more. She went to the library last week, and I've almost convinced her to join a bridge club."

Ghislaine gave an impatient snort. "I don't understand why you concern yourself with your ex-mother-in-law."

"She's lonely, Ghis, and that's something I understand." Veronique tugged the duvet up around her neck. "She and Stan moved here from Toronto just to be near Graham and me. Since Stan and Graham died in the plane crash six months ago, she has no other family or friends. She used to be so fun-loving, and now she doesn't want to do anything. But she's very kind. When I first came here, she was the only one who even tried to speak to me in French. Not more than a badly mangled word or two, but she tried."

"Come home, Vero."

The warm, enveloping sound of her sister's voice tightened the gossamer threads that bound Veronique's heart to a place thousands of ocean miles away, making it ache with an almost physical need to rejoin her family. "Soon," she said. "I promise."

Tears trickled from the corners of Veronique's eyes and seeped into the pillow. The tremor in her sister's voice was echoed in hers as they said goodbye.

Veronique lay on her back and stared at the damp patch on the ceiling where the rain had soaked through a leak in the roof. Was it really less than a year since she'd left Tahiti?

The tiny island had been her home since the age of ten. She'd gone back to France once, to cooking school in Paris. On her return she'd taken a job at the Club Med, working her way up to sous chef. Five or six years went by and she'd become bored and restless.

Bored? Ha! If only she'd known then how much she would yearn for her old life. But she'd longed for change. Any change. And fate had sent her a brown-haired, blue-eyed Canadian businessman on holiday. His looks had been more intriguing than handsome, but the physical chemistry...*oh la la.* He'd charmed her with passionate glances and long-stemmed red roses. Where he'd found roses in the tropics she couldn't guess. Nor could she ask. Unable to speak more than a few words of English, she'd simply smiled, dazzled by his romantic gesture.

They hadn't needed words to snorkel on the tropical reef or to lie in each other's arms on the beach in the moonlight. And all the English she'd needed was *yes* for him to whisk her away from her beloved home to this foreign country, foolishly believing his perfect manners and charming smile were the reflection of a beautiful soul. Foolishly thinking, too, that a change of scenery would banish her ennui. Only she found she'd exchanged one tiny problem for a set of massive ones.

Veronique pushed back the comforter and crawled naked out of bed. She'd taken this apartment on the third floor of an old house because the heater was set permanently at eighty-five degrees to allow heat to reach the basement suite. Even so, her flesh rose in goose bumps as soon as she left the warmth of her down comforter. She dressed hurriedly, pulling on stockings and a straight skirt the color of black coffee and then buttoning a cream silk blouse over her bare breasts. She slipped a chocolate-colored cashmere sweater over her head, tugging the cuffs down till a thin line of cream silk showed below the brown. The cheval mirror by the old-fashioned wardrobe reflected the warmth of the apricot walls, a profusion of greenery on the windowsill, and a short, slender woman dressed in bargain-basement chic. Pursing her lips, Veronique turned to study the back view. Okay, she would do.

Her sheepskin slippers didn't match the elegance of the rest of her outfit, but they shielded her feet from the cold tiled floor of the bathroom. While the water ran from cold to hot, she used her fingers to untangle her thick, wavy hair. Shoulder-length was impractical for a chef, but she couldn't bring herself to cut off the sun-bleached tips of her honey-dark curls. They were the last tangible reminder of her life in Tahiti.

Veronique's fingers stilled as she stared at the sad sack reflected in the mirror. Loneliness hung around her like the leaden clouds that clung to the coastal mountains. What she hadn't told Ghislaine was that Marion was *her* only friend, as well. Her attempt at a smile turned into a grimace, and she had a sudden, terrifying mental image of her *self* being washed away by the endless rain.

She could not spend another winter in this cold, damp country where the sun disappeared for months at a time. She needed warmth and sunlight, friends and family, people who shared her language and her culture. People who understood her and loved her for who she was.

She needed to go home.

Veronique splashed warm water on her face. With her eyes shut she could almost imagine it was the tropical ocean.

She would go home.

The possibility of happiness unfolded inside her like the *tiaré* flower after the rain. This afternoon she would give notice at Le Soupçon. This morning she would tell Marion of her plans.

Her excitement withered at the thought of how the older

woman would be affected by her news. Since the deaths of their husbands, they had become closer, relying on each other for company. Perhaps too much so. She suspected that some weeks she was the only person Marion spoke to other than the mailman or the grocery clerk.

Veronique made herself coffee and toast in the small kitchen, which was hung with copper-bottomed pots and strings of garlic and chili peppers from the market. Then, with professional efficiency, she whipped up Marion's favorite cake. When it had baked and cooled, she packed it into a wicker basket along with a book of crossword puzzles. Outside her Kitsilano apartment, she caught a bus that carried her over the bridge, through the city and over another bridge to her mother-in-law's house perched high on the edge of a cliff in West Vancouver.

Veronique stepped off the bus. Head down, shoulders hunched against the rain, she jogged the short distance to Marion's gate. Rain-soaked pansies lined the path to the bright red front door, but Veronique didn't spare their drooping velvet heads more than a glance. Huddled under the gabled overhang, she lifted the brass knocker and tapped three times.

CHAPTER TWO

THE DOOR OPENED A CRACK, and one gray-blue eye peered over the chain. "Is that you, Veronica?"

"*Bonjour,* Marion. Yes, it is me, Veronique." As always, she emphasized the correct pronunciation of her name, but she did so with a good-humored smile.

The door shut. Veronique heard the chain slide back, then Marion, well-groomed as usual in a tailored maroon shirtdress, swung the door wide to welcome her in.

"Hello, my dear." Marion smoothed her carefully styled gray hair and adjusted the belt of her dress. "You shouldn't have come all this way in the rain just to see me."

"Poof! The bus, he goes practically door-to-door." Veronique breezed inside and lightly kissed Marion on both cheeks. The first time she'd done that Marion had recoiled in surprise, but now she seemed used to what she once regarded as Veronique's excesses.

Marion frowned in concern. "Your voice sounds odd, Ronnie. Are you all right?"

"I think I am coming up with a cold." Veronique sneezed twice, rapidly.

"Coming *down* with a cold. I don't know how you can catch a cold when your apartment is as hot as Hades. It's a wonder you're not sick!"

"I *am* sick." Sniffing, Veronique unbuttoned her soggy wool coat and peeled it off. "Yesterday I miss my bus and was caught in the rain, hopping mad like a wet cat. My dress, she stick to me, and the water it pours down my back... *Attention!*'' She shook her head like a Saint Bernard, and Marion stepped back quickly, away from the spray.

"You need to dress for the weather, my dear." Marion took Veronique's coat and hung it over the open door of the hall closet to dry. "And find a place to live that doesn't leak. I don't know why you sold your house after Graham passed away." She paused. "You could move in here with me. This house is far too big for one person, and goodness knows I could use the company."

Oh la la. Veronique twisted the gold bangle on her wrist. Selling Graham's house had been the first step toward going home. Here was the perfect opportunity to tell Marion she was returning to Tahiti. She just wished it hadn't come up so soon. "That is very kind of you, but—"

Marion cut her off with a self-deprecating laugh and a flutter of her blunt-fingered hand. "Oh, I know you wouldn't want to live way out here with an old woman."

Veronique captured her hand and gave it a squeeze. "Just look what I've brought." She lifted her basket up and peeled back the blue-and-white gingham. "Your favorite, almond torte."

Marion leaned over the basket and inhaled with obvious pleasure. "Oh, and a new book of crosswords, too. You're so sweet, Ronnie."

Veronique shrugged. "It is nothing."

"You're always so thoughtful and kind. When I think what a good wife you were to Graham, it's all I can do not to weep." Marion tucked her bottom lip tightly beneath the top one. "Such a short time together. It's so...s-sad."

Veronique knew from experience Marion would dissolve into tears unless she acted quickly. "You mustn't upset yourself over me," she said, pulling Marion into a hug. "I am fine. No, don't cry, *chère* Marion. Think how puffy your eyes will get. Is that coffee I smell?"

She didn't want to talk about Graham and feign a grief she didn't feel. He'd been controlling, manipulative and cruelly unsympathetic to her feelings of isolation. All this she might have borne if it hadn't been for... Her mind skittered away from bad memories. She'd been packing her bags to leave him when she'd received the hysterical phone call from Marion telling her that the light plane carrying Graham and Stan to a remote fishing lodge had crashed in the wilderness of northern British Columbia. She couldn't bring herself to disillusion Marion about her only son, so she'd kept quiet, but Marion's peace of mind had come at a price. If Graham was the one thing they had in common, he was also the barrier to her and Marion becoming true confidants.

"It's French roast," Marion replied, dabbing at her eyes. "Your favorite. But first, I have something for you."

She led Veronique into the living room with its sofa and chairs in a matching floral print and wooden lamps with the plastic still protecting their shades. Folded on top of a knitting caddy beside the couch was what appeared to be a sweater made of ivory-colored silk wool.

Marion handed it to Veronique. "I hope it's not too big. I wanted it to be a surprise, so I had to guess at the size."

Veronique held the sweater out in front of her, admiring the simple lines, then put it to her cheek to feel the caress of its slippery softness. "Silk! It is beautiful! *Merci, merci.* So warm, so soft. You did not have to do this, *chère* Marion." She reached up to kiss her again.

Marion's cheeks flushed. "It's just something to do while I watch TV. I'm glad you like it. Now, come and have some coffee." Her head a little higher, she led the way down the hall to the spotless and gleaming kitchen.

Veronique draped her new sweater over the back of a chair and placed her basket on the counter. She carefully removed the plate with the almond torte while Marion poured cream into a dainty floral creamer.

"After we have coffee, perhaps we go to the seniors' center," Veronique suggested. "As the bus passed I saw a notice saying the bridge club meets today. You play bridge, *non?*"

"Yes, but… Oh, my dear, I don't know. I'm not a joiner. Never have been. Stan was all I ever needed. Why, he and I—"

"Marion." Veronique took a step to lay a gentle hand on the older woman's arm. "Stan is gone. You need to get on with your life. You need to make friends. Everyone needs friends. Especially when they have no family."

"I have you. We've got each other." Marion's wistful smile went straight to Veronique's heart.

"Yes," she agreed quietly, and dropped her arm. "We have each other."

Veronique cut the cake while Marion poured coffee into Royal Albert china cups and set the creamer and matching sugar bowl on the lace tablecloth in the dining room.

When they were both seated, cup and cake before them, Veronique put her hand over Marion's. Her mother-in-law's long, thin fingers felt cool and papery. Her solemn gray-blue eyes looked a question. On the mantelpiece, a small ormolu clock ticked quietly.

"I'm going home, Marion."

Marion gave an almost inaudible gasp, then glanced away. "You mean, to your apartment? Did you forget something?"

Veronique noted the pink in Marion's powdered cheek. She'd glimpsed the shock in her eyes. Marion hadn't misunderstood.

"No, I mean to my real home—Tahiti. I can't stay here any longer. I'm sorry. I will miss you. I hope you will come and visit me. It is very beautiful there.…"

"It's beautiful here, too." Marion gazed into her coffee.

Veronique watched helplessly as a large tear rolled down the older woman's cheek and dropped into her cup, spreading ripples in the dark, creamy liquid.

"Do you really miss it so badly?" Marion asked softly. "Your parents don't even live there, you said."

"They went back to Bordeaux, it's true. But my sister and her family live there. And my parents spend the winter there every year since they retired. It's my home. I did most of my growing up there."

"I grew up in Toronto—I guess we're both out of our element," Marion said a little too brightly.

Perhaps. But Marion didn't know what it was like to be in a place where no one spoke your native tongue. No one she knew, anyway. Even when she'd learned the language, she'd still felt like a stranger in a strange land. Especially living with a husband who hated everything foreign about her.

A husband who'd left her a sizable sum of money she didn't want to touch.

"Before I go, I want to sign over to you the money Graham left." She held up a hand when Marion started to object. "*Non,* I insist. I have saved all my wages from the restaurant...."

Marion shook her head. "With Stan's estate and the insurance money, I have all I could possibly need."

Veronique sighed. Perhaps if she explained why she didn't want the money... But she couldn't. She wanted to be completely free of Graham, but without hurting Marion.

"I have Sunday off," she said, squeezing Marion's hand. "Why don't we go somewhere interesting? The museum? The art gallery? Perhaps a walk in the park if it's not raining."

Marion drew herself up and dabbed at her eyes with a tiny paper napkin. "You know I don't go anywhere on Sundays," she scolded with a brave smile. "My favorite program is on in the afternoon."

"*Strange Lovers*? You could tape it."

"*Lovers and Strangers*," Marion corrected her with a laugh. "Oh, I never could work out how to use that thing. Stan always did that."

"I'll show you." Veronique wasn't sure how to do it, either, since she didn't own a TV, but it couldn't be that hard to figure out.

"I was also going to take down the drapes in the living room on Sunday. They need to be dry-cleaned."

"But no!" Veronique exclaimed with an alarmed glance at the nine-foot ceilings. "How will you reach? It is too dangerous."

Marion gave a tinkling laugh, as though confident in her ability to take care of her home, if nothing else. "I've got a stepladder. I've done this sort of thing before."

"Okay," Veronique said dubiously. "If you're sure you can manage." She paused, thinking about how she might still get Marion out of the house. "I know. You could drop the drapes off at the cleaners on your way to my place."

"Or," Marion replied, "since you're not doing anything that day, you could come over and watch *Lovers and Strangers* with me, then take the drapes with you when you go. If you don't mind, that is."

Veronique laughed. "All right, Marion. Unless I develop pneumonia or become swept away by the flood, I will come. Be careful on the stepladder. Maybe you'd better wait till I get here, so I can help you."

"Oh, don't worry about me. I'll be fine."

"WELL, ERNIE, I THINK that about covers the general routine around the station." Burton leafed through the papers on his desk for the list of shows he was currently producing. "How's your work space? Okay?"

Ernie sat on the edge of the guest chair with the eager air of a puppy. Behind his round, wire-rimmed glasses, his myopic gaze was fixed expectantly on Burton. "Yessir. It's fine."

"Ah." Burton pulled a sheet of paper out from under a chunk of the Berlin Wall he used as a paperweight and handed it to Ernie. "Familiarize yourself with this schedule." He frowned. "Scratch that bottom item and add 'cooking series.' We'll call it…oh, I don't know… *Flavors.* Dumb name for a dumb show."

"Sounds good to me, Mr. O'Rourke." Ernie pushed his glasses up his nose and scanned the list.

"Call me Burton. The cooking show is a last-minute item, but it's top priority. Preproduction tasks we normally do in months, we'll have to accomplish in weeks." Burton tapped his pen against his temple. "I'm thinking we'll do it live-to-tape in front of a studio audience."

"Live-to-tape?" Ernie repeated, his voice cracking slightly. "I know I haven't been around long, but isn't that kind of risky for a cooking show?"

"It is unusual," Burton admitted, "but we need something out of the ordinary to warrant prime-time exposure. Graham Kerr did it successfully in Seattle. If it worked for him, we can make it work for us."

Excess energy propelled him to his feet. In spite of himself, he was getting enthused—as he always did when planning a new show. No doubt Murphy had counted on that.

"Get straight onto Research," he continued. "Ask for everything they've got on the top chefs in Vancouver. I want James Barber or Susan Mendelson—someone well-known who can draw an audience. The ratings have got to go through the roof on this one. All right, off you go."

Ernie jumped up. "Yessir. Right away."

Burton smiled. The boy reminded him of himself as a cadet reporter at the *Vancouver Sun* almost fifteen years ago—eager to learn and desperate to make good. "Relax,

Ernie. This isn't the army. If I'm sometimes abrupt, well, it's just the way I am. Don't take it personally.''

Two hours later Burton was striding down the carpeted corridor toward studio one, where taping of his weekly soap opera, *Lovers and Strangers,* was due to start in ten minutes. Ernie trailed behind, his short legs working to keep up.

"What big-name chef did you come up with, Ernie?" Burton said over his shoulder.

"None, Burt."

Burton froze in his tracks. Burt? Ernie? Pivoting on his heel, he saw Ernie's moon-shaped face gazing up at him with complete innocence. "Don't call me that again or I'll have to fire you."

"But you just hired me!" Then comprehension sparked behind his round glasses. Ernie chuckled. "Oh, I get it. Burt and Ernie. Say, that's pretty good, Burt."

"Ernest," Burton growled in warning. If he didn't nip this in the bud, it would be all over the station. He could already hear the comments around the water cooler.

"Okay, boss, I'll try to remember."

"Good. So who have we got?"

Ernie shrugged his plaid-flannel-covered shoulders. "I told you. No one."

"You tried Barber and Mendelson? How about Umberto?"

Ernie shook his head. "No, no and no. They all have commitments for the next six months at least. You can't get chefs like that on short notice."

Burton snapped his fingers, thinking hard. This show had to work or he'd never get *Lost Harvest* off the ground. "Okay, forget the big names. We need someone new, fresh, innovative. Get me a list of the hottest restaurants in town with bios on all their chefs."

"Male or female?"

"Doesn't matter." Burton resumed his long-legged

charge toward the studio. "Attractive wouldn't hurt, but it's not essential. Spark is what sells."

"Say, Bur—Burton," Ernie amended hastily. "There's this great Greek restaurant Rita and I go to near my place in Surrey…"

Burton glanced at him with interest. "Rita? Not by any chance the same Rita who works here in makeup?"

Ernie blushed.

"Come on, why the big mystery?"

"You know office gossip. We didn't want everyone to know we're going together." Ernie's smile was shy but proud. "Don't tell anyone, but we're engaged."

"That was quick work," Burton said. "You've only been here half a day."

"We met at a dog show last fall," Ernie explained. "She's got a standard poodle—you know, one of the big ones. Took first prize over my dog. She was really nice about it."

"I'm sure she was. What kind of dog do you have?" Burton's interest was piqued at the idea of Ernie and his canine companion pursuing romance with the diminutive Rita and her giant poodle. He pictured the two of them occupying the basement suite of a Vancouver special, raising a clutch of tiny, timid Ritas and shy little Ernies. Dog shows on Saturday and roast beef at the in-laws on Sunday…

"Border collie. Smart as a tack. As I was saying," Ernie continued, "the chef at Stavros is a real character and—"

"We're talking prime time," Burton cut in, not unkindly. "We can't use some never-been from the burbs."

"Why not?" Ernie said, puffing a little in his effort to keep up with Burton. "He does unbelievable things with grape leaves."

The sign above the studio door flashed Five Minutes to Air. Burton gripped the doorknob and gazed down at his assistant. He liked the boy's doggedness, but he was a little wet behind the ears.

"Stuff the grape leaves, Ernie."

Ernie's round eyes widened. "That's what Tony does—"

Burton bit back a smile. "Greek food is old hat. I want *Nouveau*—something or other. And I want it quick."

"Okeydokey, boss, I'll get on to it right away."

Ernie turned to leave, but Burton reached out and clapped a hand on his shoulder, gently steering him through the studio door. "After lunch, hotshot. Right now we've got a show to do. Get the talent out of their dressing rooms and onto the set. It's vital we stick to our schedules, Ernie. He who comes in under budget survives to produce another day. Remember that."

BURTON RIFFLED THROUGH the file Ernie had put together while his assistant put a tape into the VCR in the second-floor screening room. It was late afternoon and the building was relatively quiet, a brief hiatus between the taping of a kids' game show and the evening news.

"Good work, Ernie," he said, scanning the contents. "Smart thinking to include cooking instructors, as well as restaurant chefs."

Ernie's face glowed. "Wait till you see the tapes. I got Research to pull all the interviews the station's done with local chefs over the past three years." He clicked the button to start, then backed up two steps to pull up a seat beside Burton. "First up is Bud Perry, seafood king."

"Sounds good." Burton settled back in his chair as the monitor came to life.

Five minutes later he was stifling a yawn. "Forget it, Ernie. Bud has a delivery like a sea cucumber on Valium. Next!"

Between tape changes he scanned the newspaper clippings of restaurant reviews, discarding most while putting aside a small pile for a closer look. The stack of tapes dwindled without a single chef striking him as having television potential.

"What is this obsession people have with food?" Burton grumbled half an hour later.

"Gee, Burt. You have to eat to live."

"These people seem to live to ea—" He froze and glanced up. "What did you call me?"

Ernie cleared his throat. "Burton?" It came out as a squeak.

"I sincerely hope so, Ernie. Is that all?" He glanced at his watch and started to rise.

"Wait. This is the last interview." Ernie removed his glasses and polished them on his shirt, an anxious smile on his homely face.

Burton resumed his seat, but with little hope. While Ernie fast-forwarded through the host's introduction, he flicked through the rest of the file. Hmm, he thought, pausing at an ad for a cooking class led by an elegant-looking Englishwoman. Possible, possible.

Then he heard the Voice—French, female and throaty. His gaze flashed upward, his attention instantly riveted by the woman on screen. Her face was animated, her hand gestures dramatic, her body movements fluid and graceful.

"Stop the tape. Stop right there."

Ernie pushed the pause button, freezing the frame just as the woman chef turned to gaze directly into the camera. Burton leaned forward to study the face beneath the thick, curling mass of caramel-colored hair.

Her nose was a bit too big, her mouth too small, but there was a light in her vivid green eyes and a sparkle in her dimpled smile that made such deficiencies seem trivial.

"Hit Play," Burton urged, keen to hear her voice again.

And what a voice, he thought, as the tape rolled forward. Blithely ignorant of the rules of English grammar, she was laughing and assertive, seductive and mischievous. The lively, wildly exotic purr of a tiger kitten. Charisma with a capital *C*.

"She's perfect!" Burton jumped to his feet. The file folder spilled off his lap onto the floor, scattering contents that had lost all relevance. Mesmerized, he touched the TV screen with splayed fingers, as if he could feel the silk of her blouse, the soft curve of her hip through the glass.

"Absolutely perfect," he repeated softly. He turned to Ernie. "Who is she?"

"Veronique Dutot," Ernie replied, reading from his notepad. "Second chef at Le Soupçon on Granville Island."

Burton paced the tiny room, able to take only two steps in either direction. "Nouvelle cuisine, no doubt. No one stays that slender on cream sauce and filet mignon."

He reached for the telephone on the desk and punched in a number. "Lillian! Get me Veronique Dutot at Le Soupçon restaurant."

Unable to sit still and wait, Burton headed for the stairs. Ernie ran after him. When they arrived at reception, Lillian was making sympathetic noises into the receiver. Burton stood over her, jingling the change in his pocket. At last she put the phone down.

"Well?" he demanded.

Lillian gazed up at him. "It seems she gave her notice this afternoon. Her boss sounded pretty annoyed."

Burton frowned. "What does this mean? Is she available? Or is she going to another restaurant?"

Lillian shook her spiky head. "Apparently she's from some French island in the South Pacific and is going back there to live."

"Damn!" Burton spun on his heel to pace the lobby, then strode back to Lillian. "Make me a reservation at Le Soupçon for eight o'clock, please. No," he said, remembering his grandfather's will, "better make it nine-thirty."

A GENTLY CRACKLING FIRE warmed the lawyer's book-lined study. Old Mr. Bingham droned on in legalese.

Burton's head drooped. His day had started fourteen hours earlier and it was far from over.

As he'd expected, his mother inherited what little money Granddad had left after taxes had eaten away at it over the years. There would be worse to come now that Granddad had died. The old man used to say the government stayed up nights thinking of ways to squeeze farmers off the land.

Burton had no expectations for himself and no desires other than the chess set. His main purpose in being here was to provide moral support for his mother. She had lots of friends, but times like this made him realize it was family that was important. Catherine sat beside him, a tall, trim figure in black, dark hair swept off a face whose natural humor had been subdued by grief. One hand clutched her leather handbag, the other clasped his.

He was starting to drift off when the sound of his own name made his eyes snap open.

"And to my beloved grandson, Burton William O'Rourke, I bequeath my two-hundred-acre property in Langley, including the farmhouse, the outbuildings and all of its chattels."

THE RAIN HAD SLOWED to a steady drizzle by the time Burton parked on a side street on Granville Island, a small plot of land in False Creek. Located next to Vancouver's business district, it was home to theaters, markets, restaurants and trendy shops.

Ducking through the glass doors of Le Soupçon, he entered a foyer of dark wood, gleaming brass and luxuriant green foliage. The coat-check girl took his damp raincoat with an inviting smile. Burton returned her smile and under other circumstances might have asked her name, but tonight he was a man on a mission. He needed a chef-presenter, and Veronique Dutot was his last, best hope.

He bribed the maître d' to give him a table near the

kitchen, then ordered a Scotch straight up from a young man with a stubby blond ponytail and a three-day beard.

The swinging doors of the kitchen were hidden by a potted ficus, but as the waiters went to and fro he heard snatches of muffled orders interspersed with the faint clang of pots and pans. In the center of the dining room, a pianist tinkled out soft jazz, which mingled with the muted conversation of diners. The walls were hung with Gauguin prints, visual promises of tropical paradise in warm, bright colors and languid women with bare, brown skin. Burton sipped his drink and felt it settle in a pool of heat in his empty stomach. Tahiti was an inviting thought on a cold, wet night in the town they called the "village on the edge of a rain forest."

He swirled the Scotch in his glass. Hard liquor wasn't his usual indulgence, but he was still reeling from the shock of inheriting the farm. He was touched and honored Granddad had entrusted it to him. A thousand good memories were attached to the two-story farmhouse with its orchards and acres of rolling pasture and cropland.

But what on earth was he going to do with it? Plenty of people commuted to Vancouver from the Fraser Valley, but with the long hours he worked, he needed the convenience of his West End apartment. Nor could he afford to keep up both residences. A farm required maintenance. Granddad had done his best these past years, and Burton had helped out when he could, but the barn needed painting, and the fences…well, the fences didn't bear thinking about.

Dinner came, and he put his worries away to concentrate on an excellent fresh halibut in a delicate sauce spiced with curry and something else he couldn't identify. He'd just run the last forkful of fish through the last drop of sauce and placed it in his mouth when the sudden crash of breaking dishes made him glance toward the kitchen. Somewhere out of sight, a woman exclaimed loudly in French, her words followed by a burst of throaty laughter.

Veronique Dutot. Her voice conjured up the after-dinner delights of strong French coffee laced with Benedictine.

The crash of dishes was possibly not a good sign, but his photographer's eye had appreciated the color and presentation of his dinner. It had tasted fantastic and was exotic enough to appeal to an audience weaned on fresh ginger and cilantro.

"That was great," Burton said when his waiter had taken his plate and returned with a cappuccino. "Who's the chef?"

Blond Ponytail scratched his jaw under its layer of peach fuzz. "Veronique is on fish tonight. Veronique Dutot. Was there anything else you wanted?"

"Just the bill. And if I may, I'd like to give Ms. Dutot my compliments in person."

"I'll let her know," the waiter assured him, and hurried off.

Burton lingered over his coffee. Fifteen minutes passed and she still didn't appear. He ran his fingers through his hair and his tongue over his teeth, and tried to feel charming and persuasive, instead of annoyed and desperate. Each time the kitchen door swung open, his heart sped up. And each time, he had to remind himself the anticipation he felt was strictly business. For distraction, he pulled out his pocket calculator and juggled numbers to see how far he could stretch the programming budget to entice Veronique to stay in Canada.

His head was down, his pen scribbling over a notepad, when the doors to the kitchen swung open. A variegated blond head and one angular shoulder clothed in starched white linen poked through.

Veronique paused to scan her apron front for spillage, then hissed over her shoulder to Glenn, the waiter, "Which table did you say?"

"Forty-two," Glenn said, layering loaded plates across his left arm. "Over in the corner. A guy on his own. I think he's about to leave."

Bon. Veronique was not averse to compliments on her cuisine, but tonight she just wanted to get home and nurse her cold in a long, hot bath. Stepping around the potted plant, she entered the dining room.

At that moment, the man at table forty-two glanced up and looked straight at her.

Her heart stopped. Blood drained from her face, her fingers went cold and her breath stuck in her paralyzed lungs. *Mon Dieu!* It was Graham. Impossible. He was dead. But…the hair, the eyes, the shape of the nose, the slant of the jaw…all exactly the same.

And it was just like this she'd met her husband, coming out of the Club Med kitchen to accept a compliment…. Déjà vu washed over her in sickening waves.

He'd seen her! He was getting up.

Panicking, she backed into the kitchen, yanking furiously at her apron ties. "Louis! I am leaving," she called in French to the master chef.

Glenn, his arms laden with soiled plates, stepped out of her way. "Hey, did you talk to that guy?" he asked.

"I cannot!" she cried distractedly, conscious only of an overpowering need to escape. Tossing her apron into the basket of dirty linen in the corner, she ran from the kitchen, grabbed her coat and small leather backpack from the locker room and dashed out the back door. Picking her way through puddles, she rounded the corner of the building and followed the path to the street.

CHAPTER THREE

BURTON WATCHED VERONIQUE'S hasty retreat in astonishment. He checked his shirt for curry sauce, glanced behind him… Nothing seemed out of the ordinary.

Blond Ponytail went by with a load of desserts.

"Excuse me," Burton called.

"Be right there," the harried waiter called back.

He returned in a few minutes with the bill enclosed in a discreet black folder and placed it on the table.

"Did Ms. Dutot say when she'd be out?" Burton asked, reaching for the bill. "I thought I saw her, and then she disappeared."

Ponytail grimaced. "Uh, sorry. She just left."

"What!" Burton pushed back from the table, causing his empty cappuccino cup to clatter onto its side in the saucer. This was the only address the station had for her. If he didn't catch her here, he might not find her again. "Did you tell her I wanted to speak to her?"

"Yeah, but she wasn't feeling well."

"Thanks, anyway." Burton pulled out a couple of twenties, threw them on the table and dashed out of the restaurant.

His gaze swept the length of the brightly lit, rain-soaked street. Pedestrians dotted the sidewalk. Umbrellas jostled for position in a queue outside the Granville Island Theatre. Cars swooshed by on pavements glistening with rain and reflected light.

A half block away, he spotted a small, dark figure hurrying along, shoulders hunched against the rain. Her hair, coiled and frizzing in the moist air, gleamed as she passed beneath a streetlight. It had to be her; everyone else on the street seemed to be in pairs or groups.

Burton ran, dodging pedestrians, till he drew up beside her. "Excuse me, Veronique Dutot?"

She cast a startled glance sideways at him, the way a woman does when approached by a stranger. Instead of softening to cautious curiosity, her expression turned to shock—eyes wide, mouth open in a silent scream.

He backed off a step. "I didn't mean to startle you...."

But she wasn't listening.

She blinked hard, rubbed her eyes with her fists. Stared. Then abruptly dropped her gaze. With a shaky hand, she sketched the sign of the cross over her breast, and low, mumbled words seemed to spill directly from her heart.

For once in his silver-tongued life Burton had no idea what to say. "I'm Burton O'Rourke," he managed to say at last, and held out his business card. "Producer at Channel Seven Television."

She squinted at the small print, which was rapidly becoming blurred by raindrops. In the light of the streetlamp, her eyes were dark and her face as pale as a ghost's. "Who are you?" she whispered.

"Burton O'Rourke," he repeated. "I asked to see you in the restaurant.... Is something wrong, Ms. Dutot? Are you ill?"

Instead of answering, she tugged her collar higher around her neck and, with one last wild-eyed glance at him, hurried away.

What the hell? Burton shoved his card back into his pocket and started after her. "Wait. Please. I just want to talk."

The mist coalesced into drizzle and trickled under his collar. Damn. He'd forgotten to get his raincoat from the coat check. Ignoring the cold drops snaking down the back of his neck, he lengthened his stride.

"Ms. Dutot?" he said when he'd caught up with her again.

She sneezed violently. "Go away!"

"I didn't mean to frighten you. I won't hurt you. I'd just like a chance to tell you more about the cooking show before you make up your mind."

Slowing a little, she cast a white-faced glance at his chest. "Cooking show?"

"Yes." He slowed to a halt to keep her in one place, thankful she seemed to be comprehending at last. "My secretary talked to your boss about it this morning. Can we talk?"

"*Non.* In two weeks, I will be gone from this country." She flung her hand out in a dismissive gesture, then again hurried away.

A gust of wind buffeted his back and a sudden cloudburst drenched him with chilling rain. Burton turned his face into the deluge. *Anything else you'd like to hit me with, Big Guy?*

Ahead, a bus pulled around the corner. Veronique picked up her pace, boot heels clicking on the pavement.

"Fine," Burton called out, throwing up his hands. "But if you change your mind and want to talk, call me. Okay?"

She broke into a run.

He watched, mentally calculating the speed of the bus, the speed of the woman and the angle of their respective trajectories. He knew the race was futile even before she shook her fist in a gesture of despair and defeat. Belching diesel fumes, the bus rumbled past the empty stop.

Her arm fell to her side. Her shoulders slumped under her black woolen coat. Even her curls seemed to have lost their spring.

She covered the few yards to the bus shelter, which offered little protection from the gusty, wet wind that blew in off the Pacific. Burton saw her shoulders hunch and heard the muffled sound of a series of explosive sneezes. She reached into her pockets. Her hands come away empty.

He didn't want to harass the woman. He ought to just leave her alone.

But she needed him.

Burton walked to the shelter and approached her cautiously, as if confronting a frightened, wild animal. She looked pathetic—and appealing. From an inside pocket he produced a clean cotton handkerchief and silently held it out to her.

She looked at it suspiciously, then slowly reached out. Her fingers were surprisingly long and tapered, her nails short and very clean. A Band-Aid, not a wedding ring, circled the third finger of her left hand. Not that he was interested in her marital status.

"*Merci,*" she said in her husky voice. She blew noisily, then looked uncertainly at the handkerchief.

"Keep it," Burton said. "I've got plenty. My mother drummed certain things into me as a child. Always carry a clean hankie, never go to bed with wet hair and—"

Miraculously the corners of her lips curved upward. "My mother told me that, too."

Burton smiled back, encouraged, even though her gaze had yet to rise higher than the second button on his jacket.

"Do I look like an ax murderer? Is that it?" he said humorously. "Because, you know, if you don't like my face, I could change it."

Her smile vanished. "You look like my late husband. Exactly like him."

Burton spun away in a quick double-take. No wonder she'd acted as if she'd seen a ghost. "I'm sorry. I had no idea."

"You could not know."

She stared at his feet. He stared at her pinched white face. "You missed your bus."

She glanced at her watch. "There will be another in twenty minutes."

The drizzle had turned to steady rain. "Can I buy you a cup of coffee?"

"Thank you, n—" She broke off as a sneeze convulsed her body.

"You really ought to get out of the rain."

She hesitated, glancing at her watch again.

"Look, there's a coffee shop across the street. You can watch for your bus from there."

She sniffed, then sighed. "Okay."

At the all-night coffee shop, pink neon winked in the window and a Formica counter ran parallel to a row of booths upholstered in red vinyl. An old man nursed a cup of coffee at the counter, and a young couple dressed completely in black were engaged in a passionate discussion in one of the booths.

"Two coffees, please," Burton said to the waitress filling napkin dispensers behind the counter. He slid onto the bench seat opposite Veronique at one of the booths.

She shrugged off her coat and with her fingers shook the water out of her hair. The rain had darkened it to amber, and her skin looked pale in the harsh fluorescent lighting. Her face wasn't any more beautiful in person than on tape, but she had a certain something that snagged his attention and wouldn't let go. That something would catch the attention of the viewing audience, too.

"Ahhh—" she pressed the hankie to her nose "—chieu!"

"Bless you." Burton couldn't help smiling. She even sneezed with a French accent. "That's a very bad cold."

Her eyes pressed shut, and she massaged her temples. "It is this awful weather."

"You should be at home in bed, instead of running around the streets on such a wet night."

Veronique's fingers froze. *Mon Dieu.* That sounded exactly like something Graham would say. Who was this man, and what was she doing having coffee with him?

Once again she tried looking at his face, but her gaze jumped away automatically, as though physically repelled. She stared, instead, at the crumpled wet cotton in her hands with its monogrammed *B* in one corner. Graham had not used cotton handkerchiefs. He'd kept a little plastic pack of tissues in his briefcase, and a box in the car, plus one in the bathroom. In Tahiti she didn't get colds. Here, it seemed, she got one a month.

The waitress brought their coffee, steam rising from thick white mugs. No caffe lattes or cappuccinos in this establishment. Across the table from her, the man's long, blunt fingers tore open a sugar sachet. "When you say I look like your late husband, what exactly do you mean?"

Oh la la. What a question! Her heart beat fast as she remembered the moment she'd spotted him across the dining room. This man Burton had the same downward slant to his mouth, the same long nose and pugnacious jaw. The same short hair—although more coppery than Graham's—and the same intense blue eyes.

Veronique's covert glance across the scarred Formica table confirmed what her rational mind knew must be true—he wasn't Graham. Her husband had had a mole on his left cheek. This man had none. Between Graham's eyebrows a pair of fine lines had frequently deepened in disapproval. There were no such lines on Burton. Perhaps she simply hadn't encountered them yet. He seemed kind, but then, so had Graham at first.

Veronique took a sip of her coffee, strong and black, and it bolstered her enough to answer. "Your *visage*…your face, is very similar. Although he did not have this curl—what-you-call-it?—on top of the head."

"Cowlick."

In her peripheral vision she glimpsed dark eyebrows angled in a frown, then his firm voice became comically lamenting. "I've tried barrettes, but they're just not me."

It was so unexpected, she laughed.

"My hairdresser suggested using a gel," he continued, "and then I had three cowlicks instead of one."

In spite of herself, she chuckled again. Graham, although charming when he wanted to be, had taken himself too seriously. The thought of her dead husband sent a wave of cold anxiety washing over her, and she reached to the back of her neck to twine a long curl around her index finger. *Non!* She would not think about Graham, not ever again.

"I must go," she said, and started to rise.

"I really enjoyed the halibut."

It was probably the only thing he could have said that would have made her pause. She knew her cooking was good, but direct feedback was rare. *"Merci."* She cast a brief smile in his direction, then reached for her backpack.

"The curry I detected right away," he added as though she wasn't putting on her coat and preparing to leave. "But there was something else, almost a licorice flavor." He leaned toward her over the table. "What's the secret ingredient? I promise not to tell a soul. I won't even make it myself, since I'm completely hopeless in the kitchen. Please, just satisfy my curiosity."

She knew exactly what he was doing of course. But this recipe was her newest creation. How could she resist? Slowly, she sat down again, although she didn't remove her coat. "Fennel. You chop the bulb very fine and sauté in just a little butter before puréeing."

"Ahh. I don't know much about cooking, but I know what I like." He paused. "And I would really like you to consider doing this cooking show."

She focused on the gold pen peeking out from a breast

pocket behind the vee of his pullover. "*Monsieur,* I do not know if you have noticed, but I cannot even look at you. How could I possibly work with you?"

"I could hardly not notice," he said, sipping his coffee. "It's the worst blow to my male ego since Sissy Jamieson wrote 'Burton is a blockhead' all over the bathroom wall in grade four. But I got over that, and I'll get over this. The question is," he finished gently, "would you?"

Would she? Could she? Or would she remember the pain and humiliation of her life with Graham every time she looked at Burton O'Rourke? She pushed her hands into her hair, unable to answer.

"Has it been very long since…?"

"Six months."

"Oh. I'm sorry." His voice was filled with compassion. "I guess the sight of me would be painful."

Not in the way he obviously thought. She hesitated on the brink of telling him she'd hated, not loved, her late husband. But explanations would only cause her pain, not to mention be irrelevant to him. "I am not over him," she conceded.

"I know how hard it is to lose someone close to you." Pain hid behind the sympathy in his voice.

"You do?"

This time, he looked away. When he spoke it was to his rain-streaked reflection in the window. "My grandfather."

Veronique studied the taut line of his jaw. "I'm sorry."

He shrugged.

The waitress came by and refilled their cups. She dropped a handful of creamers onto the plate between them and moved on.

Burton picked up a creamer and peeled back the plastic lid. In silence he tipped the tiny container over the rim of the cup and cream swirled through the black. "I saw the interview you did with Rafe Corrigan on the morning program," he said after a pause. "You looked great in front of the camera. I think you'd enjoy this cooking series we're putting together. It'll be prime time, live audience...."

Veronique's nerves stood on end. Live audience? He thought that would entice her? Before the *Vancouver AM* interview—which Louis had arranged—no one had mentioned the terrifying sound of hundreds of pairs of hands clapping in the darkness. Or how petrified she would feel being the object of scrutiny for rows upon rows of total strangers.

"If the show is so special, why do you ask me? Why not someone like Susan Mendelson?"

"All the well-known chefs are committed for the next six months and beyond," he admitted. "But that's good," he added quickly. "I've decided I want someone fresh."

He really knew nothing about her, yet he was eager to take her on. Again, like Graham. What kind of man proposed after knowing someone only a few weeks? What kind of woman accepted? She had learned a lesson from her impulsiveness. Granted, this man wanted her as the presenter for his TV show, not as his wife. But still.

"And...colorful?" Veronique asked, sipping her coffee. "I suppose you think I'm colorful." At first, Graham had thought she was wonderfully colorful. Then, later on, too colorful. Like a Hawaiian shirt he'd bought on holiday only to find it didn't fit in with his urban executive wardrobe.

Burton shrugged. "*Colorful* is probably not a word I would apply to anyone other than a member of a mariachi band, but I would say you're definitely photogenic."

She heard the admiration in his voice, and like everything else, it reminded her of Graham, whose admiration hadn't lasted. Maybe her antagonism toward Burton was unreasonable, but his appearance recalled memories she'd rather forget. Like Graham ridiculing her poor English, yet not wanting her to take a night course to learn to speak better. Or turning off the French radio so he wouldn't have to listen to that "gobbledygook." Or badgering her to hang up whenever she talked on the phone to Ghislaine. He couldn't bear not knowing what she was saying. Couldn't bear not being in total control.

"I'm going back to Tahiti soon," she reminded Burton.

"There's only thirteen segments. The whole thing will take no more than a couple of months," he said persuasively. "We'd be finished taping by July. You could enjoy the summer here and be back in the South Pacific come fall."

"I know the summer here," she said dryly. "I don't enjoy the rain."

"This summer will be good," he assured her, not having given it a thought before now. He sipped at his coffee. "How long have you been in Canada?"

"Eleven months, ten days and—" she checked her watch "—forty-two minutes. I must go."

Burton glanced out the window at the bus stop across the street. "Relax. There's not a bus in sight. You speak English very well, considering you've been here less than a year. Why are you in such a hurry to leave?"

"I work very hard to learn English. I only come because my husband have a business here. His home is here, so my home is here. Now he's dead, I go." She pushed her cup away and got to her feet. "I really must go."

Burton slid along the bench and followed her up. "I'll drive you. I haven't even mentioned the perks of the job like, like…free publicity and, uh, extra money for location work—"

"No. Thank you." She wound a black woolen scarf around her neck and slung her leather backpack over her shoulder. At the doorway, she paused. "Goodbye, Monsieur…"

He fished his card out of his pocket and, before she could protest, tucked it into a side pocket on her backpack.

"O'Rourke. Burton O'Rourke. Just think about the show, okay?"

A bus swung around the corner and this time slowed to a halt in front of the stop to pick up a pair of teenagers. Without answering him, Veronique ran outside to the bus and up the steps. The doors closed behind her with a clang.

Burton had followed her out and he watched until the bus pulled away. His last view of her was of a white face pressed against the window, as though only from the safety of distance and a glass barrier could she bring herself to look at him.

She must have really loved the guy. Head down, Burton walked back to the restaurant to retrieve his coat. He felt hollow and deflated, as though he'd somehow missed out on something good. And it wasn't just a presenter for his cooking program.

A WELCOME BLAST OF WARM air hit Veronique when she opened her apartment door. She shrugged out of her damp coat, kicked off her boots and slipped into the sheepskin slippers that waited by the door like a faithful pooch. By the light of a single table lamp, she crossed the worn Persian carpet to the built-in teak shelving next to the mantelpiece. She'd given Graham's CD player to Marion, but she'd kept the cassette player, scorned by him, for herself. She touched a few buttons, and a moment later Piaf's throaty voice purred out a torch song.

On a side table, the answering machine's red light blinked. Ignoring it, she crouched low to open the bottom drawer of an old wooden file cabinet she'd bought at an auction, much to Graham's disgust. He'd tried to stop her, but she'd persisted. Once she'd sanded it down and applied new varnish, it looked better to her than his brand-new metal cabinets.

She leafed through the hanging folders and soon found what she was looking for—her work permit. Burton's mention of the approaching months had made her curious. The expiry date on the permit was June 2—less than four weeks away. With Graham's death, her application for immigrant status had been automatically canceled. Without it, she couldn't renew her work visa.

Veronique slid the folder back into place and shut the drawer. Well, no matter. In two weeks, she would be going home.

Rising to her feet, she went to the kitchen and filled a copper watering can from the tap. Caring for her collection of tropical plants was a ritual she never tired of. She murmured sweet nothings to each as she moved around the apartment, dreaming of the garden she would grow one day soon in Tahiti.

"How are you tonight, my lovely?" she murmured to her favorite, a sweetly scented gardenia with glossy leaves and waxy white flowers. "Graham said I would never get you to grow, but he was wrong, wasn't he? He didn't know what a little love can do for a hothouse flower."

Graham. Burton. She shivered despite the warmth of the room and clutched the watering can to her chest. How was it possible another man could look so much like her late husband?

At least she could walk away from Burton without repercussions. Knowing she would never see him again gave her a sense of freedom. Freedom from the confused mix of anger, resentment and bitterness Graham had ultimately inspired in her. Feelings Burton had so unexpectedly caused to well to the surface.

Did those feelings include attraction? Desire? The thought startled her. It had been so long since she'd even thought about love. But after all, it had been Graham's physical type that had drawn her in the first place.

Veronique stood very still, eyes closed, and plumbed her first reaction at seeing Burton O'Rourke. That swift rush of adrenaline, the way her heart raced and her palms had grown suddenly damp… No. Not desire, surely. Simply a response to being startled. And a reminder of the unhappy past.

Opening her eyes, she released her breath and moved again among the rows of plants banked against the bay window. Her head brushed a mobile of brightly painted wooden fish, which twisted and swam as though trying to break free of their vertical school.

"Non, je ne regrette rien…" she crooned along with Piaf. Then sighed. If only it was true that she regretted nothing. But she had many regrets. Worst of all was the loss of that brief, glorious fraction of time when she'd believed herself and Graham to be truly in love.

Veronique passed the answering machine on her way to refill the watering can. The red light blinked reproachfully. *Oh la la.* She ought at least to listen to it.

The usual series of clicks and whirs sounded when she punched the replay button. After a moment, her travel agent came on to confirm Veronique's flight to Papeete with stopovers in Los Angeles and Hawaii.

Oui! Veronique spun around, hugging herself. She was going home at last!

Another series of clicks and beeps indicated someone had called but not left a message. Veronique started to move away. Then came another abrupt click. She heard Marion's voice. It was fraught with fear and pain.

"Veronica? Are you there? I need you, dear." Marion gasped, a soft, raspy sound barely audible above the static on the tape.

Veronique walked back to the machine and stared at it, goose bumps rising on her arms.

"Ronnie? Where are you? I thought you'd be home by now." Marion's voice was high-pitched, ready to crack. "I was taking down the drapes…the stepladder…I reached too far…it fell. I fell.'' A sob, tightly held in check, then, ''I think I've broken something, Ronnie. It's quite…painful. I called 911, but can you come? Please come, Ronnie. Please. I can't move.''

CHAPTER FOUR

IN THE CONTROL BOOTH high above the studio floor, Burton donned his headset. He scanned the bank of monitors that relayed shots of the kitchen from each of the three cameras set up at different angles. A fourth, "to air" monitor, displayed the scene viewers at home would see, an ever-changing composition he would create as taping progressed. Burton had a chair, but he preferred to stand and pace while directing the technicians in the booth or conferring with Vince, the floor manager. He glanced at his schedule, then at the digital chronometer on the table, which ticked away the time in hundredths of a second.

"Ready one," he said clearly but quietly, alerting Mario, the vision switcher, and Bill, head camera operator, to begin with camera one. "Pan up...left. Whoa. Good."

Next to Mario sat Kate, the audio technician, who watched the needles on a series of dials and adjusted the sound level by sliding buttons around on a large panel.

Burton spoke into his headset again. "Stand by." Down in the studio, Vince held up a sign reading 30 Seconds to the chef behind the makeshift kitchen counter.

Three weeks had passed since the night Burton had had coffee with Veronique. Since she hadn't contacted him or shown up for the advertised auditions, he presumed she'd gone back to Tahiti. Well, so what? he thought for the twentieth time, trying to banish her image from his memory banks. He would cast Emily Harper-Smythe, a poised and efficient Englishwoman who'd auditioned the day before. A cooking instructor of some repute with experience on cable TV, she filled the bill to perfection—if only she had a little more pizzazz.

"Roll tape," Burton announced, and Vince began his countdown.

The final chef to audition was a hulking man with hairy black knuckles. Burton watched him prepare his first dish with growing impatience. Chef Wareneki mumbled into his mustache, and the chef's hat he'd insisted on wearing kept slipping forward and obscuring his face. The audience, a mix of retired folk, housewives and the underemployed, was getting restless. So was Burton.

"Cut!" Burton barked into his headset to Vince. Then he burst out of the control booth and skimmed down the sharply spiraled staircase to the set. Murphy and his damn cooking shows!

Camera operators and stage hands parted as he crossed to the kitchen. "Take five, everyone." He went up to the chef. "Mr. Wareneki, we need to talk."

One hand resting on the chef's burly shoulder, Burton steered him aside where they couldn't be overheard. "I'm sorry, but we're running out of airtime."

Chef Wareneki's thick black eyebrows disappeared beneath the starched white brim of his chef's hat. "But I still have to demonstrate my individual chocolate soufflés. They are already in the oven to bring out later."

"Don't worry about that. I've got enough on tape to make my decision."

A movement near the bleachers snagged at his peripheral vision. Another person leaving? He turned. And his heart leaped.

Veronique. She wore a black, long-sleeved dress that hugged her slender, curvy figure. The burnished tips of her softly curling hair spilled over elegant, angular shoulders. Plain, simple, undeniably chic. Her bright green eyes glanced in his direction, then quickly away.

Adrenaline sent his pulse into high gear and nearly had him striding across the studio floor toward her. Then he caught himself. He already had his chef.

Anyway, Ernie was taking care of her.

He turned back to Wareneki with a consoling remark, all the while keeping his eye on what was happening across the room. Veronique had rested one slim hand on Ernie's arm and was gesticulating with the other as she spoke. Hmm. Ernie's gaze was riveted on Veronique as though she were Mata Hari, the Virgin Mary and Marilyn Monroe all rolled into one. His chest was puffed out, and somehow he seemed to have grown taller.

"Excuse me," Burton said to Wareneki, and headed over. Master Ernest was far too impressionable to be left alone with Veronique. Before he could say "bouillabaisse" she would have him wrapped around her little finger.

"What's the problem, Ernie?" he said, clapping a friendly hand on his assistant's shoulder.

"No problem." Ernie didn't take his eyes off Veronique. "Your chef has arrived."

"My chef!" He glanced at Veronique. Her gaze darted between Ernie and the studio floor. Anywhere but at him.

"Ernie, go help Mr. Wareneki organize his stuff to leave." He turned back to Veronique, arms crossed over his chest. "My assistant was out of line just now. The successful candidates were chosen last week to do a live audition this week. I'll be choosing my presenter from among them."

"But I have changed my mind," she said, gripping the strap of her leather backpack. "I want to do the series."

And God help him, he still wanted her to do the series, too. Emily Harper-Smythe might be poised, but Veronique was dynamic. Where the Englishwoman was pleasant-looking, Veronique was magnetic. She might not be able to look him in the face for more than a split second, but he couldn't keep his eyes off her. And he knew the audience would feel the same.

But he wasn't ready to let her know that. He had to be sure that if he hired her, she wouldn't let him down. Why was she here now? And how badly did she want the job?

"Well, now, I don't know," he said, uncrossing his arms to scratch his jaw. "Wareneki was the last to audition. The boys will be wanting to pack up the set."

"But you offered me the series."

Was that desperation in her voice? "You turned it down."

She shrugged, a fascinating, complicated gesture that involved not only her shoulders, but her head and all her features—the eyebrows raised, lids lowered, mouth pursed.

"I did not say I didn't want to do it. I said I could not."

She held her elbows in tight to her sides. Talking to Ernie, she'd been fluid and unconsciously graceful. With him,. she was all angles and nervous energy. He found himself wanting to change that.

"I've made my decision." He added a dash of regret to his voice.

"Not Monsieur Wareneki, surely." She sounded deeply offended.

"No, Emily Harper-Smythe. Englishwoman, very elegant."

Her hand flipped up, and a thin gold bangle slid over black cashmere. "Poof! The English do not know how to cook." But her lightning glance at his face held a trace of uncertainty. "Was she any good?"

Burton smiled cheerfully. "Terrific. Very professional. Her Thai vegetable curry was delicious." He patted his stomach at the memory.

Veronique straightened her shoulders. Two small spots of red burned in her cheeks, enhancing her vivid hair and brilliant green eyes.

"It is only right you give me a chance to prove myself,"

she said, glaring at his chest. "You beg me to do the show. I come all the way down here to tell you I will consider it, only to find you have hired someone else!" One hand swept dramatically skyward, and she burst into a torrent of excited French.

God, she was gorgeous. And if she would only look him in the eye, she'd know he thought so. She'd also know he'd give her whatever she wanted, including an audition.

Ernie was at his sleeve. "Hey, Burt. The guys want to know—"

He spun around. "'Burton,' you dolt!" He stopped short and took a deep breath. "Tell Vince to hang tough for a while."

He took another breath and turned back to Veronique. "One—I never beg. Two—I haven't hired anyone yet—"

"You should not talk to him like that." Veronique's frowning gaze followed Ernie. "He is a sensitive young man."

Burton gritted his teeth. "Tell me, what made you change your mind about doing the show?"

Again that hint of desperation in the ragged, in-drawn breath, and the shaky hand through tangled curls. "My mother-in-law, she break her hip. She must stay in hospital for some weeks. She have no one to help her but me. Already I quit my job at the restaurant, and there is nothing else available, so…" She trailed off, looking embarrassed.

"So you thought you'd fill in the time with my cooking show." *Look at me.*

"We help each other, I think." She stared fixedly at his shirtfront. A tiny twitch started at the corner of her nostril.

Behind him, Ernie cleared his throat. Burton started. "What is it now, Ern?"

"She could fill in the rest of Wareneki's time slot. You know, sort of a minishow. One dish."

"Thanks for the suggestion." His dry tone went right over Ernie's head.

"Any time, boss." Ernie smiled at Veronique.

Veronique beamed back at Ernie. *"Merci."*

Burton felt an uncomfortable twinge somewhere in mid-chest. Him, jealous of Ernie? No way.

"All right," he said to Veronique. "Since Wareneki's out of the running, you can finish his segment. Ernie, go tell Vince we'll shoot one more set. Let's get moving before we lose the rest of the audience."

Veronique glanced at the bleachers, and a shiver skittered through her. She'd come to the studio today expecting a brief chat to negotiate money and menus. Now her sure thing hinged on a public performance. "But I have nothing to prepare!"

Burton's chest, and the arms crossed in front of it, looked unsympathetic. "You can prepare whatever Wareneki was going to make. Chocolate soufflé, I think he said."

Veronique didn't respond. Maybe it wasn't too late to call Louis and ask for her old job back. Though in truth, she'd been glad to leave Le Soupçon. Louis had hands like an octopus and the morals of an alley cat.

"Chocolate soufflé," Burton repeated. "Can you make it?"

Her head snapped up. "But of course. Every apprentice chef knows how to make that." But her mind went blank even as she mentally reviewed the recipe. How many eggs, exactly? How much cream?

Then Burton was leading her across the floor. She'd meant to tell him right away about her work visa running out, thinking maybe he could help. Now it was too late. Everything was happening too fast. People were all around them, Burton issuing orders as they went. So many cameras and wires and lights…

"Nervous?" Burton murmured.

"Not at all." Never would she admit such a thing!

"Don't worry. You'll be fine. Just remember to look directly into the camera. Don't look at the audience."

They stepped onto the set. The floorboards sounded hollow beneath her feet. The "kitchen" looked like a department-store display. There was a fake window with a light behind it and some fake plants hanging from the fake ceiling. She felt like a fake herself.

"But these people are right in front of me, watching what I do," she protested in a low voice. "How can I not speak to them?"

"Trust me on this. Your real audience is the people at home in front of their television sets."

She glanced around the kitchen and wiped her palms down her dress. Everything looked so small. So unfamiliar. "Go on," she said.

"The ingredients are in the fridge. The pots and pans in the cupboards—"

"I am a chef. These things I know."

A white apron with a bib hung on a hook beside the stove. She took it down, inspected it for cleanliness and put it on. Then took a deep breath. "I am ready."

"Great. In just a few minutes the floor manager…that's Vince there with the red baseball cap…will begin the countdown, at first out loud, then like so—" He broke off with an exasperated sigh. "Veronique, you're simply going to have to look at me!"

Taking another big breath, she raised her eyes—and exhaled in relief. All she was expected to look at was his hand. He counted down the seconds by folding his fingers back one by one.

"When he claps the board together—" Burton illustrated that, too "—you're on." He moved around the set as he spoke, straightening some pots, whisking a dirty cloth out of sight. He stopped in front of her to tuck a strand of hair behind her ears, his fingers cool and impersonal. She tensed, remembering touches that had nothing to do with Burton. Her confused senses wanted to attach the scent of English Leather to him, but all she could smell was the merest whiff of sandalwood. And chocolate soufflé.

Veronique swallowed. "He does not say 'action'?"

He laughed, a warm, melting chuckle. "That's only when making movies. You've got twelve minutes to complete the segment. I'll be in the control booth." He indicated a glass-fronted room high on the opposite wall. Then he walked off the set and disappeared into the crowd of camera operators and assorted others whose position and function she had no idea about.

Twelve minutes! *Oh la la.* Self-consciously, Veronique began to assemble the utensils she would need to create a soufflé. In her nervousness, she banged the top of a double boiler into its base with a clang. Chocolate soufflé! She did not want to do someone else's dish. That would not show Monsieur Burton what she could do.

"Thirty seconds to air," announced an unsmiling man with headset and clipboard.

Banks of bright lights flared on, making her squint. Three cameras were positioned, to her right, left and dead center. Her stomach flip-flopped like a lobster in a pot of boiling water.

"Ten…nine…eight…"

This was even worse than preparing *choux* pastry in front of Maître Chef Duxelles at the Cordon Bleu in Paris.

The floor manager's voice stopped. She saw his hand go up, fingers outstretched.

"Five…four…"

Blank. Her mind was completely blank.

"Two…*one.*"

She gazed into the camera directly in front of her. It seemed to engulf her, sucking her down the round black hole into a tortuous maze of shutters and lenses. Veronique stared into the unseeing eye, paralyzed.

Was that herself reflected in the dark glass? It reminded her of Marion, small and pathetic in her high hospital bed. Marion needed her. She, Veronique, needed this job. She hadn't wanted it, but now she had to do it.

"Bonjour."

Merde. She'd croaked like a frog! Swallowing hard, she cleared her throat and spoke again. "My name is Veronique Dutot. I am to prepare a soufflé."

She could not speak to the camera; it was too alien. Her gaze went to a woman in the front row who wore her hair in a similar style to her aunt in Bordeaux.

"The soufflé is a very special dish," she confided to the woman, and imagined Tante Hélène nodding in agreement. "With all that cream and eggs the soufflé can be very heavy, but no, she must be light as a cloud. And she is very versatile. You can make dessert soufflé. *Par example,* chocolate. But I don't care so much for chocolate soufflé. Let's see what else we have in the refrigerator."

With a silent prayer, she opened the fridge door. Thank heaven! On the otherwise bare shelves were several plastic-wrapped parcels of vegetables. They must have been left over from the Thai curry. *Pah!* She could do better than the Englishwoman, even with leftovers.

Transferring her bounty to the kitchen counter, Veronique beamed at the audience. "This is the test of a true cook—to make a delicious meal out of whatever you happen to have in the cupboard. Today I will show you how to make…ah, spinach soufflé."

A movement caught her eye, and her gaze flicked up to the control booth. Burton was at the window, frantically making a cutting motion with his hand. *Mon Dieu,* but he made her nervous. Raising the bunch of spinach, she blocked him out of her vision.

"Come closer. Please…" She waved her arm at the scattered groups high in the bleachers. "Come where you can experience the colors, and the aroma of the cooking."

She didn't wait to see if they would follow her directions but quickly unwrapped the vegetables and placed them on the chopping board. With nothing prepared in advance, she had no time to waste.

"Okay, first the garlic. Lots of garlic." Her hands flew, smashing the cloves, ripping the skins off and chopping furiously. "Onions…" She peeled and sliced faster than she ever had before. "Into the pot with them…" Bits and pieces flew everywhere. *"Oop, et là!"*

"I never cook on TV before," she confided to the audience with a laugh. "Okay, add a big knob of butter…." She turned on the gas flame under the pot, and the garlic and onions began to sizzle. "What a beautiful aroma. *C'est fantastique, non?*

"Now some flour, stir it around…. This is called a r-r-roux." She rolled the *r* till it swallowed the vowels.

This might be fun, after all, she thought. If only she wasn't so conscious of Burton O'Rourke watching from on high. She wouldn't look at him again. Glowering like that, he was sure to make her forget some crucial ingredient.

"Now, we need eggs. Maybe six eggs yolks, and nine or eight eggs whites." With one hand, she separated the eggs into two bowls while with the other, she stirred the roux. The familiar movements helped to relax her.

"You know why the best chefs are women?" she asked the audience with a grin. "Because they can do more than one thing at a time. If I had a baby under my arm, I would look just like my mama when I was a little girl in France, and she cook for me and my three sisters and Papa."

She glanced into the pot. *"Alors.* Now we add milk to make a thick béchamel sauce—about a cup…." She poured straight from the carton. "A little at first, so it do not go lumpy. Stir hard. Then more…*oop, et là!* Too much. Never mind. Let it thicken, turn the heat down…now, to the spinach.

"Wash it well…chop it roughly…put it in the pan and turn up the heat." She shook the pan vigorously. "Wonderful food, spinach. Make you strong like Popeye."

From the corner of her eye, she caught a glimpse of someone to the left of the stage signaling to her. She glanced at the control booth. Burton wasn't there so that meant… Yes, it *was* him. His short, coppery hair was tossed like a salad, and he held up one hand, fingers outstretched. What did that mean? Surely not "five minutes." She still had so far to go, and a soufflé could not be rushed.

Steam billowed out of the spinach pan when she lifted the lid. "Done!" she proclaimed, and scraped the wilted greens into the pot with the sauce.

"Now to beat the eggs whites. A copper bowl is best—" she glanced around "—but this will do." She grabbed a stainless steel basin.

She poured in the egg whites and picked up a large wire whisk. "You can use an electric beater, but beating by hand is better even though it is slower." She heard a groan from the darkened sidelines and ignored it. "Start slowly to beat, breaking the whites, making them foam. Then, a little faster, then very fast." She glanced up at the audience. "Who needs the dumbbells, *hein?*"

Chuckles rose from the blackness beyond the lights and gave her heart.

"To fold the eggs whites into the sauce require a light touch," she explained, holding the bowl up so the audience could see. "A big spoonful at first, mix lightly, then fold the rest in carefully. Now to prepare the soufflé dish.

"Dishes," she amended, catching sight of a half-dozen small ramekins. "Normally, I make this in one large dish. But—" she shrugged "—we make do. Always we make do. Grease them with butter and dust with grated Parmesan.…"

Veronique searched the fridge. No cheese. "Never mind," she said cheerfully, "just remember to add the

Parmesan when you make it at home. Mushrooms or ham are also good with spinach. Now, plop, plop, into the little dishes it goes. *Et voilà,* they are ready to go in the oven.''

Veronique loaded the soufflés onto a baking tray and carried it to the oven. ''About thirty minutes in a moderate to hot oven and…'' She removed another pan of ramekins containing barely risen chocolate soufflés, and held them up for the audience to see.

''These are…not what one expects from a spinach soufflé. But—'' she beamed a smile to the audience ''—if you follow my instructions, your soufflé will be high and puffy, like white clouds on a sunny day.''

Through the shadows behind the set, she sensed Burton coming closer.

''If I had a few minutes more, I could show you some simple garnishes…''

''*Cut!*''

The overhead banks of lights switched out with a series of loud thuds. Veronique leaned against the counter and wiped a dishcloth across her damp forehead. It had been terrifying, but she'd done it. Done it? *Mon Dieu,* she had triumphed!

''Well,'' she said, turning to smile at Burton's left shoulder as he strode onto the set, ''what do you think?''

''What do I think?'' he repeated, his eyes round and harried. ''I'll tell you what I think. You don't follow instructions. You can't stick to a schedule. And you talk way too much!''

Her hopes collapsed like Wareneki's pathetic soufflés. Eyes burning, she stared at his chest in silence. She would have to go back to Louis the Octopus. And beg.

''Burt, hey Burt.'' Ernie tugged on Burton's elbow.

''Ernest!''

''Sorry, Burton. But look!'' Ernie pointed to the audience.

The scattered groups of people had voted with their feet,

gathering into one enthusiastic knot in the front two rows. Contrary to Burton's opinion, the majority was overwhelmingly in favor of Veronique.

"Oh, great," he muttered, pushing a hand through his hair. "Exactly what I'd hoped for."

Veronique saw it, too. Exhilaration bubbled unexpectedly through her. They liked her.

BURTON HAD BARELY BEEN home from work twenty minutes when the doorbell rang. It was his mother, with a large paper bag containing something that gave off a delicious savory aroma. As always, Catherine O'Rourke was stylishly dressed, in black jacket and pants. Burton was relieved to see she'd recovered some of her bounce. Maybe too much bounce, he thought darkly as she sailed through the front door and headed straight for the galley kitchen at the back of his one-bedroom apartment.

Catherine cast a pitying glance at his half-eaten plate of baked beans on toast. "I brought you some homemade chicken soup. You can still get a cold this late in the season, you know."

Burton took the bag from her hands and placed it on the counter. He drew her into a hug. "Thanks, but I'm thirty-four—much too old to be receiving care packages from my mother. You just look after yourself."

She eased out of his arms and gestured to his open briefcase and the stack of papers spilled across the two-person table. "Why are you still working at this hour?"

"I've got scripts to approve for tomorrow." Burton sat down again and scooted his chair in.

Catherine shed her damp trench coat and sat down opposite him, crossing one leg over the other. "Honestly, Burton," she said, flicking a wisp of dark hair off her forehead. "What's to become of you? You're all work and no play. How long has it been since you've done anything for fun? Taken any photos? And what's happening in your sex life?''

"Mother!"

Catherine carried on, unperturbed. "Have you called Beth's daughter for a date yet?"

"No, and I don't intend to. Beth is your friend, not mine." He took a mouthful of beans and toast.

"I want grandchildren, Burton, while I'm still young enough to enjoy them."

Swallowing, Burton raised a warning finger. "Don't start." Then, to distract her, he leaned forward confidingly. "I've got a new PA at the station. His name is Ernie and he keeps calling me Burt."

Catherine laughed and flapped a well-manicured hand. "Oh, that's too funny. Burt and Ernie. Is he short?"

Burton nodded, grinning. "And he's got a round head with fuzzy dark hair that sticks out in tufts over his ears."

"He doesn't!"

"Well, not quite. His hair is light brown and slightly wavy, although he does have a round head. He's a good kid. He's going to do fine."

Catherine laid an elbow along the back of her chair and rested her jaw on her knuckles. "So tell me, have you found a chef for your cooking show?"

His smile faded. Burton sliced savagely into his beans and toast. He didn't want to be reminded of Veronique. The audience had responded to her exactly as he'd expected, but what he hadn't expected was…was… He didn't even know what to call the crazy way she made him feel.

"Burtie!"

His head came up with a jerk. "I beg your pardon?"

"You're woolgathering."

"Woolgathering?" His eyebrows rose. "Have you been reading Jane Austen again?"

The mixture of irritation and motherly indulgence on

Catherine O'Rourke's face disappeared abruptly. She looked down at her well-manicured hands. "It's the only thing that completely absorbs my mind," she said, her voice quavery.

Burton understood; photography did the same thing for him, though it had been ages since he'd taken his camera out. Just one more thing he never had time for anymore. He reached for her hand and gave it a squeeze. "Sorry."

"It's okay." She straightened with a shaky but determined smile. "You were telling me about your new chef."

Burton scowled. "The test audience was riveted. Ernie was practically in a swoon—and he's supposedly engaged to be married. Even Murphy thought she was—"

"She?"

Burton swore he could see antennae rise out of his mother's sleek pageboy hairdo. "Murphy," he said, stressing the name with a warning frown that told her to keep any further remarks about his love life, or lack of it, to herself, "thought she was a corker. He actually used that word. The entire camera crew is completely infatuated."

"And you're not?" Catherine cast him a shrewd glance.

"Definitely not. She didn't listen to a word I said. She had no concept of time— Wait a minute, I'll show you what I mean. I've got a tape of her audition." He pushed back his chair. "Come on."

"What about your dinner?" she said, jumping up to follow him into the living room.

"It'll keep." Burton plugged the tape into his state-of-the-art video player and sat on a stool to fast-forward to Veronique's segment. Catherine sat on one of the two chairs of vaguely Swedish design that made up the only large furniture in the room.

"There, that's her," he said, stopping the tape. "The one with the hair and the voice."

"You mean the woman in the chef's apron, behind the stove?" Catherine remarked dryly.

They watched for a moment in silence. Behind Veronique's charm, Burton could see a woman clinging to the edge of control. She'd held it together, he had to give her that, but it had been a close thing. He glanced at his mother to check her reaction and was surprised to see her leaning forward with a smile that blossomed every now and then into a chuckle.

The taped segment ended, and the small audience broke into enthusiastic applause.

"Burton, she's wonderful!" Catherine said, turning to him. "So full of life. So confident—"

"Confident? She was terrified."

His mother waved this away with a flick of her perfectly manicured fingers. "She has terrific rapport with the audience. And she made do wonderfully with what she had. Women can relate to that."

Burton jumped to his feet and began to pace the small living room. "She didn't have to 'make do'! That's not the way a TV cooking show works. Everything is planned, prepared and premeasured to ensure nothing goes wrong."

"Nothing did go wrong," Catherine insisted.

"That depends on your point of view. The show has a tight schedule, an even tighter budget. Plus, it'll be taped before a live audience. There's no room for retakes if she screws up. If I don't make this work, Murphy will scuttle my plans for *Lost Harvest*."

Catherine twisted in her chair to look at him. "You took risks with *Lovers and Strangers*. Look how well that paid off."

"Going on location for a daytime soap is a far cry from letting a deranged Frenchwoman loose in front of a live audience."

Laughing and shaking her head, Catherine got to her feet. "Sounds to me like this is more personal than professional. Are you sure you're not just a little interested in her?"

Burton glanced away. Mothers and their sixth sense. "I hardly know the woman. I was ticked off when she turned down my first offer to appear on the show. Now I'm wishing she hadn't changed her mind. People like her are hell to work with. I'm responsible for bringing the show in under budget. It's me who has to fix things if they go wrong."

"It was only an audition. She'll learn."

Burton leaned over and pushed the eject button to retrieve the tape. "Maybe. She's coming in tomorrow to talk it over."

Catherine handed him the cover. "If you really feel she won't work out, I'm sure you can persuade Ed Murphy you should hire someone else."

Burton shook his head. "That's the trouble. She's got style, she's got pizzazz, she's warm and human and funny. She'll be really popular and the ratings will go through the roof."

"Then you should count your blessings."

"I'll be counting them from a padded cell in the loony bin before this is over," he replied gloomily. "If it wasn't for the documentary, I'd chuck it all in right now."

"You know you don't mean that." She glanced at her watch. "I'd better be going. Put that soup in the freezer if you're not going to eat it right away."

"Sure," he replied automatically. "I'm sorry I haven't been able to get out to the farm yet to help go through Granddad's stuff. This cooking show has been sucking up every spare minute. Have you got much done?"

"Not really," Catherine said, walking back to the kitchen where she'd left her coat and purse. "I cleaned out the fridge and took whatever was perishable from the pantry. His clothes I put in a bag for the Salvation Army. Oh, and I brought Rufus home with me. I didn't think it fair to leave him with the neighbors for too long."

"You brought Rufus to the city?" Burton leaned on the

doorjamb in the entrance to the kitchen. "Do you think he'll be happy there?"

She shrugged. "He seemed glad to see me, poor thing. Over at the Vandermeres he has to sleep outside and share rations with their two dogs. He's fine in the backyard, and now that summer's coming I can take him for a walk every day."

"Still."

"I know."

Their eyes met, and Burton knew Catherine was thinking the same thing he was—Granddad's absence was a tangible thing. Like a boulder in midstream, it created ripples and eddies downstream in time.

Catherine blinked bright eyes and reached for her coat. "Have you thought about what you're going to do with the farm?"

Burton heaved a sigh. "I think about it all the time, but I've yet to come to any brilliant conclusions. Living out there isn't practical, and I hate the idea of renting it out to strangers. Tomorrow I'm meeting a real estate agent to go over the property and give me an idea of its market value."

"You're not thinking of selling!" Catherine's voice rose in alarm.

Burton led the way down the short hallway to the front door. "I don't want to, but at the moment it's looking more and more like a white elephant."

"It's your inheritance, Burton. You'll marry someday, I hope. The country is a wonderful place to raise children."

He perched on the edge of the hall table. "You told me you hated living out in the sticks when you were a teenager. It was so isolated you couldn't even go to the movies."

"Things are different now. There's more development out that way. More activities for young people."

"True, but it's not the life for me," Burton argued.

"I'm no farmer. I don't have time to plant crops even if I wanted to. On the other hand, it would be wrong to let the land lie fallow, even worse to sell to developers. It's a real bind."

Catherine set her purse on the table beside Burton so she could put on her coat. "I could rent out my place and live at the farm until it suits you."

Burton pushed away from the table and held her coat while she slipped her arms into the sleeves. "And shovel half a mile of driveway every winter? What about your aerobics class? And your book club? I can't see you being happy out there, either."

"I guess not. But please, Burton, don't put it on the market without telling me."

"Sure."

She turned to face him, eyes alight with newly hatching schemes. "Why don't I get Melissa to call you?"

"Melissa? Who's Melissa?"

"Why, Beth's daughter, of course."

"Forget it, Mother." He gently steered her toward the door. "I'm not interested in meeting anyone right now. And when I am, I'll find my own dates. Thanks, anyway."

"Or what about that Frenchwoman?" she said, doing up her buttons. "What's her name?"

"Veronique?" he said. "Don't even think about it."

"She's not terribly pretty, I know, but she's got something." Catherine peered intently at him the way she used to when he was a teenager coming home late from a party. "Don't you think so?"

"I think it's time you went home and badgered the dog for a change." Burton reached around her to open the door. "Oh, by the way, did you happen to bring the chess set?"

Frowning, Catherine tied the belt around her coat. "That's the oddest thing. I looked for it, but it wasn't there."

"Not there! Did you look in the cabinet in the living room where he always kept the games?"

"Of course. The Monopoly and the Scrabble games were there, but not the chess set."

Burton scratched his jaw. "How could that be? I know he sometimes took it out to play against himself, but he was always so careful about putting it back."

Catherine slung the strap of her black leather purse over her shoulder. "I know. That's why it's so odd. I hope…" An anxious frown slanted her carefully shaped eyebrows.

"What?"

She glanced away. "Nothing."

"Come on, Mother, what were you going to say?"

"Nothing." She leaned up to kiss him on the cheek. "I'm sure it will turn up. Goodbye, Burtie darling. See you soon."

"Bye." He gave her a hug and shut the door behind her. The chess set was missing. Another loss, one that left him anxious and uneasy. But Mother had been intent on other things and probably more than a little distraught. He'd have a look for the set tomorrow, after his appointment with Veronique. It had to be there somewhere.

CHAPTER FIVE

VERONIQUE ROSE ON TIPTOES to peer through the small high window into the hospital ward where Marion lay with her broken hip. Her move to the rehab center had been postponed when a secondary infection had set in around the pins holding her brittle bones together. The delay seemed to have set her back emotionally, as well as physically. The curtains were shut, the lights were off, and Marion's eyes were open, staring at nothing.

Veronique dropped back to her heels. She twined a long curl around and around one finger. *She is giving up, I can see it happening. She will need me, and need me, and need me, forever.*

Never before in her life had friendship come with such a huge responsibility. A letter from the Department of Immigration sat in her backpack, weighing her down like a chunk of lead. She hadn't found the courage to open it yet, because she knew what it would say. The implications for herself—and for Marion—were frightening. Only a week left before her work visa expired and she would have to leave the country. But she couldn't tell Marion and add that to all her other worries.

Veronique took another peek through the window at Marion's drawn face, and her heart contracted at seeing her timid, good-hearted friend further diminished. *Pauvre* Marion. She had no one else.

With a sigh, she leaned on the door and went in.

"*Bonjour,* Marion." She spoke softly but cheerfully as

she approached the bed and set her leather backpack on the floor. "How are you feeling today?"

Marion slowly turned her head. Her eyelids fluttered as she focused on Veronique. "Not very well." It seemed an effort for her even to talk.

She has aged, Veronique thought, dismayed. Her hair color was in need of renewal and the skin on her thin hands resting on the pale green coverlet looked almost transparent. "It's only been a few weeks. Give yourself time. Did you see the doctor today?"

Marion nodded weakly. "She says I'll be ready to move to the rehab center of the hospital next week. While I'm there I'll have physiotherapy to get my joints working and learn how to walk again." Tears moistened her sparse gray lashes. "I wish Stan were here. I still can't believe he's gone forever."

She closed her eyes and the tears seeped out from beneath her lids to trickle down her pale cheek. "I'm sorry, Veronique. I know I'm a burden."

Veronique fought back a flutter of panic. "You are not a burden, Marion, but you must be brave." She spoke firmly. "This is not the end. You will grow strong again. Stronger than ever."

"What if I don't?" Marion cried in a feeble outburst of passion. "What if I have to use a walker for the rest of my life? What if I never go home? Tell me one good thing that could ever come from this."

Veronique gave her an affectionate smile. "It got you out of the house."

She walked around the bed to the window and snapped open the curtains. A dozen stories below, sunlight reflected off car windows as traffic backed up along Burrard Street. "Ah, that's better," she said. "The sun is good, no? It brightens the spirit."

Marion squinted at her, one hand raised to protect her

eyes from a shaft of sunlight. "I'm not a brave person, Ronnie. I never have been."

"Nonsense. People are not born brave...."

"They have courage thrust upon them," Marion finished in a dismal monotone.

Veronique laughed and pulled up a hard-backed chair to the bed. "There now, I was going to say the same thing, but with three times as many words. And what happens after the rehab center? Can you go home?"

"Yes, but even then I won't be able to look after myself. The nurse told me I'll be on crutches for weeks, maybe months. I won't be able to dress, or cook for myself. I'll have to get a home help."

"I will move in and look after you until you are better," she said, pushing aside worries about the uncertainty of her own immediate future. She put on a smile and teased. "Better the tyrant you know than the tyrant you don't."

Marion hitched herself higher on the pillow. "But how can you do that if you're going back to Tahiti?"

"I'm not going right away." Veronique got up to help Marion adjust her pillows more comfortably. When she'd seated herself again, she said, "I auditioned to be a chef on a TV cooking show. Maybe I will get the job. The audience liked me." She curled a lock of hair around her finger. "But I don't think he liked me."

"Who could possibly not like you, my dear?" Marion said.

"Burton O'Rourke. The producer."

"Burton O'Rourke?" Marion's eyebrows pinched together. "That sounds familiar."

"He also produces your favorite show—what do you call it—*Loving Stranger*?"

"*Lovers and Strangers*. Oh, Ronnie, how exciting!" Two spots of pink appeared in her sallow cheeks.

"I don't know. He's a very uptight man. At first I thought he was kind even though he look like—" She broke off and rose to walk around the foot of Marion's bed. "During the audition he went berserk. He didn't like that I talk to the audience. Or that I change the menu. And everything have to be timed right down to a fifth of a second," she said, tapping the face of her wristwatch. "No time to chat, or joke, or think about what is coming next. He will drive me crazy!"

Marion shifted in her bed to watch Veronique. "Give him a chance, poor man. He must have so much on his mind. So many people to organize. When do you start?"

Veronique shrugged, her mouth pursed in speculation. "I don't know yet if I have the job! His assistant seem to think I do, but *Monsieur* O'Rourke, he does not say yes or no. He just tell me to come to his office tomorrow. Today, that is."

Marion's mouth dropped open. "Goodness' sake, girl! What are you doing here? Get along to the television studio and find out."

Veronique smiled. A little vicarious excitement had brightened Marion's spirits better than comfort and kind words. "Don't worry. The appointment is for two o'clock, and the studio is right next door to the hospital."

She reached for her backpack. "Before I go, I brought you some chocolate. And a new book. I hope you haven't read it already."

"Ooh, a romance." Marion reached for her reading glasses and glanced at the title before flipping it over to read the back cover. "No, I haven't. Thank you, dear. And Ronnie…?"

Veronique glanced up from fastening the thongs on her backpack. "Yes?"

"I know you're not very happy here," Marion said, her gray-blue eyes uncertain. "You're not staying because of me, are you?"

Veronique rocked her head from side to side. "When I

got the chance at the cooking show I decided I could stay a little longer.''

Marion was silent a moment. "How much longer?''

"Until the end of summer. I'll leave before the rains come.''

"Oh, you and the rain. Weather's not everything, you know.''

Veronique smiled a little sadly. Weather was actually quite a lot when it was all you had. True, she had Marion, but although she was very fond of her, it wasn't enough. After Graham she needed love, and nurturing—preferably in a warm climate.

"I'm very glad you're staying longer, but...'' Marion's voice shook, and she paused to clear her throat. "I will get a home help. I don't want to be a burden to you.''

"You are not a burden, Marion—''

"Don't argue, Ronnie,'' Marion said with surprising firmness. "I am grateful for everything you do for me, but you're not going to bury yourself way over on the North Shore with an invalid old woman.''

"We shall see,'' Veronique said, rising. "Wish me luck.''

She put on a confident smile, but the butterflies in her stomach were already taking wing. She didn't know which would be worse—if she got the job, or if she didn't.

VERONIQUE FOLLOWED the Channel Seven receptionist down a wide corridor, admiring her spiky white hair. They stopped in front of a closed door, and the older woman knocked.

"Come in.''

Lillian opened the door. "Ms. Dutot is here to see you.'' With an encouraging smile, she said to Veronique, "Good luck.''

Veronique returned her smile and went in. She got a quick impression of wall-to-wall photos and shelves of videocassettes before her gaze lit upon Burton, who was scowling over some business papers. For one horrible second she felt as though she'd stumbled through a time warp and come across her husband seated at his desk at home. She gulped in a deep breath and pressed a hand to her chest as her heart leaped into high gear.

Then he glanced up, and it was not her husband at all, but Burton who rose to extend his hand. His palm was warm and dry, and his fingers enclosed hers completely. Her stomach flipped over, and her heart raced faster, leaving her even more confused.

"Have a seat," he said, releasing her hand to glance at his watch. He frowned. "I've only got about five minutes though before I have to leave for another appointment. If you're going to work in television, you've got to learn to be on time."

Startled, Veronique checked her watch. "It's not yet two o'clock. I'm five minutes early."

Burton frowned. "I asked you to come at one o'clock."

"I am sure you said two o'clock."

"My life revolves around schedules. I don't think I would be mistaken." He flipped his desk diary around so she could see it. "Right here," he said, tapping an entry midway down the page. "One o'clock."

Veronique leaned over the desk to look. Her name was indeed opposite the time he'd indicated.

"It cannot be right." She glanced up. Straight into deep blue eyes framed with dark, coppery lashes. Then immediately down to an argumentative jaw so close she could see the glint of coppery stubble.

"I will show you," she said, breathless. Digging into her backpack, she whipped out the envelope on which she'd scribbled the time of their appointment. The return address, the federal Department of Immigration, surfaced under Burton's nose. Quickly she flipped it over. "*Voilà.* Two o'clock."

"Proves nothing. This," he said, tapping his diary again, "is official."

Veronique stuffed the envelope back inside her pack without revealing its contents as she'd originally intended. There was no point introducing that complication until she was offered the job, which at the moment seemed unlikely.

"Your assistant was there—he can tell you," she said to Burton's left shoulder. Her English wasn't perfect, but she could hear the difference between "one" and "two."

She got an impression of dark eyebrows pulling together. "Never mind about Ernie," he growled. "We're wasting time arguing. How about coming with me? We can talk about the show while we're driving."

"Driving? Where to?"

"Langley." Burton picked up a file—one with her name on it—and thrust it, along with a stapled sheaf of papers, into a black leather briefcase. "I have an appointment at three at my grandfather's farm." He tossed a calculator into his briefcase, snapped it shut and strode to the door. "It's a nice drive. The whole thing won't take more than a couple of hours. I've got the contract with me, so if we come to an agreement—"

"Stop!" she cried, throwing up her hands. "You are rushing me. I need to think if I am free."

In truth, she didn't have to think more than a few seconds to know she was completely, utterly, depressingly free. Le Soupçon was history. Marion was being well looked after. Graham's friends never called anymore. And for the past five months she'd been careful not to make any new friends whom she would regret leaving. On the other hand, Burton was a busy man. If she left now, who knew when she'd get another appointment? Or if he'd call the Englishwoman, instead.

"I will come," she said, slinging her backpack over her shoulder. "But I must be back by six o'clock."

"No problem." He swung his coat over his arm. "Big date?"

"Ah…something like that." A date to talk to her sister halfway around the world. A date she wouldn't miss for anything.

They picked up his car, a silver Tercel, from the underground parking lot and within minutes were heading east on Georgia Street, zipping in and out of traffic like a ricocheting bullet. The sun that had briefly brightened Marion's hospital room had been enveloped by thick, dark clouds. Fat drops of rain began to splat against the windshield. Burton turned on the wipers and pressed the defog button. Two clear patches formed on the bottom of the windshield and slowly spread upward.

Jumbled thoughts and confused feelings held Veronique's tongue. She listened to the rhythmic swish of the blades and the hiss of tires on the wet road. Swept away again. No, it was not the same. Her heart was not involved, or if it was, then only to the extent she was doing this for Marion. She glanced sideways. It was easier to look at his profile than his full face, but harder to accept he wasn't Graham when she couldn't see his eyes.

"Have you seen much of the Fraser Valley?" Burton said, shifting down for a red light. His hands and feet moved in tandem, quickly, efficiently.

She watched his rapid movements and intense gaze on the road ahead. Could she work with a man so speedy and nervy? "Once we went to Harrison Hot Springs for a convention, but Graham preferred the city, where his business contacts and his friends were."

"What about you? Are you a city girl?" He shifted gears again, muscles and sinew moving under the tracings of dark hair on his lightly tanned forearm.

"I'm an island girl. A bit of city, a bit of country. But always a garden, the ocean and the sun. Freedom to wander—and a home to come back to.'' A home that was waiting for her now.

They'd left the city streets for the freeway. Veronique cracked open the window on the passenger side and inhaled deeply of the towering evergreens that lined the roadside. Houses and trees, fields dotted with horses, all zipped past as Burton picked up speed.

''I've always lived in the city,'' Burton said, ''but when I was a kid I spent most of my summers at my grandfather's farm, where we're going now. He died recently, as I think I told you, and left it to me.'' He sighed and tapped his fingers on the steering wheel. ''I used to travel a lot as a photojournalist, but I don't have time for trips these days.''

''You should make time. You are like the—what do you call them? The skinny dogs that race?''

''Greyhounds?''

''*Exactement.* Always running and running, faster and faster after the bunny.'' She made paws of her hands and paddled through the air.

He laughed. ''The difference is,'' he said, ''I get the bunny in the end.''

''My husband worked much overtime. He became vice president of a chain of travel agencies—the week before he died.''

Burton's smile faded. ''Heart attack?''

''Plane crash.'' Her gaze dropped. Although she didn't feel a speck of grief or loss, she couldn't be happy that even a rat like Graham had died.

''I'm sorry.'' His voice was low, consoling. ''At least he achieved something.''

Veronique made a dismissive gesture. ''What good is that when you're gone?''

''Who knows how far a good man's influence will extend? If everyone stopped to smell the roses, there'd be no one to tend the garden.''

"Je m'excuse?" Her mind struggled with the unfamiliar expression. She tried to recall if she'd seen anything like it in the book of sayings she'd picked up to study colloquial English.

"I mean—"

"I think I know what you mean. I was not suggesting—" she waved a hand uncertainly "—that. All I said was, you, *Monsieur* O'Rourke, are too speedy. You should relax."

"I do relax." He frowned, as if trying to remember the last time he *had* relaxed. Then he slanted her a brief smile. "If you have to judge me, I'd rather you just admired my stamina."

Veronique quickly turned to the window to hide her smile. At times he could be quite charming.

"So, are you interested in doing the show?" He came up close behind a semitrailer going under the speed limit.

"Are you offering it to me?"

"Yes." His gaze flicked from the side to the rearview mirror and back. Then his car shot sideways into the other lane and roared past the truck.

Mon Dieu! Veronique thought, clinging to the armrest. "What about the menu? Can I choose what I want to cook?"

"Yes, within certain guidelines. Whatever you plan, you'll have to run by me."

"But I am the chef." Consultation she didn't object to so much as working one-on-one with him.

"Television is a collaborative effort. Nobody gets one hundred percent say in what they do. I'm giving you plenty of leeway as it is, considering you're an unknown quantity. Emily Harper-Smythe has put out two cookbooks, you know."

If he gave the show to the Englishwoman, she, Veronique Dutot, could end up flipping burgers in a fast-food joint. She shuddered. "When I cook I have a vision in my brain," she said, tapping her temple. "Certain dishes complement each other. I cannot have you insist on…on…chocolate cake when I wish to concoct a mango mousse to finish a dinner of tropical origin."

"Let's not get technical. I'll be directing, as well as producing, because I like to retain creative control. But basically, all I'm interested in is appearance and timing. For television we need dishes that are colorful and quick to prepare. The details of what goes with what, I'll leave to you."

"That's okay, then," she said, appeased.

"If you do come on board," he said, flicking on his indicator and changing back into the left lane, "we'll get started right away on preproduction tasks—research, scripting, set design, menus and so on. Once those are complete we'll be shooting two, possibly three segments a day for one or two weeks, depending on how much studio time we can get. Do you think you can handle that?"

Her nose tilted up. "If I can handle entrées for a five-star restaurant with seating for three hundred, I am sure I can handle an hour or two of television work a day."

He swung onto the exit ramp signposted for Langley. "The show is only a half hour, but each segment takes two hours or more to tape. I can't stress enough how important it is we stick to schedule."

"I can do it."

His fingers gripped the steering wheel as they took the sharp corner on the exit ramp at ten miles an hour over the speed limit. "It's important you're totally committed to doing this series. If not, I need to know now."

Veronique made a sweeping gesture with her hand. "I cannot commit myself until I know hours, pay, conditions… What are you offering?"

The salary he named was, she suspected, lower than he was prepared to go. She responded with a tiny toss of her head. "I made more at Le Soupçon."

They negotiated upward until they reached a deal both were happy with. Under the circumstances, money was of secondary importance to Veronique, but she was too practical and had too much self-esteem to sell herself short.

Burton turned onto a secondary road edged by deep ditches and sprawling blackberry bushes. Metal mailboxes on posts appeared at intervals beside gravel driveways leading to farm buildings set well back from the road. The land was gently undulating, broken by long rows of poplars acting as windbreaks.

They rounded a bend in the road, and Burton slowed to turn into a driveway flanked by two big maple trees. He geared down again for the steep incline, and as they wound up the hill between grassy verges dotted with wildflowers, Veronique found herself craning forward for a first glimpse of the farmhouse he'd inherited.

The fitful rain had stopped, and the clouds parted, revealing tantalizing glimpses of clear blue sky. They came to an orchard, row upon row of apple, cherry and plum trees, whose rain-sparkled leaves dripped onto lush green grass. A two-story Victorian farmhouse came into view, faded yet dignified, with a wide veranda and fancy cutout trim. Sunlight glinted off its big front window and the smaller gabled windows on the second floor. It faced south over rolling farmland, past the mudflats of Boundary Bay, across the American border to where a white-peaked Mount Baker floated above the blue horizon.

It was more beautiful than she could have imagined.

Burton pulled up in front of the house and turned off the ignition, aware suddenly of a strange reluctance to be here.

His first impression as he walked toward the house was that it looked the same as always: wisteria just about to bloom around the veranda, white-painted wooden siding, green filigreed trim....

And the front step that still sagged.

The sight of it stopped him cold. He looked again. Everything was different. The windowpanes looked starkly blank and empty. The chimney didn't curl with smoke. The front door didn't stand open in welcome.

Granddad was gone.

Burton tested the broken step with his foot, and the board gave under his weight. He heard the crunch of gravel as Veronique came up behind him on the path.

"You should fix that," she said, "or someone will get hurt."

He had to clench his jaw to stop his face from contorting. He jammed his hands in the back pockets of his jeans and took a couple of deep breaths, striving for control.

"Burton?"

She didn't know how Granddad had died. "Yes?" He turned a falsely bright questioning look her way.

She frowned, and her gaze slid away. "Nothing."

He took one of the large rocks lining the flower bed and shoved it beneath the broken board as a temporary prop. Then he climbed up to the porch and pulled on the metal handle of the screen door. It opened with a creak, reminding him that as a kid he'd called it the "scream" door. Gram had laughed every time, and he'd gone on saying it long after he'd learned the correct word, just to make her happy. The memory made him chuckle and, surprisingly, eased some of his pain.

Propping the screen door open with his hip, he fished in his pocket for a ring with two keys on it and inserted one in the lock. He glanced back at Veronique. "Coming?"

She made that funny twist of her shoulders and head that expressed so much, and so little—restrained acquiescence, a kind of Gallic fatalism—and started to climb the stairs.

The door opened to shadows, a quiet hallway and the musty smell of no one home. Yet it still smelled like

Granddad's house. Memories came back in a rush, tumbling in his head. Himself as a child, as a teenager, as an adult. Warmth, love, a haven from the trials of ordinary life. Gram baking bread, Granddad stoking the wood-burning stove. Then just Granddad, but still a second home.

He turned left, drawn to the big country kitchen where he'd spent so many happy hours. He and Granddad had played chess at the large kitchen table while Gram kneaded dough and rolled it into soft, round balls which she'd cover with clean tea towels and leave to rise. As the chessboard emptied, the room would fill with their moist, yeasty scent.

He paused on the threshold, his gaze sweeping the scarred red counters, tall white-painted cupboards and round-edged appliances—forty years old if they were a day. Thick oak beams crossed the high ceiling where Gram used to hang strings of onions and garlic, and in the fall, a ham. At the head of the wide pine table was Granddad's chair, the one he'd made himself, with wooden arms and a padded, fabric-covered base that rocked on hand-carved rockers. For an instant he saw Granddad, seated before the laid-out chess set, his work-roughened hand outstretched in welcome. Heat pricked the backs of his eyes. Homecoming held a bittersweet edge.

Silently Veronique slipped past him into the room. She crossed the worn lino to push back yellow-flowered curtains, and through the big picture window he could see apple trees blooming with pink blossoms. He knew their branches and their hollows, the knots to use as steps on the way up, the best places to perch.

She glanced over her shoulder and, just for a second, looked him square in the face. "There was much love here. I can feel it."

The warmth of her tone made him confide, "One of the reasons I came out here today was to look for my grandfather's chess set. It holds a lot of special memories."

She tied back the curtains, letting in the sun. "Is it missing?"

"It's not where it's supposed to be. I'm going to search for it before the agent arrives."

"Do you mind if I explore a little? I promise I don't touch anything."

"Go ahead." He wanted to be alone for a bit, anyway.

He left her peering into the walk-in pantry and went through the arched doorway to the dining room, where ceramic ducks flew across an eggshell-blue wall above Gram's rack of souvenir teaspoons, and on into the living room.

The "games room," as Granddad jokingly called the cherrywood cabinet that held the chess set, was beside the fireplace. On the mantelpiece, dust had collected on his high-school graduation photo, Gram's Royal Doulton shepherdess and on Granddad's pipe resting in the lumpy clay ashtray Burton had made in grade two.

A huge chunk of his life was in this house. His parents had moved five times while he was growing up—this was the one constant. How on earth was he going to part with it? Or replace it?

He skirted Granddad's recliner, Gram's armless rocker where she'd spent her evenings knitting and the big comfy sofa where he'd sprawled with a book as a child or stretched out for a nap after Gram's Sunday roast. Crouching in front of the cabinet, he turned the old-fashioned key in the lock.

He hadn't really expected a miraculous reappearance, but the empty space where the chess set should have been was a blow, anyway. He ran a hand over the bare shelf. It was gone, all right. But where?

Rising, he crossed to the dining room and stood on a chair to peer on top of the oak sideboard. Nope. Not in the cupboards, either. Long, prowling steps took him back through the hall to the bookshelf in the spare downstairs bedroom. The shelves were crammed with Raymond Chandler and Jean Plaidy, copies of the *Farmer's Almanac* and back issues of *Better Homes and Gardens,* but no chess set.

He carried on down the hall to Granddad's room, his footsteps sounding too loud on the hardwood floor. He hesitated an instant, then pushed open the door and stepped inside, feeling like a kid entering off-limits territory. Quiet pervaded the monastic room. There was the old-fashioned wardrobe, the white dresser and matching bedside tables supporting family photos and a couple of paperback mysteries. The brass bedstead was covered with the patchwork quilt Gram had hand-sewn as a bride. So much he'd taken for granted. Not just the chess set had value.

There was a sound in the hallway, and Veronique's bright head poked around the door. ''Did you find it?''

''Not yet.'' He opened the door to the mahogany wardrobe and gave a start at the reflection of his tense face in the full-length mirror on the back of the door. His gaze bounced away, skimming the bare shelves and sagging rod where a few hangers dangled empty. One hanger lay on the floor.

Conscious of Veronique's watchful gaze, he left the wardrobe to pull out every drawer in the dresser. He checked underneath, then went back to the wardrobe to probe the dusty top surface. Nothing.

''Upstairs,'' he muttered, brushing past Veronique in the doorway. The faint floral scent of her perfume followed him down the hall to the staircase near the front door.

The three upstairs bedrooms had lain empty for a lifetime, waiting for the large family that had never eventuated. They were still empty of all that mattered. Veronique followed behind, silently double-checking his efforts. When Burton found himself poking through neat piles of towels and sheets in the linen closet, he gave up the search. Granddad had been occasionally absentminded, not senile.

Burton clumped down the stairs and slumped onto the third step from the bottom. The chess set was really gone. He'd never considered himself particularly sentimental, but the crack that had opened in his heart when Granddad died became a little wider.

Veronique sidled past and stood at the base of the stairs, her slender fingers curving around the newel post. "Do not worry. It will turn up. Is there an attic?"

"No, but there's a basement, although I can't believe it could have found its way down there. I'll look later," he said, glancing at his watch. "The real estate agent is due any minute."

Her green eyes grew round. "Real estate agent? Is that who you've come to meet? Don't tell me you're going to sell this wonderful farm!"

Burton shoved a hand through his hair. "What else am I going to do with it? I can't farm it, and anything else would be a waste." He was getting tired of explaining the obvious.

Veronique threw both hands in the air. "Don't give me this logic! Even I, a stranger, can see that you love this place. What would your grandfather think? He entrusted you with his home to cherish and to pass on to your children."

"How can you possibly know that?" Ignited by frustration, his temper flared. "Maybe he was just giving me a nest egg. This is a valuable piece of property."

"Of course it is valuable, but it is not worth half as much to anyone else as it is to you!" Agitated, she paced a few steps away before turning back. "How can you throw away what your grandfather worked so hard to build? Something this special doesn't come your way more than once in a lifetime. Here you can find the *tranquillité* you need."

"I haven't had a moment's peace since I inherited it." Burton got to his feet. God, he hated this. He didn't even sound like himself. The fact that she was right only made him feel worse. But why was she so het up about it?

With an upward slashing motion of one hand, Veronique turned away. "It is none of my business. What do I care what you do?"

The sound of a car crunching up the gravel drive came through the screen door.

Burton pushed it open and stepped onto the porch. A cherry-red BMW came to a stop behind his Tercel. Acid ate at his stomach, reminding him he'd missed lunch. "Here he is now."

CHAPTER SIX

A WELL-GROOMED MAN in his fifties emerged from the car, buttoning his navy jacket with one hand while he extended the other to Burton. "Afternoon, Mr. O'Rourke. Don Chetwynd, Valley Real Estate."

As Burton shook his hand, his mental VCR fast-forwarded to images of the agent bringing strangers through his grandparents' house. The sick feeling in his stomach intensified.

"Nice piece of property you got here, Mr. O'Rourke. I was real sorry to hear about your grandfather."

"Did you know him?" Burton turned and led the way back up to the house. "Watch that first step."

Don Chetwynd chuckled. "I went to school with your mom. I've been out a few times more recently trying to convince William to put this place on the market. The way housing prices are going up, this farm would bring in a tidy sum if developed properly."

Burton kept his expression cool and neutral. "This is prime farmland, Mr. Chetwynd."

"Call me, Don. Hello-o-o," he added, seeing Veronique in the doorway.

She stared back at him, unsmiling. *"Bonjour."*

Burton made the introductions, then led the agent into the house. As the screen door shut behind him he saw Veronique wander off around the house in the direction of the orchard.

They toured the farmhouse, and Burton could tell Don

Chetwynd wasn't seeing a lifetime of memories or even the beautifully proportioned, high-ceilinged rooms. He was seeing a cleared lot that would make way for new houses. He was seeing dollar signs and billboards that read Mountain View.

They went out the back way, through the kitchen and the back porch, which housed the washing machine and dryer. Behind the house, plowed fields were bordered on one side by a row of poplars, separating it from the Vandermeres' farm, and on the other by towering cedars. A creek-cum-drainage ditch ran from a small wood at the top of the hill down through the cedars.

Big red hens fluffed their feathers and scattered clucking as they walked through the farmyard, reminding Burton he ought to thank Hank and Mary Vandermere for taking care of Granddad's flock. He ought to just *give* them the chickens. Maybe he would.

"The barn needs painting," he said coming toward the old wooden structure. "I'll get that done before the place goes on the market." The words were out before he realized what he was saying. When had he made the decision to put the farm up for sale?

"I wouldn't bother if I were you," Chetwynd replied. "Whoever buys will just rip it down, anyway. Drake Developments is actively looking for land in this area. You say the word, and I'll bet my license you'll have an offer you can't refuse within the week."

Burton paused outside the double barn door. "My grandfather wasn't interested in selling to developers, Mr. Chetwynd, and neither am I. If you want to see the place so you know what to tell prospective farmers who come looking, then we'll continue. If not, we might as well call it quits right now."

Chetwynd laughed. "Just as stubborn as your grandfather. The thing about the future is, you never know quite how it'll turn out. Or how you'll feel in, say, three months' time.'' He gestured with a hand weighed down by chunky gold. "But by all means, let's continue."

Burton pushed open one of the tall doors and stepped back to allow Chetwynd to precede him into the cool, cavernous interior. Straw rustled beneath their shoes. Mice scurried. Then silence. Dust motes swam in the sunlight shafting through the high window over the hayloft.

Memories washed over him like clips from old movies—himself leaping from the cross beams into hillocks of loose hay, searching the nooks and crannies for stray eggs with Gram, watching Granddad tinker with the diesel engine on his old John Deere tractor, which was still parked to one side on the rough dirt floor. Granddad never had gotten around to building a separate machine shed.

In spite of Burton's admonitions, Chetwynd started explaining local zoning regulations. Burton ignored him and walked slowly around the barn, his thoughts puzzling over a vague notion that something about the place seemed wrong. He couldn't put his finger on it, but it felt like something was missing....

He stopped suddenly and turned, his gaze sweeping from the ancient harnesses hanging from one wall to the long-disused horse stalls lining the other, as if he could catch whatever it was in the corner of his mind's eye. Nothing. He shook his head. He must be getting fanciful. All that was missing was Granddad.

The horse stalls were filled with seed potatoes, and his mind flipped back to the acres of freshly plowed fields that rolled into the distance behind the house. It was June. Granddad had been getting ready to plant the fall crop. The magnitude of his responsibility grew, accompanied by a burst of anger. How the hell had Granddad expected him to take proper care of the farm? What did he know about sowing and harvesting?

His anger subsided as quickly as it had come. It wasn't only Granddad's fault. They all—he and Mother in-

cluded—had acted as though the old man would live forever. Why had they never talked about what would happen
after he was gone?

"Guess you won't be needing those this year, eh?"
Chetwynd put his hands in his pockets and rocked back
on his heels.

Burton's jaw tightened. "What makes you say that?"

"Hell, why plant when you're going to sell? Even your
granddad wouldn't see the sense in that."

Burton had had a gutful of Don Chetwynd. "I'm not
putting the farm on the market right away," he snapped,
making the decision on the spot. "Since I talked to you
last, a family heirloom has gone missing, and I can't sell
until it's found."

Chetwynd smoothed his lacquered hair. "I'm sorry to
hear that. But if someone comes along who's interested in
farming, I'll give you a call."

Burton was about to tell him not to bother, then
shrugged. The chess set might turn up today for all he
knew. "Just don't count on me being ready to sell."

FROM THE ORCHARD, VERONIQUE watched the real estate
agent drive away. She didn't know why she'd gotten so
angry at Burton, only that there was something about this
unpretentious yet dignified farmhouse with its lopsided
front steps, chickens scratching in the dirt and flowering
trees that reminded her of home.

Ridiculous, really, when her home was so totally different.

She pushed away from the tree she was leaning on. They
could delay no longer the decision on whether or not she
was to do the cooking show. Burton might think he had
his answer already, but he didn't know about the letter.

When she came around the side of the house, he was
standing beside a picnic table of thick cedar. Above him

spread the massive limbs of the horsechestnut tree, its spiky cones thick with frilly white-and-pink blossoms.

Her footsteps slowed. There was a contemplative droop to his mouth, and his fingers splayed across the wood as if he wished he could read his fate in its lines, like the palm of a hand. His motionless stance contrasted sharply with his earlier restless, nervous energy.

Alors, he had a quiet side. Perhaps he was not completely impossible. She wished she could bring herself to offer whatever comfort a stranger could give, a squeeze of the hand, a consoling word, but it would feel like she was offering comfort to Graham, a laughable concept. Burton wasn't Graham. She knew that, but she didn't feel it.

He turned and saw her watching him. "He's gone."

Her gaze shifted away from his face, although her attention was still focused squarely on him. "I am sorry I was angry before. I had no right."

"It's okay. Granddad taught me to play chess at this picnic table the summer I turned nine," he said. "We'd sit out here all afternoon. Gram would bring us Kool-Aid and cookies."

She wandered closer. "Kool-Aid? What is that?"

Burton's mouth twisted in part grimace, part smile. "A sweet, flavored drink for kids, but Granddad drank it, too. I took it for granted at the time that he liked it, but I suppose he was just keeping me company."

He sat and leaned his elbows on the table. Veronique sat on the other side, not directly opposite, but a little way down. The heavy planks of yellowed cedar felt as solid and unmovable as the earth beneath her feet. From the corner of her eye, she glimpsed Burton's features in the filtered green light of the horsechestnut. He was lost in the past.

She plucked a long strand of grass and crushed the sweet, juicy stem between her teeth. "You miss him."

"And her. But mostly Granddad. I was closest to him. We spent so much time together over chess."

"Perhaps he gave the set away?"

Burton shook his head. "Granddad would never do that. He promised it to me years ago when I was a teenager. Besides, it was an antique. It was valuable."

Lightly she brushed the feathery end of the grass once across the back of his hand. "It will turn up."

"I hope so," he said, his gaze following the stalk of grass. "I can't sell the farm until it does."

"Do you mean that?" she asked, slightly disbelieving.

"The chess set is the only thing of his I ever wanted. It *is* him." The sincerity in Burton's intense blue eyes matched his words. "I won't let the farm go without finding it."

"I see." She believed him.

With a whispered plop, a blossom dropped from the tree above and landed in her hair. Before she could remove it, Burton reached over and pulled it from her springy curls. His fingertips brushed her palm as he presented it back to her with a tiny smile.

"*Merci.*" Eyes downcast, she studied the frilly confection of cream and pink. The air seemed to grow stiller, heavier.

"Will you do the series, Veronique?"

Miracle of miracles, he pronounced her name correctly. At least, as correctly as an *Anglais* could.

"Yes." She nodded. "Yes, I will like to do it."

And at this moment, she couldn't even remember why she'd been so worried it wouldn't work out. Ah, yes, the menu. She smiled. What a small thing to fret about. She would create splendid food and he would adore it.

The pleasant glow of anticipation lasted only seconds before the recollection of government regulations crushed it. She tugged apart the thongs on her backpack and pulled out the letter she'd been so careful to hide from him earlier. "Perhaps you'd better read this before we sign a contract."

Burton glanced at the return address, frowned and turned the envelope over in his hand. "It hasn't been opened."

"I know what it says," she replied. "Go on. Read it."

She tucked her hands up into her sleeves while he inserted a forefinger beneath the sealed flap and tore it open. One stiff sheet unfolded in his hands. He silently skimmed the page, then glanced up at her. "What does this mean?"

"My work visa expires in a week." She explained quickly to get it out in the open and over with. "My husband's death automatically canceled my application for landed immigrant status. Without that, I cannot get another work visa. I was hoping, if you offered me the job, you could do something, call someone." Now that she said it aloud she realized how unrealistic it sounded. She wouldn't blame him if he was angry with her. "I'm sorry I have wasted your time. I wanted to help my mother-in-law, so I grab at the straws. You must find another chef. And I will have to leave the country."

"Hold on," Burton said, scanning the letter a second time. "Don't give up so easily. Could you get some sort of reprieve on the basis of caring for your mother-in-law?"

"I have already written to them, explained the situation. They refuse to give me even a little more time."

Burton folded the letter and tucked it into his pocket. "Leave it with me. I'll see what I can do to square it with Immigration."

Mon Dieu. He sounded so confident. Graham had been like that. Nothing was a problem he couldn't fix. Except for her.

Burton went to his car and came back with his briefcase. Veronique watched while he riffled through a stapled sheaf of papers, making a notation here and there in blue ink. His hands weren't like Graham's; Burton's were longer and leaner. And bare of the chunky rings Graham had had in common with Don Chetwynd.

Finally he slid the papers and the pen toward her. She paged slowly through to the end, pretending to read, rather than admit her ability to read English was so poor she couldn't understand more than one word in three. She was working on it, but she hadn't graduated from the children's books she checked out of the library, and she certainly wasn't up to legalese.

"And the menus?" she asked, hoping it wasn't spelled out in black and white.

"You'll have input, but I get the final say." He held out a pen.

Instead of taking it, Veronique wrapped her arms around her waist. All she'd wanted to do was go back to Tahiti, yet every day, every hour, led her deeper and deeper into this other new life. She was *fatigué*. Burned-out. But Marion was depending on her. And it wasn't as if she expected to *enjoy* the next two months. Happiness was just a vague promise for the future.

Burton cleared his throat, and his fingers began to drum discreetly. Not allowing herself to think about it any longer, she took the pen and wrote her signature in her squiggly, up-and-down hand, ending with a sharp dot at the end of Dutot. *"Voilà,"* she said, and pushed the pages back across the table. "We have the deal." She tried to smile, but it wouldn't come.

ERNIE HURRIED DOWN to reception to greet Veronique on her first working day at the station. She and Burton were going to plan the menus, and Burton had asked Ernie to come along and take notes. There she was, chatting to Lillian. His heart rate picked up and he lengthened his steps.

Her hair was wet with rain, and her paisley jacket drenched and dark over the shoulders, but the smile she flashed him was pure sunshine. He tugged self-consciously at the tie around his neck and wondered guiltily when he'd last dressed to impress Rita. He pushed the thought aside. Veronique was way out of his league, and nothing was ever going to happen between them. But he wanted to look his best when it didn't.

"Ms. Dutot—er, Veronique. Welcome."

"*Bonjour,* Ernie. What a nice tie." Smiling, she adjusted the knot, leaving him breathless. "Look, it is paisley, like my jacket. I just knew we were going to be simpatico."

Ernie blushed and pretended not to see Lillian's look of mild amusement. "If you'd like to come with me..." He turned quickly to hide the heat in his cheeks and led the way down the hall toward Burton's office while Veronique told him about her bus ride to the station.

"A great furry dog leaped onto the bus and put his big muddy paws on the driver," she said. "The man, he was so mad, but the dog, he was laughing."

Ernie stopped outside Burton's office. "You like dogs?"

"They are wonderful," she said warmly. "So faithful and loving."

"I like them, too," he said, smiling at her over his shoulder as he knocked. The door, which had been ajar, pushed open. "Excuse me, Burt—" He leaned around the door. No one there.

"He must have gotten tied up with something," Ernie said. "Have a seat. Can I get you some coffee?"

"Thank you, yes." She slung her backpack over the arm of one of the two guest chairs and sat down.

Ernie hustled down to the coffee room, anxiously wondering if there'd be anything left of the fresh pot he'd put on to brew earlier. Just as he came through the door, Murphy poured the last of the coffee into his giant-size mug.

Until today, he'd never encountered the vice president

of programming without Burton around to do the talking. Ernie sidled warily over to the coffee machine. The old man's temper since he'd quit smoking was already a legend.

"How are you making out, Ernie?"

The jovial tone startled him. "G-great. I mean, I'm doing okay, I think."

He slid the pot off the burner and rinsed out the dregs, his mind racing. Should he put the coffee on and go back to Veronique, then run back in five minutes when the coffee was done? Or should he wait for it and leave her wondering where he'd disappeared to? Darn that Murphy and his big mug, anyway. He ripped open a fresh packet of ground coffee.

"O'Rourke working you hard, boy?"

Ernie's hand shook, and coffee spilled across the counter. "I'm l-learning a lot. It's a little different from cable TV." Cripes, why had he gone and said that? Murphy would think he didn't know what he was doing.

Murphy uttered a sharp grunt, presumably his opinion of cable TV. "Saw Burton rushing off a moment ago to Props. The kitchen just arrived for this new cooking show. You're working on that, aren't you, lad?"

Something about the way Murphy growled the question made Ernie wonder if the big boss thought checking out the kitchen was the production assistant's job. But Burton had asked him to meet Veronique…. Unless Burton hadn't trusted him to make sure the kitchen checked out okay. Sometimes it seemed like Burton thought he was the only one who could get things done.

"You can learn a few things from O'Rourke," Murphy added, slurping loudly from his cup. "He's the best in the business."

"I will. I mean, I do, sir." Perspiration formed at Ernie's hairline. He had to get out of here, fast. Fill the jug, pour it in, switch it on…

Darn. Murphy was leaning against the counter as though he was settling in for a chat.

"So what do you think of the Vancouver Canadians' chance at the pennant this year, Ernie? You a baseball fan?"

"You b-bet I am, Mr. Murphy." He loved baseball and usually he liked nothing better than to discuss it. But Veronique was waiting.

"The station has a couple of season tickets. Fans around here get to a game or two." A phlegmy cough rumbled from Murphy's chest.

"That sounds great," Ernie said over the hacking that seemed to go on and on. He filled two cups, grabbed a handful of creams and sugars and had started to back away when he noticed Murphy looking apoplectic. "Are you going to be all right, Mr. Murphy?" he said, alarmed. "Should I call someone?"

Murphy, red-faced and eyes bulging with the strain, stopped coughing long enough to gasp on a breath. "I'm fine." He waved him away. "Go."

"Okay." Ernie turned, and shamelessly ran.

Veronique was gazing at the photos on Burton's wall when Ernie returned with the coffee. With luck he'd have a few minutes with her before Burton showed up.

"Sorry I took so long," he said. "Had to make a new pot." He set the cups on the edge of the desk. The cream and sugar spilled from his hand and fell to the floor. Flustered, he crouched to pick them up. "I didn't know what you liked in your coffee so I just brought lots of everything."

"It looks wonderful. *Merci,* Ernie."

Her voice did something weird to his insides, like going down the first big hill on the roller coaster. He removed his glasses and polished the steamy edges on his tie, taking deep breaths to control his breathing. "I was just chatting with Murphy, vice president of programming," he said casually, as though he and Ed got together every morning to chew the fat. "Burton was called down to Props. Apparently—"

"The kitchen just arrived." Burton strode through the door, and instantly all attention turned to him. "Morning, Veronique. Morning, Ernie. Ah, coffee. Any more where that came from, Ern?"

Ernie sighed. "Sure thing, boss." He slipped back out the door, hoping like hell Murphy had gone back to his office.

Burton waited until Ernie had left the room before he pulled Veronique's letter from the Immigration Department out of his briefcase. He normally wouldn't send Ernie out for coffee, but the fewer people who knew about her work visa problem, the better.

"I talked to this Ms. Papazian at the Immigration Department—boy, was she a grouch." He passed the envelope across his desk to Veronique, and her face fell. "I haven't given up. Last night I wrote half a dozen letters—to my member of Parliament, to the Human Rights Commission...you name it—explaining the situation. Stressing, of course, the importance of your ex-mother-in-law's well-being rather than the show."

"Of course. I would not be here if not for Marion."

"My plan," Burton continued, "is for my letters to initiate an investigation. And for the various government departments to get so tangled up in their own red tape that by the time they've made a decision, Marion will be well enough to cope on her own and taping of *Flavors* will be complete."

Her smile was brief and skeptical. "Thank you for trying," she said politely.

He sat back in his swivel chair and spread his hands apologetically. "I wish I could have gotten you a temporary work visa, but for now this is the best I can do."

Ernie returned with another cup of coffee.

"Thanks, Ernie. Just set it down and have a seat." Burton located the file labeled *Flavors* from among those on his desk and flipped through it. "Okay, we've got the kitchen being assembled—" He broke off to glance at Veronique. "You're going to love it—granite countertops, washed-oak cupboards, top of the line appliances." He turned to Ernie. "We can use most of the same crew as *Lost Harvest*. Did you ask Carly to start working on a script?"

Ernie nodded. "She said she'd have something ready this afternoon for you to look at."

"Excuse me," Veronique interrupted. "Why do I need a script? I am not an actor."

Burton glanced up, and as usual, her gaze slid away. A guy could get a complex about this. "While you're cooking you can ad-lib, but we need set lines for you to say at the beginning, to cue commercial breaks and to wrap up the show. You'll soon know it by heart. The biggest bit is the intro, and once we have that taped we'll just splice it into every segment."

"Oh, if that is all…" She sneezed and pulled out a hankie.

His hankie. Burton's eyebrows rose. Well, well. He was touched that she'd kept it all this time. He noticed her damp hair that was drying into tight curls, and the wet jacket hanging over the back of her chair. "Ever consider getting an umbrella?"

She shrugged. "I lose umbrellas. Are we going to talk about the menu? I have written down some ideas." She reached for her backpack and pulled out a spiral-bound notebook.

"Great." Burton noticed his untouched coffee and took a sip. "I'm a dab hand at opening cans, but what I know about cooking would fit on the back of a soup label. On the other hand," he said, rising from his chair, "I know what we need in terms of producing this sucker."

He paced the tiny space behind his desk. When his brain got active, his feet wanted to move. "I want a show that's fast-paced and colorful. With recipes that can be completely prepared and cooked within the time allotted. Minimal use of electric appliances—they're too noisy. Let's go through your list of recipes, Veronique, and decide what will work and what won't."

He paused, noticing Ernie had his head down and was scribbling industriously. "You're not taking minutes, Ern," he said in an undertone. "Just get the main points." What the hell was the kid wearing a tie for?

"Oh. Okay." Ernie blinked behind his round glasses.

Veronique consulted her notebook. "First, I thought I would like to do a risotto."

"Risotto's good," Burton said. "It's quiet." Then he frowned. "But not very colorful."

"Pumpkin risotto is very beautiful with the dark orange against the creamy rice."

"How fast is it to prepare?"

She pursed her lips. "That depend on what exactly you mean by fast."

"Say, five to ten minutes?" he suggested hopefully.

She laughed her low, throaty laugh. "First you must prepare the pumpkin. Then the rice, he must be stirred for twenty minutes—"

"That's way too long," Burton said, cutting her off. He planted his hands on his desk and leaned over it. "What about using, say, carrots, instead? Maybe stir-fry them to speed things up. Stir-fry is perfect for TV."

Veronique drew herself up, chin high in the air. "I cook haute cuisine, not TV dinners."

Burton continued to pace; two steps one way, two steps back. "I'm not suggesting you lower your standards, God no. Just…experiment a little with alternative ingredients."

"I experiment all the time. I change this, I change that," Veronique said, waving a hand to illustrate. "But the changes, they has to make sense. Pumpkin is very different texture from carrot—it is creamy like the rice, not crunchy. You cannot change one for the other because it is convenient. It would be like using pineapple, instead of corn, just because they were both yellow.'' She turned to Ernie. ''That wouldn't be right, would it?''

Ernie cast a desperate glance at Burton. With a judicious lift of his eyebrows, Burton let him know just whose hand was feeding him. ''Gee, Veronique,'' Ernie said, ''I guess not, but—''

''Nobody's trying to make you put pineapple into a stew,'' Burton said in the most placating tone he could achieve between gritted teeth. ''But I don't see the big difference between carrot and pumpkin. They're both savory, and both orange—since you seem to be stuck on the color thing.''

She half rose in her seat. ''It is not I who am stuck on the color.''

Ernie cleared his throat. ''E-excuse me, B-Burton, Veronique. I'll bet Veronique plans to, you know, cook the pumpkin beforehand and then just toss it into the risotto. That way it's even faster than carrots. Isn't that right, Veronique?''

Smiling, she touched him on the shoulder. ''But of course that is how I would do it!''

Burton stared at Ernie. The boy surprised him sometimes. To Veronique he said, ''It might have been helpful if you'd mentioned that in the first place.''

Veronique shrugged. ''It was obvious.''

For the next four hours they worked their way through the list, stopping once for more coffee and for Ernie to order in sandwiches. Burton tossed some recipes out, bullied Veronique into modifying a few and accepted her judgment on still others. Together, they organized, estimated and calculated until every dish had been planned down to the last detail, each segment timed to the minute.

Finally Burton stood behind his chair and stretched. "Well," he said, bringing his arms back to his sides, "at least that's settled." He leaned forward on the back of his chair and studied Veronique. "Your hair. It's a pretty color, but…"

"But what?" A frown appeared.

"Would you consider getting it styled? Nothing radically different, just a trim."

Her index finger curled through the long tresses at the back of her neck and tugged. "No."

Burton frowned. That multicolored mop didn't fit with the sophisticated way she dressed. He made a closer inspection of her blouse and skirt, which he was able to do because her gaze was resting on his knuckles. Maybe her clothes weren't as expensive as he'd first thought, just well put together. "Will you think about it?"

"Non."

"Okay, it was just a thought. We'll look on it as part of your exotic and eccentric personality that's going to make this show a hit."

She glanced up at him then, her face growing pale. When she spoke, it was with quiet intensity, from some place deep and hurting. "I hope your taste for the exotic does not fade before the series is over."

He blinked. What was *that* about? In the silence that followed, he could hear rain drumming on the roofs of the cars in the parking lot outside his window. "How about we go check out the kitchen? Then, Veronique, you can make a list of the utensils you'll need."

She rose, slinging her backpack over her shoulder. "I have my own set of knives."

"Great." He ushered her out with a quick prayer she wouldn't end up using them on him.

"Coming, Ernie?" He threw his arm across his assistant's shoulders as they followed Veronique out of the office. "Good suggestion back there," he said in a low voice. "You're a real diplomat."

Ernie smoothed the beginnings of a frown into a smile and made an effort not to let his annoyance show. Burton was just trying to make him feel good. But why did tall people always think they could throw their arms across the shoulders of shorter people, like they were some kind of public leaning post? Just because he was young and less experienced didn't mean he shouldn't be taken seriously. And just because he was short didn't mean he could be patronized.

CHAPTER SEVEN

SPITTING RAIN HAD DAMPENED the sidewalk when Veronique alighted from the bus across the street from the hospital. She had an hour to spend with Marion before going to the market to buy groceries for the first day of taping tomorrow. Yesterday she and Ernie had gone shopping for pots and pans and other dishes. It had been fun and Ernie had been so sweet, trailing after her loaded down with her parcels. She had to be careful not to encourage him—that wouldn't be fair. But he was such fun to tease, like the little brother she never had.

Veronique hurried through the hospital to Marion's new room in the rehabilitation center located in another wing. Marion was moving around on crutches, but she still had too much time to think and tended to fret when Veronique was late.

"*Bonjour,* Marion," Veronique sang out as she strode through the open door into the semiprivate ward.

"Hi, Ronnie," Marion whispered. She put a finger to her lips, and pointed to the next bed.

Someone new had arrived in the night. The woman occupying the other bed looked roughly Marion's age. She was thin, with long dark hair. Her eyes were shut, but the arms lying on top of the covers seemed tense and rigid, giving Veronique the impression she was only pretending to sleep.

She lowered her voice to a whisper, anyway. "*Voilà,*

Marion,'' she said, pulling a package of hair color out of her bag. ''Today you are going to the beauty parlor.''

Marion struggled to sit up. ''You really shouldn't have bothered, Ronnie. No one's going to see me in here.''

Veronique wasn't fooled by Marion's protest. She could see the gleam of interest in her mother-in-law's eyes and rejoiced at the progress. ''Nonsense. You are doing it for yourself.''

Marion glanced at her roommate, whose face had taken on an almost imperceptible frown. Marion beckoned Veronique closer and whispered in her ear. ''She was in a temper last night when they brought her in. She's had surgery. I don't know what it was, she wouldn't say, but you should have heard her snap at the nurses.''

''Perhaps she was in great pain,'' Veronique whispered back. ''Come, let us go. We can talk better in the washroom.''

Veronique pushed the wheelchair over to the bed and helped Marion into it. Placing a folded towel across Marion's lap, she wheeled her down the hall to the communal wash and laundry room where there was a wide sink and a nozzle attachment.

Veronique adjusted the temperature and directed the spray onto Marion's bent head, wetting her hair thoroughly.

''Tell me about the studio,'' Marion asked over the noise of the water. ''Have you started taping yet?''

''Tomorrow. I am so nervous my hands shake just to think of it. At least we have agreed on the menu.''

''It must be so exciting working in a television studio. Did you see *Lovers and Strangers* yesterday? I can't believe how mean that awful Tiffany is to Reilly. He really loves her, even if she is quite a bit older.''

Veronique laughed uneasily as she helped Marion sit upright so she could towel-dry her hair. ''You really must get out more. Tiffany and Reilly are not real people.''

"Oh, I know that." Marion adjusted the belt of her dressing gown and shifted her leg on the bit of the wheelchair that held it out straight. "What's it like working for an important producer? Is he nice?"

Scary was the word that came to mind. She was always afraid she'd forget and call him Graham. Afraid of remembering the past; afraid of not remembering and repeating it. Briefly she contemplated telling Marion that Burton resembled Graham. No, that would only get her started talking about Graham.

"He wants me to cut my hair!" She reached for the package of hair color and flipped the instruction sheet over to the French side. Thank heaven for a bilingual country, at least in theory.

Marion eyed her in the mirror. "It's time you got rid of those blond ends."

"Not yet." Veronique snapped one bottle into the base of the other and shook. "We will do the whole head at once, eh? It has been so long we don't need to do the roots separately."

"Whatever you think, dear."

Veronique arranged the towel around Marion's shoulders to protect her robe from spills, then pulled on the plastic gloves and squeezed a stream of gel onto Marion's hair.

Marion's eyes were shut, showing thin blue veins on her eyelids. Her hands were folded in her lap, relaxed. "You know, Ronnie, maybe you just need a holiday."

Oui. Tahiti. "Mmm-hmm."

"I mean, you haven't been away since Graham took you to San Francisco."

Veronique's hands stilled, knuckle-deep in foamy goo. "Pardon?"

"Don't you remember? It was the second weekend in February. He called to wish me happy birthday and to explain why you two wouldn't be over for dinner. I didn't speak to you, but I could hear you laughing in the background.''

Ah. Now, she remembered. How like Graham to cover his tracks so carefully. She'd spent that weekend watching old movies while he'd flown to San Francisco on a sudden business trip. Marion had heard a female voice, but it hadn't been hers. Back then Veronique had suspected he was seeing someone else, although she hadn't realized he'd gone away with the woman that particular weekend.

It wasn't the worst thing he was capable of.

''I'm sorry we missed your birthday dinner.'' She hoped her voice didn't sound too strained.

''Oh, that doesn't matter now, Ronnie.''

Veronique's fingers trembled as she worked the color through Marion's hair. Sometimes she awoke in the night and wondered whether Graham would have arranged that last-minute fishing trip if she hadn't confronted him about that other woman and told him she was leaving. She always pushed the thought away, angry with herself for feeling even remotely responsible for his death.

''Ronnie?'' Marion's voice called her back. ''Are you all right?''

''I'm fine. It's just…San Francisco wasn't so very fun for me.'' She washed her hands and arranged a plastic shower cap over Marion's hair—the type of plastic cap you got free at a nice hotel. She supposed one didn't wear plastic caps while showering with a lover. You brought them home as a souvenir for your wife.

''*Bon,*'' she said, with a sigh, and set the small kitchen timer she'd brought in her backpack. Then she took out a deck of cards, and Marion wheeled herself over to a small table for folding laundry. They played the twenty minutes away, keeping score of their crib hands in the margins of the hair-color instructions.

''I won again,'' Marion announced, gathering in the

loose cards. "You're not paying attention today, Ronnie. Something on your mind?"

Veronique was saved from answering by the timer going off. "Time to see the new you."

She rinsed and shampooed, then blow-dried, doing her best to style Marion's hair. "Life is strange, eh, Marion? A few weeks ago I was only a chef. Now I'm a TV star and a hairdresser." She poked a curl, fragrant with chemicals, into place. "Well, maybe not a hairdresser. When you get out of here, you must get this done properly."

"It's wonderful, Ronnie. Thank you." But at the mention of leaving the hospital, an anxious look crossed Marion's face.

Veronique said casually, "The nurse told me about the bridge club. They meet tonight, *non?*"

"Oh, Ronnie, I keep telling you, it's too soon after Stan's passing for me to socialize."

"Nobody's asking you to marry again. It's just a friendly game of bridge." Veronique came around the front of the wheelchair and crouched at eye level. "Please, Marion, for me?"

"For you?" Marion looked confused.

"When I go back to Tahiti…" She grasped Marion's hand as the other woman's mouth tightened. "When I go back, I want to know that you have other friends. You don't want me to worry or feel bad that I am abandoning you, do you?"

Marion smiled sadly and squeezed Veronique's hand. "Of course not. I just don't know what I'm going to do without you."

"When the time comes, you will be strong in mind and healthy in body—you will see. I talked to the head nurse here about getting you a home help. You will let me pay for it from the money Graham left— *Non,* I will not take no for the answer."

"*An* answer. Ronnie, we've settled this. Graham left that money to you."

From down the corridor came the squeak and clatter of the meal trolley. The aroma of overdone roast beef and packet gravy drifted through the open door. "Dinnertime," Veronique announced. "We'd better get you back before the new girl eats your meal."

She tossed the used hair-color box into the garbage, gathered up Marion's towel and wiped down the sink. Then she took hold of the handles and pushed the wheel-chair back to Marion's room. Her roommate's bed was empty, and sounds of running water came from the bath-room. Veronique helped Marion back into bed and ad-justed the pillows so she could sit upright.

"Do you think...?" Marion began, then stopped. "No, forget it."

"What?" Veronique took her jacket from the back of the chair and picked up her backpack.

"It's too much to ask...."

"Just tell me, Marion. I'll let you know if it is too much."

"I just wondered if I could possibly come down to the studio and watch *Lovers and Strangers* being taped some-time. When my hip is a bit better, I mean. And if they allow outsiders in."

Outsiders were allowed in. Friends and relatives of the crew came along frequently. Sometimes students from the film school. Veronique imagined introducing Marion to Burton, and Marion fainting or bursting into tears at the spitting image of her dead son. And what of her feelings? Would seeing Marion with Burton make him appear more like Graham, or less?

Veronique gazed at Marion's eager, wistful face. Mar-ion, who had so little to look forward to. "Yes, I think so," she said.

Marion smiled the biggest smile Veronique had seen

since before Stan and Graham had died. "Oh, Ronnie. Thank you so much."

BURTON PUSHED THROUGH the doors to Channel Seven. It was Wednesday morning, and with taping on *Flavors* starting today he had a lot on his mind.

He dropped his umbrella in the stand and started across the lobby to where Sylvia was leaning over Lillian's desk, inspecting a fistful of long purple fingernails. "...this guy I met at a computer course. I woulda gone out with him, but then he started going on about his hard drive." She cracked her gum. "So-o-o-o cute, but he's, like, such a techie."

"What a pity," Lillian murmured, out of sight behind Sylvia's shapely backside.

"Morning, ladies."

Sylvia straightened away from Lillian's desk to waggle her fingertips at him. "Hi, Burton."

Burton jerked to a halt. Lillian's snowy white hair was shot through at the temple with neon streaks of lime and purple. Hair whose soaring gelled spikes had abandoned all pretension to fluffiness. "I see your grandniece has advanced to hair color, Lillian."

She beamed up at him from behind the desk, patting her hair proudly. "Good morning, Burton. Yes, Sandy's been practicing again. Don't you just love it?"

"I've, ah, never seen anything quite like it on...uh..."

One gray eyebrow lifted as Lillian gazed steadily back and waited for him to finish floundering.

Burton took a big breath and forced himself to look, really look at Lillian. To disassociate himself from his prejudices about appropriate hairstyles for grandmothers. When he did, to his surprise, he saw an attractive woman having fun experimenting with her appearance.

With a genuinely admiring smile, he dropped a hot-pink

carnation into her vase. "Actually, Lillian, I think it's great."

Ernie came scurrying toward the desk, frowning down at his clipboard. "Is Burton in yet, Lillian?"

"Right in front of you, big fella," Burton said. "How's it going? Everything ready to start taping?" He clapped an arm around his assistant's shoulder and steered him toward his office. For a second he thought he felt Ernie tense under his friendly hand. Nah, couldn't be.

"The electricians have finished wiring the set," Ernie said. "Bill and the guys are setting up their cameras. We should be ready to go as soon as Veronique gets here."

"Great, Ern. With a presenter as, shall we say, unpredictable as Veronique, it's nice to know I've got a PA who can get things happening and keep everyone in line when I'm not around." He held Ernie's mild brown gaze to impress upon the boy that although expectations were high and the tasks arduous, he had every confidence Ernie would rise to the occasion.

Ernie passed the back of his hand across his forehead, which was covered with a faint sheen of perspiration. "Gee, th-thanks, Burt. I mean, Burton. I'll do my best."

From reception came the sound of throaty laughter and a melodious French accent. Burton turned. "Ah, there she is now."

Ironic that her first day on the set should be June the second, the date her work visa expired. So far he'd had no luck getting the Immigration Department to change their collective mind. He'd only succeeded in raising bureaucratic interest in her case to the point where they'd started asking him a lot of sticky questions. Like, why wasn't he hiring a French-Canadian chef, eh? Just his bad luck that the official who'd responded to his inquiries had been born in Trois Rivières, Quebec.

Veronique approached, her averted gaze skimming the framed stills from various television shows that lined the walls. How could he get her to look at him? It wasn't just his ego at stake, but the success of *Flavors* and, ultimately, his documentary.

She came closer. Ernie's eyes glazed over. Burton had a brainwave.

"Ernie, show Veronique to the dressing room and then take her to Makeup. I have to get something from Props. I'll meet you in the studio." He lifted a hand in greeting to Veronique before hurrying into his office to drop off his briefcase.

When he emerged, Veronique had caught up with Ernie and was bussing him on both cheeks. *"Bonjour, bonjour. Ça va?"*

Burton quickly turned down a secondary corridor and ran up a flight of stairs. Okay, the dual peck on the cheeks was a French custom, but she never greeted him like that. When had she started treating Ernie like a friend, as well as a colleague? Would she ever see him that way? Would she ever see him at all?

Ernie, meanwhile, was awash in body heat and Chanel No. 5. But by the time he'd figured out what Veronique was doing it was too late to press his lips against her cheek. She'd already drawn back, digging in her backpack for something and chattering about the bus, which was late, and her stocking, which had torn.

Ernie forced another image into his clouded brain. Rita. Lovely Rita, with her smooth dark hair bobbed under her pointed chin. Rita, whom he suspected of being too good for him, but who had consented to marry him, anyway.

"Uh, g-good morning, V-Veronique." He whipped off his fogged-up glasses and polished them on his shirttail. No ties today. Not even for Veronique would he wear a noose every day. "You can put your stuff in the dressing room, and after you get done in Makeup, we'll meet Burton in the studio." Makeup. The thought of taking Veronique to meet Rita made the perspiration stand out on his brow.

"Bon." With a flourish she produced from her bag a large, ripe mango. She handed it to Ernie, then pulled out a cucumber, a tomato, some green onions and a bouquet of fresh cilantro, and piled them into his unwilling hands already burdened by a clipboard and pen.

"I knew something was missing from the menu the other day when we were planning the grilled pork Polynesian," she said. "Mango salsa. The grilled pork, he must have mango salsa."

"Oh, no," Ernie said, alarmed. "Burton's not going to like adding another dish at the last minute."

"Poof. He will love it—it's colorful and quick, and low-fat, too. It has absolutely no effect on the waistline."

"It'll have a big effect on the schedule. At rehearsal yesterday, we just squeaked in on the timing." Almost dropping the cucumber, Ernie clutched the mass of fruit and vegetables tighter to his flannel-clad chest. A paper fell out of his clipboard and fluttered to the floor. "You can't add things at the last minute, Veronique. Burton won't allow it. Sure, he's a bit of a stickler, but that's why he's the best—"

She cut him off with a conspiratorial smile that made his stomach drop. "Er-r-rnie," she purred. "We will just have to surprise him. We will show him how well it works."

"Veronique!" he pleaded. He didn't like the sound of that "we."

"Don't worry, Ernie. It will be fine. The mango salsa takes just two minutes to make. Chop, chop, chop, and it's done."

Burton thought he was reliable. Burton was counting on him to keep Veronique in line. Ernie drew himself up a little taller, made his voice a little deeper. "Veronique, I forbid you to make mango salsa."

She laughed and pushed his chest lightly, dislodging the mango. Despite his desperate effort to catch it with his elbow, it fell. Veronique reached for it, trapping it against his upper thigh. "*Oop, et là.* Mustn't bruise the fruit." She glanced up at him with a sly lift of her eyebrows.

Ernie's cheeks flamed. She was flirting with him. He was gonna mess up his career. And his engagement. And he was only twenty-two. Oh God, oh God, oh God.

"Here, take these back." Ernie shoved the produce into her open backpack as if it was stolen goods, his gaze darting from side to side. The corridor was empty, but with microphones in every second room, the walls had ears. No, that was paranoid. Ernie picked up his dropped schedule and mopped his forehead. "Don't do it, Veronique. I beg you."

"Such a worry warp, Ernie." She smiled her dimpled, dazzling smile. "Now, don't tell Burton. I'm counting on you." She slung her pack over a shoulder, causing her cream silk blouse to strain across one curving breast, sublimely unaware of the havoc she was creating in his conscience-control center. "Which way to Makeup?"

Sweating profusely, Ernie led her to the dressing room where she hung up her jacket, then to Makeup. The door was open and Rita was at the counter arranging her cosmetics and brushes. Oh God. She would take one look at his guilty face and know instantly Veronique had kissed him.

"Hi, Rita." His voice cracked.

Her face lit up at the sight of him. "Hi, Ernie." Blushing, she pushed a strand of straight brown hair behind her ear and shyly braided her hands together in front of her rose-colored sweater.

His smile instinctively took on warmth. Then he quickly frowned so she wouldn't think him overly warm and get suspicious. Flustered, he motioned Veronique forward. "This is Veronique, the chef on *Flavors*. Veronique, this is Rita.'' He turned to Rita. ''Taping starts in twenty minutes. Can you get her ready, please?''

''Sure. Hi, Veronique. What beautiful hair you have.''

''*Bonjour. Merci.*'' She smiled at Rita. ''Where should I sit?''

''Right here.'' Rita spun the high swivel seat around and held it while Veronique climbed onto it. Then she tied a pink plastic cape around Veronique's neck and arranged it to protect her clothes.

All right, Ernie thought, as Rita made styling suggestions while Veronique nodded into the mirror. He smiled smugly at how well he'd handled the situation. They hardly noticed he was there.

''Shall I put your backpack someplace safe?'' he suggested to Veronique. Anything to get that mango away from her.

Smiling, she waggled a finger at him through the mirror. ''You naughty boy. You know I need that backpack.'' She glanced up at Rita. ''He's so sweet and helpful, *non?*''

Rita nodded, but a tiny frown appeared between her eyebrows. Uh-oh. Time to scram. He bade Veronique a hasty goodbye and left Rita with whispered instructions not to get talked into anything. Then he raced back to the studio where the crew was assembled, and doing last-minute checks on the sound and light equipment. Burton would know how to handle Veronique. Where the heck was he?

Someone called his name and he turned to see Vince, the floor manager, coming toward him. Vince was six foot four and sported a black handlebar mustache and a Vancouver Canadians baseball cap. When he stopped in front of Ernie, Ernie felt like a midget.

''Say, Ernie, where's Burton? And Veronique? We've got to get our asses in gear. The studio's booked for another show after lunch.''

''I know.'' Ernie checked his watch. ''Veronique's in Makeup. I'm sure Burton'll be along any minute.''

Vince lifted his cap, stroked a hand over his receding hairline and slid the cap back in place. "Okay. We're ready whenever the man shows." He returned to where the camera crew were positioned around the set.

Pausing outside the studio door, Veronique cautiously touched her hair. Rita had fluffed her thick mat of curls into a spiraling mass of blond and bronze, which gave her height and accentuated her cheekbones. The makeup she'd smoothed over her face and neck felt unfamiliar and made her feel somehow unreal, almost like an actor on TV. *Mon Dieu*, but that's exactly what she was. Her palms grew damp. This was the moment.

She pushed open the door at the back of the set. On the other side of the studio, beyond the cameras, the audience filled twenty rows on either side of a center aisle. Near the edge of the set, she saw Ernie consulting his clipboard and hurried over to him.

"Ernie. How much time do I have?"

"Hi, Veronique. Hey, you look great." He checked his watch. "You've got about five minutes till airtime. Burton hasn't arrived yet."

"I go arrange myself in the kitchen, then. I am so nervous, Ernie."

"Me, too," he blurted unexpectedly.

"You? Never," she declared. "You look so professional with your clipboard and your headset."

Suddenly the chatter from the crew stilled. For two endless seconds there was total silence. Then the buzz started again, twice as loud, like crickets in a heat wave.

"Morning, gang," Burton called in the brisk voice he used when he was in high gear. "We're running late, so let's get going."

Zut alors! Veronique blinked and looked again. She recognized him by his long legs and the black vest he'd been wearing over a white shirt, but what was that on his head? And his face!

He had on black plastic glasses with a big nose and a villainous mustache that stopped just short of hiding his mouth. Covering his short coppery hair was a multicolored wig that looked as if he'd put his finger in an electrical socket. Her hand went to her mouth to cover an unladylike snort of laughter.

Calmly he walked over, put up his hand and with a straight face asked, "How many fingers am I holding up?"

Still giggling, she said, "F-f-four."

Beneath the black plastic mustache, his mouth curved. "Good. That's how many minutes you have before we start taping."

Funny, she'd never noticed before that his smile was higher on one side than the other. Or that fine laugh lines bracketed his lips. She felt herself warm to him. He'd played the fool to ease her discomfort. It was just a trick to get her to pay attention to his instructions, but his approach was to persuade rather than coerce. Unlike the other man she'd known with eyes like his.

He touched her shoulder and his voice softened. "Are you ready?"

Swallowing a sudden lump in her throat, she nodded. Then she looked at his bulbous plastic nose and started to laugh again. Burton made a movement of his head that suggested an exaggerated rolling of the eyes and gave her a gentle push toward the kitchen.

As she moved off, Ernie came forward, his smile giving way to an anxious frown. "Excuse me, Burt...on, b-b-but—"

She glanced back. *Oh la la.* Was he going to give her away?

Luckily for her, Vince had come up to confer, and Bill, the head camera operator, stood a pace away, awaiting final instructions. Burton said, "Just a sec, Ern."

Veronique scurried off to the kitchen to quickly unload the vegetable contents of her backpack into the fridge. She kept a watchful eye out, but by the time Burton had finished with the others, Ernie was caught up in some crisis concerning the electrical lead to one of the cameras. With some relief, she saw Burton disappear up the spiral staircase to the control booth while Ernie remained on the studio floor.

Burton paced behind Kate and Mario, giving last-minute instructions, while mentally playing around with different camera angles, planning the composition of shots that would be sent "to air." He spoke into his headset. "Let's have a sound check, Vince, Kate."

On the monitors, three images of Veronique stood behind three teal granite counters, showing close-ups in right profile, left profile and straight on. Through his headset, he heard Vince tell her to say something in a normal speaking voice. She looked nervous and vulnerable and brave.

"A snitch in time saves nine," she recited. "Birds of a feather talk together."

Laughing at the way she mangled the old sayings, Burton glanced at Kate, who gave him a thumbs-up. "That'll do," he told Vince. "Okay, Bill, pull focus."

Bill zoomed camera one in on Veronique, adjusting the focus on the most sharply resolved part of the human body, the eyes. Closer, closer, till her face, then just her eyes filled the screen.

Burton knew Veronique was simply looking into the lens the way Vince had told her to, but he had the oddest sensation she was gazing directly at him. Her eyes were wide emerald prisms, fringed with dark-gold lashes. They grew large, larger, drawing him in further, deeper, till she was only a blink away. Till the dark and mysterious center silently spoke secrets meant for his eyes only.

"Burton?"

Someone was talking. Vince. With a start, Burton glanced up. Then Bill's camera zoomed out and Veronique's face grew small again. He let out a breath and spoke through his headset to the floor manager. "Stand by."

Veronique touched the back of one hand to her damp temple. Her other hand gripped the edge of the granite counter. Just for a moment, when she'd looked into the camera lens, Burton's face had flashed before her eyes. Not Graham's, not a blurry mixture of the two men. Just Burton—staring into her eyes as if he was seeing her soul.

In the darkness beyond the floodlights she could just make out the shadowy shapes of the front row of the audience. She picked an elderly man as her talking target. Then Vince held up a sign—thirty seconds.

She licked her lips. Vince made a hand motion that meant she was to get into her presentation position. Shoulders back, head high, big smile…

Her gaze flicked to the control-booth window high above the studio floor. Between the monitors, she glimpsed Burton watching her onscreen and speaking into his headset. A smile lifted the corners of her mouth. He was still wearing those silly glasses and wig.

Vince held up another sign. Ten seconds. Banks of lights blazed down, hotter than the Tahitian sun.

Oh la la. The mango salsa. Doubt crept in.

Five seconds. Vince's fingers counting down.

Two, one. She took a deep breath. Rolling.

"Bonjour, and welcome to *Flavors…"*

Veronique breezed through the crabmeat appetizer and whizzed through preparation for the Polynesian pork, trying to shave minutes to allow for the mango salsa. She hurried so much the knife slipped while she was chopping an onion, and bright red blood welled across the tip of her left index finger.

"Merde!" She sucked on her finger.

Vince made a slashing motion to stop the cameras. Burton skimmed down the spiral stairs, flinging off the plastic glasses as he strode onto the set. "How's that finger?"

She hid her hand behind her back. "It's okay. We must go on. The time."

"Let's see it." He pulled her arm around, cradling her hand in his. A line of blood seeped out of the cut. He called to someone on the floor. "Band-Aid here for Ms. Dutot."

She tried to tug away. "It won't look good."

"It'll look worse if you're bleeding all over the main course." Someone handed him a Band-Aid. He tore the wrapper off and swiftly taped it in place, his warm, strong fingers moving over hers.

"What happened back there?" he said. "Wasn't there supposed to be a glaze on the pork?"

She froze. Should she speak the truth—that the pineapple glaze had made way for mango salsa? He knew about cameras and schedules, but she was the chef, and for her, it was the food that must be perfect.

Swallowing, she glanced away. "We made a change, remember?"

Silence while he wondered. Doubted. Regained faith. "Okay." He put his glasses back on and waggled his plastic eyebrows at her. "Let's go."

Then he was gone, and Vince was counting down again. "Three, two, one...rolling."

Veronique took a deep breath. She smiled into the camera and held up her bandaged finger. "This step in the recipe, you may omit." Then she wiped down the cutting board with a clean cloth. "*Bon. En suite,* a perfect accompaniment to the succulent Polynesian grilled pork is mango salsa."

If Ernie groaned quietly on the sidelines, she didn't hear. If Burton was tearing the hair on his fright wig, she wasn't going to risk a look. The camera was rolling, and nothing short of Burton yelling "cut" was going to stop her now.

She whipped out the mango and the other ingredients, babbling nervously to the audience as she chopped them into small dice. Maybe if she'd had time to talk to him before the taping, she could have convinced him… Too late, too late.

"Mango salsa is an amazing condiment," she told the elderly man in the front row as she scored the halved mango and its pungent aroma filled her nostrils. "It contains all the tastes—salty, bitter, sweet and sour. Add to that the sensual texture of the mango, the crunch of the cucumber and the juiciness of the tomato—"

"Cut!" She heard Burton's barked command right through Vince's headset. Vince winced at the sound and brought his hand across his throat in a quick slicing motion.

Veronique threw a pleading smile in Bill's direction and kept on going. She threw the chopped ingredients into a bowl and mixed in fresh lime juice, Tabasco and cilantro. *"Voilà!"* she announced proudly to the sound of applause while Burton stormed back down the stairs and onto the set.

"Take five," he called to Vince. "Ernie, amuse the audience with one of your dog-show anecdotes."

He strode into the kitchen, snatched off his wig and flung it on the counter where it landed in a puddle of juice from the chopped tomato. "What the hell do you think you're doing?"

He spoke in an undertone that nobody else could hear, but his voice was harsh. Graham had talked to her like that, and now Burton was doing it. Veronique drew in a deep breath. "I make mango salsa, the perfect side dish for the pork. We omitted it from the menu—a mistake. I simply correct that fact."

How dare he force her to justify a culinary necessity? Couldn't he see she'd done the right thing? How could she help it if he wasn't around to give permission? Didn't he know she only wanted to please him?

Mon Dieu, what was she thinking? Aghast and flustered, she picked up the wig and mopped furiously at the tomato juice.

Burton edged in closer, looming over her. "Everything is planned down to the exact second. To a fifth of a second. You know that."

His voice was controlled, but he didn't need to yell for her to hear his anger. And she didn't need to look at him to know a storm raged in the blue seas of his eyes, like a typhoon stirring the South Pacific.

Across the vast room, she heard a knock at the studio door, not the big double doors the audience had come through, but the smaller door at the back of the set. The crew wouldn't knock.

She didn't have time to wonder who it could be. Up close and in living color, she was face-to-chest with Burton's displeasure. Unchastened and mutinous as a child unfairly accused, she twined a lock of hair with the bandaged finger while her outrage mounted, squeezing her breath into a compressed knot that prevented her from speaking. Burton had no such problem.

"Look, I'd love to let you do whatever you want," he continued. "But we've got a schedule and we've got to stick to it or else it's…it's chaos. You may think it's only a little thing, but little things add up. Sponsors have paid for airtime. If we go over, we can't cut a commercial, so out goes your mango salsa, anyway."

"You said we had plenty of time to tape the first show."

"Plenty of time relative to shows two through thirteen. And that's the taping. The allotted airtime is fixed. We can't play around with that. You can't just take it into your head to change the menu without consulting me. Why did you do that?"

"I wanted… Oh, never mind." She pushed a hand

through her hair, bringing curls flying around her flushed cheeks. *This isn't like me,* she wanted to tell him. *I am orderly and efficient, the way a good cook should be.* Her outrage subsided. She'd wanted to impress, not defy him. Just as he'd tried to ease her discomfort by wearing that ridiculous mask. It didn't seem funny now. She reached up and pulled the glasses down his nose, forgetting till it was too late whom she would see.

His eyes burned into hers. Her heart seemed to stop beating and for once she couldn't look away. *Mon Dieu.*

Burton stared into Veronique's wide green eyes, and his irritation disappeared. Her gaze held apprehension, and if he didn't know better, a pinch of…sexual awareness? Hell, he did know better, but it still looked like desire. The thought dried his mouth and weakened his knees. He was losing it. Mr. Cool-as-a-cuke was in emotional free fall. In front of a live audience.

The whole place had fallen silent. For a second he thought everyone somehow knew what had just happened between him and Veronique. Then behind him, Ernie cleared his throat.

"Excuse me, Burton…"

He spun around. With Ernie were a man and a woman, conservatively dressed, carrying briefcases. They had "faceless government employee" stamped all over them.

Except they weren't faceless. They were right here in his studio, interrupting a live taping and looking at Veronique with grave expressions. In one of those too-vivid visual flashes he was prone to, Burton imagined them escorting her to a waiting black limousine, which would whisk her straight to the airport and back to Tahiti.

"James Jackson," the stony-faced man said, extending his right hand. He had a broad face, black hair precisely cut and a heard-it-all-before tone of voice. "My colleague, Wendy Connery," he said, indicating a forty-something woman with thick chestnut hair that had a swathe of white arising from a pronounced widow's peak. "We're from the Department of Immigration. It is my duty to inform you that Veronique Dutot is illegally employed under Section 27 of the Immigration Act. Ms. Dutot, if you'd like to come with us."

Adrenaline flooded Burton's body. His first instinct was to smash a fist in the bureaucrat's pasty white face. He forced himself under control. The way to deal with this was to be rational, calm, professional. Facing the immigration officials squarely, he crossed his arms over his chest. "Over my dead body."

CHAPTER EIGHT

"BURTON!" VERONIQUE exclaimed. To the Immigration officers, she said, "I am sorry. Of course I will come with you."

"Veronique! Don't just give in like that." Burton took her arm and gestured to Jackson and Connery to follow him away from the set and crew. "I've written to you people twice now on Ms. Dutot's behalf and haven't received an answer."

"Ms. Dutot doesn't fill the criteria for acquiring residency on the basis of work," Jackson said. "Although you claim she's uniquely suited to her position, there are probably several hundred French chefs in this country, if not more."

Burton jammed his hands on his hips and took a deep breath to regain some semblance of calm. "I didn't hire her because she spoke French," he said, enunciating slowly and clearly. "By 'unique,' I meant her personality, the way she comes across on camera. But putting aside her job for the moment, don't you have some kind of leniency clause that allows people to stay on compassionate grounds? She has an elderly female relative who's an invalid and is emotionally dependent upon her."

"We are aware of Mrs. Gerritson's condition and of her relationship with Ms. Dutot," James Jackson replied. "Compassionate stay of deportation is allowed only if the person in question, that is, Ms. Dutot, is medically incapacitated. I'm afraid we have no choice, given her widowed status and expired work visa, but to deny Ms. Dutot further residency. She is required to leave the country without delay.''

Ernie, apparently out of shaggy-dog stories, had returned to stand a few paces away. At this ominous pronouncement, he gave a little gasp. Veronique tugged at her hair.

Burton held up a hand. "Pause. Rewind. Are you saying she can't stay because she isn't married to a Canadian citizen?''

''That is correct.'' Jackson turned to Veronique. "You are required to file a deposition at the Immigration office. We can accommodate you immediately.''

Before she could answer, Burton put his arm around her waist and drew her to his side. "That won't be necessary, will it...darling?'' She glanced up, eyes wide. He held her gaze, hoping she wouldn't flinch.

"Wh-what are you talking about?'' She tried to tug away, but he held her fast.

Smiling through gritted teeth, he replied, "I'm talking about our forthcoming marriage of course.''

She was speechless, thank God.

Behind him, he heard Ernie's squeak of protest.

Officer Connery spoke for the first time, her smooth face unsmiling. "I must inform you it is against federal law to marry for the purpose of obtaining residency on Canadian soil.''

Burton laughed, a bit too heartily. "It would sound fishy to you people, I suppose. But we...we're crazy about each other. We can't wait to get married.'' Good God, had he really just said that?

James Jackson and Wendy Connery exchanged a glance that suggested they didn't believe he had either. "Naturally we have criteria to determine whether a couple is marrying out of a genuine desire to be husband and wife or out of expediency.''

Burton swallowed. "Naturally.''

"There will be an investigation, and interviews with both parties," Jackson went on. "So far we've only your word for it, Mr. O'Rourke, that you and Ms. Dutot are getting married."

"Say something," Burton hissed to Veronique, willing her to go along with this. Yes, he was doing it for *Flavors,* and for his documentary on farming, and even for Marion whom he'd never met, because she was important to Veronique. But there was another reason. It had something to do with the effect Veronique had on his central nervous system, and the way her face kept appearing before him at odd times of the day and night. He didn't have time to analyze it now, he just knew he wasn't ready to let her out of his life yet.

"Are you in love with this man?" Officer Connery prompted.

Veronique swallowed, conscious all eyes were upon her. "I...ah, already sometimes I feel like he is my husband." She tugged on Burton's hand, dragging him aside. "Excuse us, please," she said to the woman. "Burton and I need to talk."

"What is it?" He took her other hand and gripped them both tightly. "We're in a tight spot here."

"I know!" she said in a hoarse whisper. For a moment she clung to his hands, then loosened her hold on him. "What you are suggesting is crazy and wrong. You don't need to do this. You can get another chef. One that will not make you so angry."

Burton renewed his hold on her hands, and despite her protest, the firmness and strength of his grip felt reassuring. It took him a moment to speak, as though he was searching for words. "I don't want another chef. I want you."

Her heart did a funny little flip-flop, but he couldn't have meant it the way it sounded. And he didn't.

"I'm not being altruistic or romantic, Veronique," he added. "I want you, because crazy as you make me—and you do make me crazy—you also have charisma in front of the audience. I need this show to be a success or I can kiss goodbye the chance to make my documentary. Now do you understand?''

Of course she understood when he put it so clearly. It was a neat, clean thrust, like a filleting knife between the ribs. "*Mais oui.* What else could it be?'' she asked with an elaborate shrug. "It's not as though I thought for a moment you might love me, or that I could love you.'' And she laughed, to prove to them both how ridiculous it was.

A small silence followed. She glanced up to see hurt and confusion in his eyes. "Is the idea of marrying me really so repugnant?''

"Repug… I don't know that word, but it means something bad, *non?* I think you are a nice man. I only know I don't want to marry anyone. I had enough of that for a while.''

"What about your mother-in-law if you have to leave Canada?''

"She will be all right.'' Marion could exist without her. Of course she could. The hospital, or a social worker, would find her a home help and make sure she had what she needed to survive. But it would be hard for her, and lonely, and she might sink further into that place in her mind where she was afraid to leave the house even to collect the mail at the end of the drive. Would a public-health worker or even a private nurse have the time to prod poor Marion into recovering her joy in life?

"Do you really think it will work?'' she asked doubtfully.

"Long enough for us both to get what we need, I hope.''

The whole idea was monstrous. Why was she even pretending to think about it? She glanced at the Immigration officers. They were watching her and Burton, skepticism evident in their expressions and body language. How

would Marion feel if Veronique got married again so soon
after Graham died? Yet how much worse would it be for
Marion if she had to suddenly leave the country?

"Veronique," Burton murmured urgently, "you've got
to make a decision." He raised her hands and kissed her
white knuckles.

The touch of his lips on her fingers sent confusion into
another dimension. She couldn't be feeling this...this...
whatever it was she was feeling. He wasn't Graham. *He
wasn't Graham.*

Somehow she got enough breath past her constricted
throat and into her lungs to say "Okay." She could do
this...for Marion.

He released his death grip on her hands to pull her into
his embrace. With his cheek on her temple, his breath
warm in her ear, she stiffened, trying not to feel the swirling heat that was filling her veins.

"Do you think you can hug me back?" he whispered.
"Make this look real?"

She swallowed a hysterical bark of laughter. She had no
idea what was real anymore. She put her arms around his
waist, and pressed her head against his chest. The cloth
beneath her cheek covered warm flesh and a beating heart.
She clung to hope, which was really only the absence of
despair, and prayed the government people would interpret
the moisture in her eyes as tears of happiness.

Awkwardly they pulled apart, but Burton kept his arm
around her waist as they walked back to Officers Jackson
and Connery. On the other side of the studio, the crew had
gathered in a low buzz of wondering. Ernie stood on his
own and appeared to be going into shock.

Burton cleared his throat. "Sorry to keep you waiting,"
he said to Jackson and Conner. "My, ahem, fiancée and I
were just discussing moving up the wedding date to accommodate the, uh, changed circumstances. We'd planned
a big church wedding, caterers, live band, the whole she-

bang, but well, the most important thing is that we're together. Isn't that right, Veronique?''

"Oui, c'est vrai." She spoke quietly, not looking anyone in the eye. It was important they be together. What did it matter what the reason was?

James Jackson handed her his card. ''You must come to the office within the next day or two and complete some forms, then we'll schedule interviews to establish your eligibility for residency. If you plan to marry, I wouldn't waste any time sending out the invitations.''

His dry tone made it obvious that James Jackson and Wendy Connery, no longer faceless bureaucrats but living, breathing enemies, wanted to give Burton and Veronique as little time as possible to cook up a story between them.

Burton left to see them out, and Ernie came up to Veronique, his young face as round and white as a bowl of blancmange. ''Congratulations, Veronique. I had no idea you and Burton were…I mean, that you two—'' He broke off as color flooded his cheeks.

''Pah! Ernie, we are not lovers.'' She spoke in a low voice, so no one else would hear her confession.

Ernie blushed harder. ''I wasn't sure. You must really want to stay in Canada.''

She threw up her hands. ''That is the last thing I want, but my mother-in-law is ill. I must take care of her.''

Ernie scratched the top of his head. ''You mean Mrs. O'Rourke? I didn't know she was sick.''

''*Mais non.* I have never met Burton's mother.'' She would have to now, she realized with a start. What a box of worms they had opened!

The studio door opened and Burton reappeared. The buzz of talk from the crew faded and died. His gaze swept over them, hardening briefly when it rested on Ernie and Veronique huddled together.

''Where's the audience, Ern?''

"I told them to stretch their legs and asked Brigit in PR to organize coffee for them."

"Good work. Gather round, folks," he said to the milling crew members. "I'd like a quick word with all of you."

Veronique moved forward with the rest. Burton came through the crowd to put his arm around her shoulders. She tried to relax but felt unnatural standing at his side pretending to be his fiancée. How would she manage as his bride?

"I guess you're all wondering what's going on." Heads nodded amid a murmur of assent. "Veronique and I are getting married. It's sudden, I know, but...well, when you know what you want, you've got to grab it with both hands and hang on tight. If anyone from Immigration asks you about our relationship, you can say you don't know anything because I am a very private individual who does not discuss his personal life with his co-workers."

"That's true enough," Vince said. He lifted his cap to smooth back his thinning head of hair. "Just one thing. I'm sure no one wants to screw up whatever you two have got cooking—if you'll pardon the pun—but what if they ask us how you two get along on the set?"

"Hmm..." Burton released Veronique to pace while he thought. "How about, we fell instantly and madly in love, but we're both strong-willed people who strike sparks off each other." He glanced around the faces before him. "Okay?"

"Oka-a-ay." Bill didn't look convinced.

"Maybe you're right. As a story line, it's a bit trite." Burton scratched his jaw, paced some more. And came up with zilch. "Come on, guys. What's the big deal? We're professionals. How do you suppose we'd act? Veronique and I aren't likely to go off in a corner and start making out, are we?"

No, no, their heads shook in agreement.

"If we're a little tense, it's because we're working out the bugs at the start of a new series."

"Aah, you're always tense," someone said from the back of the room.

"Well, thank you very much."

"Excuse me, Burt…on," Ernie piped up. "They might wonder why Veronique doesn't have an engagement ring."

"Good point, Ern. We'll take care of it right away." He spun around to Veronique.

Her face was very white, her green eyes wide and wary. Mutely she nodded her head just a fraction. Burton felt a sinking sensation in his stomach. He rarely experienced self-doubt, but marriage, Veronique, the federal government—it was huge. They were all unknown quantities, and Veronique the biggest unknown of all. Had his ego been so caught up in the challenge that he'd gambled until the stakes exceeded the prize? He wouldn't know till it all shook down, but right now, one thing was certain—he had to brazen it out.

"Okay, let's get back to work. Ernie, get Rita in here to fix Veronique's hair. Vince, round up the audience. Bill, let's set up a mirror over the range top so it'll look like we're shooting from directly above the pan. Veronique…"

He moved over to her as the others dispersed to perform their various tasks. He stood close, but without touching, afraid of touching, now that it could mean so much. "It's going to be all right."

"We cannot fool them, Burton."

"I don't have to pretend an attraction to you, Veronique."

She glanced up, alarm in her eyes. "Attraction is not love. Anyway, I don't want you to be attracted to me."

"I only meant that we can fool them. You don't have to worry about me demanding my conjugal rights. This marriage will be temporary and platonic. In name only.

Even so, we need to get to know each other in a hurry.
Are you busy tonight?''

"I am going to help Marion move to the nursing home.
She is finished with the rehab center, but her doctor doesn't
think she is ready to be on her own. I don't know how
I'm going to tell her I'm getting married again.''

He would have to tell his mother, he realized. Which
meant her book club friends and the whole aerobics class
would know. He groaned. At least it would get her off his
back about Melissa.

"Tomorrow then. Don't think about it now. We have to
finish the segment.''

He reached up to brush her cheek with his fingers,
caught her eye and was about to stop. Then he saw Bill
watching them curiously. Might as well play the part if it
made it easier for people to believe and back them up.
Deliberately he let his fingers slide through her hair to the
back of her neck, then bent his head to press a kiss on her
temple. Beneath his fingertips and his lips, he could feel
her tremble. He pulled away, not wanting to speculate on
the whys or wherefores.

She wouldn't meet his gaze, so he handed her over to
Rita, armed with brushes and powder, and walked away,
his heart beating fast.

BURTON WAS HURRIEDLY going through his in-tray, determined to have an early night for once. The first day of
taping hadn't gone too badly, considering, but what with
the mango salsa and the feds he was exhausted.

Damn, he thought, when he came across a hand-written
memo from Ed Murphy. The old man wanted to see him.
Now. The time noted was 5:00 p.m. It was now 6:15.

Murphy must have heard the news. Burton headed for
the elevators, going over in his mind various arguments
justifying his forthcoming marriage. He could either present it as evidence of supreme company loyalty, or as suc-

cumbing to uncontrollable passion. On the whole, he thought Murphy might be more inclined to buy the loyalty defense.

Burton stepped into the elevator and punched the button for the fifth floor. The one thing he must *not* do was mention *Lost Harvest* in connection with this particular escapade. It would only convince Murphy he was becoming unhinged and further jeopardize the chances of his documentary.

Sylvia had left for the day, her computer keys silent, her monitor shrouded in plastic. Burton knocked and was about to walk in when he heard Murphy call "Wait a minute."

Something odd about his voice made Burton pause, hand on the knob. "Murph?"

"That you, Burton?" Murphy said, coughing. "Hang on."

Hearing muffled sounds, Burton unabashedly put his ear to the door. A drawer banged shut, there was a faint hissing sound and then, finally, Murphy bellowed for him to come in.

The odor of fresh cigar smoke combined with pine-scented air-freshener almost choked him on the spot. He swung the door open and shut a few times before stepping into the office. "When did you take up smoking again, Murph?"

His boss glared him straight in the eye. "I didn't."

Burton glanced at the thin curl of smoke seeping out of the desk drawer. Murphy wasn't getting off this easy. He sniffed the air. "I'm sure I smell something."

The lines etching either side of Murphy's down-turned mouth sunk deeper. "Well, you don't."

Burton strolled over to the desk, affecting an air of unconcern. "What the hell, eh, Murph? They're probably wrong about smoking being bad for you. Everybody knows statistics can be made to show any damn thing at all. And if it helps you to concentrate—''

''Go to hell, O'Rourke, or you'll drive me to drink, as well. Now, park your butt in that chair and tell me what in God's good name is going on down there. Sylvia came back from coffee this afternoon babbling about how you're getting married to that Frenchwoman.''

Burton pulled up a chair and told Murphy the whole story.

When he was done, Ed just sat there, shaking his head. ''You've got yourself in a real mess this time, O'Rourke. What's the matter, can't stand your own cooking anymore?'' He started to chuckle at his own joke, then frowned as the laugh turned into a cough. ''You're not going to go through with it, are you?''

Burton got to his feet, spreading his hands helplessly. ''I don't have any choice, unless I can get someone else to marry her. Ernie might, but Rita would have my balls for breakfast.''

''Why didn't you check her residency status before you hired her, damn it? And why didn't she have the decency to mention her work visa was running out?''

''She did. She told me about it before she signed the contract,'' he admitted, scraping a hand through his hair. ''I knew it was a gamble, but I thought I could sort it out. I didn't count on red tape being so bloody binding.''

''The solution's simple,'' Murphy grunted. ''Get another chef.''

Burton shook his head. ''Veronique's too perfect. Well, maybe not perfect. In fact, she's a pain in the butt most of the time, but on camera she's fantastic. She's going to make this show.''

Murphy reached for the humidor and extracted a handful of jelly beans. ''I thought you didn't even want to do this show.''

''I'm committed now. I want it to be a success.''

Murphy chewed. "Is what you're doing legal?"

"The question is, can they prove it's not?" Burton leaned two hands on the back of the chair and gazed earnestly at Murphy. "What is love all about, anyway? How do you define when it begins? Look at love at first sight. Lots of whirlwind romances culminate in legitimate marriages."

"Which is probably why the divorce rate is so high," Murphy growled.

Burton waved the objection away and took up pacing again. "If circumstances were different—" like if Veronique didn't hate the sight of him "—I'd take her out, get to know her, quite possibly fall in love—" if he wasn't halfway there already "—and, after a suitable time had passed, I might very well ask her to marry me." At least his mother was going to be pleased, he thought. "The same scenario is happening now, except we've bypassed the dinner-and-drinks stage, and gone straight to—"

"The marriage bed?"

It was a pleasant thought, but not to be dwelled on. Not if he wanted to keep a rein on his libido. He'd promised Veronique a platonic relationship, and that was what she was going to get.

"What are you saying to me, Ed?" he said, frustration coming to the fore. "Are you telling me not to marry her? Because if you are, you're doing Channel Seven a big disfavor."

"The hell with the station! I don't want you getting burned. You barely know this woman. For all you know this could be a setup and she could take you for all you've got. Get a prenuptial agreement. Protect yourself."

Burton had always found the idea of prenup agreements abhorrent. He was certain Veronique had no designs on his bank account, but he was touched by the old man's concern. "Thanks, Murph. I'll check into it."

"Aah, it's nothin'. I want *Flavors* to be a success, too.

If it's not, I know you'll never get off my back until you get to do your damn documentary.''

''You're right there,'' Burton agreed cheerfully as he prepared to leave. ''If at first you don't succeed, try, try, again. Right, Murph?''

He saw Murphy glance at his desk drawer. The smoke had stopped, but cigars went out, they didn't burn down. As soon as he was out of the room, he'd lay five to one Murphy would be lighting up again.

''Right, Murph?''

''Yeah, yeah, right.'' With a last regretful glance at the drawer, he pushed on the armrests to heave himself up from his chair. ''Hang on. I'll walk out with you.''

IT WAS ALMOST EIGHT by the time Burton chugged up the gravel drive to the farmhouse and parked beside his mother's Volvo. Across the fields to the south, Mount Baker floated above the horizon, a white shark's tooth gleaming in a salmon-pink sky. Since he was off early and Veronique was busy, he'd called Catherine to see if she wanted to finish sorting through Granddad's things together. And if the subject came up, he might just mention that, oh, by the way, he was getting married on Friday. Would she like to come?

The door was open, so he pulled on the screen door and walked in. ''Mother?'' he called. ''Where are you?''

''Hi, Burtie. I'm in your grandfather's room.'' Her voice sounded muffled.

He walked down the hall and paused in the doorway to Grandad's room. ''How's it going?''

Catherine was kneeling on the rag rug, her head and shoulders beneath the bed. At the sound of his voice she withdrew, dragging with her a battered cardboard box. She lifted the top copy of what must have been several decades' worth of *Playboy* magazines. ''What on earth?''

''Why that dirty old son of a gun,'' Burton said with a

surprised grin. He took the magazine from Catherine's hand and flipped to the center to study Miss March, 1975. "Now, why couldn't I have found these when I was a teenager?"

Catherine rolled her eyes. "Thank heavens Dad had the sense to hide them." She rose to her feet, a hand on the small of her back. Her navy blue sweatpants and top were laced with dust. She sneezed. "You can put them out for recycling."

"Gee, I don't know, Mother. A collection like this is probably worth a mint. Will you look at that." He tipped the magazine sideways, a mischievous eye out for his mother's certain disapproval.

"Don't be crude, Burton."

Burton tossed the magazine back into the box. "I didn't think to look under the bed when I was here last. You didn't come across the chess set there, did you?"

"No," she said, dusting off her knees. "Do you remember the last time you saw it?" Her voice sounded artificially casual.

The bedsprings were old and sank beneath his weight. Had he just imagined the flicker of guilt in her eyes? "I think it was Easter," he said. "Granddad and I played a game before dinner, but I remember putting it back in its cabinet. You know how he always liked having things in their proper place."

Catherine moved to the dresser, opening and shutting drawers he knew to be empty. "Maybe he took it out later and left it somewhere. He was eighty-one. Getting a little forgetful."

"He would never have forgotten where he put that chess set." He watched his mother twitch the curtains shut against the coming twilight, then glance agitatedly around the room. Was she looking for something else to be sorted out, cleaned up, tidied away forever? "What is it, Mother?"

"I beg your pardon?" She tried for innocence, but within an instant her face crumpled. "Oh, Burtie!" she cried, and came to sit beside him on the bed. "I'm so sorry."

He put his arm around her. "Why? It's not your fault the chess set is missing."

"Maybe it is." She wiped at her wet cheeks with the flat of her hand. "The week before Dad died, I was out here. He...I...we had a fight."

"What about?"

"It was April, and he was doing his income tax. He had all his financial papers spread out on the kitchen table. I happened to see the insurance premiums that were due to be paid against death taxes." She paused, indignant. "Did you know that without insurance, when someone dies, whoever inherits has to pay tax on the property the same as if it had been sold? Do you have any idea how much that would be on a place this size? A quarter of a million, at least."

Burton nodded. "Mr. Bingham explained all that to me the day after the will was read. But don't worry, Granddad had insurance. Well, you must know, you just said you saw the papers. If he hadn't, I would have had to sell the farm just to pay the taxes."

"It's outrageous. The thing is, last year was so wet his crop was practically ruined. He had hardly any income and not enough to cover the insurance premiums. I suggested he get a loan, but the stubborn old fool wouldn't hear of it. Said he didn't want to pass on debts when he died. It was almost as if he knew he was going to go." Tears filled her eyes. "The last time I ever saw him, we fought. Oh, Burtie, if only I could live that day over again."

Burton put his other arm around her and held her, his eyes squeezing shut against the tears. "Shh, Mother, it's okay. It's okay." His voice was thick and he could hardly speak. "He knew you loved him."

Grief and love wrapped them in silence. They held each other, remembering, slowly gaining comfort from shared sorrow.

At last Catherine heaved a deep sigh and drew back. She smiled bravely and blinked away the moisture in her eyes. Sniffing a little, she continued. "I couldn't let the matter drop. I could tell he was really worried and not wanting to admit it. I told him if he wouldn't borrow, he should sell off a few acres to get the money."

Burton snorted. "He'd never agree to that. But what does all this have to do with the chess set?"

Catherine pulled at the handkerchief tucked in the cuff of her sweatshirt sleeve and dabbed at her eyes. "It was sitting on the table, half-covered by papers, one of his games against himself in progress. I picked up one of the pieces and...I don't know, I guess my subconscious was at work because I said, 'This set is an antique. It must be worth a lot of money.'"

A sudden chill prickled the back of Burton's neck. "You think he sold it to pay the insurance premiums?"

"I don't know. But right away he picked up the chess set and started packing it away, saying, 'You're right, it's worth a great deal of money.'" Then he looked me through and through with those fierce blue eyes. I swear, Burtie, I didn't mean for him to sell it. I knew how much it meant to him, and to you."

"Exactly. That's why I can't believe he would sell it." Burton rose from the bed to pace across the room. "But what if he thought *you* might sell it to get him the insurance money."

"I wouldn't do that!"

"I know. But what if he was so afraid of losing it that he didn't want to take any chances? He must have been under a lot of stress, trying to pay his taxes and insurance. What if he hid it somewhere?"

"It's possible, I suppose," Catherine said slowly. "But

if he hid it instead of selling it, how was he able to pay the insurance?''

Burton stared out the window at the barn and the chickens scratching in the dust. And thought about an old man for whom passing on his land intact to future generations had been paramount, even if it meant dying poor.

Catherine got up and put a hand on his shoulder. ''I guess the important thing is, he saved the farm. Have you decided whether to rent this place out or live here yourself?''

Burton wiped a hand down his face and moved away. Selling didn't occur to his mother as an option. He felt like a traitor even thinking of it, and he sure wasn't ready to talk about it. ''No. Let's take these boxes out, then start on the other downstairs bedroom.''

''Okay. First thing tomorrow I'll call around the antique shops just to make sure he didn't sell the chess set.''

''That would be a huge task,'' he protested. ''You'd have to check every antique store and pawnshop from Vancouver to Hope.''

''That's okay. I'll do it.''

Burton took a step back to wrap his arms around his mother, feeling her sorrow and her fear and her determination to make it up to him. He should at least tell her about his meeting with Don Chetwynd, but why add to her worries now? He wasn't going to do anything till that chess set was found.

''We'll get it back, don't worry.'' He placed a smaller box of farming magazines into his mother's arms, then hoisted Granddad's box of secret pleasure onto his shoulder. They walked out to the car and waited until Catherine had placed her load in the trunk of his Tercel for transport to the recycling depot before he said, ''Are you doing anything next Friday?''

''I'm getting my hair done in the afternoon,'' she replied, dusting off her hands. ''Why?''

"I'm getting married at lunchtime."

When her knees started to buckle, he wished he'd told her when they were in the house and there was a chair she could collapse onto. As it was, he had to take her arm and sit her down on a granite boulder by the edge of the driveway, her hand over her heart, while the grass turned dewy in the dusk and the neighboring farm dogs took turns barking the news out over the valley.

"Oh, Burtie, I'm so happy for you!" she said when at last she was able to speak. She got up again to hug him, and her eyes glistened in the fading light. "This is so quick! But Melissa is such a lovely girl. I just knew you'd like her."

He rolled his eyes at his mother's willful optimism. "I never even called Melissa. It's Veronique, the Frenchwoman you saw on tape. The one who's hosting the cooking show."

"Oh. Her." Catherine wiped the corners of her eyes with her fingertips, blinked and smiled. She was already adjusting to the news, starting to like it.

"It's not exactly a love match." He had to get that in before she started naming her grandchildren.

"What is it, then? Should I sit down again?"

"Let's go inside and make some coffee."

"Oh, my goodness, Burton! She's not pregnant, is she?"

Once he'd told Catherine the whole story, it took three cups of coffee before she calmed down. Like Ed Murphy, she was against the match. Unlike Ed, her objection wasn't over what Veronique might do to his unsuspecting bank account, but how she would ruin his chances of finding, and marrying, someone he did love.

"For crying out loud, Mother," he said finally, setting his cup down hard on the pine table in the kitchen. "This isn't till death do us part. It's just temporary, two or three months at the most. When it's time for her to go back to Tahiti, we'll just have it annulled.''

Annulled. The word had a hollow, barren sound. He'd never given marriage a whole lot of thought, but somewhere at the back of his mind he'd expected to be in love, at least. Well, this wasn't the time for sentiment. Entering a temporary marriage wasn't that big a sacrifice. Despite his assurances to Veronique, the only thing that worried him was whether they'd be able to pull it off with Immigration.

VERONIQUE WAS WORRIED, and because she couldn't pin down the exact source of her anxiety, her worry grew. She rolled her assorted problems over in her mind. There was Marion—she was an obvious source of concern. The same went for the threat of deportation and the Immigration people in general. And then there was Burton's crazy idea of forming a marriage of convenience—*oh la la.* All of these were bad, but none of them quite accounted for the nebulous feeling of disquiet that floated around the edges of her mind.

So in spite of the lowering clouds and the blustery wind, she put on her wet suit and carried her sailboard across Cornwall Avenue and through the little park to the beach. Leaving her shoes on the seawall, she hopped barefoot onto the cold, pebbly sand. Briefly, she shut her eyes, recalling the fine-grained beaches of Tahiti, black as the pearls for which the island was famous, and hot as a stovetop. Water so warm it felt like a lover's embrace.

The water of English Bay was choppy and cold, and the salt spray stung her eyes. She waded out, pushing the board before her. Icy water seeped into her suit through the ankles and wrists and trickled down her neck, making her shiver. When she was waist deep, she climbed aboard, kneeling to drag the heavy sail dripping from the water.

Wind caught the sail, and the board gusted forward on

the crest of a wave. Many times during her claustrophobic marriage she'd sought the freedom of the wind and the waves. Or like now, she'd taken to the ocean to empty her mind of the tangled details of her problems, so a solution could work its way into her consciousness.

In Tahiti she used to sail around the island or across to Moorea, wearing only a bikini, sometimes just a *pareau* knotted around her hips, while the frigate birds wheeled overhead. Here, she went back and forth across the bay clothed neck to ankles in a constricting wet suit, sometimes ending up on Wreck Beach where nudists sunbathed among the scattering of salt-bleached logs. There she would peel off her wet suit and lay naked in the sand against a giant Douglas fir. She'd never mentioned this to Graham, of course. Such freedom was just an illusion.

She hadn't told Marion about her upcoming marriage because there seemed little point. The whole thing would be over before they knew it. She was used to protecting her mother-in-law, so it wasn't this minor deception that worried her.

The wind shifted to the north, and Veronique changed tack, the muscles in her arms straining to maintain a firm grip on the crossbar as she crossed the board to the opposite side. Strength, balance, flexibility—a person needed them all.

The marriage might not even take place if Immigration denied her claim. At the moment she would almost welcome a deportation order. It would absolve her of responsibility and send her to where she wanted to go.

A sailboat came toward her, its prow dipping into the troughs of the waves and back up. Seasick, a boy hung over the rail. Veronique turned her sailboard out of the boat's path, lifting on the crest of a wave and surfing down the other side.

Marriage to Burton. He had no claim of love on her, no right to expect…anything. Except, of course, that she fulfill her contract for *Flavors*. She was surprised he'd committed himself in front of everyone, but she supposed that, like Graham, for him work was everything. Or perhaps marriage meant so little that he could treat it as mere words on paper. He, she felt certain, would have no trouble dealing with the platonic nature of their marriage.

Her sailboard cut through a white-capped wave and dashed a spray of icy saltwater in her face. Stung, her eyes shut, and the memory flashed back of that moment on the set when she'd looked into Burton's eyes and felt something inside catch fire. She flicked her head, tossing the water out of her eyes. Her anxiety crystallized. So *that* was what had sent her out here on this miserable day.

She felt something for him. But was it leftover attraction from early days with Graham, or worse—something new?

The more she went over it, the more her perceptions became muddied. She couldn't, after all, separate Burton from her image of Graham. So she blanked her mind, letting the roar of the wind and the cry of the gulls displace her eddying thoughts. At last she turned back to the beach, chilled to the bone, her arms and legs trembling with fatigue.

She had no solution to her problem, except a resolve not to let these feelings, whatever they were, grow. She was going home.

Nothing, and no one, was going to stop her.

CHAPTER NINE

ERNIE WAS WORRIED, TOO—about Rita. His first mistake was not complimenting her on her new haircut when he'd picked her up after work. *Styled,* she called what Lillian's grandniece had done to it during lunch break. He could have done better with his dad's tin snips and a jar of Vaseline. He'd liked her hair the way it was before, a soft, shiny curtain that hung to her shoulders.

Gearing down his trusty old Volkswagen Beetle at the entrance to the subdivision where Rita lived with her mother, he wondered what the big deal was about a haircut. He bet Veronique didn't fuss over her hair.

He sure knew better than to say that, because his second mistake had been to innocently agree that Veronique was chic—whatever the hell *chic* meant. He'd just wanted to make amends for screwing up on the hair thing, but right away Rita had gone all huffy. She'd crossed her arms beneath her breasts and stared silently out the window all the way back to Surrey.

Petunias bloomed in two neat circles of earth cut into Rita's front lawn and were watched over by a pair of garden gnomes in red trousers. Ernie pulled into the driveway of the two-story house and cut the engine. A marmalade tabby jumped onto the hood of his car and eyed him through the windshield. Rita's standard poodle poked her curly black head over the top of the fence separating the side yard from the front and let out a few joyous yips.

"Rita?" he said tentatively. That morning she'd invited

him to stay for dinner, but maybe she'd be in a better mood if she didn't have to cook. She didn't really like cooking, though she was pretty good at it.

Rita made a production out of getting her purse and her shopping bag full of hair-care products together. "Yes?"

"What do you say we go out to eat?" He was going to suggest Stavros, their favorite restaurant, then he remembered Burton saying that Greek food was passé. "There's that new French restaurant over in White Rock—"

"So you want French food now? Is that it?" Her voice had an injured sound, and two spots of red stained her cheeks.

"Huh?"

"You know what I'm talking about, Ernie. I saw the way you looked at her."

"Who?" he squeaked, though he knew darn well who she was talking about. He just hadn't thought he was so obvious.

"Veronique."

"I thought you liked her. You said yourself she was chic."

"Oh, Ernie! Sometimes you just don't have a clue." Rita swiped angrily at a tear that had broken free and threatened to run down her cheek. "Do you have any idea how humiliating it is for me to see you fawning all over her in front of everybody?"

"She's going to marry Burton!"

"You *know* that's just a setup so she can stay in Canada. You spent all day Tuesday shopping with her, but you never want to go shopping with me."

"We had to get things for the show!"

"Oh, sure. How do I know what else you two got up to?"

"Nothing." Then he remembered that afternoon when a mango had been all that stood between Veronique's hand and his thigh. He couldn't help it, he blushed.

Rita's eyes widened and filled with glistening tears. "Oh, Ernie!"

He reached for her, but she twisted away from him and pushed open the door. Her bag dropped and a bottle of shampoo rolled down the driveway. While she bent to retrieve it, Ernie got out and hurried around the car.

"Rita. Honey." When she straightened, he put his arms around her and her bags. She averted her face but didn't move away. "It's you I love. Nothing happened, I swear."

She looked up, her expression a mixture of grief and accusation. "But you wanted something to happen."

Maybe in some parallel universe, but Ernie knew better than to say such a thing. "No, honestly. Please, Rita, don't cry. I love you. Your hair is beautiful. You're beautiful."

She sniffed and glanced up at him beneath wet lashes. "Do you really like my hair?"

Oh, boy. Ernie took off his glasses and began to polish them, partly out of nervous habit, partly so he wouldn't have to look at her in full focus. "I…I like you *any* way you are. I really mean that."

Rita heaved a big sigh and wiped her eyes. "Oh, Ernie. I know you do. I'm sorry I got so silly. It's just…I don't know. Lately you don't seem to even see me when you look at me. I thought maybe if I did something different… That's why I got Sandy to cut my hair. I'm not totally sure I like it myself. I just wanted something different."

Ernie listened to her with a sinking heart. He didn't understand half of what she was saying, but he did hear her say she wanted something different. As in different boyfriend? No, no, no. He leaned over her bags and, ignoring the twitch in the living-room curtains, took her lips in a deep kiss. A French kiss. For a split second, a corner of his mind flashed on Veronique. He moaned, blocking his thoughts and deepening the kiss further.

"Oh, Ernie," Rita breathed when they broke apart. "I've got goose bumps."

It was Rita he wanted. No question. "So, how about dinner?"

She hesitated. "Mother's expecting us to stay in."

"She's a big girl." Then he winced, because Sheila Grafton *was* big—as in very overweight. "Sorry, I mean, why don't we see if she wants to come with us?"

"She doesn't like eating out unless it's Chinese. You wait in the car and I'll sort it out." Rita planted a tiny kiss on his lips and ran up the path to the front door.

Ernie backhanded the perspiration off his forehead as he walked back to the Volkswagen. He'd had no idea Rita was so jealous. He wasn't the type to play around, but he had to admit it was a boost to his ego that she thought Veronique would even look at him.

Rita was back in ten minutes with fresh lipstick and dry eyes. "Mom doesn't mind staying home," she said, fastening the seat belt across her lap. "She's on some new diet, anyway."

"So…have you thought about which restaurant you want to go to?" he said, starting up the engine.

She sighed. "If you really want French, I guess we'll go French."

"We don't have to go French. I like Greek, too. In fact, I like Greek better."

"Do you really?" Her glance was wistful.

"Yes."

"Okay," she said, smiling happily. "Let's go French."

Damn. Damn, damn, damn, damn.

Burton glanced at his watch as he burst out of the conference room and broke into a lope down the corridor toward his office. Today of all days, his meeting with the writers of *Lovers and Strangers* had run overtime. His mother had called at least a dozen times. And Ernie had driven him crazy by humming the wedding march all morning.

He hated being late, even for his own wedding.

He grabbed his coat and the umbrella he'd bought this morning—dark green with a varnished teak handle and brass fittings—and hurried down to reception.

"Where's Ernie?" he asked Lillian, pulling on his coat.

"Right here, boss." Ernie came puffing around the corner.

"Have you got the ring?" Lillian asked. The figure of calm, she came around her desk to straighten Burton's tie.

Burton jammed a hand into his pants pocket. "Yep."

"And the license?"

"Yep. Let's go, Ern."

"Wait a minute." Lillian picked a white carnation out of her vase, broke off the stem and poked the fresh, peppery-scented flower into Burton's lapel. "You look very handsome."

"Thanks, Lil. You're a doll." He kissed her on the cheek.

She held on to his arms and whispered in his ear, "This could turn out better than you think."

"I sure hope so." He turned to go, then on impulse, pulled the whole dripping mass of flowers from the vase. "You don't mind, do you, Lil? I won't have time to stop at a florist."

"Of course not." She helped him wrap the stems in computer paper and all but pushed him out the door.

They arrived at the courthouse, a modern hanging garden of glass and greenery, a few minutes past noon. Burton groaned when he saw his mother. She wore a dark blue suit, a silk corsage left over from Easter and a resigned smile. There was no sign of Veronique.

"Maybe she changed her mind," Catherine said, looking hopeful.

"No, Mother. She's probably just..." He broke off, having no idea what might be keeping her. Other than her visits to Marion, he knew nothing of her life off the set.

Going back through the revolving door, he scanned the sidewalk in both directions, peering through the lunchtime crowd for his reluctant bride. Why was he so nervous? It was just a piece of paper. A piece of paper that ought to stand for love and cherish till death did them part—not for the length of a television series. He paced the sidewalk, feeling like a character in one of his old sitcoms.

Then he saw her. Hurrying toward him, hair loose and glowing, the black cashmere dress he liked so well clinging to her shoulders and hips. It wouldn't have been his choice for a wedding dress, but what the hell. Maybe, he thought in a burst of optimism, when she got to know him she would like him better. After all, familiarity bred... No, no, that wasn't right. He rubbed his temples, trying to collect his thoughts.

When she got within ten feet, she looked up and their eyes met. It was hard to say if it was alarm or anticipation that widened her eyes, but for him, that instant of eye contact went way beyond platonic.

"Hi," he said, nervously smoothing back his cowlick. He handed her the bunch of flowers, then leaned over to kiss her on the cheek. Her skin was cool and soft, and slightly damp with the moisture in the air. She started to jerk away from his lips, so he whispered, "They might be watching. No, don't look around. Look at me."

She couldn't, of course. She buried her face in his shoulder while pedestrians parted around them. He put his other arm around her and felt her trembling. "It's okay," he said in a low voice. "It's going to be okay. Our kisses will only be in public."

She glanced up, brushing her curls from her forehead, and smiled briefly. "I am sorry I'm late. Thank you for the flowers. I don't think about a bouquet."

Or an appropriate dress, or anything else associated with a real wedding. He felt suddenly foolish and wanted to rip the boutonniere from his lapel. "The others are inside," he said, and guided her through the revolving door.

Ernie turned as they entered the lobby, his expression a tragicomic mixture of eager and wistful at the sight of Veronique. She kissed him on both cheeks, making him bloom with pleasure. "*Bonjour,* Ernie."

"Uh, bon-joor, Veronique."

Burton's hand tightened around hers. She still didn't kiss him in greeting. She kissed Lillian and Ernie and God knew who else, but not him. Stepping back, he said, "Mother, this is Veronique Dutot. Veronique, Catherine O'Rourke."

His mother held out her hand with a too-gracious smile and murmured a cool pleasantry. Then she took his free arm, pulling him aside. Burton glanced back to see Veronique looking at them and twining a finger through her hair.

"She's wearing black to her own wedding?" Catherine said in an undertone. "I hate to say it, Burton, but I'm beginning to think you were right the first time—this woman is trouble."

"It's just a dress," he whispered. "It's not as though this is a church wedding. Or, or…we're in love."

One perfectly shaped eyebrow arched infinitesimally. "I saw the way you looked when she kissed Ernie."

"She can't kiss me—I'm her boss," he said, not having the foggiest notion of French etiquette. He glanced over to see Veronique straightening Ernie's tie and teasing him. His blood pressure soared. She only ever looked at *his* tie to avoid looking at his face.

"So why does it make you so tense? And why doesn't she look you in the eye?" She put a hand on his jacket, imploring him. "Oh, Burtie, I don't want to see you hurt. It's not too late to call it off. You don't owe this woman anything."

"We've been through this," he said grimly. "I'm not

changing my mind." He glanced at his watch. "We'd better get down to the registrar's office. Please, Mother, be nice."

Veronique watched the exchange between Burton and his mother with a sick feeling in her stomach. But she took Burton's arm and together they led the little procession down the stairs to the basement floor where the registrar's office was located.

Two other couples and their witnesses were in the waiting room when they entered. One bride was decked out in ankle-length white muslin and had flowers in her hair, while her husband-to-be wore a tuxedo jacket over blue jeans. They sat nose-to-nose, arms wrapped around each other, giggling. The other couple was about twenty years older and more staid, but the way they held hands and the quiet glances they exchanged left no doubt of their affection.

"I am very hungry," Veronique said suddenly. "Maybe we eat lunch first, *non?*" All morning she'd been too nervous to eat, and now, when the moment was upon them, her stomach did nothing but rumble.

She hadn't meant for Burton's mother to hear, but Catherine O'Rourke slanted her son one of those arched-eyebrow looks. He just uttered a hapless laugh and said nothing.

Oh la la. Veronique shrank back, a hand to her stomach. His mother hated her, and Burton thought it was all a joke.

Still, it was thoughtful of him to bring her flowers. Avoiding their eyes, she buried her nose in the fragrant mass. And saw, half-hidden by stems and leaves, the Channel Seven logo and a few lines from one of Lillian's spreadsheets. Her empty stomach turned over on itself, and her eyes threatened to weep like the sky.

A clerk came out of an inner office and called their names.

The service was mercifully short. When the registrar

pronounced them husband and wife, Veronique lifted her head high. She was a Frenchwoman. She would fulfill her part in this marriage with no weak longings for false sentiment.

Burton touched his lips to hers and she fought to still the inner trembling, vowing if she could ever bear to go through this again in the future, she would marry for nothing less than love.

Then Ernie gave her a peck on the mouth and his eyes were moist, too. Burton glared at him but for once didn't make some snappy remark. Catherine O'Rourke's eyes were cold and dry.

"Be good to him," her new mother-in-law said, embracing her stiffly. "He's all I have."

"I do not harm him." Impulsively Veronique hugged her. Catherine had been cheated out of a proper daughter-in-law and a church wedding. She wanted the real thing for her son. What woman wouldn't?

Catherine responded with a perplexed smile. Veronique wondered if Burton had told her about the resemblance he bore to her first husband. How close was he to his mother? So many things she didn't know about her new husband. It had been the same with Graham. And it filled her with trepidation.

They emerged onto the street, newly wed. This was not the way she and Ghislaine had pictured their weddings as little girls. There was no music, no flowers, no friends and family to wish her love and happiness in her new life. Only gray, drizzling skies and the uncaring faces of strangers hurrying along crowded downtown sidewalks.

"So," Burton said, clapping his hands together with a forced smile, "how about that lunch?"

"I'd better get back to the studio," Ernie said, looking regretfully at Veronique. "Rita's waiting for me."

"See you later, then. Thanks, Ernie." Burton turned up his collar at a gust of wind and, in doing so, knocked the carnation from his lapel. He made a grab for it, but it landed in a puddle and a pedestrian stepped on it, leaving the petals muddy and bruised. Straightening, he said, "Mother?"

"No thank you, darling. I'm having my hair done, remember? Anyway, I'm sure you two will want to be alone." Catherine gave him a peck on the cheek, threw a vague smile in Veronique's direction and hurried down the sidewalk, pushed along by the wind.

Having her hair done? Veronique thought. *After* the wedding? Outrage coursed through her on Burton's behalf. Yet he did not seem concerned. It did not matter, she told herself. It did not matter.

Then they were alone and Burton was pressing something solid into her hand. "This is for you."

She glanced down, surprised. "Thank you, but…an umbrella? I lose them."

"You won't lose this one. We could go to Marietta's. I haven't made a reservation, but I know the head waiter."

This wasn't a wedding feast. "A hamburger will do."

A smile crept onto his face. A real smile. "I didn't know haute chefs ate hamburgers. With ketchup and relish and everything?"

She laughed, her mood lightening. "No, with béarnaise sauce and pickled truffles. Of course, with ketchup and relish. Just no fast-food burger. I refuse to eat off cardboard and plastic."

He tucked her hand into the crook of his arm. "Come on, then, Mrs. O'Rourke, let's go have lunch."

His warmth spread down her arm and chased the chill from her toes. But…Mrs. O'Rourke? That was his mother, not her.

Burton took her to the Jolly Jumbuck, a pub just around the corner. While he went to the bar for drinks, Veronique fingered the shiny gold wedding band he'd placed on her finger. She'd just gotten used to not wearing a ring and here she was with another. When he'd talked about rings a couple of days before, she'd suggested she wear the old wedding band Graham had given her rather than buy a new one. Burton had looked at her strangely and said "No" very firmly, adding a second later that the Immigration officials would be bound to notice the ring wasn't new. She hadn't thought of that, but most likely he was right.

"Champagne!" she exclaimed when he came back with a bottle of Dom Pérignon. Could this mean more to him than she'd thought?

"It occurred to me they might be watching," he said, untwisting the wire around the cork.

Veronique glanced dubiously around the smoky, crowded pub. "Do you really think so?"

"I have no idea, but we don't want to screw up now." He popped the cork and poured out two glasses, then clinked his glass against hers. "To us—for better or for lunch."

She smiled at that and took a sip. The bubbles tickled her nose, and the alcohol went straight to her head. It felt very strange to be Mrs. Burton O'Rourke.

"Now, let's get down to business." He pulled out a notepad and pen and began to jot down notes. "You don't like fast-food restaurants but you do eat hamburgers. Champagne, yes… What's your favorite color?" He glanced up, pen poised expectantly.

She had to laugh. "In what—clothes or flowers? Do you think you can find out all my likes and dislikes over lunch?"

"We've got to start somewhere." He ripped a page out of the notebook and passed it across the table. "You'd better make notes, too. My favorite color is blue—clothes and flowers. I grew up in Vancouver, the only child of an only child."

"Lonely child," she murmured.

"Not at all." He sipped at his champagne. "My best friend lived next door. Mother had lots of friends, many with children about my age."

"What about your father? Where is he?"

"He died five years ago of a heart attack. We weren't very close—he was away on business a lot—but we had a good relationship. Granddad was more of a father to me. Birthday?"

"December 25."

"No kidding. What a bummer." He noted it down. "Where were you born?"

"Bordeaux. My father was *capitaine* in the *gendarmerie*. The French police," she explained. "I have three sisters—I am the youngest. When I was very small we lived in Algérie before we move to Tahiti."

"Ah, Tahiti. I picture a tropical paradise with beautiful bare-breasted women lounging on the banks of coral lagoons."

She laughed. "You have been influenced by Gauguin."

"More like *Mutiny on the Bounty*," he admitted. "So what's it really like?"

Her eyes closed as she transported herself mentally. "It is paradise," she said, her voice dreamy. "You awake to the sound of the cock crowing, and every day is so warm you need put on only a *pareau*—a strip of colorful cotton, like a...sarong. Home was a Tahitian-style wooden house with big windows—no glass, you understand—but sides that prop up to let the breeze flow through and give shade. In the backyard we have an avocado tree and a mango. The beach is close by, black sand. The water is warm like a bath and the coral is many colors. Fish of all shapes and sizes flash like the neon through the clear turquoise water."

Burton had propped his chin in his hand to listen to her. "I can see why you'd want to go back. What about your family? Tell me more."

He sounded as though he was really interested. Unlike Graham, who hated to hear her talk about her life in Tahiti or her family. Or any part of her life he couldn't dominate. But then, Burton was probably interested only to the extent he needed the information for the interview.

"My parents are retired and live in Bordeaux, but they spend the winters in Tahiti. My sister, Ghislaine, lives outside Papeete. She is married and has two children, Coralie and Hugo."

"Go on," he said, writing quickly in his bold, slanted hand.

"Ghislaine is a flight attendant, but she is looking for a job closer to home. Her husband, Donaldo—his mother came from Spain—is captain on a charter sailboat. His cousin, Jean-Paul, owns a marina and is building a floating restaurant. I might get a job there when I go back."

"Oh." He frowned when he heard that, but he noted it down.

"Not everything about Tahiti is paradise," she continued. "There are tropical ulcers that take months to heal, mold that grows everywhere, and the wet season where we snap at one another's throats. And typhoons that can smash your house and scatter the pieces like twigs."

She twirled her champagne glass by its stem, watching the bubbles float to the top. "As time goes on, you learn to accept the bad with the good. My first husband didn't experience Tahiti long enough to really love it. Probably he never would have." She sighed.

There was a silence. Burton put down his pen. "I'm sorry."

Her gaze dropped. She shrugged. "Me, too."

"I think we should stay at the farmhouse," he said.

Her head came up, and her alarmed gaze danced around his shoulders. "We?"

"Our marriage won't look genuine unless we live together. My apartment only has one bedroom, and if you're going back to Tahiti it doesn't make sense for you to keep your apartment. Anyway, I've got to fix the place up before I can sell, and it's easier to do it if I'm staying out there."

She frowned. "But it is so far. I must be close to Marion."

"We'll be coming in every day for work. The nursing home you mentioned isn't far from the studio. I'll drive you or you can use my car."

"I didn't think about us...living together."

"Don't worry. The farmhouse has lots of bedrooms, so we won't get in each other's way. I'll pick you up after work. We can take some of your stuff out to the farm and stay for the weekend. Okay?"

Like Graham, he'd taken charge. She glanced around the pub, wondering if one of the gray-suited men sipping their second pint over a long Friday lunch was taking notes for the government.

"Okay."

"Good." Burton checked his watch. "I have to get back for *Lovers and Strangers*. Give me your address and I'll pick you up around six o'clock."

She wrote it down on the piece of paper he'd given her—still barren of any details of his life—and passed it back. This marriage was different to her first in at least one respect. She could not get hurt because she didn't love Burton. How could she? She didn't see him as a person in his own right.

MARION NOTICED THE RING right away.

"Some flowers for you, Marion." Veronique tucked her bridal bouquet into an empty vase and filled it with water from the bathroom. Only one flower was missing—a gardenia—which she'd pressed between the pages of the book of English sayings she carried in her backpack to read on the bus.

Marion set her crutches aside and lowered herself into a cushioned wicker armchair in the glassed-in porch that overlooked the garden. "What's that on your finger?"

"Pardon?" Veronique instinctively covered the ring, then took her hand away to regard the plain gold band with feigned surprise.

"The ring," Marion said. "It looks like a wedding band."

Veronique swallowed. *"Oui."*

"It's not the one Graham gave you. That had rows of diamonds on it."

Veronique had always hated the ostentatiousness of that ring—something else she'd never been able to say. She took a deep breath, and when she exhaled, the bare facts tumbled out. "I am married again. To my producer, Burton O'Rourke. It was this morning."

Marion gripped the arms of her chair, the bluish veins on her thin hands standing out. "Married! But…it's only been six months since Graham died." Tears filled her eyes. "Married. I wasn't even aware you were seeing anyone."

Of course Marion couldn't possibly understand. Not only did she not know the facts, Marion was a woman who talked to her husband's photo, who still had all his clothes hanging in her closet, who cooked his favorite meals even though he wasn't alive to eat them.

Veronique scooted her chair forward and placed her hands over Marion's. "Please do not distress yourself, *chère* Marion. It is the marriage of convenience only, although you must not say so to anyone."

"I don't understand," Marion said, her voice teary. She cast about for a tissue.

Veronique reached into the side pocket of her backpack and drew out the handkerchief with the letter *B* monogrammed in the corner. She handed it to Marion, wondering if she would comment on that, as well. "My work visa ran out," she explained. "The immigration officials say I must leave the country. The only way to stay was to marry another Canadian.''

''But you said you were going back to Tahiti.'' Abruptly, she lowered the handkerchief, eyes wide. ''Oh! You did it for me. Oh, my dear Veronique. You shouldn't have done that. How do you know what he's even like?''

Veronique made a sudden decision. She handed Marion her crutches and helped her to her feet. ''Come, let us kill two birds with one bone. We will get your wheelchair and take you up the street to the studio. You are going to meet him.''

''What? But I can't possibly. I don't want to meet the man who's taken you away from Graham.''

Veronique held her ex-mother-in-law's arms and looked her directly in the eye. ''Marion, Graham was a wond…won…he was your son. And my husband. But he was gone long before I met Burton. They are two separate people with nothing to do with each other, except…''

Oh la la. How could she have forgotten?

''Except what, Ronnie?'' Marion struggled to get the crutches under her arms.

Veronique thrust her fingers into the back of her hair, tugging and twining it into knots. ''You mustn't be shocked, but Burton, he look just like Graham.''

Marion laughed nervously. ''My dear, that's impossible.''

''DOES MY HAIR LOOK all right?'' Marion fretted as Veronique pushed her through the doors into the Channel Seven building.

''You look wonderful.'' Veronique wheeled her across the lobby, pausing at the front desk to say hello to Lillian.

Lillian looked up from her computer. ''Veronique! I didn't expect to see you here today. Congratulations, by the way. You may not realize it, but Burton is considered quite a catch.''

Veronique shrugged, too embarrassed to reply directly. "Lillian, this is Marion. Has Burton started taping *Lovers and Strangers* yet?"

"Hello, Marion," Lillian said warmly. "Veronique has told us all about you. I hope your hip is starting to heal."

"It gives me trouble in the damp weather, but it's on the mend, thank you." She reached back to pat Veronique's hand. "Don't know what I'd do without Ronnie."

Lillian smiled and turned to Veronique. "Taping starts in a few minutes, but if you hurry you might catch Burton in his office. I just put a call through to him a minute ago." She turned to Marion. "Are you going to watch the show being taped?"

"Oh, I would love to. It's my favorite show. I've watched it every day for the last twelve years."

"We better hurry, Marion. See you later, Lillian." She pushed on down the corridor.

"Did you see her hair?" Marion asked in an astonished whisper when they were out of earshot of the front desk.

Veronique laughed. Lillian's hair had undergone some amazing transformations in the past couple of weeks. Currently it was a luscious pale caramel color with sugar frosted tips that looked surprisingly good against Lillian's delicate skin. "Maybe we try that shade on you next, eh?"

"Not on your life!"

Ahead of them, an office door opened. Burton's door. Veronique's hands turned clammy and slipped on the plastic handles of the wheelchair. She let go and stepped forward, wishing she could somehow prevent this meeting now that it was actually about to happen.

Burton's expression when he saw her—surprise and warmth in equal parts—did something funny to the pit of her stomach. Her gaze went to the wedding band on his left hand. Somehow she'd half expected him to take it off when she wasn't around.

She glanced back at Marion and was shocked. Far from

being surprised or upset at seeing Graham's double, her mother-in-law merely smiled expectantly. *Zut alors!* Had she dreamed the whole thing?

"*Salut,* Bur-r-rton." Nerves thickened her accent. "Zis ees Marion, my ex-muzzer-in-law. Marion, zis ees Burton O'Rourke, my—" She choked over what to call him. Husband? Producer?

"Pleased to meet you, Marion." Burton bent to take her hand. "I'm sorry about your accident. Although it's thanks to you we have Veronique with us."

"It's wonderful to meet you, Mr. O'Rourke," Marion exclaimed. "I just love your show."

"Marion would like to watch *Lovers and Strangers* being taped," Veronique said. "Okay?"

"No problem." He glanced at his watch. "I'm going to the studio now. Want to come along?" And without appearing to hurry them, he had them moving quickly down the corridor.

"You know, I haven't missed an episode in twelve years," Marion said.

Burton smiled. "I'm glad you enjoy it. I've only been producing it for seven years, but it's always nice to meet a fan."

"I'm a fan, all right. Although lately that Tiffany has made me so cross," Marion complained as Veronique wheeled her along beside Burton. "Ever since she came out of the institute, she's been a different person. And so mean to poor Reilly. I had hopes they were going to get married."

Burton nudged Veronique aside and took over the wheelchair. "Can you keep a secret?" he asked Marion in a low voice.

"Oh, yes!" Marion's reply was breathless with excitement.

"Tiffany is Reilly's mother."

"No!"

"It's true," he replied. "She's keeping Reilly at a distance because she doesn't want him to find out it was she who stabbed his uncle—who is really his father—with a fondue fork."

Marion gasped. "She murdered Jonathon?"

"Don't you dare tell a soul," he warned. "Or my boss will have my head."

"Cross my heart." Marion pursed her lips tight. "I can keep a secret, can't I, Ronnie?"

Biting her lip, Veronique nodded. Then Burton placed his hand in the small of her back and murmured in her ear, "Can you keep a secret, Mrs. O'Rourke?" Her laughter vanished as a rush of pleasure spiraled through her. She drew away, murmuring something, she hardly knew what.

In the studio Burton parked Marion in a level spot and said goodbye before striding down to the set.

Veronique sat in an aisle seat next to Marion. "So, does he not look like Graham?"

Marion's thin gray brows came together as she appeared to give the question some thought. "Not really. Oh, maybe a little around the nose and the mouth."

"And the eyes and the jaw…" Veronique couldn't believe Marion didn't see it.

"No, not so much the eyes. Possibly you see more of a resemblance than I do. You see…" Marion's voice became soft. "I still think of Graham as he was when he was a little boy."

She peered at Veronique through the semidarkness. "You married him because you think he looks like Graham, didn't you?" she said gently. "Oh, my dear, I know how much you must miss him." Her glance strayed to the set where Burton had gathered the talent for a last-minute pep talk. "I hope for Mr. O'Rourke's sake he'll be able to live up to Graham's memory."

CHAPTER TEN

THE HUMIDITY IN VERONIQUE'S apartment hit Burton like a sauna. She answered the door wearing a saronglike wrap of hot pinks and orange, and a short, tight pink T-shirt that hugged her firm breasts and exposed her navel. Wow. This was not the sort of wife he'd once vaguely imagined having, but he could probably learn to live with her.

"Come in." She clutched a large copper watering can to her chest. Silver earrings tinkling, she slipped away into the apartment before he could recover enough to say hello.

Her apartment was like her, warm and bright, and there was more greenery than in the conservatory at Queen Elizabeth Park. Burton half expected to find a parrot squawking in the foliage, or an outrigger beached near the sofa. Ah, there was a sailboard propped in a corner. *Close.* He glanced around, noting the interesting bits of pottery and carved wood lining the mantelpiece and the framed watercolors decorating the walls. Nice. Very nice.

But none of it was packed and ready for the trip out to Langley.

He glanced at his watch. "Have you got any boxes or suitcases ready? I'll take them down to the car. I thought we could grab a hamburger at a drive-through on our way to the farm."

She stopped pouring water into an asparagus fern that reminded him of a Triffid, and her mouth twisted delicately in disgust. "I do not eat fast food, remember? Relax. I will be a moment only."

Relax. Sure. Like her definition of a moment was the same as his. Even though he'd allowed time for it, getting married had thrown his whole schedule out of whack. "Can I help you with the watering?"

"No, thank you. Sit down. You look tired. We are in no hurry." She moved languidly among her plants to the bluesy warble of a French chanteuse as if she had all the time in the world.

He *was* tired. Chronically tired. But he wanted to get going, get all the awkwardness over with. Yes, it was a platonic marriage, but all afternoon he'd been picturing the two of them, alone in his grandfather's house as husband and wife.... With a start he realized he was staring at her bare midriff. That did it. He'd give her fifteen minutes, then he was packing for her.

Man, it was hot in here. He removed his jacket and pulled his sweater off over his head, wondering if she'd object to him stripping down to his boxers. "Must be a helluva heating bill."

She passed him on her way to the kitchen to refill the watering can. "The landlord pays it," she said over the sound of running water. "For the basement suite to get enough heat, the thermostat must be turned way up, and so the top floor gets very hot. He had a hard time renting the place, but for me, it's perfect." She came back out of the kitchen and glanced around with a sigh. "I am going to miss it. I'm also worried about what to do with my plants. Can we take them to the farm?"

"I'm not sure they'd survive the climatic shift. Do you have a friend you can give them to?"

She bobbed her head back and forth sideways in that funny way he'd come to interpret as "I don't want to talk about it." She said, "I will ask the woman who lives downstairs to water them for me until I can find them a home." She paused in front of him, watering can in hand. "Would you like a drink?"

Burton smiled. "I soaked my roots this morning. Perhaps something cold, in a glass?"

"There is beer in the fridge. Would you like to help yourself while I finish?"

"Sure." He entered the kitchen through an arch in the wall. It was long and narrow and looked as if it had once been part of a much larger room that had been partitioned when the house had been broken up into apartments. "I wouldn't have picked you for a beer drinker," he remarked, about to take two bottles from the top shelf of the fridge. "Can I pour you one?"

"*Non, merci.* I don't drink beer."

Had she bought them for him? Or someone else? Burton put one bottle back and set the other on the counter. He pulled out his notebook and pen and flipped to the page headed Veronique. He wrote: "Doesn't drink beer."

She swished past him, as beautiful and delicately scented as any tropical flower, and set the watering can in the sink. At the sight of his notebook her eyebrows lifted. "Are you writing about me again?"

He folded the notebook and tucked it back in his pocket. "I've got a lot on my mind. If I don't write things down, I forget."

"So when Monsieur Jackson asks you a question during the interview, you will say, excuse me one moment, I must consult my Veronique handbook." She made a comical face and mimicked him flipping through a notepad. "Let's see, is it filed under *D* for drink or is it *B* for beer?" She laughed her throaty laugh.

Burton gazed at her, fascinated by the way the sarong-thing shifted on her hips, creating a shadowed crevice where cloth parted from skin over the hollow of her flat belly. He took a step closer to her.

Her laughter faded to a smile as she cast him a quick, shrewd glance and neatly sidestepped him. "Go and sit in the chair by the fireplace while I will finish watering my plants.''

Burton took his beer and did as commanded. He rubbed a hand along the wooden arm, admiring the smooth, glowing grain and even finish. The chair was obviously old, but the dark purple upholstery covering the seat and back looked new. It was similar to his grandfather's chair except that the legs were straight and not on rockers. ''Nice job on the refinishing, whoever did it.''

''I did,'' Veronique said, turning the apartment into an Amazonian rainforest with a mister.

''Very nice. And these other pieces…?'' He waved his beer bottle, indicating a refinished coffee table and a wooden stool with a puffy fabric top. Nothing matched, but the polished wood and the traces of dark purple that ran through fabric and pottery tied everything together.

''I did them all. Graham called it junk, but they have much character. Better than that awful modern stuff.''

Burton thought of his spare teak furniture he was rarely around long enough to sit on. It was comfortable enough but utilitarian rather than inviting. Not like this. He leaned back in the chair and shut his eyes. He drifted. The bluesy music, the steamy heat, the scent of tropical flowers… His mind conjured up a sultry evening in the French Quarter of New Orleans, a doorway, and leaning in it was an exotically beautiful woman with bewitching green eyes. She spoke and her voice was a purr. ''Do you like French music?''

''Love it,'' he murmured. Without opening his eyes, he lifted his beer to let the icy bitter liquid slide down his throat.

He wanted to reach for her, but his arms were too heavy to move. With a throaty laugh the woman drifted away down the street, her curving backside briefly illuminated by a street lamp before she disappeared into swirling mist.…

He slumped further into the chair, hovering between consciousness and sleep in a dreamlike trance, vaguely aware of Veronique moving around the room. At some point the bottle was removed from his hand and placed on the stone hearth. The quiet sound of things being shuffled into boxes and the faint clang of clothes hangers skipped off the surface of his deep relaxation.

He had no idea how long he sat like that, neither awake nor asleep. Eventually he surfaced into consciousness to the aroma of butter and garlic and the sound of something sizzling in a pan. Blinking, he sat up and stretched, yawned, and was instantly alert, more rested than he'd felt in weeks.

Veronique peeked in from the kitchen. "Ah, you are awake now."

"Yes. Are you cooking?" He tried not to sound too hopeful, but the rumbling in his stomach threatened to drown him out.

"Just an omelet. Come and eat."

Just an omelet turned out to be a creamy concoction of eggs and wild mushrooms and some savory green bits that made it into one of the most delectable dishes he'd ever eaten.

"Fabulous," he said, tearing off a chunk of crusty baguette and layering on thick, sweet butter. If he had to marry, he could have done worse than to marry a chef. "What is that herb? I know the taste—I just can't remember the name."

"Tarragon. I grow my own herbs. They are coming with me, so I hope you don't mind."

With a nod of her head, she indicated two big cardboard boxes loaded with potted herbs. Beside them was another box containing copper-bottomed pots and a knife block bristling with deadly culinary weapons. Beside that, a huge, soft-sided suitcase that bulged like a pregnant horse.

He swallowed. All this was supposed to fit in his Tercel—a small car already packed with his gear?

"Uh, sure. Whatever we can't take tonight we'll come back for tomorrow."

"Did you ever find your chess set?" she asked, laying knife and fork across her empty plate.

"No. My mother thinks Granddad may have sold it to pay some insurance premiums."

"What do you think?"

"I don't think he would sell it for anything. But I haven't a clue what could have happened to it." He pushed back from the table. "I'll do the dishes."

"Thank you." Veronique stretched, showing a tantalizing length of rib cage. "I like the cooking, but not the cleanup."

Burton made a mental note to install a dishwasher at the farm. He liked to eat, but also not "zee clean-up." If possible, he'd encourage the one without incurring the hassle of the other.

"Tell me," he said, rinsing a soapy plate under a stream of hot water, "how do you eat like that and stay so thin?"

Veronique shrugged. "I work long hours in hot kitchens. I do the furniture. I windsurf. I am never, how you say, 'lazing about.' But mainly I don't eat a lot—just well." She leaned an elbow on the table and propped her chin on her hand. A tiny smile played around the corners of her mouth. "Aren't you going to write that down?"

"Good idea." Burton drained the water from the sink and, quickly wiping his hands, left the dishes to dry in the rack and pulled out his notebook.

"Non, non, non." Veronique was on her feet and grabbing for a dish towel.

Burton stopped writing. *"Non?* What do you mean, *non?"*

She extracted her expensive chef's knife from the drying rack and brandished it at him. "You wash up in my kitchen, you always, but always, dry the knives immediately.''

''It's just a knife…'' he started to say, then thought better of it. It was her kitchen, her knife, and the French, he seemed to recall, were known for crimes of passion. ''I'll make a note of that.''

He started to write, then stopped. ''Say, do you have any photograph albums? Pictures of your childhood? Your family? I would remember pictures far more clearly than words.''

Veronique slid the knife back into the block of wood. ''But of course.''

Going to the living room, she pulled out a thick and battered photo album from the bookshelf beside the fireplace and sat on the couch. With no other option, if he was to look and she to explain, Burton sat beside her. They were far enough apart that they didn't need to touch, yet close enough for him to be fully aware of her warmth, the bare skin of her arms and her intoxicating scent.

''What's that perfume you're wearing?''

She cast him a shy smile. ''It's not really perfume. It's Monoï, pure coconut oil perfumed with petals of the *tiaré* flower, the gardenia of Tahiti.''

''May I?'' he asked, and gently lifted her wrist to press his nose to her skin, which was pale and soft on the inner surface. ''It's very nice,'' he said, feeling a little faint. Before he knew what he was doing, he brushed his face along her inner arm to the hollow of her elbow, touching his lips to her skin for one shuddering second. It was more than wanting to kiss her—he wanted to inhale her.

''You're tickling me.'' She laughed, a nervous sound, and took her arm back. Yet when he looked up, she was staring at him, eyes dark green and intent.

She glanced quickly back at the photo album. ''This is in Algérie with my sisters,'' she said, pointing at a faded photograph. ''I was four and a half.''

He squinted down at the album. "Is that a parrot on your head?"

She laughed. "They are peacock feathers we found on the lawn of the French Embassy. We played dress-up while the grown-ups had a garden party." She turned the page. "Here are my mother and father."

"Your mother looks like she enjoys a laugh, though I couldn't say the same about your father. Is he as forbidding as he looks?"

"He is a good man, but sometimes he wears his *képi*, his policeman's hat, at home, as well as at work. We were scared of him when we were little. Now we tease him and don't let him take himself too seriously."

She turned to the next set of photos, and a look of bittersweet nostalgia that might have been mistaken for physical pain crossed her face. "That was my home in Tahiti. Look at the bougainvillea," she said, pointing to a profusion of scarlet-and-fuchsia-colored flowers massed along a low stone wall. "That is me on my Vespa. I must have been on my way to work at the resort on the other side of the island. And there is Moustache, my little cat. Ghislaine has him now."

"Moustache," he repeated. "Is that…mustache?"

She beamed. "That's right. See his long whiskers? But you must be *exactement* with the pronunciation. Moostash." Her lips pushed outward, making a kiss out of the word, then retreated, causing him to ask her to repeat it. "Moos-tash," she obliged.

"Teach me to speak French," he said, enthralled.

"*Non.* What for?"

"I mean it. I know the basics everyone learns in school, but I've always wanted to be able to converse in French."

"Yes?" She was still skeptical.

"Yes," he said. "Please?"

She gave a little shrug. "Okay."

Burton went back to poring over the photographs. He

actually wanted to speak French, she marveled. She was
thrilled by his absorption in her island—and reluctant to
believe in it. How much of his interest had to do with
getting past Immigration?

"What do you do for entertainment?" he asked. "Are
there theaters, nightclubs?"

"Papeete has all sorts of modern entertainment. But
mostly we come together with friends and cook a big feast.
Maybe one of the guys go to the wharf and buy a fish
freshly caught, and we prepare it with some nice sauce.
We drink a little, we talk a lot. We have a good time. The
night breeze is so soft and warm we sit outside. Someone
have a guitar…"

She broke off with a shrug. How could she convey the
feeling of life in Tahiti to someone who thought a freezing-
cold rain shower was refreshing?

"I went to Bali once for a little R and R after covering
the war in East Timor," he said, stretching an arm along
the back of the couch. "No telephones, no computers, no
hurry, no worry. If Tahiti is even half as nice, you're lucky
to be going back there. The French love of food and culture and the island way of life—what a great combina-
tion."

He didn't sound like Graham, Veronique thought, aware
of the gentle touch of his hand in her hair. He wasn't
scornful, skeptical or disparaging of her language and culture. Cautiously she glanced sideways at him. At that moment he hardly even looked like Graham. At least, he did
look like Graham on the surface, but she seemed now to
be seeing past the familiar features to something deeper.
It was so confusing. Confusing, too, were the threads of
desire weaving themselves into the erotic tapestry his fingertips made as they lightly stroked the nape of her neck.…

"Maybe I'll come for a visit sometime," he continued.
"Would you show me around?"

Veronique went very still, remembering. *Maybe you*

could show me around, Graham had said after complimenting her on the *poisson cru.* Now she bobbed her head
sideways. *"Peut-être."* Maybe.

She turned another page, and instinctively flinched.
Burton's fingers tightened on his side of the album. Graham's tanned face gazed up from every photo.

There was a close-up of him smiling at her over lunch
at the resort. Graham coming from the water, snorkel gear
in hand. She and Graham on the beach at Venus Point, his
arms wrapped around her while she gazed adoringly into
his face. It hurt, that one, because they looked so very
much in love. Ten months later she'd cut up her wedding
dress for kitchen rags.

"You can see the resemblance?" she asked. Marion
might not think Burton and Graham looked alike, but Veronique would dare any stranger to tell them apart.

"Yes, it's uncanny. Spooky, even." He stroked back a
lock of hair from her cheek, exposing her face. "Are you
all right?" he asked, so gently she almost wept.

She shrugged, wishing she could go back to that time
when love was simple and desire an emotion she wel-
comed. Burton's other arm was around her shoulders now,
pulling her toward him.

"I know it hurts," he said, "but don't be sad."

And then his lips were coming closer to hers, his blue
eyes familiar yet newly dazzling.... God help her, she
wanted to kiss him. At the last second, Graham's face su-
perimposed itself over Burton's. She turned away, gasping
for breath. *Oh la la.* Just who had she been about to kiss?

"Veronique?"

She picked at the edges of the plastic sheets holding the
photos in place. "Just because we are married doesn't
mean we are husband and wife."

"I know." Rebuffed, his voice was no longer gentle.

Veronique made a move to replace the album in the
bookshelf.

"Wait. We can use those photos of you and Graham," he said, still in that hard voice she'd never heard before. "It'll look to Immigration as though we've known each other longer than we have."

"Non!" She clung to the album, appalled. It was bad enough marrying a stranger who resembled her hated late husband. It would be quite impossible to look at the past and smile.

He eased it from her grasp. "I know you're not over him," he said, compassion softening his voice. "Maybe you never will be. But think of Marion."

Knuckles clenched in front of her tightened mouth, she watched as he tore back the sticky pages and peeled off photo after photo of her and Graham. Oddly enough, it seemed to pain Burton, too, for two sharp lines had appeared between his eyes.

Burton grimly completed his task, feeling like the biggest jerk who'd ever lived for what this was doing to Veronique. He didn't know why the hell it should hurt him so much. Ego, he guessed. When he was done, he offered Veronique the loose photos for safekeeping, but with a burst of fresh tears, she pushed them away. Frowning, he tucked the photos into his breast pocket and carried his rival's image like a ghostly doppelgänger next to his heart.

VERONIQUE OPENED HER EYES and, for a moment, didn't know where she was. In the center of the white-painted plank ceiling squatted a pearly pink glass light fixture that seemed to double as a fly trap. Ah, the farmhouse.

She put on blue jeans and thick socks, a turtlenecked shirt and Marion's big ivory sweater, and went out to the kitchen. She made herself coffee and toast, and sat down in the upholstered wooden rocker. It would be very nice sanded down and oiled, she thought, chipping at the peeling varnish with her thumbnail.

Burton came in, buttoning the sleeves of his tan corduroy shirt, his coppery hair wet and gleaming. "Good mor—" He stopped short.

"Bonjour," she corrected him, then noticed the odd expression on his face. "What is it?"

He gave his head a little shake and moved toward the counter and the coffeepot. "That was my grandfather's chair."

She sprang out of it. "You don't like me sitting there."

"No, it's okay. It's just…when I saw you there, it reminded me that now we're living here and he's gone."

She went to stand on top of the heating vent beneath the window to warm her feet. "You sit there. It's your chair now."

His chair. His farm. He realized suddenly the source of his ambivalence. He wanted the farm, but he wanted it the way it was when he was a child—worry free. He didn't want the responsibility of hundreds of bushels of seed potatoes waiting to be planted, later to be harvested. If he sat in Granddad's chair, he had to walk in Granddad's shoes and ride Granddad's tractor….

The phone rang.

He walked over to where it hung on the wall and picked up the receiver. "Hello?"

"Burton? Don Chetwynd here. Glad I caught you. Listen, I've got a couple of young fellas in my office right now, brothers they are, who're looking to buy a parcel of land in your area."

"I told you I'm not ready to—"

"Sell. I know, but just hear me out. These boys are just starting out, pooling their resources to buy some land. Their daddy's got a farm over near Chilliwack, but there are four sons and they all want to farm."

"Look, Mr. Chetwynd—"

"I've told them you're not ready to vacate, and they're willing to let you stay in the house till the end of the year, just so long as they can start working the land. Now, do yourself a favor and think about it. I can bring 'em by for a look any time you say. No obligation. I'm not trying to pressure you, but you don't know when you'll get another offer like this.''

''They haven't made an offer.''

''I'm betting my bottom dollar that once they see your property, they're going to make you that offer. Whaddaya say? Shall I bring 'em by?''

It seemed the perfect solution. Granddad's place would remain a farm, and he could go back to doing what he did best with a clear conscience. But in spite of what Chetwynd said, Burton did feel pressured. ''I'll have to think about it and call you back.''

Hanging up, he took a cup from the cupboard and poured himself a coffee. Veronique had returned to the table to sit on a straight-backed chair with her knees tucked up to her chest. Her hands were wrapped around her steaming cup, and her face held a mildly questioning expression.

''That was the real-estate agent,'' he said. ''He's got an interested buyer. Farmers.''

''But you haven't found the chess set.''

''That's why I put him off.'' Burton spread jam on a piece of toast and walked over to the window. The orchard which his grandparents had planted nearly fifty years ago would be spared the ax. Yet even selling to farmers was hard to accept. Was he just hanging on to childhood memories? Was he having trouble letting go of the last link to Granddad? The path toward the future suddenly seemed muddy and indistinct. What if he took a wrong turn and there was no way back? He hated this feeling of weakness and indecision. He needed to do something.

He took his cup to the sink and brushed the crumbs from his hands. ''I'm going to fix the front steps,'' he said. ''Make yourself at home. Do whatever.''

She uncurled her legs and tipped her cup to drain the

last of her coffee. "Would you like me to help? I can use a hammer and a saw."

Frowning, he shook his head and started to leave the room. "This is something I need to do myself."

"Burton?"

He paused at the doorway and looked back.

"Do not be too hard on yourself. You will make the right decision in the end."

He nodded, oddly touched by her confidence. And grateful that although she thought he was wrong, she didn't feel the need to keep telling him so.

Granddad's tool chest was in the barn, along with the ten-foot length of two-by-six lumber with which he'd intended to replace the broken step. Burton had stored it in here after the ambulance had taken Granddad away. Now he hoisted it to his waist. It was awkward and unwieldy, but not that heavy. Not for a man who'd spent his life doing physical labor. Maybe the doctor was right, and Granddad's heart attack was a fluke of timing. It was a consoling thought, even if it didn't help Granddad.

Burton carried it back across the yard and around to the front of the house, visualizing Granddad making the same short journey. Had he staggered the last few steps? Had he felt a stab of pain in his heart as he fell? What were his thoughts in those final seconds? If Burton had turned up half an hour earlier, could he have been saved?

He dropped the length of wood to the ground with a thud, flattening the grass beside the path. Then he set to work prising the nails out of the broken board to lift it off and make way for the new. He'd measured and cut the new piece of wood and was setting it in place when Veronique came out the front door, her backpack slung over her shoulder, the umbrella he'd given her in hand.

"I'm going to walk down to the farmer's market we passed last night to get some things for dinner," she said, pausing at the step above the one he was working on.

Burton pushed the hair off his forehead. "Take the car if you want."

"Thanks, but I like to walk. Guess what? I found five new eggs in the henhouse. And one of the hens is nesting. I wonder who has been feeding them."

"The Vandermeres, our neighbors to the east," he said. "I really should get over there to thank them and let them know we're here."

"I also found a few vegetables out back. Someone had a garden there between the orchard and the house."

He straightened and went to rummage through the toolbox for a level. "My grandmother. She grew everything under the sun. Canned most of it, too."

"The soil is good," Veronique said. "It wouldn't take much work to make again the garden. Tomatoes would grow well by the side fence. And there is room for lettuce and peas...."

Her excitement seemed to check midsentence. "Well, I better not get carried away."

Burton could see what she was thinking—whatever she planted she wouldn't be around to harvest. Nor would he. The seed potatoes weighed on his conscience.

She stepped over the loose board to the bottom step, and down to the ground. "For dinner I am thinking perhaps some asparagus with hollandaise sauce to start, followed by chicken grilled à la diable. Accompanied by the baby potatoes roasted with rosemary and garlic."

Burton squinted at the liquid-enclosed bubble floating dead-center in the level atop the new board. "Sounds great," he said, beginning to salivate. "You know, you don't have to cook...." He broke off at the hurt look on her face.

"I love to cook," she said, "especially in a real country kitchen. But it's no fun cooking for just myself..."

"I guarantee I'll be appreciative."

"You better," she teased, bopping him lightly with the

umbrella as she turned to leave. "Or next time you get tuna casserole."

THE MARKET OFFERED less choice in imported fruits and vegetables than the city, but the produce was as fresh as if it had come out of the field that morning. There was also a small butcher-cum-deli where she picked out a plump chicken. On impulse, she bought some packets of seeds and a tray of marigold seedlings to plant beside the front door.

Her laden backpack was starting to feel heavy by the time she turned into the driveway. Behind her, a horn beeped and a white pickup truck rolled to a stop, its motor idling. A woman of about her own age with an open, friendly face and short dark hair escaping from a ponytail poked her head out the window. "Hop in. I'll take you up to the house."

"*Merci.*" Veronique laid the seedlings on the floor of the truck, hoisted her backpack onto the seat and climbed in. "Are you—"

"Jill Vandermere, from next door. I was coming over to feed the chickens." She put the truck back in gear and started up the hill.

"So it is you we have to thank for taking care of them. I am Veronique. I am…staying here with Burton for a while."

"Great. It'll be nice having another woman my own age close by. We can always use new blood around here."

Veronique's eyebrows rose. "New blood?"

Jill laughed. "It's just an expression."

"New blood. That's good," she said, smiling. "I collect expressions."

Jill's brown gaze strayed to Veronique's wedding ring. "Are you and Burton married?"

"Sort of."

Grinning, Jill shook her head. "I didn't know there was

such a thing as 'sort of' when it came to marriage. You're either in it or you're not. I'm married to Rick, Hank and Mary's son. It's their farm, but we're gradually taking it over. We'd like to expand, but—'' she shrugged ''—it's hard to find land close by.'' She glanced down at the seedlings. ''I see you're planting flowers. You're welcome to come over and take cuttings any time. We've got a huge garden.''

Veronique smiled at her and at the serendipity of their instant rapport, knowing even without further words they would have things in common. There could be details and confidences exchanged…if. Always the *if*. She thought of the seed packets tucked in her backpack and felt unaccountably sad by what could and could not be allowed to grow. ''Thank you,'' she said, ''but I probably won't be here very long.''

When they arrived at the house. Burton was nowhere in sight. But as Veronique got out and set the marigolds beside the newly repaired step, she heard the sound of hammering coming from the barn. More repairs. She admired the fact that he did the jobs around the farm himself. Many men would have disdained dirtying their hands or simply not known how to use the tools. His grandfather had taught him well.

She went back to the truck where Jill waited, the engine running. ''Would you like to come in for coffee?''

''Thanks, I'd love to another time. But if you don't need me, I'd better get back and help Rick and his dad finish planting the potatoes while the weather's clear. They say more rain is on the way. Oh, by the way, tell Burton we'll bring back the…''

She broke off as a pale blue Volvo came up the drive and parked beside the truck.

Another neighbor? Veronique wondered. The real-estate

agent with someone to view the property? The car door opened, and a tall, dark-haired woman holding a brown paper bag emerged.

Zut alors. It was Burton's mother.

CHAPTER ELEVEN

CATHERINE O'ROURKE WORE a cherry red linen dress, the simple lines of which accented the smooth sweep of her shoulder-length dark hair and elegant gold jewelry. She had style, Veronique gave her that. And from the size of her smile, she clearly intended to be a good mother-in-law.

Veronique said *au revoir* to Jill and, as the truck rumbled back down the hill, went to greet Catherine. *"Bonjour,"* she called cheerfully, equally determined that discord not originate with her.

"Hello, Veronique."

Veronique's eyebrows lifted. This mother-in-law actually pronounced her name correctly. She felt Catherine's bright blue gaze, disconcertingly like Burton's, inspecting her. "Burton is in the barn," she said, hoping she'd want to see him right away.

But Catherine proceeded to the steps, pausing to test the new board with one black patent pump before continuing on into the house. "I'll wait for him to finish. I know how he hates to be disturbed when he's working. Here, I brought you a little housewarming gift."

"How thoughtful…" Her voice trailed away. The bag contained something heavy, solid and still warm. She heard the clink of a lid against its base and caught a faint but distinctive aroma.

"Tuna casserole," Catherine said with a bright smile. "Burton's favorite. I know you must be too busy to cook."

"Merci bien," she murmured, forcing a smile in return.

She was never too busy to cook. But she stepped back so Catherine could precede her down the hallway and into the kitchen.

At the counter, she slid the casserole out of the bag onto a hot mat and gave a little gasp of surprise. The dish was not Pyrex but pottery, the glaze a medley of natural greens with dark brown accents. She turned to Catherine, her smile genuine. "It is beautiful."

Catherine waved a hand. "One of the ladies in my book club makes them. After all, you missed out on wedding presents."

Her tone was faintly accusatory, as though Veronique had caused her own misfortune. Who did Catherine imagine would keep the casserole dish when the marriage was over? Veronique wondered. Her son, whose idea of a good dinner was dinner out? Or Veronique, who would soon be shedding belongings in preparation for departure? Still, it was a nice thought. Maybe. She cast a sideways glance at her new mother-in-law. She wasn't quite sure about Catherine.

"You will stay to dinner, of course?" Veronique picked up an oven mitt and lifted the lid by the cluster of acorns that formed the handle. On top of the casserole was a layer of…crushed potato chips? *Mon Dieu.* Quickly, she put the lid back on.

"Oh, I wouldn't like to intrude…." Catherine said, moving toward the sink.

"*Non,* I insist. You will stay for dinner." If for no other reason than to help them eat this…this… Veronique switched on the oven, placed the casserole inside, then turned to Catherine. "Would you like a glass of wine?"

Catherine was filling the kettle. Faint color rose in her cheeks, matching her dress. "Oh, I'm sorry," she said. "I grew up in this house. I guess I haven't adjusted to it not being my home anymore."

Her sigh was just loud enough to be heard, yet not so

loud as to sound complaining. *Formidable.* "But of course it is your home," Veronique said. "It certainly is not mine, though I like it very much." She threw down her oven mitts and faced Catherine squarely. "I know you are worried about Burton, but I am not the problem."

Catherine looked taken aback. "Well, I know he's upset about the chess set and his documentary. But if I may speak frankly, I don't feel this is the best time for him to take on a wife, especially one who's not in love with him."

"He does not love me, either." Surprisingly it hurt a little to say that. "We have the understanding. I do like him, and I wish him well. That is why you must talk to him, convince him that even after he finds the chess set, he should not sell the farm."

Catherine laughed shortly. "Burton would never sell the farm."

"The real-estate man called this morning to say someone is interested in buying. Burton is thinking about letting them come and look."

Catherine's face went pale. She reached for a chair.

"You did not know?" Catherine shook her head. Veronique threw up her hands and burst into an impassioned tirade in French about *les hommes.* While she ranted, she got out a glass tumbler and a bottle of cognac, and poured Catherine a stiff drink.

Catherine took a big sip. Coughed, blinked and gave her head a rapid shake. "That's better, thank you. I agree men can be pigs, but I rather object to being the mother of a swine."

Heat rose in Veronique's cheeks. "You understood?"

"Oui." A faint smile appeared on Catherine's face. "I majored in languages at university," she continued in French. "And did a year as an exchange student in Paris. I'm a bit rusty."

Rusty, perhaps, but it was music to Veronique's ears. She pulled up a chair and poured herself a small cognac.

"You speak very well," she said in French. "I can't be-lieve Burton didn't tell you he was thinking of selling the farm."

"He talked about the impracticality of living here, and how he didn't like the idea of renting, but I didn't ever think he'd seriously consider selling. But you say he's had an offer?"

Veronique shook her head. "It hasn't gone that far yet. All he said was some farmers were interested in looking at it."

"If he sells to anyone it will be to a farmer." Cather-ine's manicured fingernails tapped the table in little clicks of frustration. "I'd hoped he would marry and have chil-dren and raise them out here on the farm." She sighed. "I'm not wrong to want that, am I?"

"No," Veronique said slowly, "but perhaps that is not his dream."

Catherine snorted. "Burton dreams in Technicolor, with his finger on the fast-forward button."

Veronique laughed. Her eyes met Catherine's and the other woman gave her a warm smile, the first genuine smile since they'd met.

Catherine reached for her hand and gave her fingers a squeeze. "Slow him down, Veronique," she said, her voice suddenly urgent. "Slow him down long enough for him to find out what his dream really is."

Veronique's smile disappeared. "We are husband and wife on paper only. I cannot influence him."

"I think you can. I've seen the way he looks at you." She paused. "His father died of a heart attack when he was fifty-five. Burton's not like Tom—he doesn't drink much or smoke, and he doesn't overeat—but he pushes himself too hard. Maybe I'm just being a typical mother, but I worry about him."

Veronique tugged at a lock of hair. She and Burton would have to be far more intimate than they were, or were likely to be, for her to affect his future. Such intimacy was impossible for her, and possibly damaging for him, if what Catherine said about the way he regarded her was true.

"You could persuade him better than I—" She broke off, hearing his footsteps outside on the porch. Already she recognized his walk.

"Speak of the devil," Catherine said wryly, reverting to English. "Burton hasn't listened to his mother since he was a teenager."

"I heard that," Burton said, coming down the hall into the kitchen. Two pairs of curious female eyes turned at his entrance. He stopped short at the unlikely sight of his mother and Veronique gossiping over a drink. Suddenly wary, he fought the impulse to hightail it back to the barn.

"You were supposed to. Because it's true, isn't it, Burton?" His mother's voice held an undercurrent he couldn't place.

He laughed the fatalistic laugh of the doomed. "I refuse to answer on the grounds it might incriminate me." He went to the sink and washed his hands. Drying them on the towel, he sniffed the air. "What's that?" he said, glancing at Veronique. "I thought you were making some fancy—"

Her warning glare cut him off. "Your mother very kindly brought your favorite dish."

Funny, it didn't smell like grilled chicken with French mustard, the latest in a string of new favorite dishes, each a product of Veronique's mastery in the kitchen and worth pulling rank over the camera crew for.

No, it smelled like…tuna casserole. His favorite, all right. When he'd been ten years old. "Thank you, Mother. You really didn't have to."

"It was meant as a housewarming gift, but apparently that's not exactly in order." Catherine twisted her nearly empty cognac glass. "Why didn't you tell me you'd taken steps toward selling the farm?"

Burton glanced at Veronique. For once she met his gaze head on, transmitting waves of courage and support. It was only for an instant, and then she disappeared out the back door with a murmured comment about picking something or other.

He got a beer from the fridge and sat in the chair Veronique had vacated. She'd abandoned him to his mother's reproach, but it didn't matter. They'd just exchanged their first ever silent communication.

"I kept hoping I'd come up with another solution," he said, twisting off the cap, "but there are only so many options."

"You could have talked to me about it," Catherine replied, sounding hurt. "You don't have to take the whole burden on yourself."

"I was going to that night we were out here, but I thought you had enough to worry about. Or maybe I just knew you'd be unhappy about it and I didn't want you to try and talk me out of it." Before she could do so now, he went on. "I think I've figured out what Granddad sold to pay the insurance premium on his death taxes."

"Oh?"

"The pick-planter."

Catherine looked taken aback. "The machine he used to plant potatoes? It's gone, too?"

"Yep. I knew something was missing from the barn the first day I came out here after he died, I just couldn't put my finger on it."

"He sold the pick-planter when he had a barn full of seed potatoes and a crop to put in," Catherine said slowly. She slapped her hand down on the table. "That just shows you how much he wanted to hang on to the farm. Don't let him down by selling out."

Guilt propelled Burton to his feet, and his chair scraped backward against the lino. He paced across the room to grip the side of the window frame. Outside, in the remnants of Gram's garden, Veronique was picking something and putting it into her wicker basket. "For God's sake, Mother, I'm not a farmer and I have no intention of becoming one."

"I wasn't suggesting that. But you could still live here."

"It's too far from my work."

"Maybe you work too much." She held up a hand. "Okay, I won't start on that. But you could always rent it out."

"And have to deal with strangers living here? People who might wreck the place?" He rubbed his temples, feeling the beginnings of a tension headache.

"There'll be strangers living here if you sell," she replied sharply.

"Drop it, Mother. We've had this argument before."

"All I can say is, your granddad was lucky he didn't live to see you disappoint him."

He shot her an angry glance and she covered her face with her hands. "I'm sorry, Burtie. That was an awful thing to say."

"I didn't know this place was so important to you," he said stiffly.

"It's not for myself," she replied, wiping her wet eyes with her fingers, "But for you and your children. If you ever have any, that is."

"Definitely don't start on that, Mother. If it makes you feel any better, I'm not selling until I find that chess set. And at my present rate of success that could be well into the next century."

The back door creaked and Veronique came in through the laundry room, her basket filled with delicate green stalks.

"Oh, you found the asparagus bed!" Catherine exclaimed, getting up to look. "I can't believe it's still going. My mother and I planted that together over ten years ago."

"It needs some thinning and some weeding, but it grows

beautifully,'' Veronique said, holding up a stalk and pretending not to see Catherine's red-rimmed eyes. ''Asparagus with lemon butter will go nicely with tuna casserole, *non?*''

''Perfect,'' Catherine said.

''Perfect,'' Burton echoed, thinking longingly of hollandaise sauce and poulet à la diable.

DUSK WAS FALLING when they stepped onto the front porch to wave Catherine off. Veronique hung back, but Catherine came up and gave her a hug. ''*Bon chance,* my dear,'' she whispered.

Veronique saw her own emotions reflected in Catherine's clouded blue eyes—confusion, worry and hope. ''*Merci.* Good luck to you, too.''

Catherine turned to Burton and he gathered her into a hug. ''Oh, Burtie,'' she said, ''I know it's a dilemma. But please, don't be afraid to talk it over with me.''

''I won't,'' he said gruffly. ''As long as you remember it's my decision.'' With one last squeeze, he released her.

Catherine started down the steps. When she reached the one Burton had repaired, she glanced at it, then at Burton. As Veronique watched, an odd look passed between them, a baffling exchange of some deep emotion. She glanced away, unwilling to intrude, but curious to know more about this family she'd married into. The more she learned about Burton, the more she liked and admired him. He'd not only eaten his mother's tuna casserole without a grimace—an action as courageous as it was caring—but even when Catherine had gone out of the room briefly, he hadn't betrayed her by expressing his true feelings. Feelings that were obvious to Veronique after witnessing the gusto with which he devoured her meals.

Veronique and Burton watched in silence as Catherine's car disappeared down the gravel drive.

The clouds had disappeared, leaving the pearly sky

streaked with salmon and aqua. Shadows stretched across the grass, but the air was balmy and softly scented. The perfect summer evening beckoned.

"I guess I'll go look in the cellar for the chess set," Burton said, but he made no move to leave. He turned to Veronique and in the dusky twilight his eyes were a deep blue.

A shivery anticipation raised gooseflesh along her arms. This...attraction she felt for Burton didn't mesh with her plans. She was falling for him when she should be keeping her distance.

Yet she was loathe to part with his company. "What is it about that step?" she asked, gesturing to the bottom plank.

Burton jammed his hands into his back pockets, and his gaze swept past her, across the farmyard and up the green slope behind the barn. His shirt flattened against his chest as he sucked in the soft evening air. At last he said, "My grandfather had a heart attack while repairing it."

"But—"

"I was supposed to be helping him, but I was too busy." His voice was bitter with regret.

She could see it was eating him up inside.

"And you think it is your fault he's dead." She kept her tone flat, used deliberately stark words.

"No! Okay, I did at first," he admitted. "But when you put it like that...well, it's nonsense." He sighed. "I just wish we'd had time to talk about some things."

She placed a hand on his forearm, feeling the texture of the dark hairs laid over his skin and the muscle underneath. It was the first time she'd voluntarily touched him. "It is natural to wish for more time."

"I guess you know what it's like to miss someone." His gaze, responsive, flicked down to her hand before meeting her eyes.

"Don't go into the cold, dark basement on such a beautiful evening," she implored. "Stay. Enjoy the sunset with me."

Her words brought a warm, glad smile to his lips. He moved closer, till she was sure he was going to take her in his arms. Wanting, yet fearful, she held her breath, a wave of anticipation thrilling through her.

Then, inexplicably, he backed away. His hands dropped to his sides and his fingers curled into his palms. "Don't tempt me," he said with a short laugh. "It's hard enough—" He cut it short and abruptly turned on his heel.

The screen door banged shut behind him.

Veronique put a hand to her forehead, feeling the adrenaline subside, cooled by his curt reaction. What was happening to her? When had she started craving his touch? Part of her longed to run after him. She took a step toward the front door, then stopped herself. If he was strong, she could be, too. This temporary marriage, this situation, would only work if they didn't let their attraction grow.

Keeping busy would help.

She found Burton in the laundry room putting new batteries in a flashlight. The door leading down to the basement was open.

Veronique hovered on the kitchen side of the doorway. "Do you have sandpaper?"

"Sure, what for?" He didn't look at her, just clicked the battered steel flashlight on and off, testing the light.

"If you don't mind, I would like to refinish your grandfather's chair. I think it is oak underneath."

"You'd be wasting your time," he said shortly. "Everything will go when I sell the farm."

"You might be foolish enough to let this farm go," she said gently, "but you will never get rid of your grandfather's chair."

He smiled and shook his head. "Okay, you got me there. But you don't have to do this. It's too much."

She shrugged. "I enjoy the work. It gives me satisfaction to restore something to beauty and usefulness."

"Go ahead, then," he said. "Just don't give me any more lectures about working too hard."

They laughed together, and although she felt a pang of loss for what hadn't happened, Veronique was relieved she and Burton were still friends.

The big hand on the clock over the stove moved slowly around to the next hour while she sanded down the chair arms to a pale, wide-grained wood. Outside the kitchen window, night fell. The house was quiet and peaceful, but for the rasp of sandpaper on wood and the faint sounds of Burton moving around in the basement.

When she'd finished the arms, she rose, stretched and made herself a cup of tea. Sipping it, she studied the chair. To sand the base properly she'd have to take off the seat cover. She had an idea the springs needed replacing, anyway, so hard was the seat. Setting her cup on the table, she grasped the chair at the top of the rockers and turned it over. Oof, it was heavy.

Using a pair of pliers and a hammer, she pulled out the upholstery tacks that held the worn fabric in place. They came away easily, and she noticed curiously that there were sets of tack holes in the wood; apparently the cover had been pulled off and replaced sometime in the past.

The last tack came out and she popped it into a glass jar with the others. Righting the chair, she peeled off the old fabric. Underneath lay a thick layer of foam padding, which she lifted off so she could get at the springs.

Mon Dieu! What was this? She let the square of foam drop to the floor and leaned over to lift a large wooden box from inside the base of the chair. It was heavy and old, with squares of light and dark wood inlaid in an alternating pattern. It rattled when she picked it up. The chess set. Her heart beating fast, she fumbled to undo the metal latch at the side.

Veronique picked up one of the large, elaborately carved chessmen and slowly turned it in her fingers. They were very beautiful, definitely old, and it was quite believable that Burton's grandfather, or anyone, could have sold them for a lot of money. Burton would be so happy to have them back. He would...

She gripped the black knight so hard the tip of his lance bit into her palm. He would sell the farm.

Her first instinct had been to run to the top of the basement stairs and shout out the good news. Now she went very still and thought of a mother's plea for her son. She agreed with Catherine that the farm was good for Burton. If only he lived here a little longer, she was sure he would decide to keep it, whatever the cost.

It wasn't her decision to make, a little voice told her.

In the end, she argued with herself, he would have the chess set *and* the farm.

Not daring to let herself think any further about what she was doing, she placed the knight back in the box and relatched the lid. Silently she tiptoed out of the kitchen, the box clutched to her chest to stop it from rattling.

She was halfway down the hall when she heard his footsteps coming up from the basement.

For a moment she couldn't move. Then with a burst of energy, she ran the rest of the way to her bedroom. Swiftly she opened the cupboard and shoved the chess set into her empty suitcase, then threw some dirty clothes on top. She stood back, breathing hard and telling herself it was for his own good.

She had other reasons, vaguely formulated, that had nothing to do with Burton's needs and everything to do with her own. Perhaps she was projecting on him her own longing for a place to belong. She didn't want to think about it too deeply. She only knew she wasn't ready for Burton to sell the farm.

Burton came into the kitchen and saw Granddad's

disassembled chair spread over the floor. He went through to the hallway, brushing cobwebs off his shoulders. "Veronique?"

She came out of her room, shutting the door behind her. Her face was pale and she licked her lips nervously. *"Oui?"*

"Is something wrong?" he asked.

"Non, what could be wrong?" She walked past him back into the kitchen, took her place in front of the chair and started to sand the base around the tack holes. Without looking up, she said, "You did not find the chess set?" Her voice was curiously flat, making it more a statement than a question.

"I found cobwebs and dust and a lifetime of stored junk, but no chess set." He noticed the worn and discarded upholstery fabric tossed to one side. "My grandmother kept fabric remnants in the cedar chest in the dining room. You could probably find something in there to recover the seat."

She nodded and kept on sanding, scraping away the varnish in large sweeps of the gritty paper.

Burton leaned back in his chair and tried to cast an objective glance around the room. Maybe he should paint the walls and replace the lino with something more modern. On the other hand, whoever bought the place would want to choose their own color scheme and floor coverings. It was the land that was worth something, not the house. Not to anyone but him and his mother, anyway. And, it seemed, curiously enough, to Veronique.

"We should talk some more about the interview with Immigration," he said.

"You want some more facts about me?"

"No, this time I want to know how you think."

She glanced up, almost, but not quite, looking him in the eye. "Do you mean like, what do I think of the Middle

East situation, or do you mean, if I had to come back as another animal, what would I choose?''

He smiled. ''I was thinking of something closer to home, such as…oh, why is it you don't like the rain?''

She laughed huskily. ''You have to ask? Because it is cold and wet. I get the cold and the sneezing. All the time.''

''Viruses cause colds, not the weather. Once you adapt to the different bugs here, you'll get fewer colds.''

She tossed away the worn piece of sandpaper and sent him a skeptical sideways glance. ''I do not intend to adapt to your bugs. Anyway, it's not just the rain, it is the constant threat of rain.''

''It must rain in Tahiti.''

''Yes, but it's a warm rain,'' she said, taking up a new piece of sandpaper. ''In Tahiti, everything you touch is warm. The sand, the trees, the buildings.''

''It does sound nice. Is there anything you like about Vancouver?''

''Oh, yes. The mountains, the cherry trees that line the streets in spring, so pink and fluffy and sweet-smelling. And the air is very fresh and energy-giving.'' She started to scrape again. One leg of the chair was bared to the pale gold wood beneath.

''What would you like to come back as?''

''A seabird,'' she said without hesitation. ''One that could fly all the way to the South Pacific.''

He had to ask. ''I'd come back as a horse.''

''Why a horse?''

''Granddad used to keep a couple of Arabian horses. He taught me to ride, and whenever I came to visit I'd take off for hours of cantering along the road or through the fields. It was great.''

Veronique turned the chair and started another leg. ''And you think the horse shares your enthusiasm for running all day?'' she said humorously. ''What you really want is to relive your boyhood.''

He thought about that for a moment. ''I think,'' he said slowly, ''that what I'd like is to take the best bits of my boyhood and incorporate them into my adult life. Do you think that's possible?''

''I think they are already there, in your memory and in your imagination. It is what you choose to do with them that counts.''

He saw where this was leading, right back to his plans for the farm. Rising, he strode across the room. ''Maybe we should concentrate on our recent history. We'll have to show Immigration it's plausible for us to have fallen in love.''

''How do we do that when we are not always at ease with each other?'' she murmured.

''You're right, we have to deal with that. We need to do something physical together, to be comfortable touching without one of us jumping out of our skin.'' He thought for a moment. ''I've got it.'' Striding back to where she was sitting, he took the sandpaper from her hands and pulled her to her feet.

Alarm leaped to her eyes. ''What are you doing?''

''It's an exercise I learned in a management course.'' He led her to the middle of the living-room floor, then turned her so she was facing away from him. Beneath his hands, her shoulders trembled. With the interview less than a week away, it underscored just how far they had to go.

He stepped back a pace. ''When I count to three, I want you to fall backward, arms at your sides, as though you were falling into a swimming pool or onto a bed. I'll catch you.''

''But—'' Her head swiveled around, eyes wide.

''Marriage is based on trust. I'll catch you.''

''Trust,'' she repeated, sounding agonized. ''I will try.''

She clenched her fists, then unclenched them. Started to fall, then caught herself, tottering a little.

"Come on. You can do it. I'm right behind you."

"That's what I'm afraid of," she muttered.

"One, two, thr—"

"*Attention!*" she cried, and fell backward, straight as a ramrod.

Burton caught her easily, his arms tightening around her waist. Through her silk sweater he could feel the warmth of her body, and the soft fabric slid sensuously beneath his fingers. Her head fell back on his shoulder, sending the scent of her hair into his nostrils and directly to his brain. He'd barely managed to resist kissing her earlier. Now that she was in his arms...

"Let me up!" she cried.

Reluctantly he set her back on her feet. "Are you okay?" he asked, wishing he could remember an exercise for establishing and maintaining eye contact.

"Yes," she said, her cheeks pink. "Do you do this with Ernie?"

"Ernie doesn't have a problem trusting me. He almost hero-worships me."

"Sometimes you are too much making the joke with him," she scolded gently. "He is sensitive."

"He can take it." Burton turned his back to her. "Now, you catch me."

"*Mon Dieu!* You are so tall. But I will try."

"Maybe this isn't such a good idea," he said, starting to have second thoughts. "You are a lot smaller than me."

She braced one foot in back of the other and held out her arms. "You can squash me like the bug, but I will not let you down."

"Okay, here goes." But he couldn't move. Her imagery had set off a vivid motion picture of real damage in his mind.

"Come on," she urged. "Don't be a baby."

"I'll hurt you."

"No, you won't. I am very strong. I lift the big pots, I beat the sauce. *Un, deux, trois…allez!*"

Without allowing himself to think about it another second, Burton put out his arms and fell back.

She let out a soft grunt as the full impact of his height and weight landed on her. Gripping hard to support him, she staggered backward, preventing him from regaining his balance.

"Let go—"

"Oof!"

They were both down. Veronique lay motionless beneath his back. He rolled off immediately, but her eyes were wide and staring. He gathered her up in his arms, and then they were on their knees, facing each other. Her mouth opened, her hands clutched at his shirt, but she couldn't speak.

"Are you all right?" he asked urgently. "Breathe out slowly. Now in. Do it again. Okay?"

She nodded. He released his own breath, relieved. He didn't know which had taken the greater act of faith—for her to catch him or for him to fall. But amazingly, she was looking straight at him without flinching. More than that, for the second time tonight there was a light in her eyes and a tremulous smile on her lips. He just had to believe she wanted him to kiss her.

"You're so beautiful," he whispered. And lowered his mouth to hers.

This was no chaste kiss meant for public consumption. He tasted her eagerly and she responded. For weeks he'd hungered for this, and now she was in his arms. Her lips were heaven and earth combined. While his head spun in starry infinity, his blood flowed hot and thick as lava. And when he gathered her closer still, feeling her slight body press against him, passion warred with tenderness, until passion threatened to overwhelm.

She eased away a little, her breath both warm and cool on his moistened lips. He pressed her head onto his shoulder and stroked her hair. They were both trembling. Shock. Nerves. Desire. Suddenly he didn't want to look into her eyes. Afraid he might see that her feelings didn't, after all, match his.

"Burton?"

"Yes?" He loosened his hold and slowly met her gaze.

Her face was alive with wonder; her skin flushed and glowing. "I caught you."

He smiled into his wife's eyes. They were shy, but welcoming. He could hardly believe his good fortune. Wanted to kiss her again. "I knew you would."

She laughed, a rich, throaty sound. "You did not."

"I wanted to believe."

"Maybe that's enough."

Drawn by the way her mouth moved, he leaned closer. "I can do better if you want me to."

They hovered on the brink of another kiss. He was willing; she seemed to be debating. Private kissing hadn't been part of the deal. But things had changed since he'd said that. He'd changed.

"I think...I think I'm falling in love with you." His voice was husky.

Her gaze turned wary and she pulled away a little more. Within the space of seconds, the mood changed abruptly. Then it hit him. Maybe all the time she'd been kissing him she'd been thinking of Graham. The thought made him feel sick.

"I know you miss your husband...." he began, his voice tight.

She swallowed hard.

He was in agony but compelled to continue. "I think it's fine and right that you loved him so much you can't be with another man so soon. But I can wait, because—" with a finger he lifted her face to his and couldn't stop the yearning note from entering his voice "—when I kiss you I want it to be me you're making love to, not the memory of your dead husband."

Her eyes widened in horror, reminding him of the night they'd met. "You have it wrong," she said in a choked voice. "The reason I couldn't look at you is not because I miss him. His memory fills me with rage. I didn't love my husband, I hated him."

Burton couldn't breathe. Couldn't comprehend. Janus-like, his image of Veronique turned on itself and showed the opposite face. All this time he'd thought she'd loved her husband and was grieving his loss. Instead—what did this mean? That when she looked at him she saw not the painful memory of someone loved and lost, but…a man she hated?

The thought was staggering, the situation appalling. One look at her stricken expression assured him she hadn't de-liberately misled him. Still, he felt horribly tricked. It was all an optical illusion. He'd been looking at the outline of the vase when he should have been seeing the image of opposing faces.

One thing hadn't changed—Graham still stood between them.

Love or hate, Burton thought fiercely, he would over-come her memory of her late husband. He would make her see him for himself, and love or hate him on his own merits.

Veronique couldn't look one more second at the tur-bulent emotions blowing across Burton's face. He obvi-ously thought she was a monster, but she couldn't explain. She hardly knew what to make of her confused longing for him; she only knew she couldn't allow herself to feel this way. Or for him to know and feel encouraged.

"I'm sorry," she cried, forgetting he had no knowledge of either her feelings or her betrayal. She got to her feet and ran. And when she'd put the length of the house and a locked door between them, she fell on the bed and sobbed. For herself, for Burton and for what might have been.

CHAPTER TWELVE

ANOTHER MONDAY MORNING. Rita turned at the knock on the makeup room door, half hoping, half afraid it would be Ernie. Lately nothing seemed right between them. But it was Veronique, coming to have her hair and face done in preparation for the taping of the fifth and sixth segments of *Flavors*.

"You have changed your hair!" Veronique said, walking around Rita to see the back. *"C'est fantastique!"*

Rita blushed under Veronique's admiring gaze. "Lillian's grandniece, Sandy, did it." Rita pulled at one newly dyed reddish lock uncertainly. "Do you think it suits me?" Part of her hated asking her rival to bolster her confidence, but it wasn't Veronique's fault Ernie was acting so dumb. Veronique always looked good no matter what she wore, and Rita would have given anything to know how she did it.

"But of course! The color brings out those pretty amber lights in your eyes." Veronique plopped down in the makeup chair and swiveled to the mirror. "Don't you like it?"

Rita got out the plastic cape and tied it around Veronique's neck. "Er... My boyfriend thinks it's awful. He didn't actually say so, but I could tell." It hurt, especially when all she'd wanted was for him to notice her again.

"Poof! What do men know? He will get used to it." Veronique flipped her hair out from under the plastic collar. "We must be quick, please. When I checked the kitchen this morning, the food had not yet been delivered and I forgot I need to prepare the pomegranates *en avance*. Burton is already in a terrible state."

"I can imagine," Rita said, rolling her eyes. "Oops, sorry," she added, a hand to her mouth. "I forgot you two are married now."

"It's all right. You can talk to me the same as before."

Well, that was hardly true, even though everyone at the station knew the real reason Veronique and Burton had gotten married. But Rita kept her mouth shut and her expression bland as she smoothed on the Pan-Cake makeup. She'd gotten some practice at that when those government people had come snooping around. Like everyone else at Channel Seven, she'd said nothing that could work against Burton and Veronique. "Do you want the Fresh Melon lip gloss or the Succulent Succotash?"

"*Oh la la.* You decide, Rita. You have good color sense. I am used to putting food in my mouth, not smearing it on my lips."

Through the mirror, Veronique saw Ernie go by the open door. "Oh, look, there's Ernie. He will know what to do about the food. *Salut,* Ernie!"

Rita ground her teeth at the warm familiarity in Veronique's voice. Sometimes she wished she and Ernie had made their relationship public. She didn't seriously think Veronique was interested in Ernie, but she could be awfully flirtatious. Okay, she was French, but that didn't make it any easier to bear.

Ernie poked his head around the door. "Morning, Veronique," he said in that deep-voiced unconscious imitation of Burton he only used around Veronique. Then he squeaked back to normal. "Hi, Rita."

Rita felt a flood of misery and jealousy at rating second.

Veronique was oblivious, of course. "Ernie," she said, "do you know if the food has arrived?"

"Yes. It's all laid out in the kitchen."

"You are *très* genial!" She blew him a kiss in the mirror.

"Uh, I gotta go," he said, his cheeks reddening. "One of the mikes is on the blink." He waved and disappeared out the door.

Veronique waved back. "He is sweet, *non?*" she said to Rita.

Ernie didn't have a chance of resisting a woman like Veronique. Rita dug the comb in harder than she meant to. "As sweet as Burton?"

"Ouch!" Veronique cast her a surprised glance in the mirror.

Rita felt ashamed and angry at herself. "Sorry," she muttered, on the verge of tears.

"So tell me about your boyfriend, Rita, the one who does not like your new hair?"

Rita darted her a pained glance in the mirror. "It's Ernie." Her tone said, *Of course you know this.*

"Ernie?" Veronique looked astounded. "Burton's Ernie?"

"My Ernie," Rita asserted. "We're engaged."

"Engaged? How wonderful." Her brilliant smile lit her face. Then she sobered. "You mustn't take any notice of the way I tease him, Rita. As for your question, Ernie is as sweet as apple tart, but for me, Burton is breakfast, lunch and dinner."

A weight seemed to lift from Rita's heart. "Really?" Then her smile faded and she sighed. "Ernie is really special, you know? He's just not very…assertive. He's easily led."

Veronique patted her hand. "Give him time. He will gain confidence."

Rita untied the cape and removed it, careful not to get any dustings of powder on Veronique's dress. "It's not just that. Lately he doesn't seem to appreciate me. I…I was wondering, actually, if you would give me some fashion tips. You always look so great.''

"Moi!" Veronique exclaimed, laughing. She slipped down off the chair. "I am glad to help if I can. Turn around. Yes, with legs like yours the skirt should be shorter. Tuck in at the waist, like so. You have a wonderful figure, Rita. All you need to do is show it off."

Rita stood in front of the mirror, feeling quite racy with her skirt hiked up and her sweater cinched in. Could she do it? Yes. To keep Ernie, she could do anything.

Veronique gazed at her, smiling, and her next words seemed to mirror Rita's thoughts. "Don't underestimate Ernie's love for you. I bet if he thought he was losing you, he would do anything to get you back."

CHAOS. HE WAS SURROUNDED by chaos. Burton ran down the spiral staircase, his headset looped around his neck, his feet barely touching the steps. He took a flying leap off the third to last stair and landed running. With a commanding flick of his hand, he summoned Vince and Ernie.

"What's the holdup?" he demanded. "Is that microphone working yet?"

Vince lifted his baseball cap to run a hand over his scalp. "We pulled one off another set. It's being hooked up."

"Good. Ernie, what's the status of our chef? Is she ready yet?"

He could see Veronique over in the kitchen, making last-minute preparations. She'd hardly spoken on the drive in this morning, and not knowing where they stood was making him very tense.

Ernie pushed his glasses up his nose. "It's kind of complicated...."

"Just give me the facts," Burton snapped.

"She's ready, but the pomegranates she ordered aren't

ripe enough. She can't start the appetizer till we get some more."

"Have you got someone onto that?"

"I sent Joe down to Granville Market as soon as I found out."

"Okay, fine." Burton tried to think calmly. "We'll just have to begin with the main course."

Ernie shook his head. "Problem is, boss, she needs pomegranate juice for the main course, too. She's making some Persian lamb thing."

"In that case, we'll start with dessert."

Ernie consulted his clipboard. "Uh, that would be the pomegranate granita."

"What!" It was all a bad dream, and any second he would wake up.

"Granita is a kind of icy, sherbety thing—"

"I know what granita is," Burton said, pinching the bridge of his nose. "What I don't understand is why we have three dishes all using pomegranates! Did I approve this?"

"Yessir. You liked the idea of a theme tying the show together. I think your exact words were 'That's the most sensational—'"

Burton cut him off by starting toward the kitchen at a fast clip. "In the future, Ernie, when I start tossing around superlatives, give me a swift kick and remind me of the time I allowed an entire show to be based on one temperamental fruit."

"Yessir." Ernie hurried along beside him.

"We're doing week six this afternoon, right, Ern?"

"Yes, but—"

"So we'll switch the order and do it this morning."

"I don't think she'll go for that," Ernie said. "Part of week six's menu builds on something she makes in week five."

Burton stopped in his tracks. "She's not constructing a

fourth lane for the Lion's Gate Bridge, for crying out loud.'' He took a deep breath. ''I'm almost afraid to ask… Week seven?''

''We don't have the ingredients. I told you it was complicated.''

Burton resumed his long-legged stride toward the kitchen. ''No, Ernie. Calculus is complicated. Einstein's theory of relativity is complicated. This is chaos. Chaos, Ernie. To be avoided at all costs.''

''Gee, sorry, Burt.''

Burton had neither the time nor the inclination to take notice of Ernie's slip. The crew dodged him and cameras rolled out of his way. None of it was her fault, he reminded himself. Not the pomegranates, not the farm, not even the fact that he was falling in love with a woman who hated the sight of him.

Veronique watched his long-legged approach, her stomach fluttering nervously. *Oh la la.* All that energy and tension was not good for him. But it made her feel justified for hiding the chess set and delaying the sale of the farm. Then he was stepping around the counter, and the tiny kitchen was filled with his overwhelming aura of urgency.

''I understand the pomegranates haven't arrived.''

Her fingers formed a death grip around a wooden spoon. ''Ernie has ordered more.''

''When you auditioned, you said 'A good cook makes do.' Can't you substitute something? Raspberry juice?''

The suggestion brought on a near-hysterical burst of laughter. She'd stayed out of his way yesterday but still slept badly last night, and this morning Burton had hardly spoken to her. They couldn't go on ignoring the kiss. She was frazzled and tired and she had a horrible feeling Rita had applied her makeup unevenly. ''Raspberry juice is no substitute for pomegranate juice, which is tart, not sweet. More pomegranates are coming. We can wait a few minutes, *non?*''

"No." He rubbed the back of his neck. "We don't even have time for this discussion. Is there anything we can do?"

She thought for a moment. "We could start the Lamb Faisinjan, I suppose. The pomegranate juice isn't added until about halfway through."

"Now you're talking. I'm going to stay on the floor while we retape the opening sequence. It wasn't bad the first time, but now that you're a little more practiced, I think we can make it even better. Do you still remember it? Good." He adjusted his headset and started to back off the set. "Veronique, can you look at me?"

Something in his voice, some hint of hurt quickly covered up, made her look. For an instant their eyes connected. *Mon Dieu.* He still thought she was seeing her first husband.

She twisted a lock of hair at the back of her head around one finger. "Yes, Burton, I can look at you. But about the other night—"

He glanced at his watch. "Can we talk about this later?"

"All I want to say is, I don't think we should talk about it. I think we should forget it happened."

"Forget we kissed? I don't know if I can." He stepped forward again to tucked a strand of hair behind her ear, barely skimming the lobe with his finger. "What if I said, The appetizer made me ravenous and I'm ready for the next course?"

"Then you better eat somewhere else," she said quietly, her skin still tingling from his touch. "In three months we divorce."

He wasted five whole seconds just looking at her. "We're not going to last even three months if we don't convince Immigration our marriage is genuine. Like it or not, we have to pretend we're in love."

TWO HOURS LATER, the gofer Ernie had sent to the market reported back after making the rounds of Granville Island,

New Westminster and Lonsdale Quay Markets, plus dozens of produce outlets in between. The pomegranates he brought back would be ready tomorrow at the earliest, Veronique declared, and not a minute before.

Burton had nothing else scheduled and was too frustrated by the delay to sit at his desk doing paperwork, so he consigned the half-finished lamb to the fridge and took off with Veronique for the farm.

"Are you still angry?" Veronique asked as they pulled off the freeway and onto the exit ramp for Langley. Burton hadn't said a word since they left the station.

Startled out of his worries about mountains of sprouting potatoes, Burton said, "Angry? No. It wasn't your fault. It's a bad season for pomegranates or something."

"I do not mean the pomegranates." She cast him a sideways glance that slid away even as he turned to look at her.

"Oh, that," he said with a wave calculated to look more casual than he felt. "Don't give it another thought." He didn't see any percentage in further exposing his feelings. His misunderstanding about her husband aside, they'd both made it clear from the beginning that the arrangement was short-term. Today she'd confirmed that; in spite of their kiss, nothing had changed. He was still determined to make her see him for himself, but he wasn't so pathetic he had to beg for it. And he wasn't going to mention the word *love* again. Ever.

"You were so quiet," she persisted, "I couldn't help wonder…"

"I was planning the rest of the day."

And then there was more silence. It was just after noon when he turned the car into the driveway. The sky was overcast but the air temperature warm, and rain looked some way off. After a quick lunch of reheated soup, Burton went out to the back porch and stuck his feet into

Granddad's gum boots. He came back through the kitchen pulling on a pair of worn leather gardening gloves.

"What are you doing?" Veronique asked lazily. She was still seated at the pine table sipping coffee, her feet tucked up under her on the chair.

"The pomegranates defeated me, but the potatoes won't. I can't look at those empty fields another day. If Granddad were still alive he'd have the whole crop planted by now."

"How you going to plant potatoes without the machinery?"

"The old-fashioned way. By hand."

"Are you crazy?"

"Probably."

She put her feet down and drained the last of her cup. "Then I will help you."

In the barn Burton loaded potatoes into a wheelbarrow while Veronique shook the straw out of some buckets she found in a corner and filled those, too. With the barrow bumping over the rough ground and buckets in hand, they walked out to the plowed field that rose in a gentle slope behind the barn and the house.

Veronique scanned the long rows of turned dirt that stretched ahead of them to the horizon and for hundreds of yards to the right and left. "How many acres did you say?"

"Two hundred," Burton replied, "but only one hundred are plowed." They turned and headed for the row of poplars that marked the eastern boundary. "Granddad would likely have put the rest into corn, but I'm not going to worry about that now."

Only one hundred acres, Veronique thought. For two people to plant a field that size by hand would take weeks. But she said nothing. This exercise in futility—and her willingness to help—had nothing to do with growing potatoes. Burton needed to do this one last thing for his grandfather. To make amends, to carry on, to somehow keep the old man alive through working his land. And she had this idiotic desire to spend time with Burton. To be physically close to him. *He was falling in love with her.* She couldn't get his words out of her mind even though she prayed he wouldn't utter them again. Head down, once again avoiding his eyes, she stepped clumsily through the soft hillocky dirt in Burton's grandmother's big rubber boots.

At first they tried planting side by side on parallel rows. Burton showed her how deep to plant, how far apart. It was not so very different from growing potatoes in her kitchen garden. Bend, scoop out a hole, drop the potato in, shovel over the dirt. Bending and straightening, inching along, it was backbreaking work. After twenty minutes she paused to stretch, pushing a hand into the small of her already-aching back.

Burton looked up. "Go back to the house. You don't need to do this."

"Perhaps if we work together," she suggested. "You dig the holes and I put in the potatoes."

"Let's try it."

They worked in short sections, Burton hoeing a trench while Veronique followed, dropping in the potatoes at regular intervals. Then she shoveled the dirt back over them while Burton hoed another trench. The method was a little faster, a little smoother, and as they progressed, they developed a rhythm. Hoe, plant, shovel, hoe, plant, shovel...

"Do they not need fertilizer?" Veronique asked, pausing to separate two potatoes whose sprouts had tangled and grown together.

Burton leaned on his hoe. He brushed a gloved hand across his forehead, leaving a dirty streak in its wake. "Granddad did things the old-fashioned way. He grew peas in this field last year—they add nitrogen to the soil."

"For someone who is not a farmer, you know a lot about it."

He seemed a little surprised himself. "I guess I've spent so much time here over the years some of it rubbed off." He sunk his hoe into the dirt and, with a grunt, dragged it along, furrowing through the dark, rich soil. "Doesn't mean I like it."

Veronique turned away to hide a smile. "No, of course not."

Eventually they had planted one entire row. Standing at the top of the slope, Veronique gazed at their accomplishment with silent pride. A warm hand gripped her shoulder, and she glanced up into Burton's smile. "Pretty good, eh?" Burton said.

"It's very good." She didn't point out the hundreds of rows left to plant. Or the fact that tomorrow they'd have to leave it and go back to the studio. They both knew the magnitude of the job and the impossibility of finishing. Nor did she suggest he rent a picker-plant, or whatever they called it. Maybe later he would get the machine and finish the job properly. But she could see that for now he felt good to have simply made a start. And she felt good for having helped him.

"Tell me about yourself," Veronique said when they'd started back hoeing and planting. "What do you like to do when you're not working?"

He told her he liked listening to blues, but not country and western; when he read, it was science fiction; and he'd seen every Hitchcock film half a dozen times. His friends were scattered over the globe, a legacy of years on the road as a photojournalist. He kept in touch, but visits were sporadic, and although he didn't come right out and say so, Veronique got the impression he would have liked to have a circle of friends closer to home—if he wasn't so busy with his work.

She was pondering the similar gaps in their lives when a gust of wind caught her across the cheek, and a cool, wet drop splashed onto her nose. She glanced up. Dark streaks of heavy rain were slanting across the base of the mountains, and in the middle distance, a bank of black clouds was rolling in across the valley. A storm was heading their way.

"Burton," she called, but he'd already seen it.

"You head in," he said. "I'll just finish this row." They were about a third of the way through the fourth row, heading toward the house. Finishing the row together would take an hour; twice as long if he did it by himself.

"Are you crazy? You'll get soaked." Drops were falling steadily now.

He shrugged and dug a trench with his hoe. Reaching past her for the bucket of spuds, he placed it in the trough between the rows and picked up the shovel. "Go on," he said. "Just because I can't leave a job half-done doesn't mean you should suffer."

She wanted to leave, but she couldn't let him do this alone. She was married to a madman, but he was her husband—for better or worse, for colder and wetter, in sickness and in health....

Wresting the shovel from his hands, she began to mound the dirt around the seed potatoes nestled in their earthy beds. He frowned and started to say something. She lifted her chin, silently defying him to try to make her go back. His brief smile warmed her through despite the chilling drops falling on her neck and hands.

The rain poured down. The soil became wetter, heavier and more and more slippery. Rivulets snaked down the slope between the rows, and Veronique discovered that her boots leaked. It was hard to shovel, hard to see, hard to stay upright. Twice she slipped and fell into the soft, wet dirt and had to struggle back up, aided by a strong hand from Burton. Rain soaked her thin jacket and her jeans, got in her eyes, dripped from her hair. Conversation ceased in their determination to get the row planted.

She sneezed twice, jamming wet, mud-streaked fingers

against her nose so Burton wouldn't hear and tell her to go in. She'd built up a sweat that, added to the chill and wet, made her feel feverish.

Finally, soaking wet, muddy from head to toe, backs aching, they reached the end of the row. This time when Burton told her to go inside while he put everything away, she didn't argue. Sneezing and shivering and aching in her bones, she ran splashing across the yard to the house.

Merde, she thought, another cold.

THE NEXT DAY STARTED badly and got steadily worse.

Veronique awoke with a congested nose and a prickly feeling at the back of her throat. Burton loaded her up with cold remedies she didn't want to take and dropped her off at the nursing home with a terse "If it's raining, call me. I'll come and get you."

She paused at the half-open doorway to Marion's room. Her spirits sank further when she saw Mother-in-Law Number One in her wheelchair staring morosely out the window, her hair uncombed, her face pale and unmadeup. Depressed again.

Suddenly Veronique felt unbearably burdened by the task of coaxing Marion into a happy, functional future. Why had she taken it on? Why had she even thought she was capable of it? Every week seemed to be one step forward and two steps back. Getting Marion to join the home's bridge club, her goal for today, now appeared to be monumentally out of reach.

"*Bonjour,* Marion," she sang out with determined cheerfulness as she gave a knock and entered the room. "How are you today?"

"Oh, hello, Veronica." Marion turned, mustering a feeble smile. Her eyes were bright, as though she'd been crying. "I guess I'm fine. Janice, my roommate at the rehab center, came to visit me. She's back in her apartment, fully recovered." Marion went back to staring out the window.

"She came to visit? But I thought you did not get along."

"Oh, she's quite nice once you get to know her. It's just that she was in such a lot of pain at first."

"I'm glad. It's not right that you sit here by yourself. Hey, you know what? There is a bridge club here, too. They meet this morning. I am going to get your brush and your lipstick and a mirror, and we will get you ready. *D'accord?*"

"Oh, I don't know," she said listlessly. "I won't enjoy it."

Veronique felt like screaming, she was so frustrated. Maybe she was wrong to jolly Marion along. Maybe she should stop pushing and let the woman take responsibility for her own happiness. Then again, maybe if she persisted just a little longer, Marion would make a breakthrough. It was so hard to know what was right.

It wasn't until she'd brought the toiletry bag from the bathroom and handed it to her that she noticed something in Marion's lap, half hidden under her palm. "What is that?"

Marion turned her hand over. Photographs. Graham as a boy. Graham as a teenager. Graham and Veronique on their wedding day. Graham and Stan, smiling widely, all decked out in their fishing gear. Dressed for death.

Marion sifted through the photos, selected those that didn't include Stan and handed the rest to Veronique. "I'd like you to have these."

Veronique didn't know how to refuse, only that she had to. "*Merci,* Marion. But I cannot take them from you. Please, you keep them. I have others." More than she wanted.

"Not of him as a boy. See, he doesn't look like your nice Mr. O'Rourke in this picture, does he?"

Veronique held the photo closer. Perhaps not surprisingly, there was little resemblance between the ten-year-old and Burton, although it made her wonder what Burton had looked like as a boy. The longer she knew him the less he reminded her of her first husband. That was both a blessing and a danger, she was just beginning to realize. "No, he doesn't."

"Well, then, you keep it. I know you said you married Burton to stay in Canada, but I can't help think you chose him because he looks like Graham. I understand, I really do, though I worry about you. I'm too old to think about marrying again, but you shouldn't live in the past."

Veronique pulled up a chair and sat down facing Marion, their knees nearly touching. "Your life is not over. You must believe that. Also, you must not worry about me."

"You're grieving over Graham," Marion replied. "It's natural, but is it fair to Mr. O'Rourke?"

Mon Dieu. She could not let Marion go on thinking this way. "Marion, there is something I must tell you," she said gravely. "It is not easy for me to say, and it will not be easy for you to hear."

"What is it?" Marion's face looked naked and vulnerable.

Veronique took a deep breath and clasped both of Marion's hands in hers. "I married Burton not because he looks like Graham, but in spite of it."

Marion's brows knit together. "I don't understand. Didn't you like Graham's looks?"

"Yes, at first. You see…" She hesitated. How little did Marion need to know to understand? How much could she say without Marion hating her?

"At first, Graham and I were very much in love," she began again. Marion smiled. "But we didn't really know each other. We married too quickly."

Marion nodded wisely. "You did it again."

Veronique made a face in frustration. Marion was still having trouble with the concept of a temporary marriage.

"Forget about Burton for now. The truth is…" Suddenly she was fed up with pussyfooting around. "The truth is, when Graham and I got to know each other we discovered that our love was not real and lasting."

Marion slipped her hand out and patted Veronique's. "You don't know what you're saying, my dear. You're rationalizing your new marriage. You and Graham would have gone on forever."

"*Non!*" Veronique jumped to her feet. "I am telling you, I did not love Graham. He did not love me."

"Graham adored you."

"He didn't even *like* me. He was horrible to me. I was going to leave him."

"No!" Marion's denial was firm and swift, but traces of anxiety creased her gentle face.

"He cheated on me."

"Not my son—"

"And he hit me."

"Stop!" Marion burst into tears and covered her face with her hands. "Oh, please stop."

Veronique hugged her arms around herself. She hadn't meant to say so much. Marion was sobbing, and tears streamed from her own eyes, as well.

"I'm sorry, Marion," she said, kneeling to put her arms around the other woman. "I didn't want to hurt you."

"He really…hit you?" Marion's face was wet and pale, her voice trembling.

"Once." Discovering the other woman had made her pack her bags; the blow he'd struck had made her impervious to all pleas, threats and demands. Thank goodness they'd had no children.

Marion was shaking her head, tears streaming. "Not Graham. Not my sweet little boy. He'd never do anything like that. I can't believe it. I won't believe it."

Marion wept as though she'd lost her son all over again. She voiced her disbelief over and over, until Veronique wondered who she was trying to convince, herself or Veronique. Veronique held her, wishing with all her heart she hadn't destroyed Marion's image of her son. Being understood wasn't worth taking away Marion's happy memories when memories were all she had.

"I'm sorry, Marion," she said, stroking her hair back from her damp face. "I should not have told you this. I'm sure Graham was a good man," she lied. "We just weren't right for each other."

Marion's sobs slowed. She took the handkerchief Veronique held out and dried her reddened eyes. "Don't go trying to make it out to be nothing now that you've said it."

The harshness of the reprimand chastened and surprised her. With Marion, she sometimes felt as though she were dealing with a child. Now the tables had turned. Inflicting wounds had taken away Veronique's authority; receiving them had given Marion dignity. The last, at least, was good, but it was so unfair. Veronique had been hurt, too.

"He was a good son," Veronique offered meekly.

Marion clutched the photos of Graham to her breast, and fresh tears filled her eyes. "Of course he was a good son. There was never any question of that."

"Come," Veronique said. "I will help you to the bathroom to wash your face. Maybe the bridge club will take your mind off this."

Marion's face set mulishly. "Don't push me, Veronica. When I'm ready to go to the bridge club, I will, and not a moment sooner."

"Yes, Marion."

There was no answering squeeze when Veronique bent to hug her goodbye. Veronique felt a sneeze coming on and pressed a finger beneath her nose. "My handkerchief," she requested. It was too wet to use, but too important to lose.

When she stepped outside, rain was pouring onto the

city from the dark clouds banked against Grouse Mountain. Half a block away, a bus swooshed in close to the curb. With no time to open her umbrella, Veronique ran for it. She was soaked, but she got aboard. Her change clinked down through the cash receptacle, and she swung into a seat as the bus swayed back into traffic.

The vinyl seat was cold beneath her wet stockinged legs. She hooked the umbrella over the seat back in front. Only then did she remember Burton telling her to call him for a ride. Oh, well, she thought apathetically. She would be there soon enough.

Misery and habit sent her thumb curving repetitively over the monogrammed *B* in the corner of the handkerchief. She'd hurt Marion—maybe even set her recovery back. And in the process, she'd hurt herself.

If a lie had bound them together, the truth had set them adrift. She felt as though she were bobbing lonely on the open sea, with Marion moving away in the distance like a sailboard that had been knocked out from under her. For, like a sailboard, Marion had been both drag and lift—responsibility and support. Veronique wished she could transfer her guilt and Marion's pain into anger at the man who had created this situation, but he'd become a speck on the horizon, too insignificant to attach any emotion to at all. She shut her eyes and tried to pretend she was floating on the warm waters of her homeland. She would give anything to see her sister, to be back in the loving embrace of her family, to let her weary soul make landfall on the warm sands of Tahiti.

CHAPTER THIRTEEN

BURTON STOOD AT HIS DESK, rapidly dividing papers between his out-box, his still-to-do box and the circular file on the floor. He checked his watch. Veronique should have been back by now, but maybe she'd probably gone directly to Makeup. Taping of *Flavors* was due to start in five minutes, and after yesterday's fiasco, the budget couldn't afford another minute wasted.

Ernie poked his head in the door, puffing as though he'd been running. "Hi. The crew's ready to go. Where's Veronique?"

"What! You mean she hasn't shown up yet?" Burton threw down his papers. "She said she'd only be a few minutes at the nursing home. I knew I should have waited and driven her to the studio."

"Maybe she missed her bus," Ernie suggested.

"Maybe she isn't paying attention to the time," Burton countered, scowling. He was annoyed she was late, but he was even more worried something could have happened to her. When had that started? He checked outside the window. Raining. What a summer. At least she had her umbrella.

"Let's get down to the studio. I want everything double-checked," Burton said, coming around the desk. "By the way, everything okay between you and Rita?"

Ernie, about to stride off, stopped so fast he wobbled on his cross-trainers. "Y-yes, why do you ask?"

"Rita came to me yesterday asking if it was really your

job to be running around after Veronique's pomegranates.''

"Isn't it?" His voice came out on a squeak.

"It is. But Rita's a nice girl. You don't want to lose her by making a fool of yourself over an older woman." Burton scowled again. "A married woman."

"Gee, Burton, I thought you and Veronique weren't really...I mean I thought your marriage wasn't r-real...." Ernie's glasses started to fog up.

Burton stepped to the doorway and loomed over him. "As long as she and I are together, the marriage is real. Got that, Ernie?"

Ernie's Adam's apple bobbed up and down. "I g-got it, boss. Nothing's going on between me and Veronique."

"I know that. Maybe you should let Rita know, too."

"Yessir. Right away, sir." Ernie shot off down the corridor.

Burton followed, feeling worse, not better, for having slapped Ernie down. The kid didn't deserve it, and Burton knew his own obsessing over Veronique was not good. She wanted to forget the kiss he couldn't get out of his mind. With that kiss, he'd kissed goodbye any objectivity he'd ever had about her as an employee. With that kiss, he sealed his fate—he was no longer the reluctant bridegroom, but a frustrated lover. He groaned. Why had he gone and said he was falling in love with her? Ernie wasn't the only one in danger of making a fool of himself.

Burton was pacing the set like a trapped wolverine, snarling and snapping when Veronique arrived twenty minutes late. She was dripping wet and sneezing, her hair a bedraggled mess, and her clothes, which ought to have been adequate for June, were drenched through.

He stood back and took deep breaths while Lillian brought her a cup of hot tea with lemon. He paced some more while Rita whipped the hair dryer into action. He ground his teeth while Ernie fussed over her and handed her a tissue every time she sneezed. Thin-lipped and silent, he waited till the others had finished with her, then he shooed them out of earshot.

"What happened?" he said, his voice low and tense. "You told me you'd only be a few minutes. You're late. And you're soaked. Where's your umbrella?"

Veronique's hand went to her mouth. "My umbrella! I must have left it on the bus. Oh, I am so sorry. It was your wedding gift to me."

A wedding gift for a nonwedding. Burton tried to contain his irritation, to keep it separate from the job. So it hadn't been a romantic present or anything she'd wanted, just something she'd badly needed. So what? Why should she take care of it? Just because it had been the nicest-looking, the highest-quality, the absolutely best umbrella he could find.

"Forget it," he said, tight-lipped. "We have more important things to worry about. Like the fact we're now half an hour behind schedule. Do you know what overtime for an entire crew does to a programming budget?"

She bit her lip and looked away. "I am sorry."

Hell, now she was going to cry. "Don't do that. Your eyes are red enough as it is. Did you have to go and get a cold just when we're in the thick of taping?" He remembered too late that she'd caught the cold by helping him carry out his insane notion of planting potatoes by hand.

He was about to apologize when she snapped back, "Yes, I got a cold—just to annoy you. What do you think?"

"I think you're not taking this show seriously. Yesterday was a mistake. But today? Running around in the rain, getting soaked, leaving your umbrella on the bus—" His voice had become more strident with every word. He broke off and shoved a hand through his spiky hair. He was losing it. Really losing it.

"I had to see Marion. You knew when you hired me she was the only reason I am here. And now…and now…" Her eyes filled with tears, but she set her shoulders defiantly. "You are upset over a lost umbrella when she is struggling just to cope. I am struggling to cope…."

"I am not upset about the umbrella. It's just…it's typical of your ambivalence—toward me, toward the show, toward this whole damn country." He flung an arm wide. And almost clipped Ernie on the nose.

"What is it, Ernie?" he barked, turning on him.

"Don't yell at him!" Veronique shouted. "If I am so ambi—ambilva…" Her hand flew upward in a sharp gesture. "Whatever it is you say—maybe you should find another chef."

"Maybe I should," he snarled.

Outrage flashed in her vivid green eyes. "I will not hold you to our contract. Call Monsieur Mumbling Mustache. Better still, call Madame Emily Up-Herself. She is the one you really wanted, *non?*"

"No!" At his protest, Veronique seemed to have no trouble looking—no, glaring—him in the eye.

"Excuse me, B-B-Burt…on," Ernie cut in again. "We're ready to start."

"Not now, Ernie." Burton took his eyes off Veronique for only a second, but when he looked back, she was striding away, waving her hands, turning the air blue with her French.

He charged after her and caught her by the arm. "Where the hell do you think you're going?"

"I'm quitting," she snapped. "You don't care about me, or the farm, or anything but the show and your career. You think I need you, but I don't."

"Without me and my show, you'll be deported."

Veronique went pale. "Then I will be deported. I am going back to my apartment. *Au revoir.*"

Burton threw his hands in the air. "Fine, go. I don't

need prima donnas around here. I'll find another chef, no problem.''

He watched her walk away, their angry words echoing in his ears while a sick feeling formed in the hollow of his stomach.

Au revoir. Finis.

ERNIE THREW A FURIOUS glare at Burton—how could he just let her go?—then took off after her himself. He caught up with her in the corridor, a little way down from Makeup. He glanced nervously at the open door, wondered where Rita was right now, and decided it couldn't be helped. *Flavors,* everything, was at stake.

"Veronique!" He reached out to touch her arm. "Don't go."

"He sent me away. I have no choice." Her shoulders lifted in a careless shrug, but her face was white.

"He didn't mean it. He's like that, sort of abrupt. He does it to me all the time."

"Ah, but he doesn't appreciate you, Ernie." Veronique touched him on the cheek. "He doesn't take you seriously."

Ernie couldn't help himself, he leaned into her palm. "He does. He just doesn't always show it."

Part of him wanted to trash Burton, instead of defend him, but he liked his job, and Burton really was a pretty great guy, and Veronique wouldn't ever go for him, anyway, and it was Rita he wanted to marry, and…oh, hell, it was all so complicated.

"Goodbye, sweet Ernie." She put her hands on his shoulders and kissed him one, twice, thrice, on the cheeks.

"Bye." Ernie watched her go in a kind of swoon.

"Ernie."

Oh, no. He'd never heard quite that mixture of anger and anguish from Rita. Slowly he turned to face her.

THURSDAY AFTERNOON, two days since Veronique's defection. Burton had a lot on his mind—all of it bad. The potatoes were still unplanted and his admittedly sketchy efforts to locate a pick-planter and someone to operate it had so far met with failure. The two young brothers Don Chetwynd kept pestering him about had seen the property and made an offer. Burton was sorely tempted to hand over the farm and be done with it, but the chess set still hadn't turned up.

At work, things weren't much better. He'd gotten a tentative agreement from Emily Harper-Smythe to take over on *Flavors*. All he had to do was pick up the phone and confirm. But if he went that route, it would mean starting over practically from scratch. He'd never complete *Lost Harvest*. At least not this year.

Plaguing his mind through it all was the image of Veronique alone and sick. He told himself he was being ridiculous; she was made of some steely Gallic wonderstuff that was as robust as French roast. But he'd been too harsh. Too caught up in his own problems. She'd been right about that.

And she was his wife. He had an obligation to look after her. After all, who else did she have? Veronique's only friend and relation required full-time care herself.

A knock at the door brought his weary head up. "Oh, hi, Ernie. No, I don't know when we're going to start taping again."

"It's not that. Some of the gang are going to the pub for a drink. I just wondered if you wanted to come."

"Thanks, but no. I've got to haul my sorry ass out of this pit I dug for myself." He leaned back in his chair and with a vague gesture indicated the paperwork on *Flavors*. He could take legal action against Veronique, and she'd have to come back to work, but she'd hate him for it, and what was the point of that? Then there was their interview with Immigration tomorrow, and he couldn't imagine what he was going to say to Officers Jackson and Connery. If they even went through with the charade. Maybe even now she was packing her bags to return to Tahiti. The thought made him groan.

"Why don't you go see her?" Ernie suggested, looking sympathetic. "Ask her to come back?"

"I don't beg."

"Nobody's asking you to beg. Just talk to her."

Burton hated having anyone suggest what he'd already decided to do on his own. "Is talk working with Rita?"

Ernie looked away. "She gave me back my engagement ring."

Burton sighed. "Sorry, Ern. I didn't mean to rub it in. Go drown your sorrows. I'll…" He didn't want to say what he was planning to do in case he failed. "I'll figure out something. See you tomorrow."

"Why don't you come? Just for a while."

Burton looked at Ernie more closely. His round face seemed gaunt and haunted. Sort of the way he himself had felt these past few days. "What the hell," he said, pushing back his chair. "I guess one won't hurt."

"ANOTHER ROUND, ERNIE?" Burton raised his hand and caught the eye of the waiter circling the crowd with his drinks tray. They sat on high wooden stools, their elbows resting on a narrow shelf overlooking the sunken central floor of the bar. Great view, if there'd been anyone he wanted to see.

"My turn, Burt," Ernie said, digging his hand in his pocket. "Whoops, sorry, Bur-ton."

Under the influence of two and a half beers, Burton waved a benevolent hand. "Just call me Burt. It must be some natural phenomenon too powerful to fight." Someone caught his eye in the far corner. "Is that Rita? She looks different. She looks great!"

Ernie glanced over to where Rita was laughing with the

guys from research. "You mean this is the first time you've seen her today?"

"Yes. What happened?"

Ernie frowned into his beer. "Apparently the hairstyle wasn't enough. Veronique gave her some fashion tips, and she's gone hog-wild buying new clothes. Rita's changed, Burt. Says she doesn't need me."

Burton used the bottom of his beer glass to make soggy circles on his paper coaster. "Veronique said she didn't need me, either. Love is a mug's game, Ernie. You have to be crazy to get involved, and insane not to be grateful when it's over."

"So it's really over between you and Veronique?"

"Veronique is not only finished with the show, she's finished with our marriage." He pulled on his beer. "It may have been a phony arrangement, but I can't get her out of my skull. Do you know what I do at night? I watch tapes of the show. I pause the tape in the middle of one of her fabulous smiles and just stare at her. Or I replay over and over that cute way she has of tossing her head from side to side."

"She's so great," Ernie mumbled morosely into his beer.

Burton put down his glass and turned to look at his companion in misery. He could almost forgive the guy for his crush on Veronique. "Listen, I..." Damn, this was hard to say. "I realize you're missing Veronique, too."

Ernie glanced up at him. "Oh, hey, no. I've gotten over missing Veronique. It was Rita I was missing just then." His head dropped again. "It's Rita I'm always missing."

A sweet-looking girl with long, blond hair walked slowly past their table cradling a half-pint mug to her pink angora sweater. As she glanced around for a place to sit, she cast them a shy smile and continued on.

Sensing a diversion, Burton nudged Ernie in the ribs. "Ernie, you devil. That little fox had her eye on you."

Ernie's gaze strayed, wavered, then snapped back to the far corner. "Forget it. I love Rita."

"Listen, pal, if you want Rita, you've got to go out there and win her back."

"Yeah, how?"

Burton scratched his jaw, thinking. "You say she's changed? Show her that you can change, too. You have been a tad neglectful lately, right?"

Ernie squirmed uncomfortably on his bar stool. "Maybe a little."

"Okay then, listen up. I'm going to let you in on the Secret."

"The Secret?"

"Yes. Not many men know about it, but the ones who do have no trouble at all in the love department."

Ernie's face scrunched in confusion. "But you say *you* know it…?"

"Yeah, well, maybe I've been a little slow in applying it," Burton said, testily. "You want to hear this or not?"

"Go on," Ernie said, looking attentive.

"Okay. The Secret is really very simple. You've got to give your woman, not a little, but a lot of tender loving care. Show her she means something to you. Show her she's the one in a million made just for you."

Ernie's shoulders slumped. "Rita would walk all over me."

Burton jabbed a finger at him. "Now that's just what you can't let her do. You've got to go in strong, like you deserve to be with her. Self-confidence is a major turn-on with women. Not arrogance, they don't like that. Just know your own worth."

Ernie lifted his head and eyed him skeptically. "That's it? That's the Secret?"

"Its beauty lies in its simplicity. Treat her like a million bucks. Then act like she's lucky to have you. Which she is, goddamn it."

Ernie took a sip of beer, looking thoughtful as he licked away a trace of foam mustache. "You might have something there."

"Now, here's the most important part," Burton said, and leaned in closer. "The secret to the Secret is not to use it as a pickup scam to get women into bed. You've got to live it, for that one special woman in your life."

"Live it," Ernie repeated.

"That's right. Actions speak louder than words."

"You really think it'll work?"

"I know it'll work," Burton said, crossing his fingers under the table.

Ernie straightened his spine to sit taller. "I could request her favorite song."

"That's the idea."

"I could buy her a rose from that flower girl who's making the rounds...."

"Yeah, go on." Burton was busy thinking about what he could do to win Veronique back.

"Then I'll go over there and ask her to dance as if we'd never met." Ernie's cheeks grew flushed with excitement. "I could join her table— No, wait. I'll ask her to come to me."

"Now you're talking." Burton clapped a hand on his shoulder.

Ernie stiffened. He drew back and looked Burton straight in the eye. "You know, Burton, I really hate it when you do that."

Three things flashed through Burton's mind simultaneously. One, Ernie had called him Burton for the first time without being prompted. Two, his assistant was displaying uncharacteristic, but not unwelcome, assertiveness. Three, it was far too easy to slap a short man on the back.

"Sure, pal," he said, a little dazed by all the revelations. He held out his hand. "I gotta go. See you Monday."

Ernie blinked, smiled and shook hands, man-to-man.

On the way over to Veronique's, Burton stopped off at
his apartment to change his shirt and pick up a package
from the freezer. Then, because it wasn't raining and he
wanted time to think, he set off on foot over the Burrard
Street bridge. At a brisk pace it would take him no more
than forty minutes to reach her apartment on the other side
of English Bay.

Fluttering red-and-black banners announcing the annual
Salmon Festival lined both sides of the bridge. High in the
night sky, stars peeked out between towering clouds of
luminous gray-white. On the far shore of Burrard Inlet, the
Planetarium squatted like a UFO about to take off.

At the crest of the bridge, Burton leaned on the rail and
gazed beyond the bay into the blackness of Georgia Strait.
What the hell was he going to say to Veronique? Stay a
month and finish the series? Stay a year and give our relationship a real shot? Stay a lifetime because I already
know I want you forever?

He sucked in a lungful of the moist night air and moved
on. What had happened to old "love 'em and leave 'em"
O'Rourke? When had his emotions gotten involved and
made it all so tangled and complicated?

Twenty minutes later he leaned his forehead against Veronique's door and imagined he could feel the warmth of
her home right through the wood. He could hear the indistinct murmur of her voice, made lower and huskier by
her cold, speaking to someone in French. A visitor? A stab
of possessiveness made him feel like a real husband.

He knocked.

A moment later she stood before him, wearing a beige
cashmere shawl over her pink T-shirt and colorful *pareau.*
"Come in," she said, her gaze wary, her mouth unsmiling.

Entering the relaxing warmth and humidity of her apartment, Burton had to force himself to remember that once
again he was a man on a mission. Bring Veronique back
to the studio. To the farmhouse. He knew better than to

think she'd come to his bed, but he couldn't help thinking about that, too. In fact, he thought about it almost all the time.

He laid the back of his hand on her forehead. "Shouldn't you be in bed?"

"I am much better. This cold was a mild one. You have been out drinking?"

"I had a couple of beers at the pub with Ernie."

"How is Ernie?"

"The worm has turned."

She raised her eyebrows, said "Ahh" and smiled mysteriously, as though she knew all about it. Damn. Just when he thought he had women figured out.

She turned and walked back to the living area. "Have you eaten?"

"I brought you some soup. My mother made it, but it's good." He handed her the paper bag with total confidence in Catherine's chicken soup—both for its restorative powers and its acceptability. There were no shortcuts here, no canned cream soup or crushed potato chips.

She pulled the frozen Tupperware container out of the bag. "I'll heat it up."

He followed her into the kitchen, pausing to take off his jacket and drape it over the back of the sofa.

The microwave hummed. Veronique stretched to reach into a top cupboard for bowls. Turned to say something and broke off in surprised laughter at the sight of his colorful Hawaiian shirt. *"Oh la la!"* she exclaimed. "You want a *pareau?*"

"I don't think I'm quite ready for that, but thanks, anyway." If he could still make her smile, hope was not lost. He came a little closer. "I'm sorry about the other day."

Her shoulders went up in a full body shrug. "You had some right to be angry. But it does not change anything. We make a big mistake—"

Burton touched her arm and felt the warmth, the softness

of her skin. "Let's not talk about it just yet. Rejection doesn't sit well on an empty stomach." He sat on one of the mismatched kitchen chairs, and that reminded him of Granddad's rocker. Would she come back and finish what she'd started to refinish?

"I had an offer on the farm."

She went still, her hand in the cutlery drawer. "Oh?"

"Those brothers from Chilliwack. Chetwynd called again, so I let them have a look."

She pulled out a couple of spoons. "What did you say?"

"I told him I needed more time." Her face went suddenly pale under the fluorescent light. "Maybe you shouldn't be doing this. Sit down. I'll get it."

"I'm fine, really." She set the spoons on the table and went back for water glasses.

Burton shook his head and got up to guide her to a chair. "Sit. How is Marion?"

"Not so good. I told her the truth about Graham. About why I was going to leave him."

Burton felt an irrational tug of sympathy for the luckless Graham. "Why exactly did you hate him so much?"

Veronique's shawl slipped over one shoulder as she reached up to tug on a curl, and her mouth pursed in remembered pain. "You don't want to know."

"Yes, I do," Burton said, taking her hand in his. "I want to know all about you. What makes you laugh. And what makes you cry. And then, if I can, I want to stop the tears."

At that, moisture welled in her eyes and a smile spread across her face. Laughing, she brushed the tears away. "There, now you have both. You make me feel so…"

Burton brought her hand to his mouth and pressed his lips against her knuckles. "What? How do I make you feel?"

She glanced shyly up at him. "Opposite to what I felt for Graham."

Warmth rose like a flame in Burton, sending heat pulsing between them. Then he said, "Exactly why did you hate Graham?" and it was as though he'd dashed cold water over her.

Veronique's smile faded. Frown lines appeared between her brows and she pulled her hand away to tuck it in her lap. "A few months after Graham and I were married I discovered he went back to an old girlfriend."

"The man must have been insane."

Veronique threw Burton a grateful smile. "I told Graham he must give her up. He just laughed and said the French have an easy attitude to that. It may be true for some, but not for me. I said I would leave him. He couldn't stand that—not to have control over me. He said my family wouldn't want me back after I ran away from them. I didn't care what he said anymore. I went to pack my bags…he followed me into the bedroom…" Her eyes became bright with tears, and she blinked angrily. "And then…and then…"

"What?" Burton was full of foreboding.

"He told me to put my things back in the closet, and when I wouldn't—" she took a deep breath "—he hit me."

Burton felt the impact of her statement like a hard right to his gut. Adrenaline poured through his veins. He clenched his hands into fists and got to his feet, wanting to smash a dead man into pulp. Instead, he pulled Veronique, his beautiful, precious Veronique, into a protective embrace. "Oh, God, Veronique. That bastard."

He held her tightly, and gradually her arms slipped around his waist and she was holding him tightly, too. She was very still. Then he felt her breathe a deep sigh, and when she drew back there was moisture in her eyes—and a greater closeness between them.

"Were you badly hurt?" He hated even talking about it, but he needed to know.

"No. A bruise here," she said, touching her left cheek-bone. "It healed faster than my heart or my pride." She looked down. "I've never told anybody all of it. It was hard to tell you."

"I know."

"He tried to make me feel like I deserved it—"

"No!" He pulled her close again.

"Maybe I was weak to allow it to happen and—"

He put his fingers against her lips. "The man was a Neanderthal. Evolution should have weeded him out at birth."

She giggled. "Don't tell Marion that." Then her smile faded and her chin came up. "I am not a victim."

He pulled her into another hug. "I wouldn't think that in a million years."

She laid her head on his chest and sighed again. "Thank you for understanding." Her arms tightened around him. "You are a good man. I...I like you very much."

Then she eased away. Burton watched her move across the kitchen to get a jug of water from the fridge. No wonder she'd hated Graham. But wasn't love the opposite of hate?

"It must have been hard for Marion to hear that about her son."

"I should never have told her," Veronique said. "She refused to believe me, and so she pushed me away, her closest friend. But I think deep down she must believe me. She never say a word against her husband, but once I came into their house—the door was open and they didn't hear me knock—and I saw Stan holding her arm so tight she had tears in her eyes. I was shocked. I didn't know what to do. I tiptoed out and knocked loudly before coming in again."

"Did you ever ask her about it?"

"Yes, but she made some excuse to cover up for Stan. Now she covers up for her son. She doesn't want to admit the truth because if she does, it will destroy one of her few comforts, her fond memories of Graham."

Burton took the jug from her and set it on the table. "She's deluding herself. The truth will make her stronger."

"I thought it would break the barrier between us, but it seems to have created a bigger one. And I have lost a good friend. I should go see her again, but I dread it."

The microwave beeped. She took the container out and stirred it. While she ladled soup into two bowls, Burton thought about Veronique and himself, and how this Graham character had more than one barrier to answer for.

"I don't want to talk about Graham anymore," she said. "Did you get another chef?" A tiny crease formed between her eyes.

"Nothing has been finalized," he said cautiously. "Do you—"

She placed a bowl of fragrant, steaming soup before him. "Eat first. Then we talk turnip."

He laughed. "Turkey. We talk turkey."

"Whatever." She tasted a spoonful of soup. "This is good. Was it still raining when you came?"

"No, it stopped. You know, Veronique, I hate to think you're getting such a bad impression of Vancouver. This is an unusually wet year."

She laughed. "Everyone I meet tell me the same thing. Then I ask Tom—"

"The station's weatherman?"

"Yes. He show me graphs of rainfall. This year is not so very different from last year. Or the year before. Which reminds me." She jumped up, went into the other room and returned brandishing her umbrella. "Look," she said, pushing it open. "It was in the Lost and Found at the bus station."

She did care, Burton thought as a smile started in his heart and worked its way to his lips. The Lost and Found was in the main bus terminal over on Cambie, several miles and at least two bus changes away. A trip she must have made in the pouring rain and sick with a cold. He ought to scold her for going out in the weather, but instead, he said warmly, "I'm glad you got it back. Now furl that thing or you'll bring us bad luck."

"Can it get any worse?" she said with a grin. "What else has happened while I am away?"

He pushed his empty bowl to one side. "Well—"

"Wait." She rose and took his hand. "Come and sit where it's more comfortable."

Burton leaned against the cushions in one corner of the sofa. Veronique put on some quiet piano music, then tucked her legs beneath her *pareau* and rested against the other arm, facing him.

He told her all the gossip at the station: Sylvia had a new boyfriend, Murphy had turned into a rabid antismoker, and Lillian's grandniece, Sandy, was coming in at lunchtime to do female staff members' hair in the makeup room. They chatted and laughed, and Burton silently admired the gleam of lamplight in Veronique's hair and on the ridge of her collarbone, and wished he could trace his tongue down that smooth path to dip into the shadowed hollow....

"Come back, Veronique," he said, leaning forward to clasp her hands and pull her closer. Breathing in her scent, he pressed his mouth to her inner wrist, to the hollow of her elbow. This time she didn't pull away.

Her eyes closed. "To the studio...or the farm?"

"Both." He felt her quickened pulse beneath his lips. "I need you."

Her eyes, still half closed, lifted to meet his. "You, the producer, or—" her voice dropped to a purr "—you, the man?"

"Again, both. But the man takes precedence."

He bent his head, and she lifted her mouth to meet his. Sensation focused, then diffused, till he was enveloped by warmth. Desire grew and expanded, like a living thing.

"Who do you...?" His voice cracked.

She knew what he meant. "I see you, Burton. Only you."

They moved closer on the sofa. The scent of *tiaré* was gradually replaced by the musky aroma of two bodies entwined, the quiet strains of Debussy overcome by breathless sighs and gentle moans. Her *pareau* parted just where he knew it would, a tantalizing revelation of slim brown thighs. His hand slid up that satiny skin to the source of her warmth, and wonder of heavenly wonders, encountered soft, moist curls, instead of panties. Here at least, there were no barriers.

His fingers found her breasts beneath her shirt, and they, too, were bare. And full and firm and... He drew back, breathing deep. "Is this what you want, too?"

Wordlessly she nodded. With one hand, she pressed his fingers against her hardened nipple; with the other she palmed his aching groin. She pressed and half rose to her knees, swaying toward him. Her *pareau* fell further open. Then, her open mouth hot and wet on his, she slowly slid his zipper down.

VERONIQUE AWOKE AS DAWN filtered through the chinks in the curtains. The previous night came back to her in a rush of aching limbs and remembered pleasure. She turned over to gaze across her pillow at Burton. His dark copper hair clashed with her hot pink comforter, and stuck up in spikes and cowlicks, but this was the most peaceful she'd ever seen him. Having him in her bed flooded her with warmth and made her smile. Such a sweet, silly grin he wore. Must be a nice dream.

Mon Dieu, but he was adorable. He might do everything else in a speedy fashion, but when it came to making love he took his time—and was very thorough. Thinking about it made her wriggle closer. She contemplated waking him up, but the poor man needed his rest.

Close up, he looked nothing like Graham. He had a different body—strong, but sleek rather than thick-set. What a pity that hatred of Graham had kept her from really seeing Burton for so long. Now, when they had just a short time left, she wanted to look her fill.

She thought of the chess set suddenly. She should tell him. She must tell him. But she hated the thought of anything disturbing this newfound closeness between them, even though their relationship would only last until the cooking series was over. Then she would go back to Tahiti. He would keep the farm or he would sell it. Either way, he would finish his documentary and move on to something else. They would sign divorce papers sent through the mail. Someday he would meet someone else, fall in love and start a family....

No, she couldn't bear to envisage such a future for Burton. All she wanted to see was the present, with her in it. The immediate present, to be exact. His nose twitched, and he scratched it in his sleep. There was that grin again. It made her want to touch his lips. Perhaps she would allow herself just a little stroke across his full lower lip....

Burton's eyes opened. Their direct blueness stopped her breath. *"Bonjour,"* she whispered.

"Bonjour," Burton replied, and laughed. "My accent is terrible."

"No, that was pretty good. Now say, *Tu es une femme formidable,* Veronique." She couldn't resist teasing him.

"You are a formidable woman, Veronique," he agreed in English. He shifted closer and nuzzled behind her ear, while his fingers slid up her rib cage to cup her breast.

"I thought you wanted to learn French," she reproached him.

"Let's start with the language of lovemaking," he murmured, his warm breath bathing her ear.

Suddenly she was afraid of how badly she wanted him, and how soon she would lose him. She rolled onto her back and stared up at the ceiling. "Our marriage is only temporary. I don't want either of us to get hurt."

"We won't, as long as we keep doing these wonderful things to each other." he stroked a hand up the inside of her thigh to illustrate.

"You're not taking this seriously," she said, even as her eyes closed and warm tendrils of desire curled through her. "Last night was *fantastique*, but—"

He kissed her nose. "No 'buts.'"

She grasped his hand to still it and opened her eyes so he could see she was serious. "Before you arrived last night, I had a call from Ghislaine."

"What did she have to say?" he asked, paying more attention to the movement of her lips than her words.

"Do you remember I told you about the floating restaurant in Papeete? Jean-Paul has offered me the position of head chef."

His smile faded. "Are you going to take it?"

"Such opportunities do not come often in Tahiti. I always said I would leave at the end of the summer." She bit her lip, glancing away. The pain was already starting.

"So you did." His voice sounded strained. "What about *Flavors*?"

"I will finish the series," she whispered, on the verge of tears. "I cannot promise more."

He ran the back of his finger down her cheek, his eyes sad. "In that case, we'd better make the most of the time we've got."

With a sigh, she shifted closer to rest her head on his chest. She breathed in his scent and smoothed her palm across the ridges of muscle and bone beneath his skin.

Already she missed what she was losing. "Let's just hold each other."

He slid an arm around her back and rolled to face her. "I'd like that."

Their bodies touched all down the front. Some places touched more than others. "Can't help it," he murmured as he grew hard against her.

Neither could she help the melting heat softening her womb, spreading through all her secret places. With a moan, she wriggled closer, pressing her breasts and hips against him.

"One of us has got to have some willpower," he complained even as he spread his hands over her hips to pull her in more snugly. "Our appointment with Immigration is in an hour."

"You're the man. You're supposed to be strong." She stroked a hand down his buttock to the back of his thigh.

"Not when it comes to you." His kisses began with her lips and drifted downward, lingering in the hollow of her hip before searing a path to the moist cleft between her legs. "How do you say in French 'I want to make love to you'?"

She whispered the words and more besides, crooning the soft, musical syllables of her passion while his lips and tongue spoke directly to her heated flesh.

"Don't stop," he murmured when his intimate kisses had reduced her to speechless desire.

"Don't stop," she begged in turn, and urged him on with a throaty description of the way he was making her feel, and the pleasure she would give in return. For the moment, at least, there was no more talk of the future and their diverging paths.

CHAPTER FOURTEEN

WENDY CONNERY SLIPPED the pair of glasses that dangled from a black plastic chain around her neck onto her rather pointed nose. With silent deliberation, she read through the contents of the manila folder she'd brought with her to this small bare box of an interview room. Veronique sat opposite her in one of the two hard plastic chairs and studied her bent head from across the table, noting where the thick streak of white hair fanned out and blended by degrees with the dark.

Somewhere down the corridor, in another room such as this, Burton was undergoing a similar ordeal at the hands of James Jackson. Her heart and mind called out to him, recalling the encouraging lift of his mouth and warm wink before he was led away. Just before they'd left her apartment Burton had taken the photos of her and Graham from his pocket and laid them facedown on the mantelpiece, saying, "I don't want to ever pretend to be him."

Wendy Connery cleared her throat and raised two sharp gray eyes to peer at Veronique over the top of her reading glasses. "You married Burton William O'Rourke on June 4. Is that correct?"

"*Oui*. That is correct." Veronique tugged on a curl of hair.

"Where and when did you and Mr. O'Rourke first meet?" Mrs. Connery went on in her spare, clipped voice.

Veronique and Burton had decided in the end to stick to the truth and not to worry if they didn't know every detail about each other. Their lovemaking seemed to lend legitimacy to their relationship—regardless of how long it was destined to last.

"May 3," Veronique replied. "Burton was dining in the restaurant where I worked and asked to compliment the chef. That was me." It was, strictly speaking, the truth, if not quite the whole truth.

Connery checked her file again. "You remarried six months after losing your first husband and only four weeks after meeting Mr. O'Rourke." Short black lashes narrowed over slashes of eyes. "Would you say you are impulsive by nature, Ms. Dutot?"

"It's Mrs. O'Rourke." Wendy Connery was probably a nice woman, just doing her job, but Veronique didn't care for her attitude. "I knew my first husband only two weeks before I agreed to marry him." She smiled. "When it comes to love, it would seem that, yes, I am impulsive."

"Or very determined to stay in Canada."

Veronique shivered. "*Non,* absolutely not. I wanted to go back to my home in Tahiti, but...love happens."

Wendy Connery had undoubtedly had a lot of practice perfecting that skeptical noise she made in the back of her throat. "Do you and Mr. O'Rourke reside at the same address?"

"Yes. Burton's grandfather died just over a month ago and left him a farm in Langley. We've moved out there until it can be sold."

"Yet I understand you've kept your apartment on Cornwall Avenue." Her severe, dark eyebrows slanted with suspicion.

Veronique shrugged. "I have many tropical plants that would not take well to a move. I wait until Burton sell his farm and we decide which of our apartments to live in before I give up mine."

"I see." Connery made a note on the form. "Do you share a bedroom?"

Since last night. "Yes."

"And the marriage has been consummated?" The question was clipped and impersonal, as though she was inquiring into Veronique's choice of laundry detergent.

Veronique felt her cheeks grow warm, not with embarrassment, but remembered desire. *"Oui."*

Something in her voice must have penetrated Mrs. Connery's bureaucratic consciousness. She glanced up and took stock of Veronique. "Are you in love with him?"

Asked point-blank, Veronique was astonished to find she could lie with ease. In fact, she liked Burton so much it didn't even feel like lying. "Yes," she replied warmly, "I love him very much."

"And is your marriage based on this love?"

Down the hall, Burton was presumably undergoing a similar interrogation. "Not entirely."

"Oh?" Wendy Connery's features sharpened.

"I also respect and admire him. He is a good friend, not just to me, but to the people he works with. He is funny and kind. He has his faults—like being too much in a hurry sometimes, and he is also a little stubborn. But I would trust him with anything. He is an honorable man and an honest one."

"I see." The Immigration officer's face softened thoughtfully. "And Mr. O'Rourke shares these feelings?"

"Yes, he does," Veronique replied without hesitation. Burton might pretend the marriage was only one of expediency, and there might have been a time when it was true. But she knew another side of him now. No man could be such a tender and passionate lover and be indifferent. Besides, he'd said... She pushed the thought away, annoyed with herself for yearning after what she couldn't have. He'd had plenty of opportunity to say he loved her again last night, or even this morning, yet he hadn't.

Wendy Connery scribbled something at the bottom of

the page. "Thank you, Mrs. O'Rourke. That's all for now. We'll be in touch if we need further information."

Burton was waiting for her outside. He opened his arms and she practically leaped into them. He kissed her on the mouth, on her cheeks and on the tip of her nose till she was laughing and giddy.

"How did it go?" he demanded.

Gleefully, she danced him around in a circle. "I think we're going to make it."

"I do, too. It was easier than I thought. They didn't even ask me what color of lipstick you wear."

"I don't wear lipstick, silly, except on the show." She stopped laughing and stood still. "I guess we'd better go to the studio. We've missed two days of taping."

He shook his head. "You're sick."

"I am not. I feel fantastic."

"Your voice is still husky. You should rest it over the weekend. I'll call Ernie from the farm and get him to organize the crew to resume taping on Monday. Come on," he said, tucking her hand in the crook of his arm. "Let's go home."

HOME. IT WAS NATURAL for Burton to call it that, but Veronique hadn't expected the strong sense of homecoming she felt as they bumped up the long gravel driveway to the farmhouse. She wanted to run to the orchard and see if the blush was on the plums, to stroll by the henhouse and see if the chicks had hatched. To dig in the rich earth of the garden, to feel the soft grass between her bare toes. To come out on the porch at dawn and see Mount Baker drift like a mystical white sail on a rose sunrise. Only a week and already she'd ceased to view it as Burton's grandfather's home. It was Burton's home…and hers.

Ridiculous, she tried to tell herself. Her home was thousands of miles away, and the sooner she got there the better. Once she'd honored her commitments and tied up the loose threads of her life in Canada, she would be on the plane to Tahiti. For now, she followed Burton up the steps to the porch.

He opened the squeaky screen door and put the key in the lock. "First thing I'm going to do is put some oil on that hinge."

"No, it isn't," she said, tugging on his wrist to pull him back outside. "First thing you're going to do is…"

His arms swept around her. "Make love in the long grass?"

The murmured suggestion made her heart beat faster. The threads that bound her to him were not so loose as she might have liked. "No, silly. Go for a walk and show me around the farm."

"You've already seen most of it." His eyes narrowed as though he suspected a plot.

She smiled innocently back at him. *Of course it is a plot, you big, foolish, beautiful man.* A plot to remind him how much he loved this place. So that when he got his chess set back he would take down the For Sale sign from the fence by the road, and keep the farm—for himself, for his children and his children's children.

"I want to see it all. Every acre, every tree, every special spot you knew as a child. I want to see it through your eyes."

Burton gazed at her and realized suddenly that he wanted her to see his farm. Relating to James Jackson the story of how she'd worked by his side in the mud and the rain had made him understand for the first time how marriage could be a partnership. But that hadn't expressed everything he felt, so he'd tried to put into words the sunshine she'd brought into his life, the warmth and companionship, the excitement and anticipation of each new day together. He'd been surprised by his eagerness to talk about her, just saying her name gave him pleasure. He wanted to know all about her, not just for Immigration, but for himself. And he wanted to share with her the things that were special to him.

"Why not?" he said with a smile. "Hang on—I'll get my camera."

Burton was in his grandfather's room, slinging the camera strap around his neck, when he heard the sound of a diesel engine coming up the driveway. He walked quickly back down the hall and pushed through the screen door. Veronique was on her knees in the flower bed, inspecting her marigold seedlings. She got to her feet as he came down the steps, and together they watched a big green tractor come over the rise. In the driver's seat was a burly man in his fifties, wearing a jeans jacket and a red Mack hat. Behind the tractor, he was towing another piece of farm machinery.

"Hank!" Burton called, recognizing his neighbor.

Hank Vandermere brought the tractor to a halt outside the barn. Switching off the ignition, he climbed down and came forward to clasp Burton's hand in an iron grip. "Sorry to hear about your granddad. He was a real fine man. We'll miss him around here."

Burton nodded. "Thanks. I miss him, too. So how've you been? How's Mary? This is Veronique. Veronique, Hank Vandermere."

"*Bonjour,*" Veronique said. "I met your daughter-in-law, Jill."

"She mentioned that," Hank replied with a friendly grin as he shook her hand. "Said she was glad to see another young woman close by. Kinda misses her city friends. Mary's fine," he added, getting around to Burton's question. "She said to say hello and ask if there's anything she could do to help."

"Tell her thanks, we appreciate the help with the chickens, but everything else is pretty much under control. Everything except the potato crop, that is. You don't know where I could beg, borrow or steal a pick-planter, do you?'' He glanced hopefully at the one Hank was towing.

Hank scratched his head under his cap. ''Well, now, I feel real bad for keeping your granddad's machine this long. Been meaning to get over here for some time, but this damn rain's slowed everything down. I did come by once or twice just to say hello, but you weren't around.''

Burton's head jerked in surprise. ''Wait a minute. Did you say 'Granddad's machine'?''

''Yeah, didn't he tell you he rented it to me? Sure was a help. Rick and I were able to get the job done a lot faster…. Say, are you all right, son?''

Burton was walking openmouthed toward the machine attached to Hank's tractor. ''This is Granddad's pick-planter?''

''Yep. My south-facing slope is drier'n his field here, so I rented it off him to use first. Didn't figure on keeping it this long. Hope I haven't held you up.''

Burton dragged a hand through his hair. He glanced at Veronique and they burst out laughing.

Hank rubbed his weathered jaw. ''Is there some joke I'm missing?''

''It's a long story,'' Burton replied, still chuckling. ''I'll tell you sometime, but I've got to warn you, it's not really funny. Rented, you said.''

''Yeah. I paid him up front. Said he needed the money for something.''

Insurance premiums, Burton thought as another piece of the mystery fell into place.

Hank went around to the back of the trailer and started to unhitch the pick-planter. ''We're all done over there. You want some help getting your spuds in the ground?''

''You bet I would,'' Burton said. ''Just let me know what it's worth to you.'' Together they pushed the pick-planter toward the barn while Vernonique ran ahead to open the big double doors.

As they came back out into the sunlight, Burton said, "Say, Hank, you've been farming a long time...."

Hank rubbed a hand over a neck reddened and roughened by years of exposure to all kinds of weather. "All my life. Just like my father before me. In a few years, Rick'll take over."

Burton grinned. "How'd you like to be on TV?"

Hank let out a snort of disbelieving laughter, but when Burton explained about his documentary, he readily agreed to participate if it would mean raising the profile of farming in the valley.

"That's great," Burton said, shaking his hand to seal the deal. "Thanks again."

Hank climbed back on the tractor and turned the key in the ignition. "No problem," he said over the noise of the engine. "Rick'n I'll be over first thing Monday to start on your fields."

Burton and Veronique waved him out of sight, then, hand in hand, they walked along the fence line bordering the potato field. Veronique gazed over the endless rows of plowed land and gave a half laugh, half shudder. "I can't believe we thought we could plant the whole thing by hand."

"I knew better," Burton said. "I was just...possessed, or something. I'm sorry I dragged you into it. It was a stupid idea—"

"No, don't say that. It was important at the time." She paused. "You know, Burton, you are looking for another farmer to replace your granddad in the documentary, and I guess that's a good idea, but—" she squinted up at him "—it makes sense to interview yourself, no? You are part of the new generation that is moving off the land for one reason or another."

The sting of truth made him turn from her gentle questioning gaze. How could he presume to lecture others? What would Granddad think of him right now? "You're right. I keep telling myself I'm helping work toward a solution when really I'm part of the problem.''

She squeezed his hand. ''Nothing's black and white, and I do not judge you. I just think you would regret letting the farm go.''

''I already regret it,'' he said quietly, and walked on.

In silence they continued their climb to the top of the ridge, their footsteps falling in the uneven ruts left by the tractor. ''At least this year's crop is taken care of,'' Burton said. ''Now if only I could find out where Granddad hid the chess set. I've searched practically everywhere. Where is it?''

It was a rhetorical question, and he'd been speaking half to himself, but Veronique made no response at all, quite unlike her. He tugged on her hand, needing to feel her presence. ''Hey, you with me?''

She gave him a weak smile and changed the subject. ''If Hank and his son plant the potatoes, will they also harvest?''

Burton shrugged. ''I guess so, if I ask them to. Or maybe I'll sell the crop in the field to those guys from Chilliwack along with the farm. When I was a boy, Granddad always said, A man with land is a rich man.'' He chuckled. ''I thought he meant rich as in money and imagined granaries heaped with coins, like Scrooge McDuck's money vault.'' His laughter faded. What Granddad had left him was more valuable than mere money. Did he have the courage and the vision to take it on?

Walking the land on this balmy summer day brought back memories of childhood, of days when he'd been intimately aware of his natural surroundings: the heavy drone of bees among the clover, the slither of a garter snake in the thick grass beside the ditch, the earthy scent of sun-warmed dirt in the plowed field, and the sight of sun-haloed dandelion seeds drifting on the light breeze. Burton walked his land with a slow pace, breathing deeply, taking in every nuance of light and color, every sight and smell. Veronique's delighted reaction to his special spots put a gloss on the day.

He showed her the creek that dwindled to a trickle in August, and the banks of clay that could be molded by small hands. The stand of quick-growing alder that hadn't existed when he was a boy, and the giant maple that had split in two when the tail end of Hurricane Frieda lashed Vancouver the year he was born. They stopped at the fallen trunk for a rest, and Veronique sat cross-legged on the log, braiding a daisy chain. He told her stories of making forts among the fallen branches, of hurling chestnuts and brandishing fern swords at imaginary invaders. Later, as a teenager, he'd sat up here out of sight of the farmhouse and coughed over his first, and last, cigarette.

Now, as a man, he raised his camera and looked through the lens at the woman who for some unfathomable reason seemed to belong to this place almost as much as he.

Engrossed in weaving starry white flowers into a circle, Veronique wasn't aware he'd taken her photo until the shutter clicked. Then she glanced up, startled, and the second shot he got was of a comical face with a tongue sticking out. He clicked again, and she became demure, hiding behind a strand of curling hair that glinted like gold in the sun. He moved to a different angle and she posed outrageously, one elbow crooked behind her head like an old-fashioned movie star, with a smirk that said she wasn't taking any of this seriously.

Then her arms dropped, and she looked straight into the camera, her mobile face composed in an expression both winsome and grave, and so light it might change with the breeze. Yet laughter lurked in eyes the color of the grass at her feet. And—dare he believe it was for him?—a loving tenderness that made him feel ten feet tall, ready to slay the advancing hordes with his fern swords and horse chestnuts.

He slowly lowered the camera, still gazing at her. His mental VCR fast-forwarded, and with a catch of his heart, he saw their child, tousled blond head and grubby, tanned limbs, playing at her feet. For an instant, time compressed and light expanded; the past, present and future composed a picture of love so tangible he wanted to reach out and touch it. Family. His family. His future.

"Burton? Are you okay?"

He lowered the camera to the ground. "Yeah, I'm fine. Just fine."

Still in a dream, he walked over to the log. He took the completed circle of daisies and placed it on her head. Then he pulled her down to the grass to lie by his side, and memorized the shape and color of her face the way he'd memorized the topography of the land that had been passed to him for safekeeping. He loved them both. Unbelievably, he was going to let them go.

"Make love to me," she murmured, touching his cheek with the tip of one finger.

Slowly, tenderly, with smiles and whispers, they joined together there in the grass, warmed by the summer sun, buoyed by the solid, patient land. It was a marriage of body and soul, more real than any piece of paper, more binding than any legal document. He touched her with the exquisite care he'd use if she were made of fine china. When she came, he came, too, trembling and in awe.

"Heaven on earth," he murmured, gazing into her eyes.

Afterward Burton slept, his head resting on her breast, while she lightly stroked his temple. The soft, throaty sound of a French lullaby mingled in his consciousness with the whisper of the wind in the trees and the distant thrum of a tractor turning over sun-warmed earth. When he awoke to long shadows and the imprint of grass stems on his skin, he was rested soul-deep.

"I had the most fantastic dream," he told her excitedly as they walked back to the house. "I was a young teenager again, living here at the farm. One night a spaceship landed in the potato field. Don't laugh, I'm serious. It was like a movie, and even in my dream, I remember thinking, this would make a great teen drama series...."

COCOONED IN THEIR farmhouse, tending to garden and chickens, Burton and Veronique spent an idyllic weekend, choosing by mutual consent not to speak of the future. By Monday morning, Veronique had an abundance of ripe pomegranates, and taping of week five proceeded without a hitch. The rest of the week passed in a blissful haze, as the series progressed through to week eleven.

Veronique knew she ought to go see Marion, but the pain of their last meeting was still too raw, and she kept putting it off. She was hurt, too, that Marion had made no attempt to call her. Finally, around midweek, she rang the nursing home only to be told Marion was napping. Marion never returned her call.

She tried not to mind, to concentrate, instead, on life at the studio and at the farm. In the long golden evenings after work, Burton would film Hank and Rick planting potatoes, afterward capturing their thoughts and fears and dreams for the future of farming on video and audiotape. Murphy hadn't officially given him the okay, but he was doing it, anyway, getting in the footage while the sun shone and the tractors were running. Whenever he had a spare minute, he searched the house and even the barn for the chess set.

During those times, Veronique always found something else important to do. Every day that passed without her returning the chess set made the act harder and harder to initiate. Their happiness was so short-lived, and so fragile. She knew the moment she gave it back would mark the beginning of the end. So she puttered around the farmhouse, fixing up a holder for her many spice jars, finishing Granddad's chair...and thinking about her own hopes and fears for the future. Nights were sweet. Burton never again said he was falling in love with her, but his gentle touch and passionate response conveyed the message that he was already there. She cherished the time with him, knowing it would be all too short.

As the days passed and they approached the end of their third week of married life, Veronique knew if anyone was living in a dream world, it was her. The series was almost over. Marion didn't seem to need her anymore. She and Burton couldn't ignore the realities of their lives for much longer. Soon it would be time for her to go home.

That Sunday night, she prepared one of Burton's favorite dinners. All through the rainy summer afternoon he'd been plotting a pilot episode for his sci-fi series. Now he rocked back in Granddad's chair, sipping cold beer and munching prawn crackers while she ground aromatic spices together with fresh garlic and chili in a mortar and pestle.

"Your idea sounds good," she said when she had a chance to get a word in. "You have the perfect place to film, right here."

His smile faded. "The farm won't belong to me by the time this series is produced."

He hadn't mentioned selling for so long she'd begun to think he'd given up the idea. "Even now you want to sell? After this wonderful time we've spent here?" She tossed the spice paste into a heated wok and stirred rapidly, speaking above the hiss of oil and pungent steam. "How can you sell your past, Burton? How can you sell your children's future?"

His beer glass came down hard on the table. "How can I make the farm a viable part of my present? Tell me that."

She tossed fresh prawns into the wok, flicking him a disappointed glance. The prawns turned pink as she stirred them into the spice mixture, and she dumped in cold, cooked basmati rice and a generous slurp of *ketjap*—In-

donesian soy sauce. "I don't understand you," she exclaimed, giving the mixture a vigorous stir. "You said you
wouldn't sell until you found the chess set."

His shoulders hunched over the table. "I didn't know it
would take so long. Maybe the set isn't even here. I've
decided to give myself till the end of July to find it. That
way I'll have a month or two to put the farm on the market
before the autumn rains come."

Veronique lifted fragrant, steaming spoonfuls of Indo-
nesian fried rice into wide, shallow bowls and topped them
with fried eggs and chopped cilantro. Burton pulled in his
legs as she placed the bowls on the table and sat down
catercorner from him.

"It's like I always say, you are in too much of a hurry."
She picked up a fork and poked at her rice. "I thought
about you living here and I thought, just thought, that if I
stayed in Canada, this is the sort of place I could live—
with land, and animals, and real neighbors. A place
with…community."

Burton sat up straighter. "Do you mean…?"

Her sharp glance was curiously painful. "I said, *if* I
stayed."

He stabbed a forkful of rice and vegetables and poked
it into his mouth. When the autumn rains came, Veronique
would be gone. The thought hung in the air between them
like low-lying cloud. He would move back to his lonely
apartment and concentrate on his career. His mother would
go back to matchmaking. Veronique would prepare delicious meals for strangers.

Burton toyed with the idea of himself in Tahiti, lazing
in the tropical sun by day, making love to Veronique by
night. It sounded like the perfect vacation. But that was
all it could be. She wouldn't stay here, and for him to go
live on a tiny island in the middle of nowhere would be
professional suicide.

He took another bite of the rice, but the taste had gone

out of it. If he told her again he loved her, would she stay? Or would she run that much faster?

"Tomorrow we tape the last two segments." He spoke impersonally, as he would to a mere colleague, not the woman he'd made love to dozens of times. "You'll need to stick around for another week until editing is complete in case something has to be redone. After that you'll be…free to go. Have you made plans yet?"

"It will depend on Marion." Veronique, too, sounded stiff. "I will see her tomorrow, make a decision."

For a moment he thought of playing on her sympathy, trying to convince her that Marion shouldn't be left, but it wouldn't be fair and would only delay the inevitable. "You've done all you could. Far more than you had any obligation to do."

She stared at her untouched plate, making no pretense at eating. "I have done wrong things. I have tried to play God, thinking I know best for people. Instead, I have messed everything up."

"You did what you thought best at the time. That's all anyone can do. But I agree you should talk to her again. Don't let her drive you away. That will only make her feel worse in the long run."

"I am so ashamed." Without warning she burst into tears.

"You didn't do anything wrong," Burton said, at a loss to understand the outburst. "Marion will be all right."

"You don't know." She snatched up the gingham napkin from beside her plate and wiped her eyes, struggling to regain control.

Pushing his plate away, he held out a hand, thinking to comfort her the best way he knew how. "Come to bed?"

She let him pull her to her feet, then let go his hand without meeting his eyes. "Tomorrow is the last day, and we must be up early for work. I'll stay in the other bedroom tonight."

"Stay with me," he urged softly. "I'll let you sleep."

"You know it's not a good idea." Her wet-lashed glance conveyed love and desire, sorrow and regret, all at the same time.

His heart thudded dully, heavy as stone in his chest. Was it over so suddenly? The sense of loss was achingly powerful. "This time together has been…wonderful and—" He stopped. Words were so damned inadequate.

"Shh, Burton." Her fingers, light and cool, touched his lips. "You are wonderful. It is I who… Tomorrow I will go to my apartment. It is time I made arrangements for my plants. Thank you, and…forgive me." She turned and disappeared down the darkened hallway.

Forgive her? he thought, gazing after her. For what? For making him love her? For leaving him? For showing him he would be nothing without the farm, and her, to fill his life with meaning? The honeymoon was over. She was easing herself out of his life, and there was not a damn thing he could do about it.

Early the next morning, before Burton was awake, Veronique took the chess set out of the bottom of her cupboard where she'd hidden it and put it on the kitchen table. Then she called Ernie, who answered the phone sleepily and thought at first he was still dreaming when he realized who it was. She asked him for a ride to work, as soon as he could possibly get there.

Veronique hoisted her suitcase and walked down the long, gravel driveway, away from the farmhouse and everything that mattered. The fresh summer morning was breathtakingly beautiful, but she barely noticed the pink blush of dawn or the riotous chorus of birdsong coming from the broadleaf maples lining the road.

She could delude herself no longer. For Burton, putting his inner visions on film was top priority. If he wouldn't compromise his career for the sake of the farm, there was no way he would give it up to come to Tahiti with her.

Nor would she ask him to. He was not her husband, not really. His home was not her home, after all. Hollow and dejected, she sat down on her bag to wait.

Before too long, she saw Ernie's rusty beige Volkswagen put-putting down the narrow country road, watching for the driveway. He had been courting Rita all week, but as far as Veronique knew, Rita, although encouraging, had yet to commit herself. Veronique suspected she was enjoying the attention and didn't blame her a bit.

Veronique stood up and stepped onto the road to wave at him. He slowed to a stop and got out, leaving the engine popping and spitting in the still morning air, to help her with her bag.

"*Salut,* Ernie," she said, kissing him on both cheeks. "I am sorry to get you up so early. You look tired."

"I don't mind, honestly." He yawned and tried to cover it.

"You should," she said severely, then smiled.

He opened the door for her, then went around to the driver's seat. "Are you okay, Veronique?"

She knew her eyes were red, but she just shrugged and made a production of rolling the window up and down to clear it of condensation. "I am okay."

Ernie put the car into gear, checked the rearview mirror and putted back onto the road. "Did you and Burton have a fight?"

"No. Yes. I don't know. We haven't had the fight yet, but it's coming." She glanced at him. "How are you and Rita doing?"

"Good." In spite of the circles under his eyes, he looked very happy. "We were up till two last night, hashing things out."

"And…?"

A smile split his round face. "She took my ring back. We've set a date for next April. Rita wants to be married in spring."

"Oh, Ernie, I am so happy for you!"

He heaved a sigh. "Oh, boy, me, too. You wouldn't believe what a rough couple of weeks it's been."

"True love is not easy, Ernie."

"You're telling me." He stared straight ahead. "You know there was a time when—"

"Non." She cut him off firmly. "Some things it is better not to say. Part of growing older is learning the difference between the puppy-dog love and the real thing."

He sighed. "Maybe you're right. Anyway, I've got Burton to thank for setting me on the right path." He glanced over at her. "Do you think you two will, you know, stay together?"

She sighed. "Who knows, Ernie. Who knows."

BURTON OPENED HIS bedroom door and a note fluttered to the hardwood floor. He picked it up.

"Dear Burton, I've gone in early with Ernie...." Burton almost crumpled the paper then and there, but there was more. "You are right, I cannot wait any longer to talk to Marion, but I will be on time today, I promise! Look on the kitchen table. Sorry, sorry, sorry. Love, Veronique."

Sorry for what? he wondered, but he appreciated that she'd made him breakfast. He was probably being incredibly chauvinistic to want a woman who was a fabulous cook, but as long as he didn't say it aloud, maybe he'd get away with it. Humming, he strolled down the hall to the kitchen.

"SHE CAN'T BE GONE," Veronique insisted. "She doesn't go anywhere by herself."

The nurse on duty at the home just shook her head and repeated what she'd already said three times. "She went out with Mrs. Webster after an early breakfast."

Janice Webster. Marion had said that her old roommate came by to visit, but if she, Veronique, couldn't entice

Marion out on an outing, how could anyone else? There had to be something wrong.

She glanced at the clock on the wall behind the reception desk. Taping of *Flavors* would start in just thirty minutes, and first there was makeup.... "When are they coming back?"

"She didn't say. Our residents are free to come and go—in fact, we encourage independence. They need to learn to cope on their own before they leave here. Why don't you check back, say, at lunchtime?"

"I'll do that." Veronique started toward the front door, then stopped. "But could you ask her to call me at Channel Seven if she comes in before then?"

"I wouldn't worry so much, Mrs. O'Rourke. A sixty-one-year-old woman on crutches can't get far."

"She could fall again and hurt herself."

The nurse's face was patient. "There comes a time when you've got to let go. Let her stand on her own two feet."

Veronique blinked. Wasn't that just what she'd been trying to do all this time? She was glad Marion had taken her first steps toward self-sufficiency.

She hurried down to the station and through the revolving door. Lillian's latest hairdo was a soft, white-blond version of the latest fashion. It made her look ten years younger.

"Oh la la!" Veronique exclaimed. "Your niece is a genius. Perhaps I get her to do my hair before I go ba—" She broke off, unwilling to destroy the fiction of her marriage and her life in Canada quite yet.

Lillian's eyebrows rose slightly, but she merely opened her drawer and handed Veronique one of her grandniece's business cards. "Burton is in his office. He'd like to see you before the taping."

Veronique walked slowly down the corridor. She was not looking forward to this encounter. When he found out how long she'd had the chess set he was going to be very angry.

She knocked lightly at his door and poked her head around the corner.

"Come in."

His voice sounded distracted, but when he saw her, he leaped up and came around his desk to spin her around in his arms. "You wonderful, wonderful woman," he said, interspersing his words with kisses. "Where on earth did you find Granddad's chess set?"

Veronique couldn't reply, partly because he was still kissing her and partly because she was trying to think of a reasonable excuse for not telling him about the chess set sooner. But after a bit she needed to take a breath, and so did he. He drew back, still holding her hands, and gazed at her expectantly.

"It was in your grandfather's chair. When I took out the bottom to change the fabric on the seat cover, there it was."

"In the chair! I would never have thought of looking there."

"It was a good hiding place." She waited for him to realize the significance of the timing of her discovery.

Too excited for that, Burton snapped his fingers and paced across his office. "So I was right. He must have been afraid Mother would sell it to raise money for his insurance premiums, so he hid it in the bottom of the chair."

"Your mother wouldn't have taken it, would she? Not without telling him."

"No, of course not. But aside from Mother and me, the farm and the chess set were the only things that mattered to him. He wouldn't have taken chances on losing them. I guess we'll never know exactly what went through his mind. But it doesn't matter now that we've got it back." He strode quickly back to where she stood, kissed her hard again, then pushed her toward the door. "Quick now, you've got to get down to Makeup."

"But—"

"Go on. We'll talk some more after the show."

Oh la la. His pleasure and excitement would make her betrayal seem so much worse when he finally realized the truth.

As she entered the makeup room, she put aside her worries. "Congratulations, Rita, on your reengagement. You've made Ernie a very happy man."

"I'm just so excited," Rita said, bubbling over with happiness and a new self-assurance. "Ernie's changed. I'd just about given up on him until that night he went to the pub with Burton. Ever since then he's been so romantic. Thoughtful and considerate, too, and…oh, I don't know, strong, without being domineering."

"That's wonderful, Rita. I'm thrilled for you."

"You've got to come to the wedding," Rita said, getting out the Pan-Cake makeup. "I told Ernie I wanted to be a spring bride. It's my favorite season, but also it gives us a little more time. I mean, I'm sure about him, but I don't think it hurts to be absolutely sure."

"I think you're very wise, Rita." Veronique played with the hem of the plastic cape and decided this wasn't the time to mention she wouldn't be around in the spring. If she thought about leaving Burton, she'd burst into tears, and Rita would have to do her face all over again.

Rita babbled on about her and Ernie's plans, fortunately not noticing that Veronique hardly said a word. When she finally stepped down from the chair, Veronique gave Rita a hug. "You will make a beautiful bride."

"Thanks, Veronique. It might not have happened if not for you and Burton. Apparently Burton told Ernie the 'Secret,' or something mysterious like that. He wouldn't tell me what it was. Do you know what he's talking about?"

Veronique shook her head, mystified. "Never heard of it."

Rita shrugged. "Must be a guy thing. See you later."

When Veronique opened the door to the studio, the crew was already hyped at wrapping up the series. The buzz of conversation was louder than usual, and the atmosphere was charged with excitement. Burton had his headset slung around his neck, and his long legs carried him from group to group with purpose and energy. He was scanning his clipboard and was laughing at something Vince said when Veronique stepped inside, but with his uncanny instinct, he turned to her at that exact moment.

Burton's smile died on his face, and his eyes turned cold. She knew then he'd figured it out. The light seemed to go out of the room. Her heart seemed to shrivel, like an apple left out to dry. Deliberately Burton turned his back on her and began issuing directions to the crew. People began to move into place.

Mon Dieu. She hadn't realized till now how much she'd come to depend on his good nature and caring. How much she'd taken his affection for her for granted. How much she…loved him. The shattering realization flooded her with the bittersweet agony that came from knowing she herself had destroyed her chance at happiness.

She loved Burton. And now he hated her.

Ernie waved her over to the set. Chin up, smiling and chatting on her way to the kitchen, she didn't dare glance at Burton again. These past two weeks, all the joy and laughter they'd shared, the tender moments, the whispered confidences in the dark of night, the plans hatched at dawn—all that was over. *Finis.*

Burton stood to one side as Bill moved around her, checking the settings on his light meter. The sound man handed her the tiny microphone to clip to the front of her blouse.

Then Burton came up to her, his impersonal gaze sweeping over her for stray hairs or a shiny nose. "You started working on that chair almost three weeks ago," he said in an undertone, his voice colder than winter rain. "I remember because that was the day Don Chetwynd called to say he had a potential buyer. Why didn't you tell me you'd found the chess set? You knew how much it meant to me. All this time you knew where it was."

She wanted to reach out and touch him, to feel his warmth, to stroke his cowlick back from his forehead. All she could do was listen to a litany of her sins and try not to cry. She'd been so naive, thinking he would forgive her anything.

"And that night I came to your apartment—" he continued, still in that cold, horrible voice.

The night they'd first made love.

"I told you I had a definite offer. Yet still you didn't tell me. Why, Veronique? I could have sold the farm if it hadn't been for you."

Enough. She slammed a pot onto the stove, grateful for the anger that superseded pain. It was anger directed at herself, but that didn't matter. "That's exactly why I didn't tell you. Okay, I was wrong. I'm sorry. But I couldn't let you sell your farm when it means so much to you." And to her, she thought, but she couldn't say it. She had no right.

"How dare you make that decision for me?" As well as anger in his voice, there was now hurt. "You knew I didn't *want* to sell. You knew why I thought I had to. Why did you keep that chess set from me? Why?"

She put her hand on his where it rested on the granite countertop, conscious of the crew standing by, conscious of the urgency and inappropriateness of this time and place for the end of a love affair. Conscious of her desperation. "Because I love you."

Pain flashed through his eyes and tightened the muscles along his jaw. "Lousy timing, Veronique."

"This isn't a TV show!" she cried, furious with herself and with him. And petrified because with every word she spoke, his expression just got harder and colder.

Deliberately he removed his hand from beneath hers. "If you loved me, you would have given me the chess set."

"I should have. I see that now. Please, Burton..." Too choked up to continue speaking, she gazed at him, silently pleading for the light of love to come back to his eyes. Her heart beat hard and fast in a chest tight with pain. She longed for a wink or a smile, something to let her know she still had a place in his heart. Nothing.

"Can we talk about it later?" she begged.

"There's nothing left to say." He gave a sharp nod to Vince, and the floor manager motioned the camera operators back into place. Without a backward glance, Burton strode across to the spiral staircase and went up to the control booth.

Taping went smoothly, considering. Gradually Veronique relaxed enough to smile and joke with the audience while she cooked. She'd done this enough times to be able to call upon a certain detachment between her inner self and the woman being filmed. Her glance went repeatedly to the control booth, hoping for a sign of forgiveness and receiving none. On the back burner of her consciousness, thoughts of Marion simmered.

She wrapped up the last dish for that segment, the audience applauded, and the banks of floodlights went out with a series of heavy thuds. Lunch break. Veronique hurried to the dressing room to call the nursing home.

After a few words with the nurse receptionist, Veronique put the phone down and tugged on a curl. Marion had come in twenty minutes earlier, gotten her message and gone straight out again. What could she be doing? All the walking would tire her out, and make her hip sore. Why hadn't she called her? Veronique couldn't take back what she'd said about Graham, nor, now that she'd said it, did she want to. But she wanted Marion safe and sound. And she wanted her friend back.

Lunch hadn't improved Burton's disposition, and she suspected he hadn't even eaten. He used to be first in line to sample her food with the rest of the crew. Now he didn't even show up.

She stopped at Makeup for a touch-up, then went back to the studio. Ernie was talking to the audience, making jokes and telling stories till the crew was ready to shoot again. Veronique took her place behind the counter and checked that the ingredients were arranged the way she wanted them. Burton seemed to be everywhere but where she was, and she half feared, half hoped he'd forget to do his usual check of her before they started taping.

And then, still talking to Kate, the audio technician, via his headset, Burton came onto the set. His mind clearly elsewhere, he straightened Veronique's collar, then paused, his fingers lightly resting on her shoulder while he listened intently to whatever it was Kate was saying. Barely breathing, Veronique trembled on the verge of tears. He had no idea what he was doing to her. Indeed, he seemed hardly aware of her, so intense was his concentration.

He nodded to his unseen discussion partner, then his full attention focused on her. "Murphy's on his way down. There's someone in the audience cheering for you. This is our last show. Let's make it good."

She nodded and smiled tightly, fighting the urge to reach for him. He smiled back, but it was the smile of someone who had lost faith, who'd found to his cost that there was no such thing as eternity when it came to heaven on earth.

She watched him run up the stairs to the control booth and turned away to dab at her eyes with a tea towel. Then she took three deep breaths to calm herself and smiled out at the rows of seats. What had he meant, "Someone in the audience"?

She scanned the rows, and just before the banks of lights

snapped on, she saw Marion in the front row, beaming up at her. Astonished, Veronique smiled and blew her a kiss. But how? She glanced up at the control booth and directed a questioning lift of her eyebrows at Burton. He gave a two-fingered salute, then stepped out of sight before she could blow him a kiss, too.

His generosity gave her strength. Knowing Marion was in the audience gave her hope. She put all her energy into her performance, cutting off worries about the future to make the most of the present. This was the last show; she would go out with a bang, not a whimper.

Afterward, amid the applause, Murphy stepped forward from the sidelines to congratulate her. Burton came down to the set, and everybody crowded around, shaking hands and hugging and clapping one another on the back. Murphy predicted the ratings would top the charts. He declared to all present that Veronique would be the next Julia Child, and that anything Burton set his heart on was his for the asking.

The audience was filing out of the studio. Veronique saw Marion making her way slowly through the seats to the central aisle. Veronique glanced at Burton. He jerked his head, indicating she should go after Marion. But she wanted to talk to him, too. She tugged on her hair. Which way? Marion paused at the end of the row of seats and looked expectantly at her.

Veronique waved to her, then ran back to Burton. Silently, her heart breaking at his stony expression, she kissed him farewell, once, twice, thrice, on the cheeks. His eyes pressed shut, and she thought she saw a line of moisture beneath his lashes. But he didn't reach for her, and Marion was waiting.

CHAPTER FIFTEEN

MARION LEANED ON HER crutches with a welcoming smile. "The show was wonderful, Ronnie, dear. I'm so glad Mr. O'Rourke invited me to come and see it."

"I'm glad, too," Veronique said, kissing her on both cheeks.

"You remember Janice, my roommate at the rehab center?" Marion nodded to a thin, dark-haired woman standing to one side.

"How do you do?" Veronique said. Janice Webster didn't look nearly so grouchy without those tubes stuck in her. In fact, she had quite a nice smile.

"I'm fine, thank you," Janice said. "And please thank your husband for our tickets. It was a wonderful treat." She glanced at Marion. "I'll wait outside."

"Okay. I won't be long."

"I'm so glad you're all right," Veronique said when Janice had left. "I was worried when I didn't know where you were."

"I'm so sorry you were worried. I called the studio this morning. You weren't here yet, but Burton suggested I come down for your last show." Marion glanced around. "Could we sit down? My hip is a little sore."

"Of course." She helped Marion into a seat on the aisle, then slid into the one directly in front and twisted to face her. Lines of fatigue were etched around Marion's eyes and mouth, but Veronique noticed the new lipstick, gold earrings and matching necklace. "You look well."

"Thank you, my dear. I'm feeling much better." Marion put a hand over Veronique's where it lay on the seat back. "I want to apologize for the way I treated you last time. You took me by surprise. I'm so sorry, Ronnie."

Veronique looked down. "I should be the one to apologize. I should never have burdened you with Graham's wrongdoings."

"I thought so, too, at first. I was so angry at you for saying those things about my son. But gradually I cooled down, and then I just felt badly that he hurt you. You see—" Marion's voice wavered "—your accusations shocked me, but they didn't really surprise me. I know you must think Stan and I had the perfect marriage, but it wasn't. He could get very impatient with me...." Her words trailed off as tears filled her eyes.

"Marion," Veronique said urgently, "Stan's temper, his need to always be the big boss, was not your fault." Veronique had to make her believe this, if nothing else.

Marion stared at her, astonishment overtaking her anguish. "How did you know what he was like?"

She shrugged. "Graham must have gotten it from somewhere, and it certainly wasn't from you. I'm truly sorry if that hurts you."

Marion sighed heavily. "It's all right, Ronnie. In spite of everything, I did love Stan. But I'm grateful you brought things out in the open. It's made me think. In a way, it's freed me to be me. If Stan wasn't always right, then it means I wasn't always wrong—if you know what I mean."

"I know exactly what you mean. I am so glad we're friends again," Veronique said, clasping Marion's hand.

"You're more like a daughter to me," Marion said, smiling through her tears. She took a tissue from her cuff and dabbed at her eyes. "There's something else I've been meaning to tell you. Janice is going to move in with me when I get out of the nursing home."

"Oh, Marion, are you sure?"

"Yes. She lost her husband last year, too. She'll help me out in the house in exchange for reduced rent. We've become good friends. We're even going to join a bridge club together."

"I…I'm pleased for you." Veronique smiled hard to hide her hurt. What she'd been trying to get Marion to do for months, Janice had accomplished in a few weeks. "You have become independent."

"If it hadn't been for you, I probably would have curled up and stayed in a corner when Stan died," Marion replied. "I was too reliant on him. Your patience and good humor taught me it's easier to get through the hard times when you've got someone to talk to. That's why I was able to help Janice. I recognized loneliness and fear underneath her bad temper, so whenever she started acting unpleasant, I'd say, 'Tell me what's really bothering you.' And we just went on from there. You know that saying, 'What goes around, comes around'? If I've learned to cope, it's only because you made me believe I could. Janice and I went shopping this morning for something special to wear here today. Do you like my new earrings? I wanted you to be proud of me."

"I am," Veronique said, tears filling her eyes. "I am so very proud of you."

Marion patted her hand. "And now that you're married again, and to such a nice man, I can stop worrying about you."

Veronique started to laugh. "You were worried about *me?*"

Marion's gaze was tender. "You seemed so lost and alone."

Veronique glanced back at the set. The crowd was breaking up. Burton and Murphy were going off together, arms around each other's shoulders. Burton didn't look back. He had performed his final act of kindness. He was free. Free to finish his documentary. Free to begin work on another of the ideas spinning in his fertile brain. Free to find himself a real bride.

"Our marriage is over," Veronique said, turning back to Marion. "I'm going home."

She tried to smile, but her heart was breaking, and Marion seemed to know it at a glance. Her hand, so cool to the touch, pressed against Veronique's hot cheek.

"Oh, my dear, I'm going to miss you. I think you're making a big mistake."

Veronique blinked back her tears. The only mistake she'd made was in coming to this country in the first place. The sooner she was out of it, the sooner she could forget.

"So now will you take back Graham's money?" she said, changing the subject. "Now that you know why I don't want it?"

Marion's mouth set in a firm line. "No. As I've said many times, Stan left me well-provided for. Whatever Graham's faults, he married you and that's a commitment he'd never made before. The money he left rightfully belongs to you." Her voice softened. "He loved you, in his own way."

It was pointless arguing that if Graham had really loved her he wouldn't have hurt her. Marion had achieved a shaky truce between reality and happiness, having arranged her memories and beliefs in such a way that she could acknowledge the truth and still live with it.

"Well, if you won't take it back, what do you think of this idea?" she said, and explained an alternative use for Graham's money.

Marion smiled. "I think it's wonderful! Be sure and let me know how it turns out." She reached for her crutches.

Veronique rose to help her up. She hugged Marion goodbye. "Come and visit me in Tahiti."

Marion kissed her on both cheeks. "Next year, if you're in Tahiti, I just might take a cruise down that way."

Veronique got her things from the dressing room and left the building. The sky had been overcast when she'd entered the studio that morning; it was still overcast when she came out. The streak of aqua and gold along the western horizon might presage a coming high pressure system, or it might be the last glimpse of fine weather before another storm. Whatever. It didn't matter. Nothing mattered anymore.

Back at her apartment, she tried to take comfort in her plants and her familiar surroundings, but it didn't feel like home any longer. When she watered her gardenia, teardrops mingled with the shower from the big copper can. And when she called her travel agent to book her flight to Tahiti, she felt no joy, only pain. She wasn't going home, she was going into exile.

Veronique hung up the phone. She leaned back on the sofa where she and Burton had first made love and brought her knees up, wrapping her arms tightly around them. She ached with missing him.

She missed his crooked smile, his bright blue eyes, even his cowlick. She missed his energy and intensity, the way he leaped to his feet in his eagerness to start something new. She missed his long, lean body and his gentle, exciting touch. She missed his generosity and his kindness, the way he could make her smile with a flicker of his eyebrows and laugh with just a word or two. She missed seeing his face grow animated as an inner vision took hold of his imagination. She missed seeing the fondness in his eyes when he looked at his mother, and the passion in his gaze when he looked at her. She missed the tender way he held her close after making love. She missed talking, laughing, walking, making plans and seeing them through with him.

In short, she missed everything about him. From her living-room window she saw the lights of Vancouver wink on as dusk fell and knew she would not stop missing him even in Tahiti. Surrounded by her family and friends, speaking her own language, basking in the heat of the southern sun and swimming in the warmth of the South Pacific—she could have all this and still miss him. She would miss him for as long as she lived.

So it was really, really stupid to even *think* of leaving him.

THAT NIGHT, BURTON wandered through the farmhouse, trying to pinpoint exactly why the place he'd known for thirty-odd years without Veronique should feel so empty just because she'd gone. How could she have made such an impact on his life in such a short time?

Everything had turned out great in the end, he told himself. He had Granddad's chess set. He had his documentary in the bag. And on his way home from work, he'd stopped by Chetwynd's office in Langley to say he was ready to accept the offer on the farm. Within two hours Don had delivered the deposit to his door.

Lonely footsteps took him to the kitchen. Granddad's chair gleamed softly with wood oil and a dark blue brocade cover he recognized as the old living-room curtains. Taking refuge in the chair's familiar embrace, he rocked back and forth, seeing all around him the ways in which Veronique had made her mark. The kitchen was as clean as it had been in Gram's time. On the counter was the old wooden bread box Veronique had rescued from the basement and turned into a spice rack. Through the open front door he could hear the tinkle of the tropical shell mobile she'd hung on the porch. From the kitchen window he could see a corner of the garden in which she'd planted vegetables and herbs she would never see to fruition.

Suddenly he couldn't bear to stay a minute longer. Not if he had to stay there without her. He called Mary Vandermere and asked if they'd mind looking after the chickens again. Then he packed his bags and headed back to town. To his real life.

But if the farmhouse was lonely, then his apartment was as bleak as a monk's cell. Not another living thing inhabited these three small rooms, he noticed—no plants, no pets—and you could hardly call what he was doing "living." He could see now how little effort he'd put into creating a home for himself. Maybe it was from living on the road for so long. Maybe it was because he had too much on his mind and not enough in his heart.

A vague rumbling in his stomach suggested hunger, so he scavenged the nearly bare cupboards. The can opener scraping around the tin of beans was surely the loneliest sound in the universe. There was a time when he'd considered baked beans adequate sustenance. Now he pushed away the unappetizing plate of food. This was not what he hungered for.

He lay on his bed and leafed through the photos of Veronique he'd developed and printed in the studio dark room the previous week. The sunlight reflected in her expressive eyes made him yearn to live that day on the hill over again. The mobile mouth he loved to watch while she talked was still, but the impression of laughter had been captured. They'd had nearly three perfect weeks together. He'd rediscovered his childhood and begun to think about the future—with her.

It didn't matter a damn about the chess set. In fact, he realized now that he'd used it as an excuse to distance himself before she left him. The real problem was that they belonged to two different worlds. A fact not even love could change.

He fell asleep still clutching her photo.

The next morning, Burton did something he'd never done before—he called in sick when he wasn't ill. He knew he was just lovesick, but he seemed to have developed a physical pain in his chest that he suspected might lead to serious illness if left untreated. Unfortunately he was constitutionally incapable of lying about. He tried rolling the TV into the bedroom but was bored within minutes. By midmorning, he got out of bed, disgusted at wallowing in his own misery. He had to get out and move—walk, run, anywhere, it didn't matter. He had to burn off this energy before it burned him up.

Snatching up his camera, he headed out the door. He walked down to Denman Street with its traffic and cafés, then turned north, his restless footsteps pulling him toward the water and the seawall that circumnavigated Stanley Park.

He felt a little better just being out in the fresh air. Summer in Vancouver could be unpredictable, but nothing beat the days like today when the air was clear and warm, the sky an infinite blue, and the mountains seemed to rise straight from the chuckling blue-green sea.

Near the yacht harbor he came upon a bent old man tossing French fries to a trio of honking Canada geese. He raised his camera and snapped a few rapid frames, then caught the old man's eye and exchanged a smile over the beautiful day.

Moving on, he lengthened his stride. Tourists dawdled and pointed to the sights; they didn't bother him. He made a game of weaving between them, outrunning his thoughts. Under the Lion's Gate Bridge, he paused to watch an Alaskan cruise liner move majestically past on its way to dock. Burton raised his camera and caught the gleaming white prow just as the ship turned toward the soaring white sails of Canada Place. Above the liner a snowy jetstream of a 747 bound across the Pacific streaked across the brilliant blue sky.

Burton lowered the camera as an image of Veronique boarding a plane to Tahiti darkened his mood. Scenery was all very beautiful, but it didn't warm your bed at night.

What the hell was he going to do without her?

Driven by the ferocity of his thoughts, he rounded Prospect Point to face the open water of Georgia Strait. There, he put the telephoto lens on his camera and shot off half a roll of film on the California sea lions basking on the rocks offshore.

Out of nowhere a bald eagle swooped for a fish in the surge at the edge of the rocky intertidal. He crouched low to get the underside of the wings as the magnificent bird lifted off into the sun. *Click, click, click.* He'd almost forgotten what it was like taking pictures, the intense concentration and the burst of exhilaration when he got a really great shot. He could easily do this for a living again.

Burton's finger froze on the button. He could easily do this for a living. Straightening, he put the lens cap back on. It wasn't like he was married to Channel Seven. However, he *was* married to Veronique. More important, he wanted to stay married to her. He wanted to marry her all over again, for that matter.

Burton pictured himself leaving the studio and striking out on his own. The thought put his feet in gear, and he headed off again along the seawall. He didn't have to wait till he was fifty to pick and choose what he wanted to do. He could do that right now. He could choose to leave. And later he could choose to come back. And if there wasn't a spot for him right away, he'd make do.

The wind gusted around his face, and he sucked back strong salt air and the invigorating tang of ozone. Excitement lengthened his stride. An image came of himself under a beach umbrella in Tahiti, clacking away on a laptop, writing the script for his teenage sci-fi drama series. Next spring he'd slap it on Murphy's desk and say, "How about it, chief?"

Next spring. Would Veronique return with him? He could only ask. Well, he could beg, too, and though he hoped it wouldn't come to that, he knew he would do it if he had to.

He suspected getting Veronique to agree to marriage a second time would not be an easy task, but it was a goal worth striving for. He glanced at his watch. If he hurried, he could catch Murphy and square things away before the old man went to lunch. With a clear head, and a heart full of life and energy and the will to be happy, Burton headed for the studio.

"*MERCI*, Lillian. *Merci*, Sandy. I love my hair," Veronique called to Lillian and her grandniece as she went out the door of Channel Seven. Catherine's Volvo waited at the curb, its motor idling. "*Bonjour*, Catherine," she said, ducking into the car. "*Ça va?*"

"*Bien, merci*. Your hair looks wonderful," Catherine said, pulling into traffic. "I might get your friend to do mine next time I need a cut."

"She's getting a lot of experience." Veronique pulled down the visor and peered into the mirror. She ran her fingers through her newly trimmed locks, and watched the thick, honey-dark curls bounce back around her nape and ears. The blond bits were gone, but they seemed unimportant now. Why tie herself to the past when the future had so much to offer?

"Thank you for giving me a ride out to Langley," she said, glancing at Mother-in-law Number Two a little shyly. "I hope I'm not keeping you from anything important."

"Not at all. I'm glad you called me, and that Lillian had my home phone number. If you can stop the farm from going out of the family like you say you can, why, I'd drive to Hope and back if I thought it would help. But now that Burton has the chess set back, I'm afraid he won't waste any time putting the farm on the market."

"I know." Veronique reached up to twine her fingers into the hair at the back of her head and found there was not enough to catch hold of. She felt more nervous than ever. Was she doing the right thing?

"I'm not even sure Burton will be at the farm," Catherine continued. "He moved back to his apartment on the weekend."

Veronique frowned. "Lillian said he phoned in sick this morning, but when I called his apartment he wasn't there. The only other place I can think he would be is the farm. Anyway, it's not necessary for him to be there for my plan to work."

"And you're not going to tell me what that is, are you."

She glanced apologetically at Catherine. "I'd like Burton to be the first to know. Everything depends on whether we stay married."

Catherine slowed for a stoplight and turned to look at her. "Do you want to stay married to him?"

"Yes. More than anything. I love Burton very much."

Catherine smiled, and her eyes became bright. Then the light changed and she hit the gas. "Burtie told me your home was very important to you. Are you still going back to Tahiti?"

Veronique shrugged. "That's one of the things we need to work out between us."

Traffic was light and they swept through the city and onto the freeway in record time. Gradually Veronique began to relax a little. Her gaze swept from the mountains, across the spreading farmland, to Mount Baker in the south. What a magnificent day! There was not a cloud in sight to dim the sun. The ice-capped peaks were sharply etched against a deep blue sky. Every leaf, every blade of lush, green grass seemed to sparkle. She had never seen the Fraser Valley quite like this. She rolled down the passenger-side window and inhaled the freshest, sweetest air she'd ever smelled. She could see why Burton loved this place.

"Beautiful, isn't it?" Catherine said. "When the sun comes out, you forget all about the rainy days."

"Like love," Veronique said, throwing her head back and smiling. The weather had changed, and so had she.

And if, at the end of it all, Burton didn't want her, he would still have the farm. She would like to do that for him, and it would wash clean Graham's money. Certainly she didn't want it for herself. Marion knew of her plans and approved. *Chère* Marion. At last they were truly friends.

She folded the leather strap on her backpack into a little concertina. Inside, next to her checkbook, was her ticket to Papeete. If only Burton would wait for her, just a little while, till she had some time with Ghislaine and the others, she would come back. It would be easier if she had the farm to come back to, but if she didn't?

She would still come back.

She would take that leap of faith because things were different this time. She was in love with Burton, whereas she'd only been infatuated with Graham. How could you love someone with whom you couldn't communicate? If she and Graham had been able to talk to each other, they probably wouldn't have married so impulsively.

Burton's resemblance to Graham had blinded her to the fact that, right from the start, it was his character that had attracted her, not his looks. In so many ways, large and small, Burton had shown her that he cared about the person she was, not the person he wanted her to be. He'd gone out of his way to make her feel special. Like giving her a hankie after she'd pushed him away. Marrying her so she could stay in the country. Bringing her chicken soup when she was sick. Even that silly wig—she laughed just to think of it.

And the fact that he wanted to learn French! What further evidence of a noble soul did anyone need? He could never *be* French, of course; one had to be born to such an honor. But he could belong. Just as she'd found she could belong out there on the farm. And best of all, they belonged to each other.

ERNIE WAS WALKING SLOWLY toward Burton's office, his nose buried in the want ads, when Burton came striding around a corner and barreled into him.

"Hey, Ernie. Watch where you're going, ol' buddy."

"I was just on my way to see you," Ernie said.

Burton helped smoothed the crumpled newspaper. "You're not looking for another job, I hope. Murphy's going to need a man of your experience around here."

Ernie glanced up to see if he was joking, but Burton's smile was genuine and encouraging. His boss's attitude toward him had changed. Nowadays he treated him, well, not exactly like an equal, but at least as though he was playing in the same league. "I was looking for a place to live," Ernie said. "Now that Rita and I are so solid, it's time I moved out of my parents' home."

Burton gave him a little punch in the shoulder. "Way to go, Ern. You want to walk as far as the lobby with me? I was just on my way up to see Murphy."

"Sure."

"So what area are you looking in?" Burton asked, striding along. "The West End is handy to just about everything."

Ernie still had to hurry to keep up, but he didn't mind so much now. "I can't move to the city. I've got a dog, remember?"

Burton shrugged. "Stanley Park is just a hop, skip and a jump away."

"Oh, no. Edward needs room to run all day, not just when I can take him for a walk."

"Your dog is named Edward? Ernie and Edward?" At his amused tone, Ernie started to frown, and Burton brought his grin to heel. "So," Burton went on, "Edward likes to live in the country...."

Ernie had been around Burton long enough to know when his mental camera had switched on, but what the boss could possibly be picturing with regard to Edward boggled the mind. "Yeah, but places with acreage are usually too expensive for one person."

"Not necessarily. Sometimes people just want a reliable house-sitter for a certain time period. Would you be interested if something like that came up? Say, on a farm?"

"Of course, if it was for at least six months. Do you know of someplace near your grandfather's farm?"

"Could be, Ernie." They reached the elevators, and Burton pushed the button. "What was it you wanted to see me about?"

"A reference, in case I need one for a prospective landlord."

Burton chuckled. "No problem." The elevator arrived and the doors opened. Instead of getting in, Burton leaned a hand against the wall and asked, "Did I ever tell you the joke about the penguin and the pogo stick?"

The elevator doors closed again, and with a quiet hum, the empty cage responded to a summons from above. Ernie glanced at his watch. "Is Mr. Murphy expecting you?"

With a careless shrug, Burton jabbed the button again. "No rush, Ern. Plenty of time." He laughed. "Not for you, of course. Once the new season starts there'll be no rest for the wicked. Or the gainfully employed." He was still laughing when the elevator returned, and he stepped inside.

Ernie stared at the closing doors. The boss had finally cracked. He was out of his ever-lovin' tree.

Poor Ern, Burton thought as he rode up to the fifth floor. He'd clarify the situation as soon as he could, but first he had to sort out a few things with Murphy. And with Veronique.

The elevator made its way slowly upward, past Research, past the cafeteria, past whole floors of offices. Burton stuck his hands in his pockets and idly studied the notices taped to the wall. They were of little interest; he wasn't going to be around here much longer.

The doors opened and Burton stepped onto the fifth floor. He hardly recognized Sylvia with her new hairstyle. She waggled dark blue nails at him as he strolled past. He smiled and nodded. "Nice 'do, Sylvia." Lillian's grand-niece was getting good.

The door was ajar and Murphy was expecting him, so he knocked once and pushed it open. The big man was standing at the window, flipping worry beads and staring out. There was not a whiff of smoke in the air. Burton cleared his throat. "Hiya, boss."

Murphy turned. "Burton, m'boy. How's it going?" He walked back to his desk and motioned Burton to have a seat.

"Not bad. So was the board happy with *Flavors* when you showed them the tapes?"

"Ecstatic. I'm giving you the official green light."

Burton's smile lingered. "For what?"

Murphy spread his arms wide. "Anything you want. Hell, the station bosses are so pleased you could write your own ticket for the next twelve months."

Burton leaned forward in his chair, elbows on knees. "Funny you should say that, Murph. I do have a certain ticket in mind."

The creases around Murphy's mouth deepened in a frown. "What do you mean?"

"My wife is going back to Tahiti soon, and once I finish my current projects, I intend to join her. I expect we'll be there for the winter at least."

Murphy snorted. "And you'll do what for a living? Nice place, don't get me wrong, but you can't even speak the lingo."

"I'm learning. As far as making a living goes, I'll free-lance for a while. I've had seven fat years—and they've been great years, Murph, don't get me wrong—but I'm ready for some lean times. Chance to take stock, explore new directions.''

Murphy rolled his eyes. ''Here I thought you were turning into a beach bum when all you're looking for is another challenge. Goddamn it, O'Rourke, you're approaching the peak of your career. Don't you get enough of a challenge around here?''

''It's not like that.'' Burton frowned. Was it? Was he going to have to consciously not look for something to do in order to slow down? ''I'll have to talk to Veronique about this,'' he muttered.

''Now, there's your problem right there,'' Murphy said with a jab of his stubby forefinger. ''You've gone and let marriage change you. You used to be my best producer—hell, you're still the best producer, you're just not mine anymore.''

''If you mean, I'm not married to my job anymore, you're right. But don't worry, I'll be back. I'll be back with a pilot script for a series that'll knock your socks off—*90210* meets *X-Files*. What do you think? Interested?''

''Hmm.'' Murphy rocked back in his swivel chair. ''You say you've got a script?''

''Not yet. I'll probably be the only beach bum in Tahiti with a laptop.''

''You are going to write it? A documentary is one thing, but…'' Murphy's eyebrows lifted in unflattering surprise.

''I'm going to take a stab at it.'' Just thinking about it made Burton get to his feet and pace across the room.

''You can't sit still long enough to write a treatment, let alone a whole script,'' Murphy rumbled.

Burton ignored the sarcasm. ''I'm thinking a rural community…a farm lad, fourteen or fifteen…bored with school…too old for 4-H, too young to drive. A hostile alien spacecraft lands in his field. Toss in an intergalactic teen romance and a ticking clock, and you've got one helluva story.''

''Sounds promising, O'Rourke. You come up with a script and I'll fast-track the proposal—if you'll stay put.''

Burton stopped short and planted his hands on the back of the chair. ''Sorry, Murph. I'm changing my life-style for a while. It might not happen overnight, but I'm going to try.''

''Nothing happens overnight, O'Rourke. It's taken me two months to go a whole week without cigars.''

''Doesn't matter, as long as you get there in the end. I'm only just starting to feel married. It's opened up a whole new world for me. *Liberating,* I guess, is the word to describe it.''

''That's not the word most men use.''

''They don't have wives like Veronique.''

''When you have kids, you'll feel differently,'' Murphy said. ''You won't be swanning off to the South Pacific whenever the urge hits. You'll be stuck in one place, ferrying the ankle-biters around to soccer games and pep rallys.''

Burton shrugged. ''I never said I wouldn't have to make sacrifices.''

''You're going into this very blithely for a condemned man.''

''Everything will be okay when it happens,'' Burton said serenely. He noticed the empty humidor. ''Have you given up jelly beans, as well, Murph?''

''Unfortunately, no. I've got a hundred-a-day habit.'' He took a big bag out of the drawer and emptied them in a steady tinkle into the jar. ''When are you leaving?''

Burton got up and peered into the jar, searching for the licorice ones. He popped a couple in his mouth. ''Now that *Flavors* is over, I should be able to wrap up *Lost Harvest* in three or four weeks. Trudy has been itching to get her hands on *Lovers and Strangers* for ages. My current contract is almost up, so as long as I'm not leaving you in the lurch, I'll be cleaning out my office before September.''

"Goddamn short-term contracts," Murphy muttered. "I knew I should have talked the board into putting you on permanent staff."

"It would have only delayed the inevitable."

Murphy pushed back his chair and got to his feet, his hand reaching for Burton's. Burton gripped his friend's hand, realizing for the first time how much he was going to miss Murphy, and Ernie and Lillian and, oh, hell, everyone in the whole damn place. "Thanks for everything, Murph," he said.

"See you around O'Rourke," Murphy said gruffly. "Give my love to Veronique."

"Will do." He started to back out of the room. "Ernie's a good kid. He's ready to take on more."

"I'll look after him. He's a baseball fan, you know."

"Thanks. Give my regards to Mrs. Murph."

"NO, NOT TO THE FARM YET, Catherine," Veronique said as they approached the turnoff to the secondary road. "Do you know the way to Don Chetwynd's real-estate office?"

Catherine laughed and obediently continued along the main road into Langley. "Of course I know the way. I used to go to high school with Don. What are you up to?"

VERONIQUE WASN'T AT HER apartment when Burton called. Nor was she at Marion's nursing home. On his way out of town, he stopped by her apartment just in case, and when he didn't find her, carried on out of the city on a stream of commuter traffic. While he had a spare moment, he'd return the deposit those young Chilliwack farmers had made on Granddad's property before the cooling-off period was over. It wasn't just that he thought he'd have a better chance of convincing Veronique to stay if he kept the farm.

He wanted it for himself, as well. And for his and Veronique's children. Surely one of their future progeny would take after their grandfather and want to till the soil.

He took the turnoff to the town of Langley, and instead of making a right onto the secondary road, he continued on into town and parked outside Chetwynd Real Estate.

"I'M SORRY, MRS. O'ROURKE," Don Chetwynd said. "It's been sold. The buyers put a deposit on the farm yesterday."

"I will offer more," she said desperately.

The bell over the doorway tinkled as someone entered the office, but no one turned to look.

"This is highly unusual," Chetwynd continued. "I think you'd better discuss the matter with Mr. O'Rourke—"

"Is someone taking my name in vain?"

They all turned.

"Burton!" Veronique cried with joy.

"Burton!" his mother exclaimed in surprise.

"O'Rourke!" Chetwynd said with relief.

"Don, here's the check back from the deposit on the farm," Burton said, his gaze fixed on Veronique.

Don wagged his head back and forth. "Those Chilliwack boys are going to be awfully disappointed. Hadn't you better think on it awhile?"

"I'm not selling."

The agent reluctantly accepted the check dangling from Burton's outstretched fingers.

"Come on, Don," Catherine said, taking her old friend by the arm. "Let's go get a coffee and let these two work things out by themselves. Call me when the dust settles," she whispered in Veronique's ear. As they went out, Don flipped over the sign on the door reading Back in Fifteen Minutes.

Veronique and Burton just stood there, gazing at each

other. There was so much to be said, so many questions to be answered, neither knew where to begin.

"You're not selling?" Veronique said at last.

"You're trying to buy my farm?" Burton asked at the same time. "I thought you wanted me to hang on to my heritage."

"I wanted to make sure the farm stays in the family. I am not going to divorce you. Sorry."

"I guess I'll get over it," he said, smiling a little. "The question is, will you?"

Her eyes were huge, and dark with uncertainty. "That's just it," she said. "I'm not going to get over you."

He shut his eyes and breathed in deeply, afraid of taking a false step. Afraid that what he thought she was saying might be just a miscommunication resulting from their different languages. Then he opened his eyes and took the leap. "I love you."

Her eyes became bright. "I love you, also."

He exhaled a relieved burst of laughter. "What are we going to do about it?"

Smiling, she said, "I don't know, but I think we must do something."

"Well, for a start..." He opened his arms.

Veronique stepped forward, and Burton stepped forward, and the distance between them was closed. He shut his eyes again, and he held her as tightly as if he'd pulled her back from a precipice. God, she felt good.

He drew back a little. "You can't buy the farm if you already own it. What's mine is yours."

She smiled. "I didn't want you to do our children out of their inheritance."

And then he knew he hadn't misunderstood. Slowly he lowered his mouth to hers. Thought became feeling, then feeling blazed into sensation, and within seconds, he not only couldn't think straight, he couldn't think at all.

"Whoa," Veronique said, pulling back, breathless.

"We cannot start with the hormones yet. We have much to discuss. I have some ideas."

"Start talking," he murmured, nuzzling her ear.

"I have it all figured out. Stop it— Oh, mmm... Are you listening?"

"Yes." Sort of.

"We will live in the farmhouse and build a French country restaurant on the property. I will be haute chef, naturally." She spoke quickly so he couldn't interrupt. "There is a helipad at the top of the Channel Seven building. To save time, you can go to and from work by helicopter—"

"Hold on a minute!" Burton said, finally waking up to what she was saying. "What's all this about restaurants and helipads, and general nesting-syndrome behavior? I've quit my job, I've psyched myself up to go freelance, and I'm frothing at the mouth to get on a plane and go to Tahiti. I haven't felt so free in years."

She drew back, her gaze uncertain. "You maybe want to be totally free?"

"Not free of you. Never that." He brushed his fingers through her short hair. "What about you? Are you pulling a Rita on me?"

She feigned indignation. "You wanted me to cut my hair."

"Yeah, and as usual, you're late." He stopped her protests with another kiss.

"Okay, what do you think we should do?" she asked a few minutes later.

"You've got to agree," he warned.

"But, of course—if I can change the parts I don't like."

"Mmm. Okay, the plan is this—we go to Tahiti, give it a year and then see what we feel like doing."

"That is a plan?" She gazed at him dubiously.

"You want something more definite? Okay, I think your idea of a restaurant at the farm is great. We could also do a second series of *Flavors*. Everything will fall into place, you'll see."

She smiled a little. "You're not the man I married."

"Lucky you," he said, and grinned back. "Murphy says he'll listen if I want to pitch my teen sci-fi series next year."

"Do you really want to stop your career for a whole year? Right now you have so much that is certain."

"I'd like to take credit for being noble, but the more I think about it, the more I feel like I'm gaining something rather than giving something up. I'll work on a script. I'll recharge my batteries. It's exciting not knowing what I'm going to be doing."

"I think it's better we stay here. What about your mother?"

"It's only for a year. And if I know her, she'll be on the next plane to Papeete, nagging us about grandchildren. If not, Ernie will love her chicken soup."

"And what about the farm while we are away?"

"Ernie's more or less already said he'll house-sit. The land, we'll lease to the boys from Chilliwack. Or the Vandermeres. How were you planning on purchasing the farm, by the way?"

"I have an inheritance, too. From Graham. But I want to give it away."

Burton laid one hand across her mouth and the other across his chest. "Never talk about giving away large sums of money so casually. You could always finance the restaurant with it. Graham owes you. But if you really don't want it, you could make a donation to the women's shelter."

"I like that idea. And maybe just a little in a trust fund for the children."

He gazed at her with admiration. "That's what I like about you. You're so practical. Veronique, will you marry me? Again?"

She tilted her head to one side and pretended to think about it. "Only if we do it in Tahiti so my sister can be matron of honor."

"I knew you'd come around to my way of thinking." His smile returned, irrepressible.

"We'll be all right wherever we live," she said complacently. "But when we're here, we must have a big, big heater."

"And plenty of umbrellas. What do I need for Tahiti?" She whispered in his ear.

"Veronique, you're making me crazy. I want you—right here, right now."

"You *are* crazy. Those vinyl seats look very uncomfortable."

"Then let's go back to the farm." He nuzzled behind her ear.

"We have no time for this," she murmured.

But he could tell by the way she slipped her hands under his shirt that she was weakening. "We have all the time in the world," he said, and hand in hand they went out of the office and into the sunlight.

Veronique's Mango Salsa

1 large ripe mango, diced
1 large ripe tomato, seeded and diced
$1/2$ small English cucumber, diced
$1/4$ cup chopped green onion
$1/2$–1 chili pepper, minced; or 1/2 tsp Tabasco sauce

juice of one lime
$^1/_2$ tsp cumin
2 tbsp chopped fresh cilantro

Mix together in bowl, let flavors marinate for 30 minutes. Serve with grilled chicken or pork.

Optional, but highly recommended: one appreciative male to share a romantic dinner for two. *Oh la la!*

Bon appétit!

HARLEQUIN SUPERROMANCE®

From April to June 1999,
read about three women whose
New Millennium resolution is

By the Year 2000: *Satisfaction!*

April—*The Wrong Bride* by Judith Arnold.
Cassie Webster loves Phillip Keene and expected to marry
him—but it turns out he's marrying someone else. So
Cassie shows up at his wedding...to prove he's got
The Wrong Bride.

May—*Don't Mess with Texans* by Peggy Nicholson.
Susannah Mack Colton is out to get revenge on her
wealthy—and nasty—ex-husband. But in the process
she gets entangled with a handsome veterinarian,
complicating *his* life, too. Because that's what happens
when you ***"Mess with Texans"!***

June—*If He Could See Me Now* by Rebecca Winters.
The Rachel Maynard of today isn't the Rachel of ten
years ago. Now a lovely and accomplished woman,
she's looking for sweet revenge—and a chance to win
the love of the man who'd once rejected her.
If He Could See Me Now...

Available at your favorite retail outlet.

HARLEQUIN®
Makes any time special ™

IN UNIFORM

There's something special about a man in uniform. Maybe because he's a man who takes charge, a man you can count on, and yes, maybe even love....

Superromance presents *In Uniform*, an occasional series that features men who live up to your every fantasy—and then some!

Look for:

Mad About the Major
by Roz Denny Fox
Superromance #821
Coming in January 1999

An Officer and a Gentleman
by Elizabeth Ashtree
Superromance #828
Coming in March 1999

SEAL It with a Kiss
by Rogenna Brewer
Superromance #833
Coming in April 1999

Available wherever Harlequin books are sold.

HARLEQUIN®
Makes any time special ™

COMING NEXT MONTH

#834 DON'T MESS WITH TEXANS • Peggy Nicholson
By the Year 2000: Satisfaction!
Veterinarian R. D. Taggart is the innocent bystander caught in the cross fire between
a blue-eyed Texas hellcat and her vindictive ex-husband. Susannah Mack Colton
inadvertently destroys Tag's reputation in what *appears* to be nothing but a vendetta
against her ex—and Tag intends to collect on his damages!

#835 THE DOCTOR'S DAUGHTER • Judith Bowen
Men of Glory
Lucas Yellowfly was always in love with Virginia Lake. More than a decade ago, the
half-Indian boy from the wrong side of town spent a memorable night with the
doctor's daughter. Now they're both back in Glory, Lucas as a successful lawyer and
Virginia as a single mother with a five-year-old son. Virginia's looking for a job—
and Lucas finds he needs someone with *exactly* her qualifications!

#836 HER SECRET, HIS CHILD • Tara Taylor Quinn
A Little Secret
Jamie Archer has a past she wants to keep hidden. She's created an entirely
new life for herself and four-year-old Ashley—a life that's threatened when
Kyle Radcliff reappears. Kyle doesn't immediately realize who she is, but
Jamie recognizes *him* right away. *Her child's father.*

#837 THE GUARDIAN • Bethany Campbell
Guaranteed Page-Turner
Kate Kanaday is a widow with a young son. Life is hard, but she manages—right
up until the day a stalker leaves his first message on her doorstep. Before long she's
forced to quit her job and run. And there's only one place to go—to the home of a
stranger who has promised to keep them safe whether he wants them there or not.
From the bestselling author of *See How They Run* and *Don't Talk to Strangers*.

#838 THE PULL OF THE MOON • Darlene Graham
9 Months Later
Danielle Goodlove has every reason to believe that marriage and family are not for
her. As a dedicated obstetrician, she's content to share her patients' happiness. Until
one moonlit night, when firefighter Matthew Creed is brought into the emergency
room. Now she wishes things could be different....

#839 HER BROTHER'S KEEPER • K.N. Casper
Family Man
Krisanne Blessing receives a call from her ex-lover, Drew Hadley, asking her to
come back to Coyote Springs, Texas. Drew is now a widower with a young son—
and he's also a close friend of her brother, Patrick. Krisanne is shocked to discover
that Patrick wants her and Drew to give romance another try. She's even more
shocked when she discovers *why* he's encouraging their relationship.